The Cat in the Cradle

LOKA LEGENDS BOOK 1

Jay Bell Books
www.jaybellbooks.com

Paperback ISBN-13: 978-1463765149
ISBN-10: 1463765142

Other available formats: PDF, ePub, Nook, Kindle, iBook

Cover art by Andreas Bell
www.andreasbell.com

Acknowledgements

Special thanks to Swimming Kangaroo Books, who first took a chance on this novel and were kind enough to let me stretch my wings. Linda Anderson and Larriane Wills, who put up with me while I was still teething. Sorry if I bit either one of you. Candace Miles for giving this book a much needing dusting off, and to my family and friends for being so wonderfully supportive and loving.

And of course Andreas Bell, my handsome husband, who spent many weekends and evenings creating the art for this book. I love you!

Last but not least, I'd like to thank Piers Anthony for being an inspiration, for showing me through fantasy that it was okay to be gay, and for being correct that those dearest to me would still keep me in their hearts.

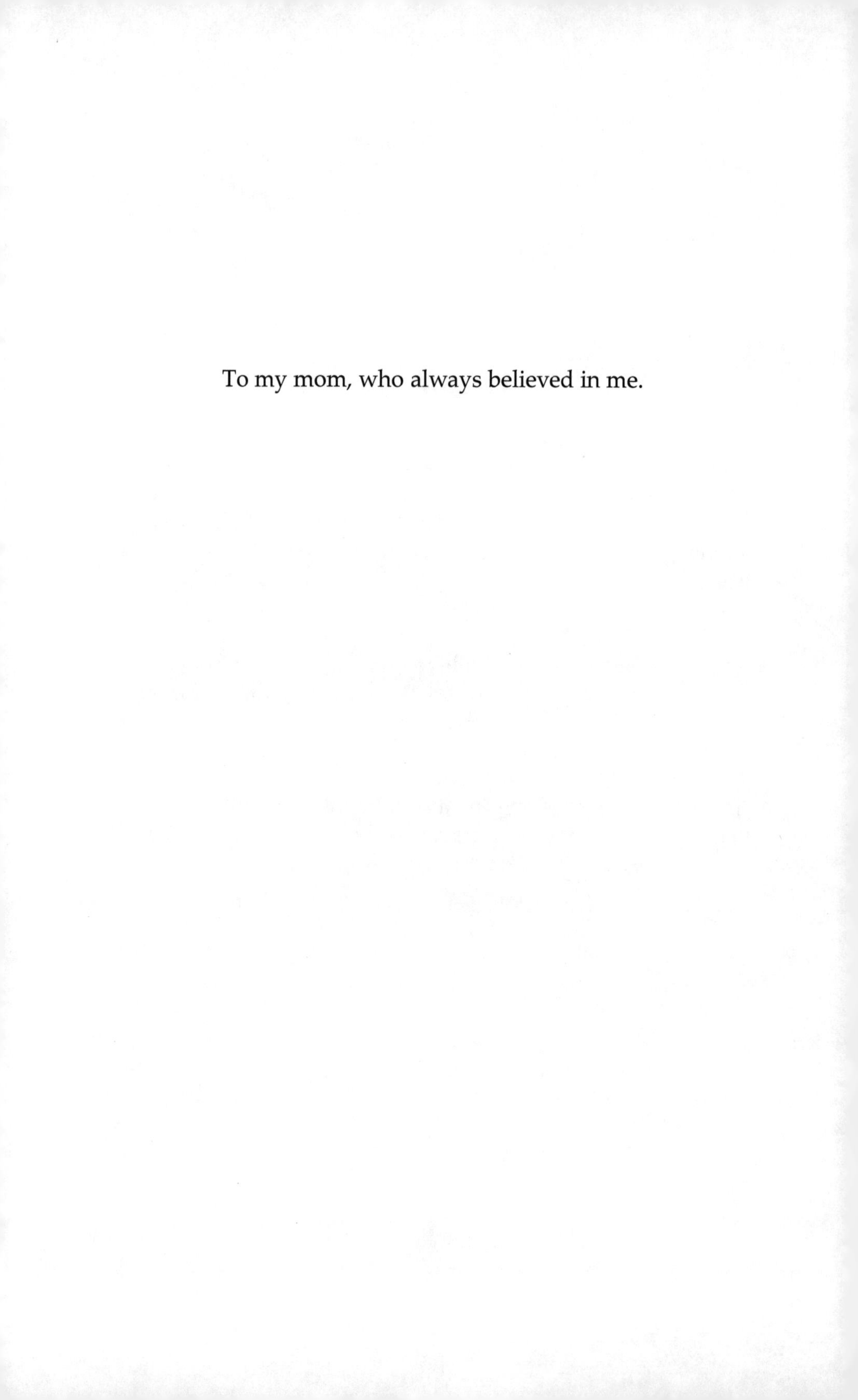

To my mom, who always believed in me.

The Cat in the Cradle

by Jay Bell

Illustrations by Andreas Bell

N
THE FIVE LANDS

Chapter 1
Departure

Humid night air danced across the rippling green waters of the lagoon, bringing with it the smells of summer and the sounds of night. Crickets competed with frogs in a contest of song, the two very different instruments blending together into a rhythmic pulse. Fireflies glided lazily through the pines and weeping willows that circled the lagoon, haunting lights that vanished before reappearing elsewhere. Sitting together on a blanket of fallen pine needles, a boy and his cat silently observed these surroundings.

The boy could hardly be called a boy anymore. Dylan was nearing his seventeenth year, and although his features were becoming more masculine, his steel-gray eyes still shone with innocence. His tanned skin hinted at a life spent outdoors, but the lack of muscles on his lean frame and the smoothness of his hands suggested that this time wasn't spent working. Messy brown hair covered most of his ears and reached halfway down his neck, adding to the evidence of a care-free soul.

Unlike the boy sitting next to him, the cat wasn't so easy to read. Kio's size made him stand out, an impressive two and a half feet from the top of his head down to his paws. He often was mistaken for a large dog. The cat's body was narrow and tight, his pure white fur short and neat. The feline mouth appeared to smirk beneath high cheekbones. Long, gently curved ears that ended in small tufts of fur twitched occasionally, orienting on distant sounds. The great golden eyes hinted at intelligence, something made plain when the cat opened his mouth and spoke.

"Out with it," Kio said, a slight purr lacing his voice.

"Out with what?" Dylan responded defensively.

"There is clearly something on your mind," the cat answered.

Dylan seemed about to say something, then shrugged, ran a hand through his tousled hair, and looked across the water's calm surface.

"You're going to make me guess?" Kio asked. "Very well. Considering that you've sighed more than six times since we arrived here, I can deduce that you are discontent with something. You've been chewing your bottom lip, which you do when mulling over some great decision, and your posture reveals to me that it quite possibly has to do with travel."

Dylan's head whipped around. "You got all that just from observing me?"

Kio snorted. "No, I got all that because you are extremely predictable. I know exactly what you are oh-so dramatically on the verge of suggesting because you do this every month."

"I may not be as predictable as you think," Dylan said, cocking an eyebrow and pursing his lips in what he hoped was a mysterious expression.

"Can you honestly say I was wrong?" Kio pressed.

Dylan struggled within himself before his shoulders slumped in defeat. "I want to leave the Lakelands," he confessed.

Kio's grin was victorious.

"Don't smile like that! I mean it this time!"

The big cat sighed. "We've been over this before. Do we really need to rehash it all?"

"Just one more adventure," Dylan said. "That's all. My lessons are finished, and Dad keeps pressuring me to train more with him so I can take over one day. If we don't go now, we might not have another chance."

"But—"

"I know, I know," Dylan waved his hand at the cat. "We have it better than anyone. I'm the son of the most prominent man around and everything is provided for me on a silver platter. I'm spoiled and the last thing I should do is take it for granted."

"So don't," Kio said with good humor.

"I won't, but before we settle down for a life of respectable maturity and constant responsibility, let's go out with a bang. Another adventure, but this time further than we've ever gone before."

"Think carefully about this," Kio said, fixing him with a gaze. "Think of the lush meals Ada always cooks for you, the silk sheets on your bed, or those lazy mornings where we don't bother rising until lunch. You really want to leave those things behind?"

Dylan didn't hesitate. "Absolutely!"

Kio groaned, dramatically falling to one side.

Dylan ignored the cat's antics. "I'm sure this has nothing to do with a certain litter box filled with pure white sand imported from the southern desert. And all this time I thought you were looking out for my best interests."

"Your welfare and mine are intertwined," the cat protested.

"No, you're right. We shouldn't take our lives for granted, but what better way of gaining appreciation for what we have than to strike out on our own?"

"You're really serious?" Kio, who had found his feet again, cocked an ear. "I have to admit the idea doesn't sound terrible. We've always had fun before. Besides, what's the worst that could happen? Aside from the time you fell into the ravine overgrown with stinging nettles. Or the time I chased that stupid rabbit into a hunter's trap and you had to buy me back from him."

Kio continued to rattle off other injuries and grievances, but Dylan didn't let it dissuade him. This was it! He could feel it in the night air. In the winter evenings, when he was returning home through the snow and heading toward warmly lit windows, there was nowhere else he wanted to be. But when the cold weather retreated and life crept back into the world, he felt a stirring in his soul; the pure potential of summer. He wanted to set out into the world, to be surrounded by the unknown and become a stranger. Only then would he be free to reinvent himself.

"Just you and me, Kio. No money, no food. A few changes of clothing and nothing more."

"All right," Kio conceded. "I'm game if you are."

Dylan scratched the cat's head affectionately. "Yeah?"

"Yeah. So where are we going? I'm assuming that we're doing this in secrecy, right?"

"Yup. It's more fun that way."

"Well, where do you plan on going that we can't easily be found?"

A yearning leapt into his chest, one that Dylan had entertained often enough in the midnight hour. Memories from two years ago rushed back at his summons; the feeling of a hand tightly gripping his, the smell of wine, a rough chin against his neck. He wanted to experience that again, to confront it instead of always hiding it away in his mind.

"Let's go see Rano," he suggested casually.

"Rano?" Kio looked surprised. "What in the world made you think of him? Although… the home of another Oligarch is probably the one place your father can't easily pry."

Kio was, of course, referring to his father's skill at blue magic. Scrying was child's play to him. Wherever Dylan went, all his father had to do was peer into his ceremonial bowl of water to see an image of Dylan's location—or anything else he wanted to observe.

"Exactly," Dylan said, happy for an excuse. "Rano is still living with his father, and Dad wouldn't dare scry there. We'll leave him a note saying we decided to camp out on the marshes like we always do. If Dad looks for us there and can't find us, he'll think his magic is on the blink or that we're already heading back. Think that will work?"

"Honestly?" Kio considered the question. "No, but when has that ever stopped us?"

The frogs let the crickets sing solo for a moment as the two conspirators silently considered their plan. Leaves rustled on the wind as if they too were impatient to break free.

"Ready?" Dylan asked.

Kio was incredulous. "You want to leave tonight?"

"Now or never." Dylan launched himself off the ground toward the trees. The cat stared after the boy for a few moments before hurrying to follow.

The moons were two small slivers in the sky, scarcely casting enough light to see by. A troublesome wind had picked up within the last hour, blowing in from the west and disrupting the waters of the otherwise calm Lake Albatross. These were ideal conditions for criminals, providing a thief with shadows to hide in and wind to mute any sounds.

Two such thieves made their way toward a rickety old dock jutting over the western edge of the lake. Stealth was not one of their concerns, as they didn't walk lightly enough to prevent the ancient dock wood from creaking. Indeed, one even burst out laughing when his companion stumbled over a loose plank and fell face-down.

"Shut up!" Dylan hissed before laughing. "We're going to get caught before we even steal the damn boat."

Kio pulled himself together enough to ask, "Is that even a crime?"

"Sure it is," Dylan answered as he stood. "Intent to steal."

"But how can they prove that we intended to?"

"Well, they can't, but what else would we be here for? They'll know we were thinking about it at any rate."

"Thinking isn't a crime," Kio replied.

"No, but in your case it probably should be. Come on."

A lonely boat bobbed in the water, bumping morosely against the dock. The boat was barely large enough to justify having a deck, the limited space dominated by a leaning cabin that looked as though it wanted to jump overboard. Its wood was weather worn, but the deck and hull were still intact.

"She's seen better days," Kio said. "Like when she was still a bunch of trees."

"She'll do fine." Dylan beamed at the boat as if it were fresh from the shipyard and patted it affectionately, causing a shower of shredded wood. "Well, maybe not exactly fine, but she'll get the job done."

"Maybe we should reconsider not using your father's resources. At least his ships have engines."

"This one might." Dylan hopped on board. Where a crystal usually sat nestled in the prow was a hole partially clogged with grass and dried mud. A little effort removed the clog, and brushing the remaining grime away revealed part of a multifaceted crystal. "It's still here!"

Dylan brought it to the shore, cleansing it in the lake's water to reveal a perfectly clear crystal, before returning to show Kio the results of his labors.

"Wow, it's really, uh…"

"Small," Dylan finished for him. "I know. The boat is too, so it all equals out."

He clambered back on board and Kio followed, his claws sending shreds of rotten wood into the air as he scrambled for purchase. Dylan ignored his friend's muttered swearing as he wiped out the empty hole and replaced the crystalline engine.

Dylan's stomach went tight as he considered the next step. The engine had not been charged for some time, meaning he would have to do so. He glanced toward the center of the boat, wishing that he had somehow overlooked a mast that could support a sail. Not that he knew how to sail, but he would have attempted it rather than use his magic.

"Don't over think it," Kio advised. "Remember what you were taught. Blue magic is fueled by intuition. Just let loose and go for it!"

Dylan knew the cat was right. After all, Kio had attended every lesson that Dylan had struggled through. It wasn't that his spells never worked, but rather the meager results that disappointed him. As son of the Blue Oligarch, the ultimate master of blue magic, Dylan couldn't help feeling that his skills were seriously lacking.

He forced the negative thoughts out of his mind, closed his eyes, and tried to silence any inner dialog. This wasn't easy with the buzzing anticipation of the voyage they were about to begin. One paltry magical feat was the final obstacle between them and adventure unknown. Taking a deep breath, he focused on building up energy within himself. He cupped both hands over the small crystal before pushing the accumulated power through his torso, down his arms, and out his hands. Dylan pushed with all his willpower until he felt purged of the force that he had created within himself.

He exhaled, removed his hands, and without opening his eyes asked, "Did it work?"

"Well, it's glowing," Kio answered.

Dylan opened his eyes, but instead of brilliant blue radiance, the crystal flickered with a dull glow as if it were about to go out.

"It's a good start," Kio said, rubbing up against Dylan's legs and trying to bolster his spirits. "I'm sure it's enough, too. Draw the water and let's get this trip started."

With a half-hearted sigh, Dylan untied the boat before placing the tips of his index fingers on either side of the crystal. This part he could handle. He frequently steered the boats at home without difficulty, although they all had fully precharged engines. With a minimal amount of concentration, he directed the crystal's energy toward the water in front of the boat. After a brief moment, pale blue light extended from the crystal to the lake. Water coursed through the light, as if flowing through an invisible pipe, until it reached the crystal and gathered there. Dylan moved his hands away just before water exploded out from where his fingers had been. Splitting into two streams, the water arced off to each side of the boat, launching into the lake and providing the vessel with propulsion.

The engines Dylan was accustomed to usually produced powerful, roaring jets but this crystal—or perhaps the weak energy he had filled it with—created wimpy streams that sounded more like someone using the toilet. Thankfully, termites had ensured that little boat was extremely lightweight, and the streams were enough to lurch the boat forward toward the center of the lake. They were finally on their way.

The boat chugged along the river, kicking up waves that rocked the sleepy fishing vessels they passed. Dylan indulged in a satisfied smirk. His skills, although far from the caliber of his father, had improved. Twice a day he refilled the little crystal engine with energy. Each time the light had been a bit brighter and the resulting propulsion streams thicker and more powerful. The necessity of putting his magic to practical use over the last two days reinforced his opinion that this trip was a good idea.

His stomach growled in complaint, reminding Dylan that not

everything was going according to plan. Living off the land, or the river as the case may be, wasn't as easy as he had expected. Preparation tripped him up the most. He had caught a fish the first morning following their successful theft of the boat—or salvaging as Kio preferred to call it. The cat insisted that stealing something nobody wanted was impossible. Regardless, when the fish had stopped thrashing on the deck, Dylan realized he had no idea how to gut it and decided to cook it whole. The end result was partly crunchy, mostly squishy, and entirely foul-tasting.

Later that day they brought the boat to shore so Kio could hunt them an alternative. He caught two large pheasants, happily digging into his own while Dylan puzzled over this even more complex animal. When he considered plucking the feathers, cutting off the head, and gutting the poor creature, he found his appetite had fled.

Instead he brought the bird back on the boat and flagged down the first merchant ship they passed. After some amateur haggling, the pheasant was traded for a loaf of dry bread and a flavorless block of cheese. He suffered them in silence, preferring them greatly to hunger, and reminding himself that better meals awaited him at the home of the Yellow Oligarch.

Thoughts of food fled, chased away by memories of Rano. They had been childhood friends, even though they didn't see each other that often. Both sons of Oligarchs, they were always paired up when Blue and Yellow met for business. When the meetings came to an abrupt end, so did the visits. Only when Rano was old enough to travel on his own did Dylan see him again, barely recognizing the handsome man as the pudgy playmate he had once known.

Dylan's pulse quickened, his mouth dry. There would be consequences to seeing Rano again, but whether they were good or bad remained to be seen. As they drew near their destination, his mind returned to the anger and regret of their ugly parting. If Dylan could recreate that night with any other, he would steer the boat elsewhere, but he didn't believe it possible. He and Rano were unique, two of a kind. There was no one else.

Then there was the letter, the one Dylan had read so many times that the paper had gone soft around the edges. He had every word memorized. Rano had written him months ago, and Dylan had poured over his words countless times, trying to decipher the reason why. The letter didn't say much of anything, simple pleasantries that were neither praising nor condemning, but these neutral words hinted that Rano was no longer angry. While the letter expressed no invitation, Dylan couldn't help but interpret it as such. If he was mistaken, confrontation lay ahead, but beyond that was the hope, however desperate, of reconciliation.

"You know, we could simply jump overboard and leave this pile of termite food to its fate."

The cat's voice startled Dylan back to the present. His subconscious had been doing the sailing, and he was surprised to see the boat gliding toward the shore. The trees lining the river had thinned and disappeared, marking the beginning of the Longlands' rolling plains. According to his map they were to head inland five miles before turning north. Yellow's home would be a few hours by foot after that.

"You really want to get wet?" Dylan asked.

"Not really. I just wanted to express my disdain for this ship one final time."

Dylan grinned and guided the boat in a diagonal line until the starboard side bumped the shore. He used the crystal one last time to fix the boat in place, sending a pole of energy straight to the shallow river bottom. He wasn't sure if the energy anchor would last for more than a day and wasn't concerned. All he could think of was how he was setting himself up to be hurt again.

Chapter 2
Yellow

The stone windmill, simple and cylindrical in shape, was unremarkable in all ways but one. It flew. The building circled through the air, its massive rotor thrumming out a rhythm. Only a thick golden rope anchoring it to the field below prevented it from disappearing high into the sky. Amazing how a building normally reserved for the working class could be transformed by this wondrous magical feat. Not only was it impressive, but it was appropriately symbolic. The Yellow Oligarch ruled over the element of air, after all.

"It's really flying," Kio said. "I don't believe it."

"Me neither," Dylan said, his awe mixed with amusement. The windmill looked like a stuffed turkey that had learned to fly backwards.

"It's positively hypnotizing." Kio blinked, forcing himself to look away. "How are we supposed to get up there?"

Dylan wasn't sure. Climbing the rope was out the question. "Maybe there's something we're missing. A way of signaling that we're here."

He headed to where the rope met the ground. Already things weren't going as planned, namely because there wasn't a plan. Dylan had naively expected to meet Rano with ease, certain that fate would drag them together again. Dylan had never visited the windmill before, but he knew of it by reputation. He should have known that reaching it wouldn't be easy.

Pointed roofs poked over the horizon. Where there were homes, there would be food. Dylan's stomach rumbled at the idea. There they could find something to eat. Plus he could make some careful inquiries. Surely villagers visited the windmill, if only to deliver food and supplies. Perhaps they would know if the mill had a regular schedule to land on the ground.

"I think we should walk to that village," Dylan said, placing his hand on the rope. "Unless you think you can climb this."

"I'd like to see you try!"

"Who is there?"

"What?" Dylan asked in confusion. "Did you hear that?"

"Hear what?" Kio responded, but Dylan waved him into silence.

His ears hadn't heard anything, but there was a voice inside his head, completely different from his internal dialog. If he focused hard enough, he could almost hear it breathing. Maybe he was hungrier than he realized.

"Is somebody there?" he tried.

"That's exactly what I'm asking you, young man. I don't have time for games! Announce yourself properly or be on your way."

There it was again, as clear as day! The impertinent voice sounded oddly familiar.

"Telepathy!" Dylan exclaimed. He had met yellow magicians before, but had never spoken with one telepathically. "So do I talk out loud, or am I supposed to think really hard? Both maybe?"

A long sigh sounded inside Dylan's skull. *"Just speak out loud, and quickly, while I still have some patience left."*

"Right." Panic shot through Dylan as he realized that he didn't have a cover story prepared. "Um, Rano sent for me. I, uh, we— That is, my cat and I, were sent for by Rano to be servants. Well, not the cat obviously. He's more of a guard dog. But a cat. A guard dog cat."

Dylan swore he could hear a puzzled telepathic pause. *"Rano isn't here. Who are you?"* The voice was shifting from irritated to angry. Obviously his attempt at lying was making things worse. He didn't have time to think up something believable, which only left one option: the truth.

"My name is Dylan. Rano visited me before, and I just thought—"

"Dylan? From the Lakelands?"

"Yes."

"You're Jack's son?" The anger in the voice had subsided a bit.

"That's right." Game over. Dylan had finally put the pieces together and knew who he was dealing with. The Yellow Oligarch, Rano's father. Dylan had hoped to avoid his notice until he could meet with Rano. Together maybe they could have travelled somewhere else, spent some time together. Now it was likely that the Yellow Oligarch would send him home.

"As I said, Rano isn't here, but I'm sure you'd like to come up for some refreshment. Something to eat perhaps?"

"Yes!" he said a little too eagerly. "Yes, that would be very nice."

"Stand well back then."

He stepped away from the rope, motioning for Kio to do the same.

"What's going on?" the cat asked as they retreated.

"Well, Rano isn't there, and it took me about five seconds to blabber who we are."

"To whom?"

"Never mind, I think the windmill is going to land."

"And then?"

"Food," Dylan answered. He stopped and turned around. He was reasonably sure they had walked far enough to be clear of the building. The windmill would probably have to make a slow descent anyway. Enough time passed that he began to wonder if anything was going to happen at all when Kio was lifted off the ground. One moment the cat was lazily licking a paw, the next he was turned on his back and yanked into the air by invisible forces.

Dylan didn't have time to react before the same fate befell him. His head swam, and his limbs felt weak as he rose faster and faster. He couldn't feel anything touching his body, but the air felt denser. Blinking away tears, he saw a barely perceptible sphere of yellow light surrounding him. So this was the magic of the Yellow Oligarch! He glanced to the left where Kio was yowling and rising along in his own flickering ball of magic before looking upward toward the windmill.

They were being brought to the windmill instead of the windmill being brought to them! The wind forced Dylan to close his eyes, but he reveled in the exhilaration of the ride, until he felt himself being lowered. Below him was a stone patio attached to the windmill's base. Kio's bubble disappeared five feet off the ground, allowing the cat to twist around in the air and right his position. He landed on his feet with feline grace. Dylan panicked, wondering if he was going to be dropped too, but he continued to sink until his rump gently touched the patio.

Before he could stand, a man stepped through the windmill's entrance. Grey-haired and of average height, his thin frame was draped in long robes of yellow silk, embroidered with various runes. Dylan recognized a few of them as symbols of air and guessed that the rest were as well. The robe was traditional, a formal ceremonial costume—exactly the sort of thing his father never wore.

"Welcome to my home, Dylan, son of the Blue Oligarch," the man said, his tones matching the formality of his clothing. His face was proud, head held high, the corners of his mouth turned down inside the neatly trimmed goatee. "Do you still remember me?"

"Of course, sir," Dylan said, realizing with embarrassment that he had been staring instead of regaining his feet.

"No need for formality. You may call me Krale." He paused, raising an eyebrow. "So you are now seeking employment as a servant?"

"What? No! Sorry for the silly introduction down there," Dylan said as he stood. "We didn't really know what to expect, so—"

"I never want to do that again!" Kio interrupted. He was lying flat on his belly, his legs splayed out around him.

"I'm afraid there was no other option," Krale said, regarding Kio critically. "It's very time-consuming to land the windmill."

"It wasn't a problem, really," Dylan said before Kio could respond. "Just unexpected."

"I see." A small smile crossed Krale's lips. "Won't you come in? You look... exhausted."

Dylan's face flushed as he realized how dirty and disheveled he must appear after traveling for three days.

The Yellow Oligarch turned and strode into his home, beckoning them to follow. Kio entered first, wide eyes regarding the open air once more before he rushed inside the windmill. Dylan followed and felt disoriented by the interior's cool darkness in contrast to the bright summer day.

Inside was a round, plain room with a dim column of light in its center, originating from the ceiling. A circular iron staircase appeared to spiral around the light to floors above. Krale led them up these stairs, each floor they passed serving a different purpose. They passed a study, and a highly decorated bedroom. Dylan peered in at these curiously, trying to imagine Rano reading a book at one of the tables, or daydreaming at a window while watching the land below. Subsequent floors were walled off to the stairwell, the doors closed.

"The baths are through here," Krale said, opening a door on the fourth floor. "I hope you find them as comfortable and modern as what you are accustomed to. The other door here leads to Rano's room. You are welcome to use it while he is away. I assume you will be staying the night?"

Dylan hadn't considered it, but by the time they bathed and ate it would be evening. A solid night's sleep in a real bed would be welcome, as well as the time to plan what they wanted to do next.

"That would be very nice, thank you," he answered.

Krale nodded. "Once you are refreshed, please meet me one floor up for dinner." The Yellow Oligarch peered at them curiously once more before turning and disappearing up the stairs.

Dylan soaked blissfully in a large tub of steaming hot water.

Such a modern set-up required multiple colors of magic, a skill only mages possessed. In this particular case, two separate magics were blended. Blue magic filled the tub with clean water, while red magic infused the water with heat that never cooled. The luxurious bathtub had probably cost Krale a small fortune.

"Any plans?" Kio asked from beside the tub as he paused from grooming himself.

"Nope." Dylan sighed. "Staying would be weird without Rano around, and it's not nearly as big here as I thought it would be."

"Strange place for an Oligarch, huh?"

"Oh, I don't know. Our home is eccentric too. Who besides us lives in a tower?"

"True." Kio stopped licking himself. "Speaking of home…"

Dylan sighed again. "This is only a setback. We just need to find somewhere else to go. Maybe one of the other Oligarchs?"

"Maybe."

"Let's talk about it after we eat," Dylan said. The truth was his heart wasn't in it anymore. Without the prospect of seeing Rano, their voyage just didn't hold the same appeal. He slid even lower into the tub until the water almost reached his nose. Maybe he could find out where Rano was and travel there instead.

Dylan's stomach growled again, so he rose from the water and changed into his last clean outfit—a white shirt and dark brown shorts. He knew a sort of blue magic that could clean dirty clothes that he would risk trying later. As he and Kio left the bathroom and headed upstairs, the water from the tub disappeared into the golden faucet it had poured from.

The next floor up was a large, open space divided into two half-circles. One side of the room was a kitchen as orderly as Krale's demeanor. The cabinets and counters curved with the shape of the outer wall, giving it a rather unique appearance, but Dylan didn't pay it much attention. The other side of the room was the real showstopper. The half circle of wall on that side of the windmill was missing. In its place was the most ambitious window he had ever seen—except there was no glass. The wooden floor of the kitchen stretched beyond where the wall wasn't, forming a wooden balcony that hung over the edge.

Krale watched him from a table on this balcony. The Yellow Oligarch had a bemused smile on his normally dour face, aware of how impressive this scene was. To his left the giant blades of the windmill's rotor turned, yet no breeze could be felt from them.

"This must be magic," Dylan said as he approached the large gap. "Otherwise the whole building would collapse."

"Of course," Krale confirmed with a nod. "Put your hand out as you approach. This is one of the finest examples of yellow magic you'll ever see, and perhaps one of the oldest in existence. As old as this building, anyway."

As Dylan's hand neared where a wall should be, he felt something resist his fingers. Soft, it soon gave way, allowing his hand to pass through. Kio did the same with his nose, his whiskers being pressed back against his face by the invisible force.

"It functions much like the pockets of air that lifted you up to the mill," Krale continued, "except in variable levels. The compression of air becomes increasingly dense as it nears the edges of the surrounding wall, ceiling, and floor, to the point that it creates enough resistance to support the structure as a physical wall would."

"Wow," Dylan said as he passed through. The sensation felt like leaning against a strong wind, if only for a split second. "I didn't know such a thing was possible."

"Only to an Oligarch, I imagine." Krale's features were proud. "Although it takes more than just skill." He dipped a hand under the table and brought out a walnut-sized diamond glowing with pure yellow light. Dylan recognized it instantly as the yellow loka. His father's looked exactly the same, although it was blue. Without the lokas, there would be no Oligarchs. Only ten existed, each a different color, and they were the most powerful sources of magic in the world. The loka disappeared back under the table, but its light left an after-image in Dylan's eyes.

A loud, wet sound filled the air, drawing all attention to the table. Kio had hopped up in the chair directly across from Krale and was noisily devouring a chicken leg. Dylan looked to Krale, whose eyes were focused somewhere on the floor. Following his gaze, Dylan saw a bowl filled with scraps of meat and a bowl of milk.

"I had intended—" the Yellow Oligarch began, his face strained.

"Uh, Kio," Dylan said, trying not to laugh. "You're eating my food."

"Whoops." The big cat jumped down, taking the remainder of the chicken leg with him. Dylan was relived to see that another drumstick remained on the plate, along with a small salad and two bread rolls.

"Sorry," Dylan said as he took his place. "He usually eats at the table."

Krale raised his eyebrows at this before steering the conversation elsewhere. "I'm afraid that I don't care much for cooking, so when Rano isn't here, I never eat a hot meal."

"Mmph," Dylan replied, his mouth already full of cold chicken. He was ravenous. Every bite tasted like heaven, which made remembering to chew difficult. Kio wasn't quite as mannerly, but the Yellow Oligarch seemed determined to ignore his existence.

"Care for some wine?" Krale asked, filling his own glass. "I have red, too, if you prefer."

Dylan shook his head, willing away memories of the last time he had drank—the smell of wine on Rano's breath, his uninhibited laughter, and the tangy taste of his sweat.

"Food disagreeing with you?"

"No, not at all," Dylan said, bringing his mind back to the present. "It's fine, really."

"Then tell me," Krale said, "why did your father send you here?"

Dylan fumbled his fork, which clattered on the plate. "He didn't!"

"Oh, come now! You haven't expressed the slightest interest in Rano's whereabouts since you arrived, not to mention this nonsense about you being employed as his servant."

"I'm being honest!" Dylan protested. "At least, now I am."

"It's really not necessary to resort to such underhanded tactics. If there's something Jack wishes to know, he need only ask."

"Kio and I came here of our own accord, without my dad even knowing. Trust me, he would never send me to spy on you." Dylan's pulse increased in his panic. He had only been thinking of his stupid desire to see Rano and hadn't once thought of the political tensions between Krale and his father. What if his presence here had serious ramifications?

"Jack wouldn't need to send us to spy," Kio said. "He could simply use his magic to scry."

"But he wouldn't" Dylan insisted. "Spying isn't my dad's style."

Krale took a sip of wine, his eyes never leaving Dylan's. "How do you explain then why you would come here, to the territory of another Oligarch, without informing your father? Especially considering that the Blue Oligarch and I are, for lack of a gentler term, political opponents."

Dylan sighed. Of course his impulsive actions appeared suspicious. The Yellow and Blue Oligarchs didn't see eye to eye on a single issue, as far as he knew. His father considered Krale's views too old fashioned, and Krale no doubt felt that Jack's were too radical. At this point, Dylan could dig himself deeper by trying to compensate with more stories, or he could lay it all to rest by telling the truth. Most of it, anyway.

"My dad doesn't know I'm here," he said. "Kio and I thought we'd see more of the Five Lands, and hoped that Rano could give us a place to stay for a while."

"I still don't see why your father couldn't be made aware of such an innocent goal."

"Well, the idea was to get by on our own instead of always depending on him."

"So you decided to leave the home of one Oligarch and head directly to that of another? That's hardly relying on one's own resources."

Harsh as the words sounded, Krale looked amused. Maybe the wine was loosening him up.

"I'll admit it wasn't the best plan," Dylan grinned sheepishly, "but this is one of the few places my father wouldn't dare scry. Especially because it's... well, *you.*"

Krale gave a short bark of laughter. "Perhaps your father sent you to charm me rather than spy. Still, I can't help but think of how Jack would react if he worried and discovered you here of all places."

Dylan knew what would happen. Krale would inform the Blue Oligarch of his son's location and could do so instantly with his telepathy.

"Why are you at odds, anyway?" Dylan asked, playing for time.

Krale regarded him a moment, as if assessing his level of curiosity. "I believe in unity," he said, lifting the decanter and refilling his glass. "I believe that the Oligarchy should be just that, a handful of people who consistently remain in power and pass their ideals down through a bloodline. This is the most efficient way to bring about change. Your father, on the other hand, is no fan of organized power and feels that each Oligarch should be subject to the people's approval."

Dylan knew this to be true. His father had already set this process in motion, allowing the people of the Lakelands to vote for or against him. Anyone had the right to campaign for his title. In Dylan's lifetime there had been only one benign competitor, but his father's re-election had been nearly unanimous.

"It seems fair, letting people choose who leads them," Dylan said.

"Indeed, it's not only fair but it works," Krale answered, surprising Dylan. "At least for the Lakelands. Your father is an apt leader, and his people would be hard pressed to find better. However, other territories in the Five Lands aren't so harmonious; places where cities are torn apart by differences of belief. In such areas an elected Oligarch would never manage to serve for more than one term, and most of that time would be spent undoing what his predecessor had changed. In a situation like that, voting works against the populace and becomes a petty game of tug-of- war."

Krale went from sipping his wine to swigging it before he continued. "I think we should circumvent all of that and have the ten Oligarchs come together to form a council to rule the Five Lands. The council would police itself, dispatching any rogue elements if need be, and elect new successors to the position when bequeathing isn't an option."

"That doesn't sound so different from what my father wants," Dylan said. "The only difference is that you want to give the vote to a council instead of the people."

"Not quite. As I said, Jack doesn't like the idea of power conglomerating in one place. He feels that power corrupts, and that the collected Oligarchy pooling their magic would be... how does he put it?"

"Playing god." Kio's sleepy voice drifted up from underneath the table where he dozed.

"Playing god, hm?" Krale shook his head. "I can see his point, but the potential is too great to ignore. Just look at what a single Oligarch can manage on his own and multiply that by ten! We could easily defend our land from those tiger people in the south, or any other threat that dare come our way, while at the same time providing the very best life for our people. Hunger, disease, even crime could be stamped out completely. The Five Lands would become one land, under one rule, and one power!" Krale's face was red with excitement, and for a moment he sat staring off into the distance, eyes wide with a private dream. Then he came back to reality, and the ruddiness of his cheeks darkened a shade as he blushed. "I'm sorry," he said. "I get rather carried away at times."

"I'm used to it," Dylan reassured him. "My dad rants about his views all the time."

"I'm relieved to hear it," Krale said gratefully. He frowned at his wine glass. "I'm afraid my ideas will never come to pass while people debate who should have power instead of focusing on the actual issues at hand."

"I don't think your ideas are so bad," Dylan said. "Then again, I also agree with most of what my father believes. I'm just glad I'll never have to decide what's right or wrong for other people."

"Then you aren't interested in taking up the mantle after your father? Rano has no interest in it either. I don't know that I can blame him. It is a frustrating occupation, always butting heads with people who have their own equally valid viewpoints." Krale managed a weary smile before finishing off his wine. "I'm afraid this old man has worn himself out." He pushed his chair back and stood. "Would you consider me a poor host if I retired early?"

"Not at all," Dylan said. He wished there had been a chance to ask where Rano was, but there would be time for that in the morning.

"Thank you." Krale waved a hand absentmindedly. Curls of wispy yellow air appeared around the table, ensnaring each dish and lifting them up. They floated, as if carried by ghosts, across the room to the kitchen. Not a single piece was broken as they dropped, one by one, into the sink.

"I'll leave the rest of the wine here," Krale said. "There's more milk on the counter if the cat needs feeding. The condition of Rano's room should be tolerable, I hope."

"Thank you," Dylan said, but the Yellow Oligarch didn't seem to hear him as he shuffled out of the room.

Rano's room wasn't the pinnacle of organization that the rest of the mill was. The small space was cluttered with cheap souvenirs collected on his travels, many of them various charms and talismans. Dylan noted with amusement that most of the magical trinkets related to beauty, charm, and romantic prowess.

He laughed as he remembered his friend's cocky attitude and tendency to strut around like a rooster. These cheap charms suggested he wasn't as confident as he liked to appear. From what he could remember, Rano had nothing that needed compensating for.

Dylan's skin tingled as he slowly inspected the room. These were the things Rano decided to surround himself with. Being in Rano's private room was somehow intimate; a way of being near Rano without him actually being there. This was a sanctuary not meant for him. And yet, here he was. Dylan flopped down onto the bed, the evening air blowing in from the window cool and refreshing.

"I'm curious about the tiger people Krale mentioned," Kio said, jumping up on the foot of the bed. "The Rasaka or whatever."

"Rakshasa," Dylan corrected.

"Yeah, them. Why don't we go there next?"

"Are you crazy? They eat humans!"

"Yeah, that's what they say, but you'd be with me. I'm probably a distant relative to them or something."

"Better send them a letter first," Dylan laughed. "Family or not, it's rude to drop in unexpectedly. No, I thought we could find out where Rano is and go there instead."

"I thought you two had a bad falling out," Kio murmured, eyelids bobbing in a battle with sleep. "Why the sudden interest to make amends?" The cat was too tired to wait for an answer. His eyes shut, and he slept.

Dylan kicked off his boots, pulled off his shirt, and stretched out on the bed, hugging a pillow to his face. He breathed in Rano's scent, closed his eyes, and let himself sink into memory.

* * *

The empty bottle of wine, knocked across the floor by the two wrestling boys, spun wildly, colliding into another that had also been drained. The outcome of the struggle was clear. Rano was both bigger and stronger, and Dylan had no chance of winning. He could only try to delay being pinned down. This was made twice as difficult by the nonstop laughter that had Dylan gasping for breath. After a valiant struggle, he gave way to exhaustion. Rano's strong legs had Dylan pinned, each hand captured in his own and pressed firmly to the floor.

The laughter ceased as they both caught their breath. Rano relaxed the weight of his body onto Dylan as they lay panting together. The rough stubble on Rano's chin tickled Dylan's neck, making him squirm. Rano reacted instinctively, pressing down with his hips to stop Dylan from moving. They noticed then that the reaction to their physical closeness was mutual. Rano raised his head and looked into Dylan's eyes with no hint of embarrassment, only lust.

What followed was a new world, wondrous and exhilarating, but most of all *right*. That was the only word for it. Dylan had found a piece that he hadn't even known was missing, and it felt right. Except right wasn't the word that Rano used the next morning. Wrong, sick, and sinful, were the kindest terms that Rano chose, and the arm that had held Dylan through the night now pushed him away.

"We shouldn't have done that," Rano kept repeating like a mantra, but soon enough the 'we' was replaced by 'you' as Rano made clear this was all Dylan's fault. Rano kept his back to him as he dressed, only facing him again when he was at the door.

"I won't tell anyone," Dylan said, but this promise didn't erase the disdain in Rano's eyes. As the bedroom door slammed, Dylan felt baffled at how something that felt like love could inspire such hate.

* * *

Dylan awoke with a start, confused about where he was. Only weak moonlight illuminated the dark room. Someone was shouting. He strained to make out the angry words when the ranting ceased. The pause lasted just long enough that he thought it was over when the voice cried out again—this time in terror.

Kio jolted awake. "What's going on?"

"I think Krale is in trouble."

A bestial scream echoed through the windmill, goose bumps racing over Dylan's skin in response. "We have to go look," he whispered.

He tiptoed to the door and opened it a crack, relieved to see the hallway empty. From the stairwell came the sound of a scuffle. Peering into its depths, he was only able to see a light from the second floor study. Kio behind him, Dylan began making his way downward, wincing with each squeaking stair.

The sounds below became so loud that there was little need for stealth. A mighty thud came first, forceful enough to vibrate throughout the entire windmill. Then Krale gave a triumphant yell, followed by the sound of stone scraping along the floor. The shouting that came next was fearful rather than victorious and strangled to an end.

Abandoning caution, Dylan flew down the stairs and plunged into the dimly lit room. The study was chaos; shattered furniture and toppled book shelves. In the corner a gas lamp sputtered on its side, its flame dangerously close to scattered books. Krale lay on the floor, only his legs visible beneath a pile of stone. Dylan whipped around, looking for the source of this havoc.

"Behind you!" Kio shouted as he leapt off the stairs.

Dylan turned to see the rubble on Krale shifting. Thinking at first that the Oligarch was alive and using his magic to free himself, Dylan rushed to help but stopped when he realized the pile of stones was moving as one, shifting like muscle, unbending and straightening. The stone was alive!

Wings unfurled from the creature's back as it turned its head to look at Dylan. The beast was bird-like in appearance, but its hide appeared to be hewn from gray rock instead of feathers. Murky red eyes peered from each side of its narrow head. Its stout beak was filled with something round, hairy, and bloody. Dylan recognized it as the back of Krale's head the moment the beast bit down, crushing the skull as if it were an egg.

Dylan was on the verge of vomiting, but the need to flee overpowered that urge. Kio, fur bristling, was already heading up the stairs. They raced one floor up before the entire windmill shook with a force that knocked Dylan to his knees. Try as he might, he couldn't regain his feet. All Dylan's strength was needed to keep from slipping down the stairs as he clung desperately to the rail. He knew that any second the creature could overtake them, and the idea terrified him.

The shaking stopped, and for the briefest moment everything was still. Dylan was back on his feet, but before he could take a single step, everything began to tilt. The slant increased until Kio slid backward down the stairs, his fall halted by Dylan, who had reached out one arm to catch the cat.

"The windmill is out of control!" Dylan shouted.

"You think so?" Kio growled.

A chorus of crashes and a bestial squawk sounded from below. With any luck the stone monster was hindered by problems of its own. Another gut-wrenching lurch and the windmill began tilting in the opposite direction until the floor was once again even.

"Go! Hurry!" Dylan yelled as he pushed Kio up the stairs.

"Where?" the cat hissed as he scuttled upward.

"I don't know. It's going to crash!"

"The windmill?"

"Yes! Now go!" Dylan took the winding stairs two, three at a time. He didn't know where they could run. The magic-fueled engines were on the top floor, Krale had told them. If the engines had been sabotaged, there might be a way to fix them, but he suspected another reason for their failure.

"Wait!" he yelled, just as they were about to pass the kitchen. "This way!"

He leapt off the stairwell and was almost knocked back by the intense winds. The magical barrier that once sealed off half the room was gone. Dylan's suspicions were correct. The Yellow Oligarch was dead, and his magic had died with him. Miraculously, the windmill was still in the air, but it wouldn't be long before it lost power altogether.

He didn't know what to do. His instincts screamed at him to escape the building before it crashed to the ground. The force of impact would shatter the entire structure, the wreckage burying them alive if not crushing them to death; but how could they escape? With no time left, he succumbed to the primal urge to flee.

Fighting against the wind, he struggled across the dining room and onto the balcony. Kio followed, fear dilating his eyes into black discs. They scrambled to a halt on the wooden balcony just as the building lurched again, tilting drastically. Dylan's feet slid out from under him. Reaching out to grip something, he found only Kio and grabbed onto the cat, his stomach turning as he realized that they were freefalling. A swirl of stars was in front of him, the wooden floor of the balcony now a wall adjacent to the sky, instead of horizontal to it. Dylan wanted to scream, but before he could his back hit the railing, halting their fall and knocking the wind out of him.

He turned his head upward, not that direction held meaning anymore, and went stiff with fear. The giant blades of the windmill's rotor were directly above him. If the windmill continued to tilt in this direction, they would be thrown over the balcony's edge and into the spinning blades. He caught his breath just as the windmill swayed, sending him rolling to the right and over the rail. He cried out in pain as Kio's claws dug instinctively into him.

The world seemed to slow as they fell toward the rotor. Dylan hoped one of the massive blades would break their fall, but imagined their bodies would be sliced in half by the gigantic knives instead. His mind replayed the image over and over again, as he pictured the two halves tumbling to the ground, one nothing more than four legs: two human and two feline.

Dylan winced as they plummeted through the rotor's vicious path, a blade passing so close that the resulting wind buffeted them like a fist. They had made it through! As they fell he watched the windmill rise away into the midnight sky and tightened his grip on Kio. He wanted to say something to the cat before they hit the ground, something meaningful before they met their inevitable end.

"Kio, I—" The air was knocked out of his lungs as he hit the ground, and when he tried to breathe in again, his lungs filled with blood.

He opened his eyes. Not blood. Water! He would have laughed if he wasn't on the verge of drowning. Somehow they had hit water! The windmill wasn't anywhere near a lake, and yet they were safe. Realizing that he and Kio had released each other, he kicked toward what he hoped was the surface. He kept swimming upward, wondering if the break into air would ever occur, until darkness engulfed his consciousness.

Chapter 3
Blue

Intense blue eyes peered from behind round spectacles, the face welcome and familiar, even the expression of concern. Dylan wanted to whisper his name, as if doing so would make the impossible true, but there was no air left to speak with. The spectacles flashed. A blue light swept into Dylan's mouth and out again, taking the water from his lungs as it went.

"Check him," his father said, stepping out of his line of vision.

The comforting green light of a healer's magic surrounded Dylan, soothing him into a blissful, dreamless sleep.

The roar of twin waterfalls brought him back to consciousness. Dylan recognized their powerful sound as belonging to one of his father's ships. No mere magician could charge a crystal like that. Dylan lifted his head and looked around the cabin. Brass and red velvet dominated the spacious room, luxuries normally reserved for a captain. The cold light outside the portholes said it was early morning. Kio was lying nearby with ears perked toward him.

"Hey, you're awake!" the cat said. "Thank the gods, too. I've been bored stiff for hours. You feeling all right?"

"What happened?" Dylan's throat felt raw and dry.

"You should have seen it! The whole thing was a lake! Under the windmill I mean. Jack used his magic to flood the entire field with water. Instant lake! Can you believe that?"

Dylan's memory of the night's events came rushing back, bringing irrational fear. His eyes darted around the room as if the stone monster would be waiting there. "What about Krale?"

"Just dandy," Kio said sarcastically. "They glued his head back together, and he's been dancing ever since."

Dylan didn't laugh. The image of the creature's beak closing and the resulting splatter of gore made him feel hollow inside.

"It's not funny, Kio."

The cat's ears sagged. "I know. I'm having a hard time dealing with it too, but hey, we came out of it alive. I'm grateful for that."

Dylan nodded. "How did Dad find us?"

"The instincts of a parent, I guess. That, and a little scrying. I didn't have time to ask many questions. After Jack made sure you were okay, he interrogated me for details." Kio adopted an apologetic expression. "I told it all to him straight. I figured it was no time to play coy."

Dylan nodded. "Good."

"Afterwards, your father put us both on this ship, and now we're homeward bound. Jack stayed behind to figure out what exactly happened."

Dylan's muscles tensed. He didn't like the idea of his father being out there with a stone creature on the loose, even with all of his magic. A loka hadn't been enough to save Krale's life. Dylan leaned back in bed and tried to swallow his guilt. If something happened to his father, all because of his irrational need to see Rano, he would never forgive himself.

Three days crawled by. Even though he was glad to be back somewhere safe and familiar, Dylan found little peace. His father had arrived back a day later—to his great relief—but hadn't spoken to them since. The door to his office was sealed off by a wall of ice, something the Oligarch always did when demanding privacy, but never had he been so distant before. Dylan wondered if this time, he and Kio had gone too far and finally exhausted his patience.

Jack didn't even show for meals, much to Ada's chagrin. The old caretaker couldn't explain his behavior either, and spent most of her time worrying over Dylan and Kio as if they were in harm's way, even at home.

Unfortunately, Dylan shared her panic. He no longer felt safe in the tower's protective walls. Situated on a small island in the middle of the Lakeland's largest body of water, the tower was only accessible by a single bridge that was neither gated nor guarded. There had never been a need before, but Dylan now knew that monsters could come from the air. Seeing the Yellow Oligarch killed in his own home had left Dylan shaken. His father had once told him that magical wards were built into the blue tower to counter-measure any attack. Dylan tried to trust his father's word, but he kept envisioning the winged beast at his window.

Despite not feeling safe at home, Dylan refused to leave the tower, even to venture out on the little island. Kio stayed with him, becoming restless, but contenting himself by taking sun naps on the balcony that ringed the tower's highest floor.

On the morning of the fourth day, Ada burst into Dylan's room without knocking. He was about to protest when he saw the tears in her eyes.

"Your father wants you," she said, clutching at him. "Don't you listen to him either. Oh!" She let go of him to wrench a handkerchief from her pocket and blew her nose.

"We're not in that much trouble, are we?" Kio asked.

"It's just—" She broke off, again overcome by emotion.

Ada looked miserable. Strands of gray hair had come loose from her normally tidy bun, and she kept wringing her bony hands. Dylan wanted to hug and comfort her, but was afraid that she might burst into tears. Then they would never get the story out of her.

"It's not my place to say," Ada said, her tone becoming angry, "but let me tell you this: You are almost a grown man, Dylan, and you no longer have to do what your father tells you." She nodded as if satisfied, turned, and marched out of the room.

Dylan pondered Ada's reaction as he went downstairs. He hadn't seen her that upset in years, and her advice to go against his father's plans was surprising. Jack wasn't a harsh man and had always punished Dylan with lectures instead of beatings. Aside from his father there was only Ada, who had raised Dylan as if he were her own son. He might as well have been, since Dylan's mother had died when he was very young, and he had no memories of her. Ada was hired shortly afterwards to be his nanny, but had long since become an honorary member of the family. A strong woman not prone to emotional outbreaks, Dylan wondered what could make her so distraught.

His stomach churned as he reached the study door. The magical barrier was gone, and the door was ajar, so he pushed it the rest of the way open and went inside.

His father's office looked as it always had. Every flat surface was piled with papers and books. Even the shelves lining the room were stuffed so full as to be on the verge of exploding. A desk was centered in front of windows on the far wall. The Blue Oligarch was sandwiched between them, the daylight from behind lending him an aura of white light.

Dylan sat down, Kio on the floor next to him, and kept his eyes on the desk rather than on his father. The desk too was cluttered by books and other items, in its center a misshapen bowl that Dylan had made when he was six years old. He had painted the clay bowl with so many different colors that they ran together to create an ugly shade of brown. The bowl was filled with water and used by the Blue Oligarch when he scried; images magically appearing on the water's surface. The blue loka hovered just above the bowl, an object of indescribable beauty spinning above a disaster of crockery.

Dylan looked to a shelf where there sat an ornate onyx bowl lined with silver. His father had used this beautiful bowl before receiving Dylan's as a present. Even though the onyx bowl was more befitting his rank, his father had never used it again. With this thought in mind, Dylan raised his gaze and met his father's eyes. Their soft blue depths radiated love and a subtle hint of anxiety.

"I'm really sorry," Dylan blurted out. "We were just out for—"

"It's all right, Dylan. You don't need to explain. Kio did so well enough the night that it happened."

Dylan reached down and scratched the cat behind the ear in thanks as his father continued in a sterner tone of voice.

"Keep in mind, though, that if I hadn't taken it upon myself to scry and find out where you were, you would both be lying dead in a field right now. Heartbreak would put an end to Ada and I shortly after. You're too old to go running off without an explanation."

"Sorry," Dylan said, not knowing how to adequately express his regret. "I love you, Dad."

"I love you, too. Both of you." His smile promised all was forgiven before he continued. "Now, down to business. I need you to cast your mind back to the events of that night and try to recall any suspicious detail; anything at all that stands out in your mind."

"More suspicious than some rock monster maiming and killing an Oligarch?" His father didn't look amused, so Dylan changed his tone. "No, not really. I've played it all back in my mind enough times to have noticed something. I mean, the windmill went crazy right after he... When the creature—"

"Yes," Jack said softly. "Perhaps Krale mentioned someone that he was having a conflict with?"

"Just you, but he was practically complimenting you at the same time. Wait, why are you looking for something suspicious? It was a wild animal."

His father raised an eyebrow. "Was it? The creature that attacked him was a wyvern. A stone wyvern to be exact, which is an exceptionally rare animal. They are native only to the northern-most point of this continent, a distance of more than five weeks by horse. I don't believe it wandered so far south by accident. No, there's little chance of that."

"So how did it get there then?" Kio asked, his eyes peering over the edge of the desk. "Did someone magic it up?"

"Most likely. It could have been brought by some magical means or perhaps even created. That's what I've been trying to discover for the last few days, but without any luck." Jack removed his spectacles and rubbed his eyes.

Dylan noticed, not for the first time, how thin and gray his father's hair was becoming and tried not to think about how old he was. More than ever he needed to believe in the fading illusion that his father was invincible. "Why would someone do such a thing?" he asked.

Jack replaced his glasses and stared at Dylan. "Haven't you guessed? The yellow loka is missing!"

"So there's a new Yellow Oligarch somewhere out there."

"Unless it was lost in the wreckage," Kio pointed out.

"It wasn't," Jack said. "A loka's magic is easy to detect. Wherever it is, the loka is long gone."

His father turned to note the sun's position. "I'm afraid we must cut to the chase. There's no doubt that Krale's murder was premeditated. Our culprit selected a creature that yellow magic would be ineffective against, thus achieving the first stage of their plan."

"First stage?" Kio's ears flattened against his head. "You mean—"

"That they intend to take similar action against another member of the Oligarchy. In fact, I am to be the next victim."

Dylan's blood ran cold.

"Let them try it!" Kio hissed.

"Why?" Dylan breathed. "Why you?"

"It's the most logical strategy. By killing Krale they ceased communication between all the Oligarchs. We relied on his telepathy to stay linked together. He was the mouth and ears of the Oligarchy, and I am the eyes. If I am killed, the remaining Oligarchs will be mute, deaf, and blind."

Dylan's stomach sank. Without his father's ability to scry anywhere in the Five Lands, finding the culprit would be near impossible. "Are you sure Krale was the first to be killed?"

"Some Oligarchs have taken great precautions to ensure their privacy, so I can't be certain. However, I was able to successfully check up on many, which brings us to the most important point. I'm sending you to stay with the Red Oligarch. Both of you," he added before Kio could protest.

"So you can stay here and face your fate alone?" Dylan said, his voice rising. "Never!"

"I won't be here either," his father assured him. "Nor will Ada. She'll be staying with her sister, and I'll be pursuing my own line of investigation."

"Then we'll go with you!" Dylan shouted.

Jack didn't reply. Instead, he stared patiently at his son. Dylan hated it when he did this. He wouldn't reply to anything Dylan said until he calmed down and spoke in a more appropriate tone. This method of discipline frustrated Dylan, but was inarguably effective.

"Please take us with you," Dylan said once he had gotten himself under control. "We can help."

"I won't under any circumstances, and I'll explain why. In the last three days, I've managed to see into the future no less than four times."

Dylan leaned forward, understanding now what his father had been so preoccupied with. Seeing into the future took tremendous magical effort, and was very time-consuming—much more so than normal scrying. Doing so once within two days was impressive enough, but more than once a day was quite a feat.

"I will not reveal the gruesome details, but in the first vision I saw you die, Son. You died trying to defend me. Armed with this knowledge, I knew how to prevent this. I looked into the future again. In the second vision, the fate befell me instead. I saw myself die defending the both of you." Jack stopped and breathed in heavily, the memory of the visions disturbing him.

"I decided then to leave this place, to hunt the killer down. The resulting vision showed my own magic being turned against me, leading to my demise."

"How?" Dylan asked.

"The details are my own," Jack said. "Finally I decided on yet another plan of action. The fourth vision I had must remain a secret if it is to come true, but is the only chance for us to survive."

"So what are we going to do?" Kio asked.

"I'm passing the blue loka on to you, Dylan."

"But that will leave you defenseless!"

"It will save my life! I'm still a skilled blue magician with or without the loka. I might not pack the same punch, but I will be fine."

"I'm not ready for it," Dylan said, shaking his head. "Squirrels make better magicians than I do."

"All the more reason for you to take it. It will see you safely to the Red Oligarch, whom I trust implicitly." He turned again to check the windows behind him. "It's time to go."

"We're leaving today?" Kio asked.

"You are leaving this moment." Jack stood and pushed a cloth bag toward Dylan to the familiar clinking of coins. "A boat stocked with provisions is waiting for you. Now, take hold of the blue loka."

Dylan wanted to refuse, to put an end to this nonsense just as Ada had suggested, but his father's expression stopped him short. Hand shaking, he plucked the loka from the air. He had handled it before and wasn't surprised to feel it vibrating with an inner warmth that made it feel alive.

"Good," Jack said. "Now you know what you must say."

"Give me a minute!"

"Say it."

Dylan sighed and promised himself this would be undone as soon as this ordeal was over. He already felt uncertain about wielding one of the most powerful magical treasures in the world, but accepting the responsibility of being an Oligarch was unthinkable.

"Blue loka, awaken for me," he said in tones that were anything but triumphant.

"Very good," Jack said.

"That's it? The loka isn't going to flash, or speak, or something?"

"Not all magic is accompanied by fanfare," Jack lectured as he rounded the desk and embraced his son. Then he stooped to hug Kio. "Take care of each other." Jack stood and looked Dylan in the eye. "One more thing. You mustn't return here, either of you. I'll come for you when all of this is over. Don't come back here for any reason, understood?"

A moment later, Dylan was standing with Kio in an empty and silent hallway, the only sound a soft humming from the glowing blue gem in his hand.

"It's inconspicuous," said Dylan.

"It's crap," Kio replied.

"It's running faster now," Dylan countered.

"It's still crap," Kio reiterated.

Dylan beamed. "It's ours!"

Kio sighed heavily. "Do you suppose this is his way of punishing us?"

"It might be."

They were aboard the same shoddy boat they had stolen a week ago. A letter from Dylan's father explained that Mr. Boyo, the original owner of the boat, had reported it stolen and asked the Blue Oligarch to investigate. Mr. Boyo was so delighted to be compensated in gold for his loss that he hadn't asked who the thieves had been. Attached with the letter was a new title of ownership, with Dylan and Kio's names scrawled at the bottom.

The boat was running three times faster, if not more. That had everything to do with the loka and nothing to do with Dylan's skill. He was nervous about using the loka for the first time, but he needn't have worried. Going about his usual method of magic, but willing his energy through the loka instead, made the engine crystal glow like a miniature blue sun. The first time the two powerful streams of water shot from the crystal, the ship almost broke apart as it launched forward.

They made good progress, winding with the curving river to the southeast where the Red Oligarch lived. The sun was now setting on the second day of their voyage, and they likely would reach their destination early the next morning. With that thought in mind, Dylan steered the boat to the river bank, performed the anchor spell, and lit the back lamp to alert other boats to their position. He didn't need to light the front lamp, not with the crystal burning so brightly. They settled down inside the little cabin, which was still cramped and shoddy, but much more comfortable now thanks to a mattress, blankets and pillows.

"It's ironic, isn't it?" Kio said as he settled down on an old favorite blanket from home, crumpled up in a corner.

"What is?" asked Dylan, who was stretched out on his back with his hands behind his head. His mattress was thin and not very well stuffed, but compared to their sleeping conditions during the last trip, it felt luxurious.

"Ironic because last week we were running away from home, and this week we've been exiled. Makes you wonder if this is all some sort of cosmic punishment."

Dylan snorted. "Be careful what you wish for? That kind of thing?"

"Exactly." Kio scratched one of his ears. "Have we ever met the Red Oligarch?"

"Long time ago, yeah. Big woman, like opera singer big."

Dylan curved each arm at his sides to indicate girth. "Loud too, but nice. You were just a kitten."

"Jack said 'him' so you must be thinking of someone else."

"Did he?" Dylan strained to remember.

"I'm certain. He was shoving us on the boat and told us to trust him."

"That's odd."

Frogs began their nocturnal croaking, causing Dylan to lapse into thought. He felt more at ease now that they were traveling. He had felt like a sitting duck back at the tower, but now that they were on the move, they would be harder to find. On the other hand, he was uneasy that he didn't have a home to return to. The tower was still there of course, but his family had gone, and he wasn't supposed to return until summoned. His dad had seen something coming, maybe the creature that killed the Yellow Oligarch. Dylan wondered if the wyvern was at the tower already, lurking in the now-empty rooms, its stone wings scraping along the floor as it patrolled hallways, searching for signs of life.

"There's something on the deck," Kio whispered.

The hair on Dylan's neck stood up when he saw that Kio was serious. The cat's ears turned as they tracked whatever was out there. Dylan didn't hear anything, but he had complete faith in Kio's hearing.

"Sounds like a human,"

"Only one?"

The cat nodded. Heady with adrenaline, Dylan eased off the mattress and crawled toward the door of the cabin. A small round window was set at head's height in the door, so he rose up from the floor and peeked out.

The man on deck was old, judging from the sparse hair on his head. Despite the shadows, Dylan could see that his clothes were ragged and his skin dirty. He shuffled around the deck in a slow clumsy circle, as if trying to get his bearings. Dylan caught a brief glimpse of his line-worn face, which was screwed up in effort or confusion.

"There's some old hobo out there," Dylan reported.

"What's he doing?"

Dylan shrugged and looked out once more. The man had finished circling and was now shuffling toward the crystal engine, his hands already raised in anticipation.

"He's going to steal the engine!" Dylan hissed. "Come on!"

Kio padded silently over to the door.

"Do your wild animal act, all right?"

"Yup."

"Ready?"

"Yeah."

Dylan threw the door open and bellowed, "Hey!" in his deepest, most aggressive voice.

As soon as the man turned around, Kio was out the door, hissing and growling as he leapt toward the stranger. He landed a few feet in front of the man, who reacted with almost comical terror as he stumbled backward and choked on his own scream. His eyes bulged like two fat grapes as he began to grasp at his throat with both hands.

"I think he's choking," Dylan said from behind.

"Or maybe he's just nuts," Kio replied.

The stranger lurched forward, falling to his hands and knees, vomiting dark syrupy fluid all over the deck. Kio's sharp instincts saved him from being sprayed as he sprang backward and landed near Dylan. He hissed and flattened his ears. "Crazy *and* drunk!"

Dylan burst out laughing, and Kio soon joined him. This guy was a nuisance, not a threat. Hopefully the shock Kio had given him would sober him up. The stranger retched again, unleashing even more bile. Dylan stopped laughing, his stomach turning at the acrid smell.

"Hey, there's something in his puke that's…" Kio trailed off.

Alive. Dylan saw it, too. Slithering back and forth in the puke was what looked like a huge snake—more than one, in fact, and they were growing longer by the second, their thick bodies still slithering out of the man's mouth.

"What the hell is wrong with him?" Kio asked.

Dylan gagged, unable to answer while fighting back his own nausea.

The stranger stood, pushing himself up with renewed energy. The two serpentine bodies, each eight feet long, rose into the air in front of the man like new appendages. What were they, some sort of parasite? Were they part of him? Their heads were flat and featureless like an eel's, their skin black and slimy. They hissed in unison, weaving back and forth as if swimming. The man glared fiercely before returning his attention to the crystalline engine.

Dylan and Kio looked at each other in shock.

"Now what?" Dylan asked.

"We can't let him take the crystal! We need it!"

"Right." Dylan fumbled in his pocket and pulled out the blue loka. He held it before him with the tips of his fingers and thumb so it could be seen. The loka was a symbol of authority, hopefully one that this creature would respond to. "Leave our ship," he said. "Now."

The eel-man whipped around. His eyes lit up in recognition of the loka, but instead of leaving, he advanced. The eels stretched out eagerly, the mouths of each serpentine creature clicking open and shut excitedly, their sharp little teeth shining in the moonlight.

"I am the Blue Oligarch, and I command you to stop!"

The eel-man didn't even pause.

"Screw that, just use it!" Kio yelled.

How? His father had taught him nothing about magical combat, not even defensive maneuvers, and the eel-man was closing in. Near to panic, Dylan summoned all the magical energy in his body and shot it through the loka. Water exploded in front of him, knocking Dylan backwards until his back hit the wall of the cabin. Ignoring the pain, he wiped the water from his eyes with the back of an arm to see the results of his magic. The entire deck was flooded with water that drained off the side of the ship. The eel-man had been knocked backward, but not as far as Dylan had been. Kio was a wet rag, hanging over one of the rails.

The eel-man stood, pushing himself up with both his arms and his eels. A deep gurgling growl came from the creature's throat as he launched himself toward Dylan, the eels stretched out arrow-straight, eager to reach him. Dylan found himself unable to move, staring numbly at the chattering triangular teeth. To hell with the loka! He shoved it back in his pocket and struggled to unsheathe his pocket knife, but he was out of time. The eels were inches away from his face when a white streak barreled into the eel-man's side.

The creature and Kio were airborne for a moment, the serpents trailing along behind like two slimy banners. The eel-man landed on his knees and skidded over the deck, stopping just short of the rail. Kio landed on all four feet and immediately sprang again, this time pouncing on the eel-man's back. The creature fell forward, knocking its head on the rail with a loud crack. After its body slid to the side and hit the deck with a thud, Kio landed gracefully and turned to face Dylan.

"You see that? I showed that little fu—"

The eels sprang to life, hissing and writhing, even though the rest of the body was unconscious. One was pinned underneath the eel-man's torso, but the other whipped out and lashed itself around Kio's neck.

The eel lifted the cat off the ground and slammed him downward toward the deck, but Kio managed to twist around so that his feet hit the wooden floor first. Snapping out of his stupor, Dylan scrambled to his feet to help him.

Dylan tried stomping on the middle of the serpent's body to stop it from rising again. It writhed under his bare foot, its slimy skin making it impossible to pin down. He slipped backward and fell to the deck, but scrambled up when Kio hissed out in pain. This time Dylan used his hands, his fingers barely connecting around the serpent's torso. He wrestled with it, Kio's claws digging into the deck as he struggled, the eel nipping at his fur but not yet his flesh. The cat wouldn't last much longer. Kio would run out of energy if he didn't run out of air first.

Dylan lifted one hand in order to reach his knife—a mistake that allowed the eel to escape his grasp. He struggled to grab it again, recognizing that holding it with one hand while cutting it with the other would be impossible. The eel was much too strong, and Kio was running out of time. Doing the only thing he could think of, Dylan bent over the eel, opened his mouth wide, and bit down. Its skin was tough and oily and difficult for his teeth to penetrate, but he kept biting. When he seemed to have broken through the outer skin, he bit down once more, this time grinding his jaw back and forth, sawing into its flesh with his teeth. A shrill screech filled the air as blood poured into his mouth, but Dylan kept gnawing into the raw meat of the eel until he heard Kio gulping in air.

Dylan looked up to confirm that Kio was free before releasing his grip on the eel. Still high on adrenaline, he stood and heaved the eel-man up by his waist. The bitten eel was almost completely severed, the other in a state of panic. Before it could recover, Dylan stepped forward and pushed the entire body over the railing where it splashed into the water.

Without hesitation, he ran to the front of the boat, magically released the anchor, and sent the boat lurching toward midstream. Kio, still panting, limped over to his side. When they were at full speed and safely away, they both began laughing.

Chapter 4
Red

Dylan awoke disoriented and covered in sweat. Thick heat made thinking difficult, but memories of last night's fight with the eel-man and their escape bobbed their way to the surface.

They had sailed throughout the night; fearful thoughts that the eel-man might follow keeping them awake and moving. By sunrise they had traveled as far toward their destination as they could by water. Anchored next to the shore, they unloaded all the essential gear and hiked three hours inland just to put distance between them and the river. Dylan had been little more than a brain-dead zombie when he had set up the tent and crawled inside.

The morning had been crisp when he fell asleep, but now the heat was becoming unbearable. He shook a still-snoozing Kio off his legs and unbuttoned the tent's flap. Stumbling outside, he saw the sun already beginning its afternoon descent.

After answering the call of nature and taking a quick swig of water, Dylan pulled out his map, which was one of the best gifts he had ever received. The magical map was made from a strange iridescent cloth no larger than a square foot. A softly glowing red light at the center of the map indicated the map holder's position. The light always stayed at the center, but the landmarks and locations shifted as he traveled. Currently it showed him so near a volcano that the little red indicator was almost on top of it.

That was their intended destination, but looking around he saw only trees. Dylan headed south as the map indicated, stopping when entering a clearing and staring in disbelief. Then he looked back at the map. The red light was now above the drawing of a volcano, making it look as if it were about to erupt. He looked up from the map again and was surprised to see how close the actual volcano was to the iconic drawing on the map—a smooth featureless cone with a wavy circular opening at the top.

Dylan shoved the map back into his pocket and rushed back to fetch Kio.

"There's no way that's natural," Kio said once he saw it. "It reminds me of the crap you used to draw as a kid."

"Hey!" Dylan scowled down at the cat.

"Anyway, how exactly are we supposed to go about this? Do we just march on in or try to send some sort of signal from here?"

"I figure that we're expected. Hopefully there's a door we can knock on."

As they neared the volcano, they could see rows of windows along its surface, indicating three stories inside. The lack of any path gave the impression that they were at the rear of the structure, so they angled off to the right and went around the base. Soon they reached a large entryway with two great wooden doors that were left wide open.

Exchanging wary looks, they continued until they were standing just beyond the doorstep where cool air flowed from inside. Dylan snorted at the volcano's domestic appearance.

Tasteful furniture and rugs decorated the large room, as well as a number of thriving house plants. Two sets of stairs ran along the curve of the inner wall toward higher floors, while a dozen steps in the center of the room led up to a stone throne set high on a dais. Cold and inconsistent with the rest of the room's decor, the throne would have been intimidating were it not for the plush rabbit currently occupying the seat.

"Not quite what I expected," Dylan murmured.

"Yeah, I was thinking fiery pools of lava or maybe some torches," Kio replied. "There's a fireplace over there, but it's not even lit."

"So why the open doors?" Dylan asked, trying to hide the unease in his voice. He couldn't help but be reminded of what happened the last time they visited an Oligarch.

"Because we're expected?" Kio answered.

"Maybe." Dylan cupped his hands to either side of his mouth. "Hello? Anybody home?"

There was a still moment in which an answer failed to manifest.

"I guess we just enter." Kio strolled in and sniffed a chair near the door. Like the rest of the furniture it was fairly modern, made mostly of twisted cast iron rather than wood.

As Dylan entered, he began to remove the loka from his pocket as a protective measure, until he realized that it might look like an act of aggression if the Red Oligarch was alive. Around, he corrected himself mentally, if the Red Oligarch was around. There was no need to panic yet.

"Hello? Anybody here?" he called out again, startling Kio.

"No answer." Kio cocked his ears in two different directions. "Shall we try upstairs?"

Dylan shrugged and led the way up the left stairway, feeling that the loka might offer him some protection that Kio didn't have. The stairs led to a hallway, featureless except for a closed door. Dylan was reaching for the handle when a whoosh from the stairway attracted his attention. Warm air blew the hair from his forehead as he turned. Flames filled the stairwell behind them. Dylan shouted in warning, watching in awe as the fire spread snarling and hissing through the air. Fire, the power of the red loka. Maybe the Oligarch wasn't expecting them, or maybe the red loka had already been taken and was being used against them.

Panicked, Dylan tried the nearest door but it wouldn't budge, even when he threw his weight against the heavy panel.

"Forget the door, just run!" Kio shouted before galloping down the hallway. Dylan struggled to keep up, barely noticing the next doorway they passed. With the fire's heat at their backs, they had no choice but to press on. They stumbled up the next set of stairs, the growling flames spurring them on.

Around another curve, past another floor, and daylight appeared like a beacon of hope. Kio had already broken free of the shadows and disappeared off to the right. After one last burst of speed, Dylan reached the exit and threw himself desperately in the same direction. He rolled over wooden planks, the bright sunlight blinding him. Scrambling to sit up, he looked back, but there was no sign of fire.

"What's the rush?" a new voice asked.

The stranger was stretched out on a wooden deck chair, sunning himself even though his skin was the color of ebony. Muscle covered his lean body, which was exposed except for the tight maroon shorts. Sunlight glinted off the red diamond between his impressive pecs, dangling from a golden chain. The red loka!

"Blue Oligarch!" Dylan gasped before another attack could come. Still winded from sprinting, it was hard to manage any words. "No fire! Please!"

The Red Oligarch considered him, his eyes hard at first. He then looked to Kio, who was still bristling with fear, before returning his attention to Dylan. Only after he looked him up and down did something in his gaze soften, albeit reluctantly.

"Weren't you expecting us?" Dylan asked in disbelief.

"Of course!" Their host grinned, white teeth brilliant against his dark skin. Now his brown eyes twinkled in amusement, as if it had all been a game.

Anger rose in Dylan. "We could have been roasted!"

"Not a chance," the Oligarch said casually. "I was in complete control the whole time. Besides, I knew you could use the blue loka if you were in real trouble." He raised an eyebrow. "Jack did give it to you, right?"

Dylan sighed. He hadn't even thought of using it in the pandemonium.

"That was all a joke?" Kio glared at the Red Oligarch. "You

really suck, you know that?"

The cocky smile swept off their host's face as he bolted upright in his seat. "You really can talk!"

"Yeah," Kio said, "or maybe it's just Dylan throwing his voice. Take your pick."

The Red Oligarch furrowed his brow before bursting into laughter. "I'm sorry," he said. "I guess it was a really daft trick to play on you."

He stood, coming close to Dylan and offering his hand. He was taller than Dylan, a little older too, but not by much. Most of him was bare skin and muscle, which Dylan tried not to think about as he accepted his hand.

"I'm Tyjinn." He pumped Dylan's arm up and down a few times before releasing him. "You've obviously had a nightmare of a trip, judging from your appearance."

Tyjinn's comment made Dylan self-conscious, so he tried smoothing down his hair while looking hopefully to Kio for some sort of cue.

"Er, you still have blood all over your face," the cat said. "Kept meaning to mention that to you."

"Were you hurt?" Tyjinn asked with concern.

"No, it's not mine," Dylan said. "It's uh, eel blood."

"Eel-man blood actually." Kio puffed up his chest with pride.

Tyjinn stepped back, and Dylan felt relieved. He had been standing so close that Dylan had felt the heat radiating off his body and could smell the sun on his skin.

"Eel-man," Tyjinn repeated with a skeptical expression. "You mean Eel Gut?"

"If Eel Gut is a guy who pukes up killer eels, then yes," Dylan said, feeling cross again.

Tyjinn seemed to be waiting for a punch line that didn't come. "I always thought that was just an old mariner's tale."

"Might be now," Kio bragged.

Tyjinn considered the cat's words before searching Dylan's eyes. "You killed him?"

"Maybe." Dylan felt embarrassed every time Tyjinn looked at him. He was handsome, which normally wouldn't be bad, but Dylan was feeling repulsive. "Do you think we can talk about this some other time?"

"Of course, sorry." Tyjinn shook his head. "I have another

Oligarch in my home, subject him to my horrid sense of humor, and then start with the interrogation. Terrible!" He flashed a wide smile at Dylan. "I've heard so much about you and Kio from Jack. I feel like I know you already. Your father was here after the first thaw helping me with some magic. Take a look."

Dylan became aware of their surroundings for the first time. They were at the uppermost portion of the volcano where the crater opened to the sky. A large sun porch had been built here, a wooden floor cluttered with chairs and a table. In the very center was a pool of water steaming with heat.

Tyjinn walked to the pool's edge, Dylan following. "The stone reservoir is natural and used to fill with rain water. When it did, I would heat the water and bathe, even swim when it was deep enough. Jack set it up so the water is always there and clean."

Dylan stared at the water longingly, the thought of jumping in nearly irresistible. The two day's worth of grime was a thick film on his skin that he was desperate to scrub off.

"Want to try it out?" Tyjinn said, glancing sidelong at him.

"I need to undress," Dylan said.

Tyjinn shrugged. "Go ahead."

Dylan's expression was incredulous enough to cause the Red Oligarch to chuckle.

"Tell you what," Tyjinn said, "I'll go sit over there with my back to the pool. Kio can keep me company while you get yourself cleaned up. Sound good?"

"Yes," Dylan said gratefully.

As soon as Tyjinn was seated, Dylan didn't hesitate. He undressed and plunged into the water, sighing blissfully once he came up for air. Practically feeling reborn, he rubbed every inch of his body clean, then contented himself by lazily swimming around the pool. As he swam, he caught snippets of Tyjinn and Kio's conversation, but couldn't follow along. Whatever they were talking about, he wasn't worried. The cat was far more clever than most people realized. Kio would come away with more information than he gave out.

When the heat of the water became too much, Dylan realized that his clean clothes, along with everything else, were still back at the campsite. He didn't enjoy wearing his dirty clothes again, but there wasn't a choice. Once he was dressed, he expressed his intention to fetch their belongings. Tyjinn offered to accompany them, but Dylan declined. He was looking forward to being alone with Kio and hearing what the cat had learned.

"Nineteen years old, lives alone," Kio reported once they were away, and Dylan was taking down the tent. "No servants. Says he prefers to be self-sufficient. You were right about the Red Oligarch having been a woman. Tyjinn took over from his mother just over a year ago. He seems awfully confident about his magical skills, considering."

"So where is she now?"

"Lives in Brandwald, a couple of miles north of here. Tyjinn has lived alone the last couple of years, for reasons I couldn't pry out of him. His mother still seems to handle all the political aspects of being an Oligarch and calls him in only when her magic isn't enough."

Dylan mulled this over while changing into fresh clothing. "So why does Dad think we can trust this guy so much? He's barely older than me." If an Oligarch with the experience and talent of his father couldn't keep them safe, then what made Tyjinn any more capable?

"Jack's never steered us wrong before," Kio answered. "If he says Tyjinn is our man, then that's good enough for me."

Dylan stuffed his dirty clothes into his pack and frowned. "That thing with the fire, though. That was seriously messed up. We could have been hurt."

"So he has a sense of humor even worse then mine. I'm sure our expressions were priceless, you have to give him that."

But Tyjinn's eyes weren't amused when they had first reached the deck. They were cold and distant, Dylan was sure of it. "I still don't know that we can trust him."

Kio's expression was sympathetic. "You're just shaken up from the wyvern and Eel Gut. Not everyone is a monster."

Dylan had to concede the point. He had witnessed a murder, been attacked by a magic hungry eel-man, and was nearly burnt to a crisp when arriving at his supposed sanctuary. To say that he was on edge was an understatement. Still, he couldn't help but feel curious about Tyjinn and why his father thought this person could keep him safe more than any other. Putting the last of their belongings away, he shouldered his pack and went to find out.

Candlelight added warmth to the otherwise cold, cavernous

room on the volcano's first floor. The rustic dining table had been set in their absence. Tyjinn reclined in one of the chairs, casually flipping through an old book without much interest. His feet were on one corner of the table, which he hurriedly returned to the floor when they entered.

"You sure cleaned up nicely," he said as Dylan took his seat across from him. "You share your father's good looks."

The comment gave Dylan pause. What had Tyjinn meant by it? Was he trying to be charming or was he teasing? The comment could be a jab at Dylan's past with Rano—if gods forbid—Tyjinn somehow knew, or as harmless as something his aunt would say. Tyjinn's face was unreadable, so Dylan turned his attention instead to the table.

A simple spread of bread and cheese was placed among the candles, along with an oily potato salad and slices of cold roast beef. A clutter of wine bottles kept a jug of beer company at one end of the table, while at the other, a third place had been set without silverware and with a bowl instead of a drinking glass. Kio hopped up on the seat in front of this setting, looking just as comfortable as he did at home.

Dylan smiled at their host in gratitude. Now it was Tyjinn's turn to look taken aback. Was it so surprising that Dylan should smile? He supposed that he had been rather moody since arriving. The fire prank certainly hadn't helped, but now it was obvious their host was doing his best to make them feel comfortable.

"It looks great," Dylan said, determined to start anew. "Thank you."

"Pour me a beer, would you, Dylan?" Kio purred.

"It's warm I'm afraid," Tyjinn said. "Hot I can do, but I'm useless when it comes to cold. Can you make ice?"

"Uh, not yet," Dylan said, wishing his answer was more impressive. He focused on not pouring too fast, even though Kio preferred a lot of foam. "Dad tried to show me, but I've never managed to pull it off."

"You might not be able to," Tyjinn said as he cut the loaf of bread into slices and passed them out onto plates. "The lokas manifest themselves in slightly different ways, depending on the person. I hear your great-grandfather could do amazing things with ice but couldn't manage a single drop of water."

"That's what they say." The conversation lulled briefly, the silence causing panic to slowly rise in Dylan. He looked around the room, grasping for some topic of conversation. The floor had caught his eye since his return. Black and glossy, he had originally thought it was marble, but the reflected light from the candles revealed a number of wavy ridges.

"Basalt," Tyjinn said, following his gaze. "Cooled lava that's been polished. It's cold on the feet in the winter, but I've grown to like it."

"Hold on a minute," Kio interrupted, his muzzle covered in beer foam. "Are you saying this place used to be a real volcano?"

Tyjinn shook his head. "Nope. It was created by a previous Red Oligarch over a century back, one with a rather dramatic flair. See the stone throne there? Aside from it and two pathways leading to the stairwells, the floor you see now was hot molten lava."

"Wouldn't the heat scald anyone who entered the room?" Kio asked.

"The Oligarch used his magic to confine the heat to the lava only." Tyjinn gestured with the bread knife toward the center of the room where the plush rabbit sat merrily on the throne. "He'd be sitting up there, and anyone paying him a visit would have to look up at him as soon as they entered. He was always decked out in red silk robes and would glide down regally to greet his visitors."

"Sounds like an impressive setup," Kio commented. "To be honest, that's the sort of thing we were expecting to find here."

"It's not very practical," Tyjinn said. "In fact, it's what did the old nutter in. A number of other Oligarchs came to pay him a visit, and while doing his usual routine of swooping down the stairs, he tripped on his robes and fell in his own lava."

Kio chuckled, and the others soon joined him.

"Funny," Dylan said, "even though I feel guilty for laughing about someone dying."

"Well, it was a long time ago." Tyjinn gazed into the air as if he could see the past. "I used to sneak around here as a kid. By then it was all overgrown. When I decided to live on my own, I thought I could bring new life to this old place."

"Still, you're a little far away from town," Dylan said. "At least that's how it appeared on the map."

Tyjinn nodded, but didn't explain. His grin almost faded

completely before he reached for one of the bottles. "Care for some wine?"

Rano! Dylan almost said the name out loud. While waiting for his dad to return from the windmill's wreckage, Dylan had thought of Rano countless times, wondering how he would cope with finding his home and family both destroyed. Who would be there to comfort him? Dylan had meant to ask his dad to scry and see where Rano was, but everything had moved so fast.

"You've been through a lot," Tyjinn said, setting the bottle back down. "Jack told me of course, but even if he hadn't, I can see it on your face."

"I'm fine."

"You will be here," Tyjinn said. "I regret my little stunt more than ever. It was thoughtless of me. I want you to feel safe here."

Dylan looked at Tyjinn and saw determination. He couldn't hold his gaze for long, so he nodded and turned his attention back to the bottle. "I guess a little wine can't hurt."

"Hell, a whole bottle can't hurt," Kio said. "Not until the next morning anyway."

They all laughed, and conversation flowed more smoothly after that. Every bite of the food was devoured as they spoke. A couple of beers later, Kio began telling tales of trouble that he and Dylan had previously gotten into. Tyjinn did his best to top Kio's stories, causing Dylan to spend most of the night laughing. Eventually, the food combined with alcohol eased them into a mellow, thoughtful mood.

As the night wore on, Dylan found his anxiety and homesickness had vanished. He *did* feel safe here. Tyjinn's self-confidence made Dylan feel protected. The idea of staying in a stranger's home until things were resolved was no longer unappealing.

"Thanks for letting us stay here, Ty," Dylan said. "It's really nice of you."

The Red Oligarch looked surprised for a moment before smiling. "Only my mom calls me Ty."

"Oh. Sorry."

"No, I don't mind! I like the way it sounds when you say it." He gave a distracted half-smile and finished off his wine. "It's just too bad that I'll be deprived of your company sooner rather than later."

"Why's that?" Kio slurred. The beer and the late hour were taking their toll on the cat.

"I don't imagine Jack will take very long to find the killer, even without his loka. It's only a matter of eliminating suspects through simple deductive reasoning."

"I didn't know there were any suspects," Dylan said.

"There are quite a few, really." Tyjinn held up the bottle of wine, and when Dylan shook his head, he poured the remainder for himself. "I'd say all of the other members of the Oligarchy are at the top of the list."

"Kio and I talked about that, but it doesn't make sense," Dylan replied. "They already have power, so why would they jeopardize it by taking down a colleague?"

"There are always people who can't get enough power," Tyjinn said grimly.

"All right, but there are plenty more ordinary people who want power," Dylan countered. "Why immediately suspect another Oligarch?"

"Because whoever sent that creature after Krale must have had potent magic at their disposal. In fact, I'd say we can narrow it down to three suspects."

Dylan and Kio both leaned forward in anticipation of this revelation.

"Considering which powers the Oligarchs have—and eliminating your father and myself of course—only Purple, Black, and Brown would be capable of organizing such an attack."

"Wait, let me figure it out," Kio insisted, always one for a good mystery. "Purple can control animals, right? So he could have magically manipulated the wyvern into killing Yellow."

"Right." Tyjinn nodded. "He's also supposed to have some sort of zoo, which means he might have such a creature on hand. What about the other two?"

Kio mulled it over for a moment and then shook his head. "I don't see it."

"What about you, Dylan?"

"Well, Brown can teleport anywhere in the world, so I guess that he—"

"She," Tyjinn corrected.

"She could have teleported up north, or wherever these wyverns exist, and then teleported one of them straight to the windmill." Dylan looked uncertain. "Can she do something like that?"

"I believe so," said Tyjinn, "although I suspect her least of all. That just leaves Black, who could have crafted the creature using his magic. The wyvern was made out of rock after all."

"Wait, that's Green's magic, isn't it?" Kio mused. "Green does all the earthy stuff like trees and rocks."

Tyjinn paused. "Maybe we should say four suspects, then. Still, that's not so many, is it?"

Any reply was halted by a loud thud reverberating throughout the room. They all looked toward the front door in time to see it burst into splinters as something large and low came trundling in. They barely had time to react before it charged, colliding with the table and scattering everything. Kio and Dylan jumped away from the table, but Tyjinn's wine-soaked reflexes failed him. He was knocked backward and now lay under a mess of dirty dishes.

The creature shook its head at the end of its long neck, dazed from its kamikaze tactic. Stunned, it stumbled around on its four stubby legs, dishes shattering underneath its clawed feet. Torchlight flickered wickedly off its scaled body as it turned in search of a new target.

"It's a freaking dragon!" Kio yelled, his tail puffed up to twice its normal size.

Panic gripped Dylan's stomach. Dragons were legendary and rare, but most of all they were deadly. He grabbed frantically for his loka as Tyjinn pulled himself up from the floor—mere yards away from the dragon—which was sniffing through its huge nostrils. It located Tyjinn just as he was tugging the red loka free from inside his shirt.

Meanwhile, a voice in Dylan's head was trying to get his full attention. An old saying surfaced in his memory: "You can always judge a dragon by the color of its scales." Usually meant metaphorically, the phrase was actually based in fact. His head made the connections as the scene played out before him in slow motion. Tyjinn had the loka out now, which was beginning to glow red. The dragon was green. This was important. This dragon wasn't a fire breather; those were red. Lightning breath? No, those were blue. Or were they gray? Dylan wracked his brain, trying to remember. The dragon had swollen with breath before starting to exhale, but nothing was visible yet.

Gas! A green dragon expelled gas! Dylan realized what was about to happen and thrust out his loka, pouring his panic through his arm and out his hand. Water exploded outward in a horizontal pillar and struck its target directly in the chest. Tyjinn was knocked backward by Dylan's magic, the fire from his loka smothered before it could ignite the gas.

Dylan then aimed the loka at the dragon and hit it with a barrage of water. This only enraged it further. The dragon lowered its head and began trudging toward Dylan, but Kio pounced on its neck before it could get close. Despite his bravery, the cat's claws and teeth were no match for the dragon's scales, and he was thrown off as the beast shook its head violently. Kio careened into Dylan, knocking them both to the floor.

Tyjinn, still soaking wet, had recovered and was reaching for his loka again.

"No fire!" Dylan shouted. "It's a gas dragon!"

Tyjinn cursed and scrambled to reach them. "Up to the throne! I have an idea. Go!"

Kio was first to race up the stairs toward the throne, with Dylan right behind him. The plush bunny was still happily smiling as they reached the top, despite the madness around it. Tyjinn followed, red light filling his fist as he reactivated his loka.

"No fire," Dylan repeated. "You're going to blow us all up!"

"No, I'm not, but have your loka ready."

The entire room began to fill with red light, all coming from the onyx-colored floor below. The basalt was beginning to heat, cracks of brilliant orange appearing in its surface. The dragon, feeling the heat through its feet, headed toward the stairs and began ascending. Dylan pressed past Tyjinn and sent a torrent of water streaming down the stairs, causing the dragon to lose its footing and slip backward. The water reacted to the hot floor, steam obscuring their vision. Smoke was added to the chaos as various pieces of furniture began to smolder.

"On my signal, I want you to completely surround us with water," Tyjinn said through bared teeth. "Give it all you've got. Fill the entire room if you can, got it?"

"Yeah." Dylan began building up his energy, unsure of what was about to happen. Smoke and steam cleared long enough to reveal the dragon slowly sinking into the ground. The floor directly below the beast was turning orange and runny as the Red Oligarch focused his power there. The dragon's legs were almost completely submerged. It let out a long painful wail as it began to sink faster, its fat belly dipping into the lava.

"Now!" Tyjinn shouted.

Dylan hesitated only a moment before unleashing all the power he had. Water exploded outward from him, lifting them all off their feet as air was replaced by liquid. Despite being submerged in water, they could still hear the loud explosion that rocked the room as the dragon's gas-filled intestines combusted. Hot bubbles of air burst through the water, and for a moment they all were boiling inside a huge cooking pot. Drained of energy and struggling to breathe, Dylan willed the water pouring from the loka to cease.

Nothing happened for a moment. Then they were falling with the water, the heat increasing as they neared the molten floor. Red light filled the water and abruptly the heat abated. With a final rush they hit bottom. The two humans pushed themselves up on their hands and knees, coughing up water and gasping for breath. Kio was carried along with the water as it poured through the broken doorway and out into the yard.

Dylan, struggling to catch his breath and his footing, pushed through the knee-high water toward the door, intent on reaching Kio. Once outside, he saw the cat sneezing and shaking on muddy but safe ground. Tyjinn also emerged unharmed, and for a while they all sat on the damp grass and focused on breathing.

Once he felt able to talk, Kio chose his words very carefully.

"Holy shit," he said.

Upon reentering the volcano, they found everything either charred, soaked, or broken. Shattered bones and fatty clumps of scale also littered the room.

Tyjinn didn't seem distraught over the mess. He launched a quick rescue of Mr. Scrumbles, the stuffed bunny, and even created mild, loka-generated heat to dry the plush animal. Aside from that, the Red Oligarch appeared thrilled with the obvious attempt on his life. He had paced back and forth on the lawn while they waited for the water to drain, ranting about the implications of the attack and what they could do about it.

Once the rush of adrenaline had left them, no one was talking much as they struggled to stay awake. Tyjinn led them to the third floor where two rooms had been prepared for them, but Kio and Dylan only needed one. Dylan fell into bed without glancing around at the room's features, and Kio took up his usual position of lying across Dylan's legs.

"I've never been so bruised in all my life," Kio murmured. "Between that eel thing and the dragon, I'm totally spent."

The cat's white fur hid the bruises from such injuries, and this worried Dylan. They'd been through so much in the last few days, and what they really needed now was a week's rest, but life seem determined to shake Dylan up every time he let his guard down.

The anxiety had returned, but Dylan felt hope now. Tonight had proven that, while they might not be able to escape the monsters, they could defeat them by sticking together. His father had chosen Tyjinn for a reason, and now Dylan could see why. As long as they stayed together, he felt sure that they would be safe.

"We're leaving right away!" The grin on Tyjinn's face suggested that this was the best news they could have received.

Dylan jabbed at his toast grumpily, doing his best to ignore any conversation. He hated cheerfulness in the morning. He glanced over at the steaming pool and considered skipping breakfast for another swim. That way he could submerge his head in the water when anyone tried to speak to him.

"Where are we going?" Kio yawned and blinked his eyes. "Into hiding or something?"

"No," Tyjinn laughed, "we're going to visit the Purple Oligarch."

Dylan put both hands over his face and rubbed his eyes. He didn't want to hear this. Perhaps if he ignored everything, the whole world would go away.

"More milk, please," Kio said, obviously with the same idea in mind.

"But Mr. Red Oligarch, sir, why are we going to see Purple?" Tyjinn said in a fake voice. "Glad you asked," he continued in his own. "Because he's most likely the bastard behind these attacks, and if he isn't, he's the one most qualified to end them." Tyjinn beamed at his two guests, both of whom broke eye contact. "No rush, I suppose. You two eat up and relax for the next hour, and I'll get everything ready. Deal? Deal." He disappeared down the stairs.

They ate in a silence broken only by the occasional sigh. After what was definitely only half the promised hour, they were called downstairs to find three packs waiting by the ruined front door. Dylan shouldered two, even though Kio would be capable of carrying one strapped to his back. Dylan didn't want the cat's injuries to be aggravated.

Just as they were turning to leave, an ominous shadow filled the doorway, barring their path. The shadow expanded as it pushed its way into the volcano. Dylan reached for his loka, and Kio let out a low growl.

"What in the five hells is going on here?" The shadow, once inside, was revealed to be a large dark-skinned woman. She was carrying an equally large basket that she dropped in shock. She raised her hands, red fire spinning around them as her wide eyes surveyed the room.

"Mama, we're fine!" Tyjinn said, and the flames extinguished. "What are you doing here?"

"I'm your mother, I don't need a reason." The woman rounded on Dylan. "And you can put that away right this moment! Don't be waving a loka around like it's a toy. Wait a minute!"

She grabbed Dylan's wrist. "That's blue! You're Jack's son! What are you doing with his loka?"

"Stop harassing my guests, Mama," Tyjinn said, taking her arm so that she was forced to release Dylan. "What are you getting so upset over?"

"Just look as this place!" She gestured broadly with both arms. If Dylan hadn't ducked he would have been knocked to the ground. "What's been going on here? Did you get in a fight?"

"No. Of course not," Tyjinn said, as if she were overreacting to a scratch on his cheek. "Dylan's new at the whole Oligarch thing, and he and I were training together. Things just got out of hand, is all. Nobody got hurt."

She peered into her son's eyes, skeptical of his tale. Next she turned to Dylan, but he couldn't hold her gaze for more than a moment. She had the same fiery, overwhelming personality her son did. Finally she turned and noticed Kio.

"Bless my gods, aren't you the cutest!" She stooped down and picked him up, not a simple feat for anyone. He winced visibly, either from the bruises or from being treated like a common house cat.

"I'm not so cute when I use the litter box," Kio said moodily.

"Still the same lip," she said, setting him down, "but my goodness you've gotten huge."

"Told you we met the Red Oligarch before," Dylan said, piping up at last.

"A long time ago, but I'm simply 'Mama' these days."

"Your name is Mama?" Kio asked with a snort.

"It might as well be when you raise seven children." She noticed the packs for the first time. "You going on a trip or something, Ty?"

"Yes," he answered. "To see Purple's zoo. Dylan is an animal lover, just like you are."

"I don't see why any so-called 'animal lover' would enjoy a zoo," Mama declared, turning a judgmental eye on Dylan. "All those poor babies trapped in cages!"

"We just want to see if there's another cat like me there," Kio said. "I'm a real rarity, possibly even endangered. I need to propagate my species, if you know what I mean."

Mama smiled broadly. "You don't get seven children by accident!" She returned her attention to the wreckage and her face grew serious. "Ty, are you being honest with me? This looks like more than a training accident."

"We'll be more careful in the future. I promise."

Mama sighed. "There's no sense in trying to clean this mess up. I hope you'll finally stop playing hermit now and come home."

Tyjinn turned away from her. "We really have to go now."

Mama considered him with parental concern. "Good thing I brought along enough food for an army." She hoisted the huge picnic basket and shoved it into Dylan's arms, almost knocking the wind out of him. "You three be careful around Purple, you hear me? That man has always given me the creeps."

"We will," Dylan promised as he stumbled out the door, struggling under the weight of two packs and one mammoth-sized basket. Tyjinn lagged behind to hug his mother and kiss her on the cheek. Dylan and Kio paused awkwardly on the path as she tried to coax the truth out of Tyjinn once more and he argued back in a low voice. When they were finished, Tyjinn walked past them, taking the basket from Dylan as he went.

"Let's go," he said, flashing Dylan a forced smile. "Adventure awaits."

Chapter 5
Purple

The Unsalvageable, as Kio introduced the boat to Tyjinn, hadn't been disturbed even though they had left it unattended for two days. Presumably anyone passing by thought it had already been stripped and abandoned. Dylan felt embarrassed about being the Blue Oligarch and owning such a boat, but Tyjinn hardly teased him about it at all.

Feeling extra nervous with an audience watching, Dylan charged the ship's engine and guided it away from the shore, basking in the impressed comments Tyjinn gave him. Together they traveled further down the river, passing Tyjinn's hometown. Brandwald was about the same size as the Lakelands' largest city, although Dylan thought it appeared wealthier with its large wooden houses nestled between pine trees. Why Tyjinn chose not to live there was a mystery.

As they travelled, Dylan began to envy the red loka. Tyjinn wielded it with confidence and ease, using it for everything from drying wet clothes to cooking the fish that he caught and gutted. Dylan tried to think of more ways to utilize his own loka. Aside from doing the dishes, he couldn't see what practical use it had.

More than Tyjinn's talent was catching Dylan's eye. Even when Tyjinn wasn't using his magic, Dylan found it hard to look away. He studied the way his strong hands wrapped around the fishing pole; admired the curve of his back as he pulled the line back in, and the shape of his dark lips when he grinned victoriously after catching a fish. Every time Dylan stared—which was often—Tyjinn would notice him looking. This was embarrassing, but Dylan couldn't resist. Half of him wished he was Tyjinn, while the other half entertained a completely different kind of fantasy.

The side effects of this infatuation were manifold. Dylan sometimes found himself bold in his attempts to impress Tyjinn; other times he was nervous and at a loss for words. Clumsiness became common place, and blushing was ever present—but occasionally, Dylan found grace. Each time that he made Tyjinn laugh felt like the greatest of achievements, and every second that Dylan captured his attention felt like a miracle.

Like all intense moments in life, time passed quickly, the little boat chugging steadily east before curving south. The woods gave way to open plains on the second day, the heat increasing as the summer sun burned toward its peak. Because the cabin was too small to accommodate three sleepers, at night they slept on deck. Underneath the stars, they stayed up to play cards, joke around, and talk until sleep overtook them.

As they neared their destination, Dylan began to wish the journey would never end. For all his mixed emotions, he enjoyed the carefree hours they spent together. Forgetting the potential danger they were heading toward was all too easy. On the morning of the fourth day, the river entered a land so thick with trees that the morning sun was invisible through the shadowy canopies above. This was the beginning of the Wildlands, a territory of mostly uncharted jungles.

The river widened until it poured out into a still, dark lake that reminded Dylan of the volcano's basalt floor. Anchoring the boat, they set out on foot, silent as they assessed this new environment. The jungle's sweltering humidity soon had them drenched in sweat as they picked their way through the dense undergrowth. Dylan, hoping to impress Tyjinn again, tried to conjure up a cooling mist with his loka. This resulted in a small geyser of water that nearly sprayed him in the face. He pretended this was intentional, washing his hands and face and watching bemused as Tyjinn did the same.

As they traveled closer to their goal, Tyjinn's bravado began to fade. This was disconcerting. His self-confidence had been like a shield for Dylan to hide behind, but now all three of them were unsure of their actions. Tyjinn asked them what they knew about the Purple Oligarch: If they had met him before, how old he might be, and how his powers functioned. None of them had any useful information. They only knew that he dealt with animals and, according to Dylan's map, he lived in these woods. One mile from their destination, they stopped to plan.

"There isn't a town anywhere near here." Tyjinn whispered as he consulted the map. "He must be some sort of recluse."

"What's the point of him having a zoo then?" Kio asked. "You would think he would want others to see it while making a few silvers."

Tyjinn shrugged. "Maybe he treats them as his army, sending the animals out to kill and bring things back for him; just like he's doing with the lokas."

Dylan and Kio exchanged worried looks. This trip had never sounded like a good idea, and the prospect of facing an army of murderous animals didn't help.

"Speaking of which," Tyjinn continued, we have one major weakness to deal with." He nodded toward Kio, who wasted no time in looking offended.

"Me?"

"Yes, you. Purple can control animals, and while you are more human than most people I know, I don't want to take any risks."

Kio looked surprised. "I hadn't thought of that! I don't want to end up in a zoo!"

"I don't want you to either, and I have an idea that might

help." Tyjinn removed his pack and started digging through it, finally revealing a small leather pouch with a string to match.

"What's in there?" Dylan asked.

"Nothing yet. I need your loka."

"What? Why?"

"Because it is hard to pit one loka against another. It's not impossible, but it takes extra effort and skill." Tyjinn tied each end of the string to the pouch as he spoke, forming a loop. "Purple won't expect Kio to have a loka, so it might be enough to protect him."

"Might?" Kio repeated.

Tyjinn offered the pouch. "No guarantees, but it's better than nothing."

Dylan realized that the red loka was too effective a weapon in combat to be sacrificed for this cause. The blue loka had faired well defensively so far, but he felt better putting their safety in Tyjinn's capable hands. Without further hesitation, Dylan took the pouch and placed the blue loka inside, stooping to hang it around Kio's neck.

"Besides that, we need to stay alert and stick together." Tyjinn reshouldered his pack. "It's three of us against him."

"Not counting a zoo full of exotic killer animals," Kio muttered.

The wind picked up, carrying the unmistakable smell of manure, straw, and sweat. The stench increased as they walked, beckoning them on like a foul-scented siren. Soon the first cage came into view. Inside its cramped quarters lay a motionless animal. Dylan initially thought the animal was covered in brown fur, but as they cautiously drew near, he saw that it was covered in so much filth that its light blue fur appeared dark. This, combined with its long thin appendages, made it identifiable as a grotter, a harmless type of monkey famous for its strange singsong voice. If it was sleeping, it was doing so very deeply, for they couldn't see signs of breathing.

More cages appeared as they proceeded. Some were made of metal, some bamboo, and a few were woven like baskets. All of them were small. To Dylan, none of this looked like a zoo. Instead he was reminded of the animals they often saw in the dockyards. Species ranging from livestock to exotic pets were shipped through the Lakelands, but such cages were meant to be temporary. If the Purple Oligarch used his powers to treat animals as neglected possessions, then maybe he was corrupt enough to kill.

They passed a medium-sized cage that was empty. Tyjinn crouched, and when he stood again he was holding a green scale. He looked meaningfully at Dylan and Kio. The empty cage had belonged to a dragon. This evidence nearly sent Dylan into a panic. Purple had to be the murderer, meaning that they should now turn tail and run. Except he didn't want to disappoint Tyjinn, who was already moving to examine other cages. Most of the animals were exhausted or worse, but some peered out at them, their eyes crazy. If they could talk like Kio could, who knew what stories they would tell?

One wire-mesh cage housed impossibly small dogs, each no larger than a fist. They stirred as Kio passed and began barking with sharp, painfully high-pitched voices. This set off a chain reaction, causing other animals to stir and growl, holler, chirp, and yowl. The thunderous noise made Dylan want to bolt for cover. If the Purple Oligarch was home, their presence was no longer a surprise.

Adopting a new strategy, or perhaps giving into panic, Tyjinn began to run toward a long squat building, the other two following. Reaching it meant passing through a ring of cages that would have been large and spacious, if not for the huge creatures shoved into them. Dylan began to fear being scorched by fiery breath or raked by claws more than being caught by Purple. A new stench, stronger than that of the animals, filled their noses. They had almost reached the house when Tyjinn skidded to a stop.

A human body lay face-down on the leaf-strewn ground in front of the house. They stared at it in confusion, panting as they considered the implications. The smell was hideously strong: the scent of death. Tyjinn shushed them with a finger to his lips, a strange request, considering the animals were creating such a racket. He pointed to the house, indicating someone might still be inside.

He crept forward and, wrinkling his nose, turned the body onto its back. It had once been a man, that much was clear, but judging more from his features was difficult. Decay, worms, and the tropical heat had done their job. Tyjinn retched, flipping the body back over before stumbling away. Dylan had the impression of parts falling off and had to turn away lest he be sick as well. Kio continued to stare, entranced and repulsed at the same time.

Tyjinn was obviously shaken as he returned. "I don't think there's anyone in the house— no one alive, that is. Surely they wouldn't be able to tolerate just leaving that there."

"Maybe we should go in the house," Dylan said, swallowing. "To get away." His stomach churned, and he felt as though he might puke at any moment.

"You should try smelling it through my nose." Kio finally turned away from the ugly scene. His tongue darted out to lick the unpleasant scent from his nose. "Let's go."

"Wait!" a deep voice rumbled, which was shocking enough even without the sudden quiet that followed. Every single animal had fallen silent.

They turned toward the sound of the voice, expecting to see the Purple Oligarch standing mere feet behind them. They saw nothing but the ring of cages through which they had passed.

"Please, wait," the voice said, this time sounding more desperate than commanding.

In the ring of cages was one made of polished metal, and it was from here the voice came. The cage was no more than two feet tall, but was as wide as a mattress. Within lay a pile of white and smoky-gray fur. A wolf's head observed them, its eyes as shrewd as Kio's.

"Don't be frightened," the wolf spoke. "I mean you no harm, nor am I in any position to cause you any."

They stared, dumbfounded.

"Who ever heard of a talking dog?" Kio said.

"Who are you?" Dylan asked in fascination. Judging by the amount of fur jammed into the cage, this was a very large animal. Or maybe the cage held more than one wolf.

"My name is Nikolai, and I know my appearance might startle you but—"

"Where is the Purple Oligarch?" Tyjinn interrupted. He strode toward the cage. "It's important we know his location immediately."

"You've already met him," the wolf said, his eyes flickering to the body and then back up to Tyjinn. "What's left of him, at any rate."

"What happened to him?"

Tyjinn's tone was aggressive, causing Dylan to wince. Why the sudden change of character? What they had seen was shocking, and they had to learn if they were in danger, but berating a caged animal was pointless. Then again, maybe he was projecting too much sympathy onto Nikolai because of the similarities to Kio. Maybe there was a reason this creature was locked in a cage.

"I haven't eaten for two weeks," Nikolai growled, "and I haven't stood for much longer than that. Get me out of this cage and I will gladly tell you everything you want to know."

"Tell us first." Tyjinn squatted down in front of the cage to be at eye level with the wolf, but Nikolai only closed his eyes and sighed.

"I'll be lucky to live long enough to tell it," the wolf groaned. He didn't say anything after that.

"Where's the key?" Dylan asked, unable to witness his suffering any longer.

Nikolai opened his eyes and focused them on Dylan. "The Oligarch used to carry a set on him. Those were taken, but perhaps in the house…"

Dylan nodded and ran toward the building, ignoring the other two as they called for him to wait. He took a slight detour to avoid passing the dead body too closely.

The front door was unlocked, the air inside stale. Clearly no window or door had been opened for many days. The interior was all shadow, but he could make out the large number of animals stuffed and mounted as decoration. Pushing angry thoughts aside, he focused on the more urgent matter at hand. He spun around once, looking for keys, and found several sets hanging next to the door. Grabbing them all, he turned to leave only to find Tyjinn blocking his path.

"Are you all right?" All traces of aggression were gone from his voice, replaced with genuine worry.

"Yeah, of course," Dylan answered, feeling a bit surprised.

"You should have waited for me. Someone could have been in here." He tipped his head toward the keys in Dylan's hands. "Are you sure this is a good idea?"

"No," Dylan admitted. He wanted to say more, explain how he felt toward this animal and all the others they had seen today, but the words were lost in his throat. Instead he pressed past Tyjinn, examining the collection of keys as he returned to the wolf. One stood out from the others—shiny and silver like Nikolai's cage. Dylan moved to unlock it, but a hand on his shoulder restrained him.

"Now listen, wolf," Tyjinn said, stepping in front of Dylan. "We're going to open this, but know that you are facing two Oligarchs. One wrong move and we will take you down, understood?"

Nikolai sighed wearily. Dylan moved forward with the key again, but Tyjinn took it from him. Dylan wanted to protest, but doing so would only delay things further. Crossing his arms over his chest, he stepped back, tense until the silver padlock finally clicked open.

Tyjinn tossed the lock aside and raised the gate a fraction of an inch. "Let's do this nice and slow. I don't want you leaping out or anything too fast, okay?"

"Agreed," the wolf said, hope shining in his eyes.

The entire top of the cage swung open. Tyjinn lifted it carefully, jumping back as soon as it tipped and slammed into the ground. Nikolai didn't stir.

"You can get out now," Kio urged.

"I think my muscles have atrophied." Nikolai's voice was strained as if fighting back tears. "Damn it!" With a painful grimace he slowly began to move. He pushed himself up on front limbs that were much too long for a canine and braced himself there momentarily. They all gaped as it became clear that they were dealing with something much larger than a wolf. Next Nikolai pulled his legs up until his knees supported him. This seemed to take the last of his energy. He looked up at them.

"Please don't be afraid," he pleaded. "I know you've probably never seen anyone like me but—"

"You're a werewolf," Dylan whispered in awe. He laughed suddenly and surprised the others by running forward to help Nikolai stand. The werewolf was equally taken aback and flinched when Dylan placed both hands under his arms and heaved. Dylan had always been fascinated with tales of werewolves, creatures that walked upright like a man but possessed the speed of the wolf. This sounded like the best of both worlds—versatile hands enhanced with claws, and a mouth that could speak or engulf an enemy's neck. Of all the monsters used to scare children in stories, werewolves had intrigued Dylan rather than frightened him.

Nikolai was mostly skin and bones, which made him easy enough to lift. He didn't smell very good, but Dylan supposed that wasn't the poor creature's fault. Locked in a cage where he couldn't even move around, he would have been forced to relieve himself where he lay. Angry thoughts buzzing in his mind, Dylan managed to get Nikolai to his unsteady feet. The creature stood an impressive seven feet tall, even while still hunched over Dylan for support. Tyjinn overcame his reservations and lent his strength to the other side of the werewolf. Together they managed to guide Nikolai into the house, a bemused Kio trailing along behind.

They had much more work to do before they could get Nikolai to tell his story. He didn't demand so much as begged, and in his poor condition, they could hardly say no. First he wanted a drink of water, claiming he had been living off rainwater for the last week. Dylan was about to search for a well, when he remembered that he could make the water himself. Apprehensively retrieving the loka from around Kio's neck, he set about filling a bowl, hoping that the wolf wouldn't want a cup any more than Kio would.

To Dylan's delight, he managed to fill the bowl without causing another eruption, though he did soak most of the floor. The wolfman lapped up the water greedily, draining the bowl. He soon became more energetic and animated. Dylan understood why. His father had long ago confided in him that water from the loka had special rejuvenating properties.

Next, Nikolai asked to check the kitchen for food. By now he was not only able to stand on his own but walk as well. The kitchen was full of rotten meat and moldy bread, but Kio did manage to sniff out some dried jerky, which the wolf devoured.

With these two tasks out of the way, as well as a second bowl of magical water, Nikolai expressed his intention to assist the other imprisoned animals, a conviction that Dylan shared. Tyjinn finally had enough and put his foot down, insisting on hearing the basic facts before anyone left the house again. Begrudgingly, Nikolai took a seat in the main room and related what he had seen.

"It's not much of a story," he began, "but perhaps it will be useful to you anyway. During my long imprisonment, the Purple Oligarch never had a single visitor or guest. He enjoyed being alone and whiling away the time playing his games."

"What games?" Kio's ears flattened as he asked the question, already suspecting the answer.

"He was a hunter. He would set some of us free and spend his day hunting us down for sport—if you can call it sport when the hunter magically stops his prey from running. When he grew bored with that he would force his favorite creatures to fight each other." The wolf's eyes narrowed. "That was how he spent his days. At night he would listen to the reports of the birds he sent out to spy."

"There are birds that can talk here, too?" Dylan asked.

"Not outside of a few trained words, but the Oligarch could understand their language."

"Communication is the secondary power of the purple loka," Tyjinn explained. "It allows the user to speak and understand all languages, even those of the animals."

Dylan had not studied the ten lokas and their individual properties for many years and had long since forgotten most of the details. He knew each loka had two attributes, one physical and one less tangible. The blue loka's attributes were water manipulation and scrying—the ability to see anywhere in the land. A sort of magic mirror basically. Purple ruled over animals and language, while yellow was the element of air and telepathy. He wondered what the second attribute of the red loka was.

"He could indeed speak with his animals, not that it increased his sympathy for us at all," Nikolai growled. "One day I was surprised to see a man arrive, one who was greeted as a guest instead of an intruder."

Tyjinn leaned forward in his chair, his eyes intent. "This would be the person responsible for killing the Purple Oligarch?"

"Correct."

"What did he look like?"

"He was draped in fine white robes. His entire head, except for his eyes, was covered in a similar material."

"Like someone from the desert," Kio mused. "So you didn't get to see his face?"

"Not at all."

"By what method did he arrive?" Tyjinn's frustration was becoming more apparent.

"That I did not see." Nikolai shifted restlessly, eager to move around more after being pinned up for so long. "It was clear, though, that this guest was expected. Purple came out to meet him, and together they entered this house. What was said was lost even to my sharp hearing. After some time, I heard an argument."

Nikolai stood and walked over to the window to peer out. He was still stiff and walked with a slight limp. "The few words I could make out had to do with power and how it would be divided. Soon after that, Purple burst out of the front door. He was fumbling with one of his key rings and heading toward his deadliest animals."

"Is that the ring of cages just out front?" Dylan asked.

Nikolai nodded without turning around. "He obviously intended to unleash one of us on the stranger, but I never had a chance to learn which. The robed man stepped outside, his demeanor calm and his eyes cold. He removed something from his pocket and raised it, and I saw a flash of light. Purple died on the spot."

Tyjinn jumped to his feet, eyes wide with excitement. "It was a loka, wasn't it? The thing he took out of his pocket. Just like the stone on my necklace!"

Nikolai turned to face him, his yellow eyes wary as they focused on the red loka. "It didn't occur to me at the time, but yes. I had never seen one until that day. Purple always worked his magic with one hand in his pocket, so—"

"What color was it?" Tyjinn interrupted.

"I am mostly colorblind in this form, so it didn't register as anything to me."

"You've got to be kidding me!" Tyjinn shouted. His hands were balled into fists, and his teeth were bared. He was beginning to look more like a wolf than Nikolai. "Are you trying to protect him or something? You don't want this guy to get caught because he killed your captor?"

Nikolai shook his head and turned away. "He was no friend to me. I called out to him just as I did to you, but he ignored my pleas."

"Well, maybe if you describe how Purple died, it would give us a hint as to which Oligarch it was," Kio suggested.

"I've already told you, he just died. One moment he was walking toward the cages, a panicked look came over his face as if he knew what was about to happen, and then he fell over dead." Nikolai stretched his entire body, the tips of his clawed fingers brushing against the ceiling. "I suppose he did make one desperate rush for the cages before he fell, but he didn't get far."

Tyjinn sat down, defeated. The killer's identity wasn't going to be gleaned from anything the werewolf had to tell them. "What did the stranger do after that?" he asked, giving it one last shot.

"Examined the body, then walked off past my line of sight. I'm sorry I couldn't be of more use to you." Nikolai moved to the door, scooping up the key rings on his way. "I'm going to see what I can do for the others. Anyone willing to help me may do so."

Nikolai stepped outside, leaving them all behind with puzzled looks on their faces. Dylan was the first to give chase, eager to do something to ease the nightmarish conditions that Purple's animals were being kept in. He found Nikolai just outside the door, surveying the task before him.

"I want to help," Dylan said.

The werewolf considered him a moment. "I'm going to need a large fire. After that, you can provide water as you did for me."

Dylan nodded and returned indoors to ask Tyjinn to start a fire. He found the Red Oligarch speaking passionately with Kio, but they both ceased talking when they noticed him.

"Out with it," Dylan said.

"Tyjinn thinks that the killer might have left behind a trap of some sort," Kio explained. "A trap, or even an accomplice."

Suddenly it all clicked into place. Tyjinn was acting so abrasive toward Nikolai because he thought he might be part of this trap. That was ridiculous! The werewolf had been weak and helpless when they had first met him. After they freed him, he had wanted only water and food and to help the others. "It's not Nikolai," he asserted.

"No, I don't think so anymore," Tyjinn agreed. "But I don't want any of those cages out there opened, especially not by you."

"I have to help give them all water, though."

"Then take Kio with you and work your magic from a safe distance."

"If I agree, will you make the fire?"

Tyjinn smiled. "You don't need to negotiate with me. I'm willing to help too. Just be careful, okay?"

Dylan beamed at him in gratitude before he and Kio set about their next goal. They started with the nearest cages, those in the ring in front of the house. The first cage held a huge beast with three heads: that of a lion, goat, and dragon, its body a conglomeration of these animals. Kio identified it as a chimera. Unlike many of the other animals, it didn't appear weakened by starvation or dehydration. It roared, hissed, and bleated continually. Rather than get too close, Dylan sent a stream of water into the air that splashed messily into the beast's trough. The chimera didn't even consider the water until they had moved to the next cage. Only then did all three heads begin lapping noisily.

The next cage contained an animal that looked like a boar, but it had a humanoid body. The creature was deep in sleep when they approached. They couldn't help being reminded of Nikolai, although they didn't think wereboars existed. When it awoke to drink its water, it didn't attempt to speak. Two of the four remaining cages were empty. The others contained an emaciated pegasus and a dead naga; a large serpentine beast with a vaguely human head. The winged horse may have once inspired awe, but its white coat was filthy, its wings molted and missing feathers. Dylan was tempted to touch the pegasus, but Tyjinn's warning sprang to mind.

After watering the winged horse they moved on to the other cages, which were scattered in so many directions that it began to appear a task without end. Almost a third of the animals were dead or in critical condition. Dylan's and Kio's sorrow reached such a depth that numbness settled on their hearts. Most traumatizing was a cage of three mountain wolves, a mother and two pups. The mother had died, and her body had been mostly eaten by her two bewildered off-spring. They barked plaintively, as Dylan gave them water. He couldn't vocalize how the unhappy scene made him feel. Kio didn't have much to say either, besides pointing out that the spirit of the mother wolf would be proud to have provided a means for her pups to survive.

Hours were needed to complete their work. More and more empty cages were discovered as they went along, either because Purple had hunted the animals, or the murderer had set them free to complete some heinous task. As they returned to the house, the delicious smell of roasted meat filled their noses. They walked faster, hunger causing their stomachs to growl, but the sight that greeted them quickly exorcised Dylan's appetite.

A pile of dead animals lay near the fire. Nikolai stood off to one side, systematically tearing the animals apart. Some pieces he skinned and set aside in a gory pile, while furs and highly decomposed bodies went into the fire. The werewolf's hands were covered in blood, despite his occasional use of a cleaver. He continued to hack at the body of a horse-sized rat as they approached.

"What are you doing?" Dylan cried out in disgust.

Nikolai looked up, his mouth also covered in blood, which only increased Dylan's revulsion. "Feeding the animals," came the answer. "There is enough feed for the likes of the pegasus, but nothing for the carnivores."

"But you are feeding them to each other!" he countered.

Nikolai stopped and considered him. "What would you have me do, hunt for meat when so much here is still good? Kill more animals and let these bodies go to waste?"

This stopped Dylan short, but his emotions still boiled inside. "Well, how did Purple feed them? There has to be something around here."

"Purple used his magic to call creatures from the surrounding woods. Against their will they marched into the cages of animals that ripped them to shreds. It was an abomination." Nikolai returned to his work, ignoring their further presence.

A pit opened in Dylan's stomach, but he knew the werewolf was right. The still-living animals were starving, and like the mother of the two wolf pups, at least something good could come from the horrid deaths that had occurred here. His heart heavier than ever, Dylan strode into the house for a much needed break.

Kio followed, turning to the werewolf as he passed. "Feed Purple to them," he suggested.

A vicious grin spread over Nikolai's lips. "I already did."

Chapter 6
Nocturnal Revelations

The moons were high in the sky before Nikolai returned indoors. The others had prepared dinner from dry preserves found in the cellar and fresh vegetables from an unkempt garden in the back, but the werewolf no longer had any interest in eating. No one had the nerve to ask how he had satiated his appetite, but at least Nikolai's smell had improved. His fur was damp, causing Dylan to wonder if he groomed himself like a dog or washed himself like a man. Regardless, Nikolai settled down in front of the fire without saying a word.

"We're leaving tomorrow morning," Tyjinn announced. Dylan and Kio eyed each other. This was the first they had heard of this plan. "I was curious what you intend on doing with yourself."

"You could come with us," Dylan offered. If Tyjinn could make plans without consulting him, he could do the same with invitations.

"Thank you, but no," the werewolf answered. "I feel my place is here."

"Are you kidding?" Kio's face expressed disbelief like only a cat's could. "You were imprisoned here, and you feel like staying?"

Nikolai shrugged. "It's as good a place as any, now that the Oligarch is gone. There is also the matter of his other victims that will need care."

"Can't you just let the animals go?" Dylan asked. He didn't like the idea of their continued existence inside such under-sized cages.

"I'm afraid not. Many of them aren't native to the Wildlands. Of those that are, most must be rehabilitated first. Then again, I can't always leave them in their cages. It is a challenging situation."

His tone of voice suggested he was satisfied with such a challenge, so they left it at that.

Dylan would have liked Nikolai to come with them, especially if they could see him shift forms. As a child he had badgered his father with questions about werewolves. He knew that the legends of them shapeshifting during a full moon were false. The primal nature inside a person triggered the transformation. Anger could bring the change, or any life threatening situation.

He wondered why Nikolai was still a wolf. He was free, and he was safe. How long had he been in that cage? Maybe so long that he had forgotten what it was to be human. Or perhaps it was his affinity with the animals that kept him from changing back. They responded to him as if he were one of their own. Dylan wanted to ask Nikolai for the answers, but there was something haunted and distant about the werewolf. He didn't rest by the fire for long before he was out the door again to care for more of the animals.

Dylan searched the room for his own animal. The big cat was curled up next to the fire, breathing the slow and steady rhythm of sleep. Dylan watched him for a moment and was considering retiring for the night when Tyjinn sprang to his feet.

"Come with me," he said. "I want to show you something." He rushed out the door without any indication of what he had in mind.

Dylan emerged into the fresh night air and shivered, taking a moment to locate Tyjinn. Hurrying to catch up, he followed him around the back of the house, through the garden, and into the darkness of the trees. He decided not to ask where they were heading, choosing instead to revel in the mystery.

The jungle had transformed into a world of tall shadows and dim beams of moonlight, the continuous chattering of insect song accompanying them as they walked. Their final destination was a small clearing that, in contrast to the gloom they had just emerged from, was strongly illuminated by the dual moons' light.

"This will do," Tyjinn said, walking to the clearing's center and dropping to his knees. "I could have done this back at the house, but the ambience here is much more dramatic, don't you think?"

Dylan came to rest on his knees just in front of him, unsure of what was about to happen.

Pulling the red loka from under his shirt, Tyjinn considered him a moment before speaking. "I need to get a message to a friend of mine. She knows the desert inside and out, and we'll need her help to cross it."

"Not that you've bothered to tell me where we're going," Dylan said pointedly.

Tyjinn winced. "Sorry. I've been living on my own too long. There are two Oligarchs in the Drylands, both of them possible suspects or victims. Whoever killed Purple was dressed in desert clothing, remember? I just assumed you'd want to go there next. I didn't mean to exclude you."

Dylan nodded. In truth he felt apprehensive about what they were doing. Scoping out Purple had been like a game before they arrived to find such a gruesome scene. The way things were going, a trip to the desert probably meant heading into even more danger. He was certain this wasn't what his father had in mind when sending him to the Red Oligarch.

"So I need to get a message to my friend as quickly as possible," Tyjinn continued before Dylan could voice his reservations, "and the best way to do this is through magic."

Dylan's worries ebbed in the face of this new topic. "Is this somehow related to your secondary power?"

"Not exactly. What we need is a little yellow magic to mentally transmit the message to her, which it just so happens I am capable of."

Dylan waited for a punch line that didn't come. "But that would make you a mage."

Tyjinn gave a cocky grin and nodded. "Sure, why not?"

There was a good reason why not. Magic wasn't limited to the Oligarchs. There were practitioners of every color, known as magicians. While a magician could never hope to reach the skill level of a true Oligarch, there was one exclusive path available to them; the study of multiple colors of magic. Mixing two styles of magic could be useful, and those capable of this were known as mages: but a person couldn't be a mage and an Oligarch. The power of the lokas came at a cost: the complete inhibition of all other magical arts. In theory, the only way around this would be ownership of multiple lokas, but such a thing had never occurred.

Until recently, he thought uneasily. Someone out there had two lokas, possibly more.

"This is the part where you demand I prove it," Tyjinn said. His loka began to glow until a small tendril of red energy snaked from the crystal. It wavered in the air and began twisting into an elaborate shape. This soon became the outline of a butterfly. Dylan watched with rapt fascination as the insect was filled with flames as easily as a glass was filled with water. The process continued until it was, in effect, a butterfly made of fire. It hovered in the air between them, gently flapping its wings. He felt like applauding. Tyjinn truly was a master of red magic!

"So now that we have the vessel, all that's left is to fill it with a message." Tyjinn let his loka thump back to his chest. He kept his hands raised, each one cupped inches away from the butterfly, and closed his eyes in concentration. Just when it appeared nothing would happen, a yellow light spread from Tyjinn's hands, enveloping the butterfly and infusing it with power. The impossible insect shook its delicate wings, crimson edged with golden light, before fluttering its way out of the clearing.

Tyjinn opened his eyes, looking rather smug. "It's done."

"You've got to be kidding me," Dylan breathed.

"Not at all. It will deliver a message that tells my friend where to meet us."

"Wait, if that really was yellow magic, couldn't you have just sent the message telepathically?"

"That's what I did, in my own way," Tyjinn explained as he settled back into a sitting position. Dylan followed suit. "My yellow skills are too limited to reach a mind so far away. What I *can* do is create a vessel that holds enough energy to support my telepathic message and carry it to wherever she is. Impressed?"

"I don't know," Dylan donned a skeptical expression. "It's fairly ingenious, I suppose, but a butterfly? That's pretty girly."

"Hey man, it looked like a moth to me," Tyjinn countered.

"Awfully pretty for a moth."

"All right, maybe it was a butterfly, but my friend is a girl, so..."

Dylan couldn't keep a straight face and laughed.

Tyjinn joined him. "I guess it is sort of girly," he confessed. "That's just the form that comes naturally for some reason."

"I like you better this way," Dylan said without thinking.

"What do you mean?"

"When you joke around. Since we reached Purple, it's like you've been someone else. I didn't like how aggressive you were with Nikolai."

"I was just trying to keep us all safe," Tyjinn said with a dismissive shrug. "It's not every day you see a corpse and a werewolf in such short succession. I guess it put me on the defensive, and I got a little carried away. Hopefully you'll forgive this small transgression."

"To be honest, it's almost a relief that you aren't perfect." Dylan laughed, but Tyjinn only looked confused.

"You lost me."

"It's nothing," Dylan said, feeling insecure. "Just a dumb joke."

"All right," Tyjinn broke eye contact with him, choosing instead to look down at the ground. "It's just that, I have this idea that I make you uncomfortable."

"That's not it!" Dylan protested.

"Isn't it?"

"No!"

"Tell me what it is then."

"There's just something about you," Dylan began, but he couldn't really deny it. He did sometimes feel awkward around Tyjinn, but not because he didn't like him. Quite the opposite in fact. "I guess it can be intimidating to be around you. I'm new to being an Oligarch, and you are too, but you wield your loka like you've been doing it your whole life. And how can you do another color of magic? It's impossible!"

Tyjinn shrugged. "Ever since I was a kid I was good at multiple types of magic. I was a practicing mage before my mother forced this position on me. The loka made other kinds of magic harder, but not impossible. So anyway, that's it? I'm good at magic, and that makes you jittery?"

Dylan couldn't answer.

"That's not all, is it?" The tone of Tyjinn's voice had changed and become serious, probing, inviting.

Dylan shivered.

"You're cold! I'm sorry."

Tyjinn's fingers brushed across his loka, causing a fire to spark into life. It burned on the ground between them, without wood or fuel. Even the grass remained unsinged. Shadows sprung up around the edge of the clearing. Dylan was glad for the warmth, but wished his face wasn't so illuminated now.

"I think we're a lot alike," Tyjinn tried.

"Oh, I doubt that." Dylan laughed without humor.

"I've seen the way you look at me."

The words stung, opening an old wound. Dylan's first reaction was anger. Who was Tyjinn to tear these truths out into the open? These were his private thoughts, hidden in a dark place and only to be looked at in the most secret of moments. He wanted nothing more than to attack Tyjinn for invading this hidden place, to tackle him and punch his mouth into silence, but the words that came next stopped him short.

"I only caught you looking at me, Dylan, because I was looking at you just as much."

Dylan risked a brief glance over the fire. Tyjinn's eyes weren't accusatory. They were hopeful.

"Or am I wrong?"

"You aren't wrong," Dylan croaked. When had his throat

become so tight?

"Since you and Kio came into my life, I've been happy," Tyjinn said, his tones confessional. "I was always so stupidly lonely, not letting anyone in, and to be honest, I planned on doing the same with you. That fire when you first arrived, that wasn't a joke. It was designed to intimidate, to make you dislike me, but when I saw you I knew."

"Knew what?"

"This!" Tyjinn gestured back and forth between them, as if something visible was there.

What was supposed to be there? What exactly did Tyjinn see, because Dylan was no longer sure. Were they even talking about the same thing anymore? Was this just about friendship to Tyjinn and had Dylan almost made a fool out of himself? "What do you want?" he asked, his jaw clenching. "I need you to say it, because I don't think I know."

Tyjinn's smile faltered. "I want to be with you. I don't just mean sex. I want you to be comfortable around me, I want to protect you, and I want to belong to you."

Dylan's mind reeled. Was he crazy? His night with Rano had already been more than he could cope with. He danced around those memories like they were explosive and had never, ever considered what Tyjinn was suggesting now. A relationship? Like any man and woman had together? The concept was alien, but already the consequences of such a proposition were rushing menacingly toward him. He recalled the hate in Rano's eyes, except this time worn by the people Dylan loved.

"If our families found out," Dylan said warily, "or our friends."

"It wouldn't be a secret." Tyjinn looked surprised. "Why should it be?"

The jungle's endless chirping, scurrying, and rustling all ceased, just for one second, as if every living creature was leaning forward to hear Dylan's response.

"No," he said, his voice much more forceful than he meant it to be.

"No?" Tyjinn's voice cracked. "Simple as that? Just no?"

"I'm sorry." Dylan stood, stumbling toward the trees.

"Hey! Hey, that's the wrong way!" Tyjinn rushed to his feet to catch him by the arm.

Dylan spun around, ready to punch him, desperate to kiss him, but instead he just sobbed. Tyjinn took him in his arms, murmuring comforting words that were mostly lost on him.

"Gods, I really know how to screw things up," Tyjinn said when Dylan had calmed down. "I shouldn't have—I don't know. I just shouldn't have."

"It's not your fault," Dylan mumbled.

"Come back to the fire," Tyjinn urged. "I don't want it to end like this. I don't want to lose you." He sounded on the verge of tears himself. "We'll sit; we'll talk about anything but my stupid ideas. Just like things were before."

"I'm tired," Dylan admitted, pulling away.

A wave of energy rushed over him, red light momentarily blinding his eyes.

"Energy, secondary power of the red loka," Tyjinn explained with a grin that almost looked genuine. He backed away and flashed another tentative smile. "Just talk to me. Please."

Dylan nodded, wiping his eyes with his arms and feeling childish. That the night could be salvaged was hard to believe, but Tyjinn managed to find his self-confident demeanor again, and with it returned his humor. In a surprising amount of time he had them both laughing, and by morning, most of Dylan's inhibitions were gone.

In a way he felt liberated. He had found a kindred spirit in Tyjinn, but one that was strangely naïve. What Tyjinn suggested was dangerously close to the concept of love. Dylan had once mistaken his attraction to Rano for that, but the pain it had caused convinced him otherwise. Love wasn't meant to hurt like that. Even if things were different, even if Tyjinn wouldn't turn his back on him, there was still his family to consider. Dylan had enough trouble accepting this side of himself. How could he possibly expect them to do the same? What a foolish risk he had taken when deciding to seek out Rano again! Ada, Kio, his father... Dylan stood to lose everyone and so did Tyjinn. If he couldn't see that, then denying Tyjinn was the only way of keeping him safe.

Chapter 7
Across the Sands

"An arid abode," the big cat purred.

"A delightful desert," Dylan replied.

Kio angled his right ear and squinted, the feline version of a musing expression. He surveyed the endless hills of glowing yellow sand, searching for inspiration. "A vivacious void," he said finally.

"Nice one." Dylan nodded. "Your turn, Tyjinn."

"I wasn't aware that I was playing."

"C'mon, give it a shot."

"Oh, all right." Tyjinn waved a hand, as if trying to waft

inspiration toward himself. "A delightful drought-hole."

"Dylan already used delightful," Kio said critically. "Not very original of you."

"Besides," Dylan added with a mischievous grin, "I'm pretty sure your mom wouldn't want you using terms like 'drought-hole' in polite company."

Tyjinn rolled his eyes. "Do you two really consider this game fun?"

"You have a better one?" Kio retorted.

"Ever hear of the quiet game?"

"How about some more water, Dylan?" Kio asked, ignoring the last comment. "Just looking at all that sand makes me thirsty."

"Sure." Dylan removed the blue loka from the pouch that had once been hanging around Kio's neck. He fingered the leather cord, strange feelings stirring in his belly that had everything to do with Tyjinn. He had told Dylan he could keep the pouch in tones that were casual, but to Dylan it felt like an important present. Often he wondered if Tyjinn had worn it before switching to the golden necklace that now held the red loka.

"Water?" Kio reminded him.

"Sorry."

Dylan pulled Kio's bowl free from his pack and filled it, proud he could now do so with precision and ease. Once Kio was lapping up the water, Dylan gazed apprehensively toward the desert. Two days trudging through the jungle had brought flat plains, and another half-day led them to the desert's edge, just as the sun was setting. Then they had camped overnight in the shade of a solitary tree, waiting for Tyjinn's mysterious friend.

Tyjinn had explained that she would help them survive and navigate the harsh climate of the Drylands. Once in the middle of all those dunes, he claimed it was easy to lose one's sense of direction. Dylan didn't think it sounded all that hard. Surely all that was required was keeping track of the sun, but when the sun came up and lit the immense landscape, he was glad they would have extra help.

He could hardly believe that anything could survive in a land so barren. He wondered what would happen if he used the blue loka to summon up as much water as he could, imagining it soaking into the sands with lightning speed, if not evaporating in a cloud of steam.

"A wondrous wasteland!" Tyjinn exclaimed suddenly.

Dylan and Kio burst out laughing.

The temperature was already blistering hot by mid-morning, when a lone silhouette crested a distant sand dune. Tyjinn noticed first and leapt to his feet. "There's my girl!" he said with a grin.

Dylan felt an unexpected pang of jealousy as he shaded his eyes and squinted to get a better look. As she neared, Dylan barely noticed her at all due to the unusual animal she was riding. The head of the creature was serpentine, connected by a long, stretched neck to the narrow, green scaled body. The front legs were bare of scales, covered instead with golden fur that suited its lion-like paws, while the back legs were slightly bowed and ended in eagle's talons. The creature's most frightening feature was the scorpion stinger at the end of a long tail that bobbed and weaved, as if it had a life of its own.

"Good," Tyjinn said. "It looks like she brought an extra mushushu with her."

Chasing along behind her was another of the strange beasts, identical in every detail except the scales were dark blue instead of green. Both creatures scurried over the sand, swiftly closing the remaining distance.

As the rider dismounted, Dylan was struck by her exceptional beauty. Her body was lean but toned, both feminine and powerful. Short platinum-blond hair appeared almost white against deeply tanned skin and her pale green eyes twinkled seductively at Tyjinn.

"Dylan, Kio, may I introduce my dearest friend in life, Lali."

Lali smiled demurely at Dylan and offered her hand. He shook it, holding her attention only a moment before she noticed Kio and squatted down to pet him.

"Oh!" she gasped. "Aren't you a cutey!"

"You're not so bad yourself," Kio replied.

Lali pulled back in surprise and laughed. "Well, well," she said as she stood. "You've made some interesting friends, haven't you, Ty?"

"I thought your mom was the only one who called you that." Dylan's words sounded more accusatory than he intended and were met by a surprised silence.

"Mama's not the only one who calls him that," Lali explained, "but she's the only one he likes hearing it from." Her tones were kind, the jealousy Dylan felt ebbing away to be replaced by respect.

"Dylan is the new Blue Oligarch," Tyjinn interjected.

"Not really," Dylan said sheepishly. "My dad is the real Blue Oligarch. I'm just doing this until the Oligarch killer is found."

"It's true then?" Lali's eyes were wide. "There have been grumblings and rumors all through the melon festival, but I couldn't believe it was true."

"It is, which is exactly why we need your help." Tyjinn handed his waterskin to her, and she drank deeply while he spoke. "You've just come from the oasis? I don't suppose you saw the Empress while you were there?"

"I was about to when you called." Lali wiped her mouth with the back of her hand. "Wow, this water is good!"

"Dylan made it," Kio said. "With magic, I mean, not the natural way. That would be gross."

Tyjinn nodded. "That's right. It's going to be a cinch getting across the desert with the three of us as a team. Dylan will provide the water, and I'll take care of the heat. With your navigation skills and the mushushus, we'll reach the oasis in no time."

"Sounds dreamy," Kio said, his eyes on the mushushus, "but what do we need these things for? As pack beasts?"

"For transportation," Lali said, wrapping an arm around the green one's neck. "Don't be scared of them. Mushi here is as gentle as a lamb."

"I'm not scared. I'm wondering how you expect me to ride."

"I'm sure we can work something out," Tyjinn said. "We can tie you on with ropes."

Kio's eyes grew huge. "Ropes?"

"You can ride with me," Lali said over Tyjinn's laughter. "It might not be the most comfortable position, but maybe you can drape yourself over the mushushu, sort of like saddlebags. Here, let's try it out."

Dylan watched as Lali did her best to make Kio comfortable. The cat was in an ornery mood, mouthing off at every opportunity he found, but Lali seemed to possess limitless good humor.

"I guess that means you're riding with me."

Dylan turned to find Tyjinn at his side, causing his heart to skip a beat. Over the last few days, the banter between them had been easy, almost as if their midnight conversation had never happened. But now the prospect of being close to Tyjinn brought Dylan right back to that night.

"I've got him on!" Lali shouted. "It wasn't easy, so I think we should leave now."

Kio was draped across the mushushu like the victim of a hunt, a dour expression on his face. Lali hopped into the saddle behind him, pulling on the reigns to turn the mushushu around.

"We can share the saddle if you stay close," Tyjinn said.

The saddle was little more than a rectangular swath of suede stuffed with some material to add padding. If they squeezed tightly enough together, they might both fit on it, but Dylan didn't trust his self-control.

"You can have it. I'll be fine."

Tyjinn broke eye contact and headed for the blue mushushu. He took a blanket from his pack, moved the saddle back, and put the blanket in its place. He patted the mushushu's haunches, causing it to sit on the ground. Then he swung his leg over and settled on the blanket. "The saddle is all yours," he said while still looking forward.

Dylan approached the mushushu with trepidation, focusing on his fear rather than the complex feelings he had for Tyjinn. Both the beast and the rider remained motionless as he mounted. Even with the saddle, he could still feel the hard bones, scales, and muscle beneath him. Tyjinn clicked his tongue, prompting the mushushu to stand again.

"You might want to hold on to my hips."

Dylan looked at Tyjinn's waist, the breath in his lungs coming short. He hesitated long enough that Tyjinn shrugged, and with a gentle kick, sent the mushushu racing forward. Dylan nearly fell backward, but before he did, he grabbed instinctively for Tyjinn's hips. As they moved into the dunes, Dylan was surprised by how smooth a ride the mushushus provided. Although their hindquarters swayed back and forth as they traveled up and down the dunes, their midsections stayed relatively still, so the riders weren't too badly jostled. Dylan basked in the experience, enjoying the wind in his hair and the way his stomach dropped with every dune they scurried over.

If the exhilaration of the ride wasn't enough, he was touching Tyjinn, grasping his hips so firmly that Dylan worried he would leave bruises. He wanted to relax his fingers, to gently move his thumb in circles across the skin of his back or maybe wrap his arms around him completely, but he didn't. Instead, he kept his hands as stiff as stones, but even this little indulgence sent his pulse racing.

Kio, on the other hand, wasn't quite so happy being draped over Mushi, who Lali explained had been her pet for eight years. He yowled and hissed with every bump. From this position he could stare sidelong at Dylan during the ride, communicating his misery with a number of facial expressions and more than one cuss word.

The mushushus carried them in this manner until the sun began to set. Lali declared they were more than halfway to their destination. Usually she would have to lead them on a detour to an oasis, but Dylan's magic allowed them all the water they wanted, making him feel proud to be so useful. Tyjinn was as handy as ever with his magic. During the day he had used it to temper off the desert heat, and as they set up camp in the evening, he encircled them all in radiating warmth. Dylan wondered how ordinary travelers dealt with the extreme heat of the day and frigid desert nights, but he was glad not to have to find out.

The food rations that Lali provided were as dry and bland as their surroundings. She had some sort of jerky that tasted about as flavorful as wood. She also had a large bag of puffed crackers mixed with dried peas and nuts. This snack was spicier than the jerky, but hardly satisfying. The mushushus, on the other hand, were treated to a ground oatmeal and raisin combination that, when mixed with water, looked much more appealing than the jerky. Too many more days in the desert and Dylan would be asking for that instead.

Kio suffered the most from these culinary limitations and wanted to stalk off into the darkness to see what he could hunt. During the day the only signs of life had been the occasional high-flying bird, but the night brought out numerous desert inhabitants.

"There are things under the sand bigger than you, Kio," Lali said, denying him permission. "They'd snatch you and drag you under before you knew it. That's why they call them draggers."

"Then why are we any safer here?" the cat asked.

"The heat. It keeps them asleep during the day. They instinctively avoid it. Without Tyjinn's magic, we'd be clustered so close to the fire that our eyebrows would singe off."

Kio resigned himself to eating more of the chicken jerky. He was unusually quiet for the rest of the night, which earned him some extra sympathy from Dylan. Kio went to sleep much earlier than usual too, perhaps hoping he would wake up somewhere better.

Lali and Tyjinn spent most of the evening talking about people and places that Dylan had never heard of. They might as well have been speaking in another language, for the little he understood. He guessed that the two friends hadn't seen each other for some time, since they had been going on like that all day, exchanging information and laughing over inside jokes. Although amusing at first, their camaraderie was beginning to grate on Dylan's nerves. He kept hoping they would run out of things to say and include him in a more neutral conversation, but before that happened he drifted off to sleep.

Dylan dreamt of the desert sand melting in the hot sun like crystals of ice, changing the parched landscape into a flowing ocean. He sank happily below the violent waves, drinking in gallon after gallon of surprisingly sweet water. Bumping blissfully along the ocean floor, he let the current take him wherever it went. Fish of all kinds swam with him in a multicolored escort while seaweed caressed his face. The ocean darkened, and he emerged from its cool depths into consciousness again; although he could still feel the seaweed tracing a line from his brow, down his cheek, and across his lips.

His eyes shot open, a face directly above him.

"Quiet," Tyjinn said, his finger pressed against Dylan's lips. "The others are still asleep."

Dylan pushed Tyjinn's hand away so he could speak. "It's still night," he complained.

A wave of energy washed through him, invigorating his body.

"Does that matter?"

Tyjinn stood and offered his hand. This time Dylan didn't hesitate. He reached out and took it, the adrenaline rush making him feel brave. Tyjinn pulled Dylan to his feet, and for a moment their faces were dangerously close. Then Tyjinn turned away, but before he did, Dylan saw a pained expression. The grimace was a reminder of the promise Dylan had made to himself. Nothing would happen between Tyjinn and him, even in secrecy, but as they headed away from the others, Dylan couldn't help but wish for another moment of weakness.

They walked together toward the edge of their encampment. Earlier they had marked an area with stones just outside the light of the fire, indicating the end of their heated magical barrier. This area also had provided them with a private place to relieve themselves that was still within safe boundaries.

"We have to stay close while we walk," Tyjinn said, placing an arm around Dylan. "I'll create a field of heat around us that will keep us safe from the draggers."

Dylan was certain that Tyjinn could create an area big enough to allow them to walk separately, but welcomed this excuse to be close. He leaned into the comforting warmth of his body, mentally whispering "I'm sorry, I'm sorry," over and over again. Tyjinn tightened his grip as if he could hear this message, even though they were walking in silence.

Occasionally they would hear signs of life in the darkness. Dylan tried to imagine what creatures were making those sounds and how they survived in the barren wilderness. Mostly it was silent, the stillness reminding Dylan of winter, the canopy of stars above like snowflakes that hadn't yet fallen. He was glad Tyjinn had woken him to see this.

"Ty?"

"Hm?"

"Why don't we travel at night? You could use your energy magic. We'd get to Green twice as fast."

"We could." Tyjinn stopped and aimed the flat of his palm at the ground. A fire appeared there. He released Dylan, and together they sat on cool sands which were soon warmed by magic. "Replenishing energy is one thing, but staying up like this still takes a toll on the mind and body. People go crazier the longer they go without sleep, not to mention how hard it would be on our bodies to walk or ride nonstop. Having infinite energy doesn't mean that muscles don't cramp and hurt. It's best saved for an emergency."

"Like tonight?" Dylan grinned.

"Well, what we're doing tonight might prove useful," Tyjinn replied. "I thought we'd try out a few magic tricks."

"Like what?"

"I'm curious to see what happens when we combine our magic. Oligarchs seldom work together. We have a unique opportunity to do so."

"Fire and water?" Dylan said. "They don't really mix, unless you are looking to make steam."

"Why not? Steam to sting our enemy's eyes. I know you can't make ice like your father does, but have you ever tried creating hot water?"

Dylan hadn't and doubted he could. His father had mastered blue magic, and Dylan couldn't recall him ever creating hot, or even warm water—only varying levels of coolness.

"All right. How do we go about this?"

Tyjinn shrugged. "No idea. We'll just have to throw caution to the wind."

They decided to use red magic to heat a pool of water created by Dylan. They dug a small hole and lined it with Tyjinn's shirt to hinder the water from flowing away too quickly. Then they set about their magic, and without much effort they had the water boiling.

"Neat, but not very useful," Tyjinn mused.

"Not outside of the kitchen. What else?"

"It could make a good weapon."

Tyjinn created a compressed field of heat so intense it appeared as a red square in the air. Dylan sent a fat stream of water directly through its surface, and for the first few seconds, only steam came out the other side. The water eventually broke through, sizzling and sputtering as it hit the desert floor. They raced to touch it before it was absorbed into the sand.

"Hard to say if it was boiling," Tyjinn said, after sucking on a finger, "but it's hot enough to hurt."

"Wouldn't it be easier just to flame enemies on your own?"

"Not if we want to take someone down without killing them. This way we could scald them and leave them wounded, rather than risk them burning to death."

"Morbid," Dylan said, feeling uncomfortable with the idea. He hoped they wouldn't have to face any enemies at all.

They spent the next few hours trying out other ideas. A few had potential, especially ones that produced vast amounts of steam. Theoretically, they could produce enough steam to obscure them from an enemy while escaping. They code-named these and a few other techniques, practicing until the eastern sky began to grow light.

"One more thing before heading back," Tyjinn said. "I wanted to talk to you about your secondary power."

"Scrying? What about it?"

"I know you said you've never been able to do it, but have you tried since becoming the Blue Oligarch?"

Dylan shook his head, the familiar feeling of insecurity welling up in his belly. He knew what Tyjinn was going to ask him to do, and he wasn't looking forward to his inevitable failure.

"I need you to try, Dylan. Events are spiraling out of control faster than we predicted. Someone out there has three lokas."

"Don't you mean two?"

"No. Someone used the purple loka to kill Yellow and a different color loka to kill Purple. They have a minimum of three."

"I hadn't thought of that."

Tyjinn nodded. "Finding out what color that first loka is would save us a lot of time. Regardless of that, we still need to see the Empress."

"And she is?"

"That's what the Green Oligarch calls herself, which should tell you something about her ego. Anyway, we need to cut to the chase. All you need to scry is which loka was used to kill Purple."

Knowing what color loka was used could keep them safe. Any Oligarch they contacted could be the killer, even the one they were about to visit.

"All right, I'll try," Dylan said. Maybe the importance of that information would motivate him to succeed this time.

"Can you do it now?"

"No," Dylan snorted. Even his father needed the better part of a day to prepare. "I'll have to induce a trance first, and that's time-consuming."

"What do you have to do?"

"There are some energy exercises, fasting except for water and raw fruits, and keeping my head clear of thoughts as much as possible, which requires silence." Dylan felt relieved. He couldn't possibly do these things while they traveled. "There's some visualization exercises, too—"

"Forget all that, it's too complicated." Tyjinn slapped him on the back. "We'll do it cold turkey. If that doesn't work, we'll get you drunk and try again."

Lali sighed contentedly in her sleep while Kio's paws twitched over invisible prey. Careful not to wake them, Dylan and Tyjinn moved off to the side after pilfering Kio's water bowl. The pink fishes scattered across its light blue surface didn't instill a sense of ceremony, but there was no other choice. Orange light crested over distant sand dunes, casting just enough light to see by. Dylan stared at the nervous face mirrored in the water's surface. He was doomed to fail in front of Tyjinn. Did his father ever scry spontaneously in an emergency? Had there ever been a need like this before?

Acting on instinct, he stirred the water with the blue loka, distorting his image. *Show me the murderer,* he thought. *If I don't know his face, show me his color.*

His reflection disappeared as the water darkened. The edges of the bowl fuzzed and faded away until all he could see was blackness. Dylan tried looking away, but the world remained dark. Tyjinn, the desert—everything, had disappeared. He was about to call for help, when a large bird attracted his attention, a vulture made completely of violet light. At least he hadn't gone blind! He could only hope that this mystical vision was a normal part of scrying.

The purple vulture was joined by others of its kind until a flock of hundreds had formed against the black backdrop. Yellow clouds spilled into the empty sky, the birds zipping around like angry bees, some sailing into the clouds and disappearing inside, tainting them a dirty brown. In other areas the clouds cocooned around the vultures, swelling and darkening to the same filthy shade. Finally they merged completely, creating a sickly haze of polluted color.

This new smog rolled like a thunderstorm until it approached a thriving jungle. Dylan delved into the green, leaves slapping his face. The jungle's scent was earthy and fertile, like the soil hidden just beneath decomposing leaves. The smog invaded, sinking heavy and bloated into the jungle. Plants came to life, swaying their branches to wave away the pollution, but the smog stuck like sticky sap, coating the foliage and causing it to wilt and dry.

Flames burst from the ground; the vile sap bubbling and popping irritably as the leaves began to burn. Then the jungle collapsed onto the flames; the ground now a mix of sap, dead plants, and ash that mixed together to become a great pool of sludge.

Dylan's perspective rose into the air. Looking down, he saw water, pure and clear. Already the sludge poured into it, spoiling its clarity. He felt sick as he watched, as if the sludge were pouring not just into the water, but into his heart.

Other colors and shapes appeared, but he was too busy fighting back nausea to pay attention. He felt bile stuck in his throat, blocking his airway. Dylan squeezed his eyes shut in an effort to breathe or vomit, but could do neither, so he opened his eyes again in the hope of finding help.

A war of colors erupted before his eyes, until gray seeped over his field of vision, obscuring everything. The grayness penetrated more than just his eyes, entering his mind and filling his body. He felt his soul would be taken next as the grayness grew in intensity.

He barely noticed that he was being shaken.

"Breathe, Dylan, breathe!"

Wasn't he doing so already? His throat loosened, and his lungs gasped in air. His vision cleared, revealing the concerned faces of his friends. He was lying on his back, Tyjinn directly above him, the other two on either side.

"Are you all right?" Kio asked, sniffing him over.

"I think so, yeah."

"What the hell were you two doing?" Lali asked. Her hair was a mess from the night's sleep, her face pale and confused.

"Trying to scry," Tyjinn answered, looking shaken. "He just stopped breathing!"

"I don't know what happened," Dylan paused, catching his breath. He felt a little lightheaded, but otherwise fine. "Toward the end, I think it was working."

"Why didn't you wake me up first?" Kio sounded both angry and concerned.

"I never thought something like that would happen. It never did with Dad."

"Yeah, well," the cat's stern expression disappeared, "I'm glad you're okay."

Tyjinn swallowed, his face lined with guilt. "You should rest now. You can tell us what you saw later."

"I'm fine, really!" Dylan sat up and described his vision in as much detail as possible. By the time he was finished, they all wore puzzled expressions.

Lali spoke first. "It's obvious the killer doesn't plan on stopping any time soon, and if what you saw is true, Green is next on the hit list."

"We still didn't see what color of Oligarch started all of this," Tyjinn said.

"Unless it was black," Kio said. "You said your vision started with blackness, and the background stayed as such. Maybe the whole playing field is his."

"What does the Black Oligarch have as his power?" Dylan asked.

"Death," Lali answered immediately.

They considered this solemnly.

Kio shook his head. "If Black can kill using his magic, why would he send animals to kill the other Oligarchs?"

"Perhaps to cover his tracks," Dylan suggested. "Maybe he used his power to kill Purple and then used that loka to go after the others."

"Maybe," Tyjinn said doubtfully. "I still think we're missing something. Regardless, we need to get to Green immediately if we're going to prevent this vision from coming true."

"To the Empress then," Lali said, rising to prepare the mushushus for travel.

Tyjinn watched her go, followed shortly by Kio who had the morning's business to attend to. When they were alone, he looked at Dylan. "You did good," he said. "I'm proud of you."

"Thanks, Dad," Dylan teased. Although he was pleased with himself, what he had done wasn't really scrying. What he had achieved was only a symbolic vision, the magic blue magicians did when practicing their own version of divination. Few except the Blue Oligarch were capable of proper scrying, and while Dylan hadn't achieved that, what he had accomplished might save a life.

For a moment he saw the flames burning in his mind again. Why had they set the jungle on fire? This had to be the power of the red loka, but that was safe in Tyjinn's hands. The flames had been extinguished shortly after. Dylan didn't like what that might symbolize. The more he considered it, the more he questioned if they should be traveling toward the one place guaranteed to reveal the truth.

Chapter 8
Green

The endless sand dunes, like waves in a sea, gradually lost their strength and flattened. Ahead was a green island ripe with thick forests and surrounded by lakes that glistened in the afternoon sun. Without any prompting, the mushushus picked up their pace.

"Strange that the Empress lives in the middle of the desert," Dylan said as they approached. "It's like she's intentionally living outside her element."

"That's the point, I think," Lali replied. "It'd be sort of like... well, you living here. Water is scarce so your power would be twice as appreciated and useful. This would all be barren desert without her, which is why people treat her like an Empress."

"Maybe I should move north to the icy mountains." Tyjinn grinned at the idea. "I'd melt the snow and create a land of eternal summer. The thankful natives would adore me and honor me with the title of—"

"Empress?" Kio interjected.

"That's not exactly what I was thinking."

After two days in the Drylands, Dylan couldn't remember when green had looked so good. The plants seemed to exhale cool, fresh air to the entire region. His eyes drank in every detail. Unlike most forests, countless species of trees coexisted in harmony, the variety so great that Dylan was hard pressed to find two of any kind.

A delicate crescent of these trees embraced the lake, its waters rippling in the desert wind. That was a bit of a puzzle. The Green Oligarch might rule over earth, but water was the Blue Oligarch's domain. How did this lake come to be here? Dylan doubted it was natural, unless oases weren't the small, struggling springs he imagined them to be. This lake was large enough to support more than the ten or so boats that currently bobbed along its surface. Surely magic was behind such a feat.

"Anybody up for a swim?" Lali called as they reached the lake's shore. Before anyone could answer she and Kio had dismounted, and Lali had begun peeling off her clothes. "C'mon," she called, as she kicked off the last thing between her and the rest of the world. "Don't be shy!"

"Don't forget Dylan's vision," Tyjinn said. "Green could be in danger even now."

"Fine, but you all are going to stink. Give me two minutes." Lali splashed into the water a few steps until she was far enough to dive in.

"You have to admit that it looks refreshing," Dylan said as he and Tyjinn dismounted.

Kio stretched, looking happy to be on his feet again. "Even I'm tempted to jump in, and I hate water."

True to her word, Lali trudged out of the water a few minutes later and began redressing, even though she was still dripping wet. Her clothes soaked up most of the water, but wouldn't stay damp long in the heat.

Dylan eyed her, trying not to be obvious. Her athletic figure was stunning. Despite not having much experience with girls, he knew a body like hers was rare. She was attractive, and yet her nudity didn't spark any urges inside him. He turned to see Tyjinn watching him with a peculiar expression. *Just double-checking,* Dylan wanted to explain, but instead he crouched to wash his face.

Instead of remounting, they led the mushushus around the edge of the lake. The babble of conversation and laughter could be heard in the distance, increasing in volume as they walked.

"Didn't you come from some sort of festival here?" Dylan asked.

"The Festival of the Melon," Lali said with a nod. "It's a month-long celebration that I never miss."

"And it's all about melons?" Kio asked. "Gosh, you desert folk sure know how to party."

Lali laughed. "Ever heard of moon melons? They only grow a short time each year and are really juicy."

"Those juices just happen to be extremely intoxicating," Tyjinn added. "Which explains why so many flock here to honor a fruit."

"If the Green Oligarch can create an oasis like this in the Drylands," Dylan said, "then surely she can grow these melons anytime she wants."

"Well, yeah," Lali said, "but she has to stop growing them in time for the festival of the beer berries the following month."

Kio appeared slightly more interested. "I'm starting to like the Empress already."

A group of men stumbled out of the forest, each holding a light blue melon with a hole cut into it. Occasionally one would clumsily hold the melon to their mouth, spilling more of the contents on themselves than they drank. They stumbled by without taking more than passing notice of them, even then only looking at Lali.

Following the path the men had come from, they entered the forest, the dark, cool interior a relief after so many days spent in the desert. The trees were giants stretching high into the sky, their tops lost in a tangle of interwoven branches. Around many of their thick trunks were wooden ramps spiraling upward.

"There's a whole village up in the trees," Lali explained, "little houses connected by platforms. That's where we'll be staying."

Lali seemed to know where she was going, and Dylan was glad to follow, since that left him free to gawk. They passed all manner of people, young and old, and even a few who weren't human at all. One wooden creature appeared to be made out of branches, but that wasn't nearly as shocking as the Rakshasa, one of the humanoid tigers who weren't known to socialize with humans. Muscles bristling with golden fur drew the eye, as did the colorful scarves and jewelry that contrasted greatly to the drab desert garb that most humans here wore.

Dylan's curiosity gave way to caution. The outfit Purple's murderer wore was the standard here. Not all had their faces covered, but they could have already passed him without knowing. Would the murderer recognize them? An attempt had already been made on Tyjinn's life, so he at least was known. Being surrounded by people usually meant feeling safe, but now every stranger was a potential aggressor.

Where the forest ended, the garden began, stretching as far as the eye could see. Bumblebees hummed happily, buzzing between flower heads the size of a plate. Nearest to Dylan was a spiky plant with angular blooms of swirled color, while violet ferns waved their appendages at Lali. Cacti wound into strange looping shapes, and trees gathered together in tiny orchards, their branches heavy with mismatched fruit. Tyjinn plucked a pear from a tree that also bore apples, peaches, and a dark red fruit covered in thorns. Kio stepped tentatively onto a carpet of soft flowers, the petals of each a different color. The viney, ground-grown moon melons lined every path.

People were everywhere, yet the garden was large enough to hold many more. Some lay in the sun, plucking at musical instruments or picnicking. Most ate directly from the fruit trees or took snacks from the berry patches around them. Dispersed among the people were more of the wooden creatures—woodworm, Tyjinn called them—although none were enjoying the festivities. Instead they bustled around the garden on their branch-like legs, tending to its needs.

Dylan remounted the mushushu that Tyjinn was leading, and from his new vantage point saw several fountains scattered throughout the garden. He wondered again how the Green Oligarch could manage such a feat, before his attention shifted to a huge mound of trees and plants in the distance. The tip of something pearl-colored poked out from its center.

"The home of the Empress," Lali said. "Or the nest as she prefers to call it."

A number of people entered and exited the nest as they approached. The Empress clearly valued entertaining over privacy. No guards were posted at the entry; no defense was visible as they entered. Inside was a jungle, the growth wound together tightly to form walls and a ceiling for the three paths stretching out before them, each leading in a different direction. Dylan was immediately reminded of a labyrinth.

Mushi pawed impatiently at the ground as Lali considered which direction to go. "I'd say she's in a social mood today, so the most direct path should be it," she said.

"You mean it changes?" Kio asked.

"Like a maze. When she wants to be alone, there's no getting to her at all. The paths change daily. I have no idea how. Maybe she talks the plants into moving."

Dylan thought this a rather dubious defense, though unlike the garden, nothing here looked soft or beautiful. Thorns, brambles, and hard bark were common, but any Oligarch could tear a path through the plants to reach her. If not with magic, then by using a simple machete. No wonder her life was in danger!

Lali had assumed correctly. The center path took them forward with minimal twists and turns, allowing them to swiftly reach the maze's center. Here was another garden, one delicate and rare. Rose bushes lined the circular clearing, their petals as transparent as glass. Ivory grass blanketed the area, its pallor disturbed by only a hint of pale green at the tip. Braided tendrils of pastel flowers draped from the branches above. Even the harsh desert sun was filtered down to a subtle sparkling light.

A seed of improbable proportions dominated one end of the clearing. Balanced on its widest end, the top disappeared somewhere in the canopy above. This was the object they had seen rising above the nest. Its shell was the pale, oily color of pearl, multitudes of gentle colors reflecting off its immaculate surface. Before this, on a dais covered in thin vines and tiny white flowers, a woman reclined.

Determining her age was difficult. As the sun danced across her features, she sometimes appeared to be in her late forties; other times not even twenty. Auburn hair flowed down her shoulders and over her breasts, the curves of her voluptuous body scarcely hidden beneath a moon-colored silk dress. The woman before them was the very essence of fertility.

A number of admirers—Dylan was tempted to call them worshipers—were sitting on the grass in front of her. One was telling the Empress a story. She smiled and laughed elegantly as the man brought his tale to its end, and Dylan couldn't help feeling envious of the man for being able to entertain her so easily. The Empress looked up as if in response to this thought, her jade eyes locking onto his. They widened in brief surprise before returning to half-lidded omniscience.

"I'm afraid I must ask you all to leave." Her gaze never left Dylan's, even though she was addressing her subjects. "All but the son of Orbsen and his companions."

As one, the followers of the Empress turned to regard them, but Dylan barely noticed. She had called him a son of Orbsen, the god he and almost everyone in the Lakelands worshiped. How had she singled him out? Could she have recognized him from somewhere?

Her court filed out, gazing at them curiously or resentfully as they passed. Even so, her eyes never left his. Her stare wasn't uncomfortable, challenging, or even searching, but as if she had known him all his life and was comfortable in his presence. Then Dylan's mushushu bucked impatiently, breaking the spell. He dismounted somewhat awkwardly and approached the dais with his friends close behind.

"You are the son... No, it must be grandson by now... Yes, the grandson of Zane." The Empress stated this rather than asked, smiling at Dylan's astonishment.

"Are you clairvoyant?" he asked.

"No, but you have his unmistakable gray eyes." The Empress straightened. "I don't suppose he is still—" The question froze on her lips.

"Alive?" Kio finished for her. "He keeled over ages ago."

"Delicately put," Dylan muttered, then said a little louder, "He passed away quietly when I was young. You knew him?"

"Oh yes!" the Empress breathed. "I knew him when he was

little more than a boy. Well, not quite a man, but certainly close enough." She smiled coyly before turning her full attention back to them. "I suppose we should concern ourselves with names from the present rather than the past. I am known as the Empress, but as you may already know, I am also the Green Oligarch."

"I'm Dylan, the Blue Oligarch."

"So, you have inherited your grandfather's legacy," the Empress said. "It pleases me to learn this. If you are anything like your grandfather, I know the blue loka is in very skilled hands." She smiled rather seductively at Dylan, prompting Tyjinn to step forward.

"I am Tyjinn, the Red Oligarch," he said, partially obscuring Dylan from view. "I believe you know my mother already."

"Ah, yes. Who doesn't know Mama? I hope she is doing well."

A smile tugged at the corner of Tyjinn's mouth. "Spirited as ever."

Kio sauntered forward. "I'm not an Oligarch, but I can talk. The name's Kio." He paused, waiting for a reaction. "I'm a talking cat?" he tried again. "Why don't you look surprised?"

"My gardens have received all sorts of visitors over the years," the Empress said. "Now if you could fly, I would be quite impressed."

"I've never actually tried before," Kio said musingly.

"And I come representing the Orange Oligarch," Lali said with a bow. "My name is Lali, and as Hasam's apprentice, I bring his respectful greetings."

Dylan exchanged a surprised look with Kio. This was news to them.

"We were just discussing the Orange Oligarch not ten minutes ago," the Empress said with raised eyebrows. "Tell me, is it true that he has gone into hiding?"

"Into hiding?" Lali frowned in confusion. "I've been traveling recently, but I don't think he has. No, of course not. Nothing would make him abandon his people."

The Empress's disbelief was apparent, but the matter wasn't pressed further. "What would the world come to if we started believing in rumors?" she said generously. "Have you only just arrived? Are any of you hungry or thirsty?"

"Both," Kio said. "I'll take any meat you have, as well as any sort of beer."

"I'm afraid you won't find any meat here," the Empress said. Kio looked deflated, so she hastened to add, "I *can* grow a type of squash that tastes exactly the same as chicken. You'll never know the difference."

She reached into the plants that formed her dais and withdrew a slender ivory wand tipped with a green diamond. Her loka flickered with the slightest green light, causing a shoot to burst from the ground. A bulb formed at its end, which grew into a full-sized fruit within seconds. The fruit resembled an eggplant, but was vaguely rectangular and white.

With a look of open skepticism, Kio approached the fruit and trapped it under one of his heavy paws. After sniffing it cautiously, he tore into it with his teeth. His hesitant chewing was soon speeded by enthusiasm. "Not bad!" he declared, despite his full mouth. "And the beer?"

The Empress gave an amused titter. "I'll have it sent for."

Dylan declined the offer of food when the others did, even though he was hungry, but he did ask for something to drink. Then the Empress flashed her green wand again, although nothing grew instantly this time.

"Please, do sit down," the Empress said.

Dylan expected something to appear for them to sit on, gigantic mushrooms maybe, but nothing did. After a moment's hesitation they sat on the grass, uncomfortable for a moment as if they were replacing the admirers who had been shooed away, until the Empress left her dais and joined them, literally, on equal ground.

They had barely sat down when the wall of plants nearby rustled. One of the woodworm stepped through with a tray and bowed so they could accept their drinks. Dylan took the opportunity to study the creature. It was indeed made of wood, although its dark, bark-covered skin looked more complicated and authentic than natural wood, as if trees were pale imitations of these creatures. Its twisted trunk torso stretched to the top of its head. It had no neck and few facial features, except for a mouth slit and two small sap-colored eyes. The woodworm didn't appear hostile, but Dylan found it frightening on a primal level. He was relieved when the creature moved away. The Empress thanked it as it took its leave, but the woodworm did not speak.

"How long have you had woodworm as your servants?"

Tyjinn asked, his voice uneasy.

"Decades now," the Empress said. "They're quite harmless when not provoked."

Tyjinn snorted. "But when they are, it's a different story."

"They make effective security as well," she admitted.

Dylan was curious to find out how, but didn't want to appear ignorant. The woodworm's spindly arms ended in long, pointed fingers that probably could be used as a weapon, although even the most basic armor should provide adequate defense. A carefully aimed kick might even break them in half, unless there was more to the creatures than met the eye.

"We can't be too careful considering recent events," the Empress added. "I must confess it's a relief to be in contact with other members of the Oligarchy. I've been running on rumors and word of mouth since Krale died. As a matter of fact, I'd heard that Blue was missing and presumed dead."

"We had to go into hiding," Dylan said. "My father scried out three possible futures, and—well, it's complicated. He's fine though. I'm sure of it."

"I'm relieved to hear the rumors were false."

"Has there been an attempt on your life?" Tyjinn asked.

"No, none at all. In fact, I'm surprised people are taking one incident so seriously. Krale was killed by an animal of some sort, which hardly sounds like murder to me, and yet everyone acts like a serial killer is on the loose. Unless my information is wrong?"

"Not wrong, but incomplete," Tyjinn said. "The Blue Oligarch's scrying is to be trusted. He foresaw an attempt on his life, which he avoided, and there was one on mine as well."

"Of what nature?"

"I can't vouch for what the Blue Oligarch saw, but an animal attacked me, too. As with Krale, it was specifically selected to take advantage of my weaknesses."

The Empress looked thoughtful for a moment. "Purple?" she inquired.

"Dead." Tyjinn filled her in on what they had learned from speaking with Nikolai.

The Empress was silent as he spoke, but looked grim as the details were made clear. Tyjinn didn't reveal Dylan's vision, perhaps not wanting to alarm her, and when he was finished, the Empress sat silent for some time.

"I don't imagine there is much more damage to be done," she said finally. "White and Black are mostly untouchable, and Gray and Brown are difficult to reach even by magical means. Regardless, they will have to be warned. They will almost certainly join us. As for Orange, it's no surprise that he's gone into hiding. Hasam has always been an alarmist and a coward. You'll excuse my candor, I hope," she said to Lali when she remembered his apprentice was present. Lali didn't look pleased.

"Did you say Gray and Brown would join us?" Kio asked. He had long since finished his meal and was grooming himself while keeping one eye on his beer. "What's there to join?"

"I assume that's why you came," she answered, turning to look at Dylan whom she had singled out as their leader. He struggled with the question before looking to Tyjinn.

"Absolutely," Tyjinn said. "We must band together and bring this to an end. If we leave early tomorrow and head west toward—"

"Nonsense," the Empress said. "We are safest here in my domain. This is where we will stand our ground. There's no need to go stumbling into any traps. I can send messengers out to the remaining Oligarchs."

"One of which is the killer," Tyjinn countered. "A messenger will only alert the murderer before losing his life. Better we travel together, picking up allies as we go until we find our culprit."

"We can discuss this later," the Empress said dismissively, looking away as if Tyjinn were no longer of consequence. She returned her attention to Dylan. "I'm glad you are here. There is work we must do. Come, let us walk together. Alone," she added when Tyjinn made to stand.

"I'd like that," Dylan said.

He couldn't bring himself to look at Tyjinn, fearing the hurt expression he might find there, but the vision of a fire burning the gardens to the ground was more upsetting. By keeping Tyjinn and the Empress apart, maybe Dylan could avoid disaster.

The Empress made small talk as they strolled through the southern gardens, commenting on her favorite areas or pointing out rare species of flora. Dylan nodded, mumbling the occasional polite reply, but most of her words were lost on him. He was distracted by the wave of response from the people they passed. Most looked on them—well, perhaps just the Empress—with awe, as if they were gods descended from the heavens to walk the earth. A few made religious gestures and fewer still dared to approach with offerings. The Empress was unabashed by this behavior, nodding and waving to everyone as she walked and gently turning away the offered gifts.

Kio struggled to keep up, a battle of will playing out on his face between staying for the idol worship or keeping an eye on Dylan. Despite the Empress's request to walk alone, the big cat had come along anyway. The Empress allowed this, knowing perhaps that she was outmatched in stubbornness.

The crowds thinned as they passed through the garden and entered woods that were identical to those in the north. Soon not a single person could be seen, and no noise could be heard from the tree huts above. An unpleasant stench lingered in the air, increasing as the wind blew. Dylan couldn't identify the smell, and the Empress wasn't telling. Her eyes were questioning, expecting him to know the answer. He didn't see how an unpleasant scent in the woods had anything to do with him. Maybe she had a stinky pet that needed washing, although the scent wasn't bestial. The smell was more elemental and wet, something that came with too much rain.

"Stagnant water!"

"I thought you'd sense it when we got close enough," the Empress said.

"It's sort of hard not to," Kio said, sneezing to clear the smell from his nose. "Everyone else sensed it too, judging from the desertion here."

The Empress nodded. "That is a problem. The tree huts in the other three quarters are over-crowded because of the smell, although that has led to some rather passionate nights recently."

Dylan tried to envision how a crowded room full of people being "passionate" might look as they came upon the lake, a mirror image of the one they had seen when first arriving. It, too, was embraced by a crescent of trees, although the water here was covered by a blanket of fragrant water lilies. The flowers filled his heart with yearning. They were common in the Lakelands, and a number of them grew around their lagoon. The flowers were meant to help hide the stagnant odor, but the result was an unpleasant sickly-sweet smell.

"It was all I could think to do," the Green Oligarch said. "I tried various forms of algae, hoping one would counteract the condition, but the results were always temporary."

Dylan wondered what was expected of him. He could refill the lake with fresh water, if it could be drained first. Unfortunately, he didn't know how to do that. The Empress might believe he could fix this, but he didn't even know where to start. This situation could quickly prove embarrassing.

"Your grandfather created this lake, you know," the Empress confided. "Before he came, the garden was much smaller and centered around a small natural oasis. He and I had the garden to ourselves back then, a private paradise just for the two of us. Zane was—" She smiled slowly as she searched for the right word.

"Always horny?" Kio offered.

The Empress laughed. "Something like that, yes."

Dylan found the topic uncomfortable. How old had his grandfather been when they were together? How old had the Empress been? Uninvited images kept popping up in his mind, so he grasped desperately for a change of topic.

"Look, I'm not sure what to do about this water thing," he admitted. "I've only had the loka a few weeks, and this is way out of my league."

The Empress was unaffected by this confession. "What does your gut tell you to do?"

"My gut? I don't know. I guess we should get Tyjinn here and hope that he knows more about this than I do."

She raised an eyebrow. "Maybe I should have asked what you feel intuitively."

Dylan sighed. He knew where she was going. His father always mentioned intuition during their training sessions, insisting that water was an intuitive element; its flow was ever-changing, the current shifting and fluctuating, and lots of other things Dylan never understood. Blue magic was meant to reflect this fluidity, so it had no standard spells or techniques, only an embracing of whatever the situation demanded.

The impromptu nature of blue magic had never worked for Dylan, so his father was forced to teach him using technique. Dylan wasn't sure how it worked for other people, but he knew he wasn't a natural. He had needed years of training to bring out the meager abilities he had, and still couldn't do a fraction of what his father could. Then again, he hadn't done so badly the other night when he and Tyjinn were training together. In fact, ever since meeting the Red Oligarch, his abilities had blossomed. Maybe Tyjinn's talent was rubbing off on him. Dylan decided to stop worrying and give it a shot.

He sat down at the lake's shore, took hold of the loka, and closed his eyes. This time he wouldn't over-think it. What he needed was to stir the water to freshen it. Mentally he reached out to the loka and through it to the lake. He heard the water respond, but didn't dare open his eyes. He increased his efforts, and so did the sound. Unfortunately, so did the smell. Dylan tried not to let this deter him, but soon it became so overpowering that breathing was difficult.

He opened his eyes to see the surface of the lake turbid with motion. Some of the water lilies had sunk while most of the rest were overturned. The condition of the water hadn't improved. He halted his magic. Kio had retreated back to the tree line to escape the stench, and the Empress's eyes were watering.

"Was that intuition?" she asked without a trace of sarcasm.

He nodded lamely.

"In that case I think it's time we try a different strategy."

The Empress pointed at the ground where two green stalks unfurled from the soil and blossomed into bright orange flowers. She picked them both, held one to her nose, and sat down next to Dylan. She offered him the other flower, and he mimicked her actions. The flower cleansed the air around his nose, making inhaling easier.

"All right," he said after taking a deep breath, "what do you suggest we do?"

"Are you familiar with magical structures at all?" she asked. He shook his head, and she sighed. "Just close your eyes and try to relax. I know this isn't going to make sense when I say it, but please, I want you to look through your eyelids."

Kio guffawed from behind them.

"*Will* your eyes to see what is in front of you, even though your eyelids are closed," she said.

Dylan struggled with the concept before giving up on understanding it. He attempted to see what was ahead of him, straining with effort. At first he squinched up his eyes, which seemed foolish, so he took a more relaxed approach and stared ahead as if his eyes were open. After a moment his point of awareness slipped upward, settling somewhere at the center of his forehead. Sudden light appeared before him. Blue lines criss-crossed through the black and formed a pattern somewhere in the water's depths.

"I see it," he said carefully, fearing that speech would cause him to lose concentration.

"Good, good." The Empress hesitated for a moment. "I'm afraid at this point I don't really know what to do myself. This isn't my style of magic either."

Dylan felt like opening his eyes so he could roll them.

"What does it look like?" she asked.

"A bunch of blue lines all jumbled together."

"Does anything look amiss about them? Any of them broken or weak?"

They all looked weak, but he assumed that was because he wasn't very good at seeing them. He started tracing individual lines to see where they led. Most of them stopped at what was probably the lake's surface, so he searched in the opposite direction. Further down the lines merged with others until eventually all connected with one of three lines. On the bottom of the lake, these three lines spun around something very faint. He needed a while to make out what it was, and he was surprised once he did: It looked like a loka. A very faint, small blue loka.

"There's only one loka of each color, right?" he asked uncertainly.

"Good! Yes! There is only one of each. What you are seeing is called a node. It's a sort of shadow loka that self-replicates its power."

"Like the crystal we use on our boats?"

"Exactly, except without the physical form."

"How do you create one of those?"

"It's complicated, but not necessary to know at the moment." The Empress's voice sounded hopeful, which encouraged him. "If it's still intact all you need to do is charge it."

For once, Dylan was in his element. He began charging the node as he would a crystal engine. The node didn't respond immediately, but he kept feeding his energy through the loka and into the node. The process took long enough that his mind began to wander. He wondered what the others were doing. Were they still in the nest, or had they gone off to explore? What if the killer was on his way to the nest and caught them there? What if Tyjinn—

The node in the water exploded with blue light as bright as the sun, the pain forcing Dylan to open his eyes. The light disappeared, but Kio's proud whooping took its place.

"Look at that! I knew you could do it!" the cat said as he pounced into him from behind.

Dylan was momentarily confused until he noticed the lake. It was just as still as before and still cluttered with lilies, but the water was now crystal clear. Even the unpleasant smell was beginning to disperse as winds blew in from the neighboring desert. Dylan looked over at the Empress, who nodded in approval, a slight smile on her face.

"Thank you," she said. "I wasn't sure if you were going to manage it, but in the end you did quite nicely."

"Of course, he did!" Kio growled happily.

"I didn't have quite so much faith in myself," Dylan admitted. "For a while nothing was happening, but then something just clicked."

"Perhaps you freed yourself from thought?" the Empress suggested.

"Not really. I mean, I wasn't exactly concentrating at that moment. I was thinking of something else entirely."

"Interesting," the Empress said. "What were you thinking about?"

It took him a moment to recall, and he blushed when he did. "I was thinking about my friends."

"What about them?"

Dylan looked up and met her eyes, not understanding why she was so interested in his thoughts instead of her now-healthy lake. His confusion and irritation must have shown, because the Empress excused herself.

"I thought it might hold some significance to your sudden success," she said. "Thought versus intuition."

"I don't follow you," he said.

"I'm referring to the five different sources that magic draws its power from."

"We've heard of those, Dylan," Kio said. "The five wells,

remember?"

"Oh yeah! What were they? Uh, intuition is one, obviously. That's what the blue loka is supposed to work best with."

"Correct." The Empress cocked her head thoughtfully. "Though perhaps 'creativity' is a better way of describing it. The invention and application of what is needed in a split second."

"Gosh, that *is* an easier way of describing it," Kio said sarcastically.

"There's also mental and physical wells," Dylan said.

"That's right. Mental wells draw heavily on intelligence and physical wells depend on the body's endurance." The Empress raised an eyebrow. "Remember the other two?"

Dylan shook his head. "Nope."

"I've got nothing," Kio said.

"The two remaining wells are spirit and emotion. The spiritual well is very akin to passion and drive."

"I bet the red loka is paired up with that one," Dylan said, thinking of Tyjinn.

"Indeed, I believe it is," the Empress said. "That leaves us with the well closest to my magic: emotion. The emotional well is chaotic and many-faceted, much like nature itself."

"Is it possible to get another one of those beers sent here?" Kio interrupted.

"As you already know," the Empress continued, ignoring the cat, "each loka functions best with one particular well. The ten lokas are split evenly in pairs that match with the five wells."

Dylan was beginning to see what she meant. "So you were trying to figure out which well I used to trigger the blue loka's magic," he said. "Normally it should be done with intuition, but that didn't work so I must draw from a different well."

"Exactly. It's unfortunate, but you shouldn't let it discourage you."

"Sorry?"

"It's a shame you don't possess a loka that suits you better," the Empress said without any malice. "You'll never reach your full potential as an Oligarch because of it."

"So you're basically saying that I'm always going to suck at magic."

"At blue magic, perhaps. Yes."

Kio's ears flattened. "You have a funny way of expressing

your gratitude, lady."

"I suppose I do," the Empress said. "My words may sound harsh, but I believe they will prove more useful to you than shallow pleasantries. I'm hoping to help you, not insult you."

"Maybe you don't recognize talent when you see it," Kio countered. "In case you didn't notice, he fixed the problem that you asked him to."

"And I am grateful, but you have to understand that this lake was created by Zane when he was Dylan's age. In this spot was nothing but sand and rock, and he created a lake that has survived for more than half a century."

"Well, you didn't ask Dylan to make a new one, did you? You just asked him to fix Zane's shoddy workmanship."

"No, she's right," Dylan said. "I struggled to recharge something that would have been child's play for my grandfather or any of the previous Blue Oligarchs."

"I suppose," the Empress said, "that Zane was simply lucky to draw from the well most preferable to blue magic. You, in contrast, have to expend extra effort, which makes your results more admirable."

Dylan wrestled with his anger and forced it down. The Empress's expression was frank, her eyes were open and calm. He believed she was trying to help, but he still didn't like hearing what she was saying. He had felt so proud of his recent successes, only to be knocked down again. Still, perhaps she could help him after all.

"If we figure out which well I draw from, do you think my magic will improve?"

"I'm certain that it will," the Green Oligarch said. "Of the five wells, we have already eliminated intuition, and you didn't mention any physical strain, so that eliminates another."

Dylan nodded in agreement.

"What about the spiritual one?" Kio asked. "The kids got spirit!"

"No, it's emotional." Dylan's face flushed, and he mentally cursed the uninvited reaction.

Kio looked at him curiously, no doubt having noticed. "How do you know?"

Dylan hesitated, wondering how he could explain it. The implications had his heart thudding, but with terror or with delight?

"I just do," he said.

"Now all that's left is to put this theory to the test." The Empress stood and gestured for them to follow.

The emotions inside of Dylan stirred. Everything was about to change.

Chapter 9
Final Evenings

The party swelled in size and noise, reminding Dylan of a wave breaking through a dam, the waters roaring and raging, movement turbulent. People danced in groups, the rhythm provided by those beating on all manner of drums. Some brave souls even attempted conversation over the din, screaming into each other's ears. Dylan couldn't see an end to the crowds and imagined they stretched far beyond the torchlight and bonfires. Despite the unrelenting mass of bodies crammed into the garden, he had managed to find solitude.

Everyone else was drinking from the blue moon melons and enjoying their effects. Dylan's thoughts were sufficiently muddled without being intoxicated, although the temptation was growing.

The only thing stopping him was the suspicion that, like alcohol, the moon juice would magnify whatever he was already feeling, and his emotions were already intense enough.

That's my well, he thought moodily. The Empress's test had been a success, but Dylan couldn't help feeling he had lost instead of won. She had led them to a small glade with a collection of flat rounded stones. This had been the spring that fed the original oasis before his grandfather had come along. Dylan's challenge was to bring the spring back to life using emotion as his magical well.

He did so. Unlike his previous attempt, he didn't need the Empress to explain what to do. This time he delved within himself, heading directly to his secret place, tearing down the walls. Tyjinn's face, the sound of his laugh, the way he clenched his jaw while working his magic, and the vulnerability that made rare appearances in his eyes. All those things that stirred strange emotions inside of Dylan, he set free.

The spring had burst into life, much like Dylan's emotions, with a strength it had never known before. Since then he had been forced to face the consequences. He was done denying who he was and what he wanted. Dylan had left the Lakelands to free this side of himself, and now his every wish had been fulfilled. What he hadn't realized was how much he would lose in the process.

He would never go home again. Dylan couldn't face his father's anger or Ada's disappointment. How could he expect them to understand? And Kio? Dylan's stomach lurched. Please let the cat accept this! He couldn't bear the idea of losing him. Kio was the one friend he hoped to take into his new life.

And what would that new life be? Joining Tyjinn at his solitary retreat? Sweeping up around the volcano and baking bread for the man of the house? The idea made him laugh, but the faces of his family quelled his amusement. This was a serious decision.

Dylan pressed his back firmly against the tree he sat under as though it could lend him strength. The world had been so simple yesterday. Funny how much difference a single day could make. A murderous Oligarch? An eel-man, gas dragon, and other killer creatures? No problem. Loving someone that you weren't supposed to? *That* was hard.

Dylan rubbed his eyes and left them covered until he felt someone watching him. Moving his hands away, his heart leapt as his stomach sank. In the crowd, standing still in the midst of dancers, was Tyjinn. He was watching Dylan with concern. Firelight played along his skin as he approached. Gods, he looked beautiful.

"Too much moon juice, kiddo?" Tyjinn joked.

"Not enough maybe," Dylan said.

Tyjinn laughed and offered his hand. Dylan's hand was shaking as he reached out, causing Tyjinn to once again look concerned as he helped him stand. "Are you all right?" he asked.

"Yeah, I'm fine."

"Seriously? Because you seem like—"

"Seriously. I'm all right."

Tyjinn scrutinized him a moment longer before shrugging. "Have it your way," he said. "I hate to point this out, but you're doing a miserable job at partying. Sitting under a tree all alone generally goes against etiquette, unless you are about to puke."

Dylan laughed in spite of himself. "Did the others send you to find me?"

"No, not really. Kio has already gathered a small following. He's somewhere that way," Tyjinn pointed to the north, "surrounded by a bunch of slack-jawed people listening to him rattle off one tale after another. Personally I think they are more entertained by a talking cat rather than his stories, but don't tell him I said so."

Dylan smiled. "And Lali?"

"She's never had any trouble attracting attention."

"I'm surprised you two aren't an item."

Tyjinn looked taken aback, almost hurt. "Not as surprised as I am that you think she and I could be together."

"Well, why aren't you?" Dylan pressed, his mind racing. He wasn't sure why he was treating Tyjinn this way. For some reason he just needed to hear him say it. Maybe because he still couldn't say it himself.

"Because she's not my type," Tyjinn said, scowling. "Not at all, in fact. For reasons I can't explain, I'm attracted to scrawny guys, preferably with brown hair and gray eyes. It especially turns me on when they are too dense to realize when someone is infatuated with them."

Dylan's legs were so weak he was worried he might collapse. "So what you're saying is that you're—"

Tyjinn grabbed him by the shoulders, pulled him forward, and kissed him. The moment seemed to last an eternity as Dylan felt Tyjinn's lips press against his. Then Tyjinn opened his mouth and closed it again, gently trapping Dylan's lower lip. The hint of stubble on his skin made Dylan want to moan with pleasure. He realized his eyes were closed and opened them, just as Tyjinn pulled away.

"That is what I am," Tyjinn said, releasing him.

Dylan couldn't speak. He wanted to cry and laugh at the same time, but most of all, he wanted to embrace Tyjinn and kiss him back, but something inside was still hesitant. He needed to explain himself first, to confess. "Ty—"

"Yes, I know. I promise to restrain myself in the future." Tyjinn turned and started to walk away. "We can still have a drink together," he called over his shoulder. "Come. Show me that I'm forgiven."

Dylan stood a moment, dumbfounded by the feeling that another opportunity had passed him by. Inside was a mixture of elation, despair, confusion, and fear. If emotion powered his magic, at this rate he'd be the most powerful Oligarch the world had ever known. Pushing all worries aside, he ran to catch up with Tyjinn.

When Tyjinn had suggested going for a drink, Dylan had imagined the typical tavern, dark and smoky. No such building existed here. Instead he was led away from the torchlight to an area lit only by the moons. Lying on a ground carpeted with clover were several people, many of them couples, who appeared to be sleeping.

They stepped over a ring of moon melons as they entered the clearing. Tyjinn must have picked up two along the way because he offered one to him. Dylan glanced about before taking the melon with uncertainty.

"One melon won't do that to you," Tyjinn said as he took a seat on the ground. He motioned for Dylan to do the same. "These people have overdone it. I brought you here because it's the only quiet place to be found."

Dylan sat down and watched as Tyjinn unsheathed his knife

and carved a hole in his melon. "Switch," he said, handing it to Dylan.

He wasn't sure if he was supposed to wait for Tyjinn so they could toast, but the idea of bumping melons sounded absurd so he tilted the fruit against his mouth and sipped. The juice was almost overwhelmingly sweet and a bit creamy. Dylan realized how thirsty he was and drank a few more mouthfuls.

Tyjinn upped his and drank it all in one go. A drop of juice ran slowly down his chin, glinting in the moonlight. Oh, how Dylan wanted to lick it off! Tyjinn finished drinking, carelessly tossing the melon behind him. "There's something important we need to talk about," he said.

"Yes," Dylan said, happy that the topic was being raised once more.

"I think we should leave tomorrow morning, head west toward Orange. It's Lali's hometown, and she has a few ideas where the Oligarch might be hiding."

Dylan nodded dumbly as Tyjinn continued speaking. He spoke of further plans and strategies, but Dylan wasn't listening. He had hoped Tyjinn was going to continue the discussion they had been having, but clearly that it was the last thing on his mind.

Dylan was a hurricane of conflicting thoughts and emotions. Tyjinn's kiss had sent him over the edge, but the Red Oligarch acted as if it had never happened. How could something that meant so much to Dylan fail to cause an equal reaction in Tyjinn? *Open that door again,* he silently pleaded. *Give me another chance to tell you how I feel.*

Dylan knew he could broach the subject again, if only he could find an adequate way to begin. *'How about that kiss, huh?'* or maybe *'A funny thing happened while working magic today.'* Neither option sounded romantic. Dylan began replaying the scene in his mind over and over, except with variations. In his fantasy he grabbed Tyjinn and kissed him back, showed him how he felt with more than words.

"Moon juice disagreeing with you?"

Dylan's conscious swam back to the surface. "Huh?"

"I asked you a question about five minutes ago. You've had the same glazed look since then. I was worried you'd start drooling soon."

"No, I'm fine." Dylan wiped his mouth self-consciously. On

the contrary, he was more than fine. His entire body hummed pleasantly, his head feeling misty and pink. Every inch of him felt content and comfortable. No wonder the people around them had surrendered to sleep. The idea sounded blissful.

"You have to keep moving once it kicks in; otherwise the buzz will work against you."

"Right," Dylan said, not understanding a word. He slipped into a daze for a moment longer, and when he came to, Tyjinn was lifting him up by the armpits.

"Up you go," Tyjinn said, his voice straining slightly as he hoisted Dylan to his feet. "What you need is a little exercise."

What followed was dancing. Tyjinn led him toward the light and noise of the party. The simple music was now more enticing, almost mystical, as if the drumbeat were the pulse of the world. They danced, spinning around each other and laughing, all insecurities abandoned. What Dylan remembered most about that night was Tyjinn's smile, the brilliant whiteness of his teeth and the alluring shape of his lips. They took breaks to drink more of the melon juice, before rushing back to dance some more.

When exhaustion came upon Dylan, it did so suddenly, his legs giving out. He found himself falling, but Tyjinn's hands were there before he hit the ground, lifting him up and pulling him into his arms. The last thing Dylan thought before passing out was how good it felt to be home.

Chapter 10
Separation

Tyjinn…

Tyjinn's eyes fluttered open in response to his name, uncertain whether he had been dreaming or if someone had spoken aloud. Pushing himself up on one elbow, he glanced around the room. There wasn't enough light to see by, so he touched the loka resting on his bare chest and summoned up a humble flame that hovered in the center of the room.

Dylan was still passed out in the bed on the other side of the room. Kio was stretched out over Dylan's legs, pinning him in place with his weight. Tyjinn couldn't see Lali in the bunk above him, but he knew from the deep sound of her breathing that she too, was asleep. He must have been dreaming.

Tyjinn...

He was awake enough to recognize it this time. Telepathy.

"Who is this?" he thought back, comfortable with this means of communication.

"Come and see who I am," the voice taunted. *"You'll find me on the bridge between the two platforms."*

Tyjinn stood cautiously and groped on the floor for his clothing, mind racing. He didn't recognize the voice. It sounded like a man, the tones gravelly and malicious, although this information was not reliable. Disguising your voice telepathically was as simple as thinking of what you wanted to sound like. The summoner could even be a woman pretending to be a man. Tyjinn would find out soon enough.

He willed the magical flame to extinguish as he pulled on his boots. Walking to the window as quietly as he could, he pressed his back against the adjacent wall and peered outside. Straining from this angle, he couldn't see much with so many branches and leaves in the way, but he could make out someone standing on the walkway connecting this platform to the next. The figure was dressed all in white.

Tyjinn was tempted to pick off the stranger from here and ask questions later. Despite what he had told Dylan, he could easily set those robes alight and extinguish them once the figure hit the ground. The only thing that stopped him was the commonness of such clothing in this region. He didn't want to be responsible for taking an innocent life. Not again.

Making sure his loka hung outside his shirt, he stepped out onto the walkway. *"Nothing personal, but so much as move as I approach and you're toast,"* he thought, making sure a telepathic vibe of sincerity was sent along with the words.

"I assure you, I wish only to talk," came the response.

The figure really was a man, Tyjinn assessed as he neared. The stranger's build was unmistakable. He didn't look very large or muscular, but he was most certainly male. True to his request, the man didn't move as he approached. Tyjinn stopped just outside the stranger's reach.

"Tell me who you are or this conversation is over," he said out loud.

"I'd rather tell you about something I have," the man replied telepathically, confirming his intent to keep his voice and identity disguised. *"Much more important than my name is the reason that you won't dare take action against me."*

Tyjinn's hand went to his loka.

"If I wasn't confident that I was safe from your formidable powers, I wouldn't have approached you as I have tonight, for I am exactly who you suspect I am."

"You better give me that reason now, you murdering bastard." Tyjinn began building up internal energy. He didn't care for games. If this creep was going to offer a partnership of power like he had with Purple, Tyjinn wouldn't hesitate to kill him. Considering that the gas dragon had been sent to do the same, he saw no reason for hesitation.

"I'm going to hold out my hand and show you something. First, I want you to know that the person it belongs to is currently in my care and unharmed. This person is being kept in a very remote location, one so hidden that if something should happen to me, she will never be found."

"She?"

The robed man carefully lifted his arm, fist upturned, and opened his hand to reveal a small golden necklace.

"Mama?" Tyjinn whispered in disbelief. He let go of his loka, stepped forward, and took the trinket from the man, who offered no resistance. He examined the gold-framed gem hanging on its chain. The fire agate sparkled—a jewel he had forged for her years before, creating first the material with his magic, then using tools to refine it into something beautiful. Its asymmetrical and slanted shape was intended to be a heart. There was no doubt that it had come from her. He pocketed it and grabbed his loka again.

"You'll burn until you tell me where she is," Tyjinn snarled.

"Or I'll quite simply leave," the man said, rising off the ground. He swept backwards and upwards like a leaf blown in the wind, with such speed that he was soon lost in the surrounding canopy. *"Do you really want to pit your magic against someone who possesses multiple lokas? I saw that glint of murder in your eye. Even if you bested me, do you trust yourself not to go too far? Will Mama slowly starve to death as you fruitlessly search the Five Lands for her?"*

In his mind, Tyjinn lashed out with fire, burning away every leaf and revealing where the man was hiding. In Tyjinn's mind, he set fire to the murderer's skin and listened to his terrified screams until he was near death. Then Tyjinn made the man tell him where his mother was; but that was only in his mind. In reality, he gritted his teeth in frustration before releasing the loka.

"Okay. Let's talk terms."

"I knew you'd see it my way."

Tyjinn floated above the gardens, the nest below him. Flight like this should have been a moment of monumental beauty. Part of him did register how exquisite the moon-bathed land below him appeared. Only a handful of torches were left to chase away the darkness, and all but the most dedicated revelers were already asleep. Dawn was only a few hours away. He should have been in bed right now, warm and safe, not here with his insides bubbling in anger and disgust. What this madman was asking him to do was unspeakable, and yet, he couldn't see what choice he had.

"I'm glad I didn't kill you," the man said. He had no need to disguise his voice anymore, knowing Tyjinn couldn't act against him. He used the magic of the yellow loka to lower them toward the center of the nest where the giant seed jutted out. "It was very foolish of me to try. Even if I had your loka, I wouldn't value my chances of successfully killing the Empress. She's very experienced, you know, and very, very old. I should like to keep her alive to find out the secret of her longevity, but I don't think that will be an option."

Tyjinn wished the man would stop talking so he could think. There had to be a way out of this. If he could trap the killer and render his magic useless, then maybe there was hope.

"When my gas dragon failed to kill you, I decided the animals were best utilized as an insurance policy." They stopped directly above the point of the seed. "Should something happen to me, they will come." His eyes locked onto Tyjinn's. "They will come and they will kill everyone in the area, if only to reach my corpse."

Tyjinn knew a response was expected, but he didn't give one. He would play this madman's game, but he didn't have to be polite about it.

"There's no way of telling what will happen once we are on the ground. I expect the Empress is already aware of our presence. Just make sure to watch my back. Keeping me alive keeps Mama alive, as well as every slumbering soul below. If you see any opportunity to finish the Empress, you take it."

Tyjinn nodded. They swept down through the foliage and landed softly on the ground. The clearing was, to his relief, dark and empty. Perhaps the fool didn't know where to find the Empress. Then what would he do? Move from hut to hut and check the beds? Tyjinn was on the verge of laughing when her voice broke the silence.

"I'm tempted to thank you for choosing such a quiet time to murder me," the Empress said as she stepped out from behind the seed. "Although I think I'll make fertilizer out of you instead."

Green light flared as she slashed her wand through the air. Vines burst from the ground around the robed man's feet and inflated into thick muscular tendrils that wrapped themselves around him. He didn't struggle. Instead he turned his head casually toward Tyjinn, who still remained free, the Empress not yet recognizing him as an enemy. She turned to look at him too. He realized she was testing him, forcing him to show whose side he was on. Her gesture was generous and made his actions all the more difficult.

Tyjinn launched a horizontal pillar of flame at her, slow enough that she was able to sidestep it. That was her warning, a message to either kill or be killed. The vines around the robed man ripped into shreds as bursts of yellow air tore through them from the inside out. He stepped free and raised both his hands, revealing both the purple and yellow lokas. The yellow blazed into life, a fierce gale knocking the Empress back against the seed, pummeling her against its surface many times until she fell to the ground.

She looked up and glared. "You can't use both lokas at once!"

Tyjinn felt hope, small and desperate. He had only seen the man use yellow magic thus far. Surely he could switch to using the purple loka, but maybe this took time. He wasn't sure how he could take advantage of this, but the Empress had an idea.

Three woodworm burst forth from the surrounding flora as more vines erupted from the ground, these spiked with long thorns that dripped a foul, no doubt poisonous, liquid. Yellow magic might be able to rip them to shreds, but only purple magic could turn away the stickmen. Their sharp fingers would pierce the robed man's throat before he had a chance to deal with them.

Mama. Tyjinn had to pretend the killer was Mama, because if he died, so did she. He screamed out in frustration as he drowned each woodworm in flames so hot they exploded into ash. The Empress turned her attention to Tyjinn, the vines changing their course to reach him instead. He brushed them aside easily with his magic, shriveling them under a scalding heat.

A burst of yellow signaled that the robed man was acting again. At first no result was obvious; then Tyjinn heard the Empress choking. She pawed at her mouth with her free hand, realizing what was happening. Just as Tyjinn could manipulate heat, reducing it as well as creating it, the yellow loka could also take air away. The Empress was being starved for air by the murderer's magic and would soon lose consciousness or die. Already she had fallen to her knees. In one last desperate bid for freedom, her wand shot forward.

The robed man lost his footing as the ground below him opened. Everything below his waist had already disappeared, his descent halted only by his stubbornly balled fists catching the ground. The Empress gasped, air reaching her lungs once again. As soon as she recovered, she would no doubt finish the job, killing the robed man—and Mama at the same time.

Tyjinn reached out with his fire, engulfing her hair and robes in flames and smoldering the wood of her wand. The loka dropped to the ground as she screamed. He raced forward to secure it, hoping that once he had the loka, she would be stripped of her power and be allowed to live. She saw what he was doing and leapt to the ground to take it first. He pounced on her and clawed at her fingers to take it from her, her flaming clothes searing him and threatening to set him alight. Feeling lower than low, he pried open her fingers one by one. Just as he was slipping the loka from her hand, it flashed once more.

"Burn in a hell of your own creation!" she hissed. A crackling noise swept like a wave through the clearing. Tyjinn jumped to his feet, the green loka safe in his hand, but now he was in mortal danger. The fire was spreading dangerously from where the Empress screamed and twisted on the ground, the dry grass erupting in flames.

Everything was dry, he realized. She had killed every plant in the area, robbing them all of life and creating the ideal timber to burn. The robed man realized this and panicked. He summoned a wind to blow the flames away from the clearing, but only managed to fan the flames and send smoke spiraling.

By the time Tyjinn had stopped coughing, the fire had spread in too many directions for him to control. The surrounding trees blazed, his own element transformed into an enemy. He ran to the robed man and grabbed his shoulder. "Get us out of here! Hurry, you idiot, before we burn!"

The man's panicked eyes squinted shut as sweat dripped into them, but he summoned his yellow magic. As they rose into the air, the screams of the Empress followed them like a ghost out of Tyjinn's past. When they ceased, Tyjinn realized with abhorrence that he had broken his own promise to himself. He had killed again.

Chapter 11
The Message

Dylan awoke to the call of loons in the distance. When he remembered he was too far from home to hear the sweet call of those birds, he pulled himself from sleep. Rubbing his eyes and groaning for good measure, he began the usual ritual of kicking his numb legs until Kio took the hint and rolled off.

"The fire can wait," the big cat grunted.

"Fire?" Dylan repeated. Come to think of it, the cries in the distance did sound like someone yelling about a fire.

"The hell?" Lali grumbled as she stirred from the top bunk bed. "Whaizzat?"

More cries joined the others, this time clear enough for even human ears to understand. A rush of adrenaline throttled them alert. Kio hopped to the floor, giving Dylan enough room to stand and look around for his clothes. Next to the bed he found his shirt and shorts neatly folded on top of his shoes. He couldn't remember getting into bed, which meant that Tyjinn had probably undressed him and put him there. He was relieved to find he was still wearing his underwear. If something was going to happen between the two of them, he wanted to be sober enough to remember it. Speaking of which—

"Where's Tyjinn?" Lali asked, voicing what Dylan had just noticed.

"He's probably the cause," Kio joked.

"Knowing him, he's down there putting it out already," Dylan yawned.

"Then you'd better hurry," Kio said, "before he steals the ultimate chance to show off."

Dawn was breaking by the time they reached the inferno, although the furious flames were casting enough light to rival the rising sun. The fire had been restricted to the nest and was currently surrounded by a crowd of people, ten rows deep. Dylan and Lali had to elbow their way through until Kio started shouting. People tended to pay attention when a talking animal made an appearance. They broke through the crowd into open air, as if an invisible moat lay between the nest and the people. At first Dylan thought the onlookers were simply being cautious, but soon saw another reason that no one approached or attempted to extinguish the fire.

A ring of woodworm protected the nest. They stood perfectly still within arm's length of each other, all facing forward. Their figures were sinister black silhouettes, backlit by the bright flames. They guarded the fire as if it were precious. For creatures made of wood, they were surprisingly calm about the hungry blaze behind them.

"Should we form a bucket chain?" Lali shouted over the crackling roar.

"They won't let anyone near enough," someone called from the crowd.

"They've gone mad," a hysterical woman shouted. "The Empress is dead!"

"She could still be in there," Kio said, blinking furiously as a breeze brought smoke into their eyes.

"So could Ty," Dylan said through a tightening throat. He found the blue loka already in his hand. Without hesitation, he opened the floodgate of his emotions. He wasn't about to lose Tyjinn, especially now. Not before he had a chance to tell him how he felt. Water burst from the loka, knocking the two nearest woodworm to the ground and causing a sizzling plume of white smoke to erupt from the fire.

Dylan stopped his magic, wanting to see how successful he was in subduing the flames. He was also concerned about the deluge washing the two fallen woodworm further into the nest, where they would surely burn. They were living creatures after all, and if that weren't enough motivation, he also didn't want the remaining woodworm to retaliate.

The smoke went from opaque to transparent, revealing that his efforts had barely made a dent. He wasn't sure if this was because the fire was magical or simply enormous. In his heart, he already knew the source of the fire. Somehow Tyjinn was involved, just as his vision had forewarned.

"Why'd you stop? Keep trying!" Kio urged.

The fallen woodworm had scrambled forward to join their brethren, but stood slightly to the side. The way was clear now; he had no reason to hold back. Dylan pictured Tyjinn trapped in the center of the nest, attempting to use his magic to draw the life from the flames but being overwhelmed.

The desperate emotions conjured by this image were enough to send Dylan over the edge. He felt his emotions pour outside of him, through the loka and into the air. Almost subconsciously, he felt the small amount of moisture carried in the air and increased it ten-fold, a hundred-fold. He fueled every speck of water with his fear, hope, and need. The air filled with blue light, becoming a ten-foot-tall wave that crashed into the flames.

The smoke was knocked away by the force of the impact, allowing Dylan to instantly see his success. A patch of charred earth had been revealed, the neighboring trees still smoldering but soaked enough that they wouldn't catch fire again. If he continued in this manner, he might be able to beat a path to the center.

He stepped forward. One of the previously felled woodworm rushed him, its arm raised, and its sharpened fingers splayed. Dylan was too shocked to move as the arm swiped toward his face. A blur of platinum blond hair and the scent of sun-kissed skin whooshed in front of him. Lali's right hand caught the woodworm's wrist, slowing but not stopping it. In desperation, she used her left hand to push its hand away, regardless of the woodworm's needle-like fingers. She cried out in pain before kicking out. Her foot connected with the woodworm's body, knocking it backward as she released her grip.

"Stop!" she snarled at it, pointing a commanding finger in its direction. "We're backing off! Back!"

Both Dylan and Kio were so stunned they needed a moment to realize her last command was directed at them. They scurried backward to rejoin the crowd, Lali not taking her eyes off the stickmen. This action seemed to appease the woodworm, who returned to their previous positions and resumed their motionless vigil.

Angry cries began to sound from the crowd, many suggesting that they drive the creatures into the flames.

The potential violence made the hair on the back of Dylan's neck stand up. "Looks like we're about two minutes away from a riot."

"It might not be a bad idea," Kio said.

Dylan nodded his agreement, but Lali disagreed. "Those things are fast and dangerous." She paused to suck on her palm where the woodworm had gouged her. "Even outnumbered, they'd still be able to kill dozens of us before they could be stopped."

Unfortunately the crowd didn't share this insight and was becoming more rambunctious by the second. Lali put two fingers in her mouth and whistled sharply.

"Listen! Listen to me!" A few angry shouts came in reply, but for the most part, everyone focused on the dynamic woman who—framed by the fire—looked like a war goddess. "Who have the woodworm always worked for? Who are they loyal to?"

"The Empress," came a few unwilling responses.

"That's right, and now they are protecting this fire with their lives." Lali paced back and forth. "That means that the Empress herself wants us to stay away from here, which is exactly what we're going to do."

"Where is she?"

"The woodworm have gone mad!"

"They've killed the Empress!"

Dylan felt uneasy with the mob's focus shifting to them now rather than the woodworm. Kio pressed against his leg, no doubt sharing similar thoughts.

"Killed the Empress?" Lali laughed. "Not likely. In fact, whoever attacked her is probably sizzling in the middle of this mess."

The crowd began talking excitedly, more than one mentioning the Oligarch killer and nodding with approval.

"Let the Empress and her guard deal with this," Lali shouted. "It was wrong of us to get in the way of her business."

"Funny way of doing business," Kio said under his breath.

"None can match the Empress's power, especially not in her own home." Lali fixed each person with her gaze as she strode past. "If the Empress were in danger, the woodworm would be at her side, even in this blaze. They have always done her will, and going against them now would be like attacking the Empress herself!"

The crowd digested this theory as Lali continued to stare them down. Many began to wander away, realizing that the show was over. Others stayed to watch the flames, but at a respectable distance, the mob mentality having dissipated.

Dylan turned his back to them and searched the relentless inferno. Before him was his vision come to life, red consuming the home of green. Like the loyal woodworm, Dylan had thought Tyjinn would always be at his side, but in his heart he knew he was gone, that the sweltering summer night had somehow stolen him away.

The fire continued to burn into the evening, the woodworm never moving from their post. Without Dylan's magic, the fire might have spread. Even with the woodworm standing guard, he was able to soak the surrounding area and put out small blazes. Had he not, the damage could have spread to the gardens and been much worse.

The Empress failed to appear, and memory of Lali's confident speech faded as panic set in. Tyjinn wasn't anywhere to be found either, but the crowd didn't know how significant his absence was. With every passing hour, Dylan's hope diminished that he would see him again, or that his protector was even alive. He threw himself into his work, dousing fire after fire and draining himself of emotion.

Sometime in the middle of that sleepless night, a tremendous thud reverberated throughout the gardens, but the cause couldn't be determined in the smoky darkness. The light of the next morning revealed that the pearl seed at the center of the nest had toppled over, kicking up ash that settled on the surrounding gardens, muting their color with gray.

Many considered this a bad omen. Before noon, multiple caravans had been organized and set out across the Drylands. Dylan could understand their fear. Even he believed that the Empress was dead. The woodworm seemed to be mindlessly guarding her last location, unable to understand what had become of their mistress. Dylan wished they would move aside and let him and his friends in. The flames had all but disappeared, and he was overcome with the morbid desire to search for bodies.

Lali was a mess. At times her hope was manic, insisting that Tyjinn was nearly invincible and would soon return. Other times she would hit bottom, saying that only death would have kept Tyjinn from rejoining them by now. Her fears only fueled Dylan's own. Over the next few days he began avoiding her, unable to stomach the same repetitive conversation that always ended with him hiding his tears. He patrolled the gardens during the day, searching obsessively for signs of Tyjinn. At night he sat under the tree where Tyjinn had first kissed him, wishing this place could somehow summon him back from the past.

Heat had settled oppressively over the gardens, silencing the few disillusioned souls that still tried to party as if nothing had changed. Dylan was lying naked in bed with only a thin sheet draped over his waist. Kio had given up his usual position at the end of the bed for the coolness of the wooden floor. Bathed in the moonlight drifting in through the windows, Dylan tossed and turned, unable to keep his eyes closed for more than a few minutes at a time.

He felt more lost than ever without the man who was supposed to be his protector and guide. Had his father seen all this when he sent him to the Red Oligarch? Was this part of the plan and was there still a happy ending in sight? Dylan doubted it.

A light breeze wafted in, blowing across his sweaty skin and giving him goose bumps. He pulled the sheet up to his chest, determined to sleep. He had almost managed to drift off when heat warmed his face and lit the darkness behind his eyelids. Startled by thoughts of fire, he sat upright. A butterfly made of light, looped upwards to avoid colliding with his head, before fluttering down to be near him again. Dylan's heart exploded with hope when he recognized Tyjinn's messenger.

He turned his attention to the room, hoping to see Tyjinn standing there, even though he knew it was foolish. Of course he wasn't there, but the butterfly made of fire meant he was alive and had something to say. Acting on instinct, Dylan held out a finger for the butterfly to land on, not fearing being burned. The butterfly responded to his offer. The second it touched his skin, and without causing pain, it began to deteriorate, its wings raining down a shower of sparks that disappeared before reaching the bed.

"Dylan, I've done something terrible."

Tyjinn's voice was perfectly clear in his mind.

"Can you hear me?" Dylan whispered, hoping that Tyjinn had somehow established a telepathic connection between them instead of sending a message, but the voice ignored his attempt.

"I should be there right now, protecting you. I want nothing more than to be by your side, believe me, but it's for the best that I'm not. I couldn't bear to see your face, to see those watery eyes judging me. You probably know already. I killed her Dylan. I killed the Empress."

Dylan's blood ran cold, his worst fear confirmed.

"I've ruined everything." Tyjinn's voice paused, struggling with emotion before he could continue. *"But it's not too late to set things right. We're travelling to the Cradle. Get out your map."*

Dylan scrambled onto the floor to retrieve the map from his pack, waking Kio in the process.

"I've got it," he said, holding it up to what was left of the butterfly. A pulse of energy beamed down into the map. The butterfly was now the size of a small moth and continued getting smaller.

"I'm sorry I failed you, Dylan, and know you probably won't believe me but I-" A sound like a sob broke the narrative, and when Tyjinn's voice resumed it was as hard as steel, causing the hair on the back of Dylan's neck to stand up. *"I won't hold back, Dylan. The next time you see me, I'll be your enemy."*

The light from the butterfly faded completely, returning the room to darkness and leaving Dylan feeling cold despite the summer's heat.

The next morning they left in a caravan with sixty other people. The colorful string of wagons failed to live up to Dylan's expectations. He always imagined little rooms inside, lined with carpets, pillows, and maybe a few small pieces of furniture for sitting and relaxing. Instead, each wagon was stuffed full of supplies for the trip and various items of trade. Some of the merchants had a tiny area to sleep in, but nothing as cozy as he had imagined.

Dylan shifted, hoping to relieve his rump. The parts that weren't sore were numb. He was riding beside Lali, each of them once again on a mushushu. Now that Tyjinn wasn't holding the reins, Dylan had much to learn, but he discovered that controlling his steed was relatively easy. The mushushu, whom he named Sapphire because of its blue scales, responded to simple leg movements. When he squeezed with his thighs, it moved faster, and when he tapped lightly with a foot, it stopped. Directions were handled by leaning left or right in his saddle.

The caravan moved slow enough that Kio could pad along beside them at a leisurely rate, which he preferred to riding one of the beasts. When he tired he would join one of the wagons, whose bored owners were glad to take a talking cat onboard. Currently he was escaping the heat by napping in a wagon's dark interior, an opportunity Dylan envied.

No one had slept much after Tyjinn's message. Dylan had struggled in the dark, trying to come to terms with what he had heard while explaining it to Kio. Halfway through telling him what had happened, Lali stirred from sleep, and as Dylan started his story over, he made an important decision. He wouldn't tell them of Tyjinn's confession. Dylan wasn't ready to say it out loud, to acknowledge an act he could barely comprehend.

"I killed her Dylan. I killed the Empress."

The words echoed in his mind, repeating over and over and leaving Dylan's emotions a tangled mess. He didn't know if he wanted to cry or scream. He had trusted Tyjinn completely, had thought him infallible until this unwelcome revelation. Why had he done it? Imagining something horrible enough to drive Tyjinn to murder was hard, especially when his victim was the Empress. Unless she was the Oligarch killer. That didn't seem likely, but what if he had been right?

Dylan knew better. Tyjinn would have stayed if he had done the right thing. Instead he had fled, leaving even his best friend behind. Thank the gods that Lali didn't know the truth. It was better to let her image of Tyjinn remained untarnished.

The map, once examined, had revealed a glowing red spot where nothing had been before. The location itself didn't look significant. It was north of the desert, located in the Longlands. Nothing was near the spot, just open grasslands. Tyjinn had referenced the Cradle, but this didn't shed any light on their destination, as none of them had heard of it.

Dylan suspected that they weren't meant to travel to the Cradle. Tyjinn's threat was surely designed to keep him away. No doubt they were supposed to send more capable forces there, other Oligarchs perhaps, but every fiber of Dylan's being yearned to see Tyjinn. He was sure that, once together again, they could make things right. This meant keeping Tyjinn's declaration of being an enemy a secret from his friends. Dylan mentally added it to all the others. He was amassing quite the collection.

The pace of the caravan was trying at best. The mushushus could travel much faster, but Lali cautioned about safety in numbers, both due to the Oligarch killer and the draggers beneath the sand. She insisted they stick with the group until the second day, when they would make their way north alone. Dylan was ready to return to the more temperate climate of the Longlands. Without Tyjinn's magic, the desert's heat was more than unpleasant.

They had planned to keep a low profile during their journey, not wanting to draw attention to Dylan's status as the Blue Oligarch, but that had proven impossible. Too many people had seen him confront the nest's flames and recognized him for what he was. A few hours into the trip, he had started receiving requests for refilled water skins or water for cooking. The notoriety left him free to use magic openly.

As the sun was settling on the horizon, Kio came strolling back to them, looking half-asleep despite having napped the entire day away.

"This heat makes it impossible to wake up," he said. "I can't get my head unmuddled."

"We'll be stopping in a few minutes," Lali said, looking toward the half-circle of orange light. "The temperature will drop so quickly that we'll soon be shivering if we don't stay near the fires."

"Is a campfire really going to be enough to drive those things away?" Dylan asked.

"The draggers? They'd barely notice a normal fire. You need red wood. Burns for days with an intense heat."

"Where do you get something like that?"

"Red magicians. Quite a few down here make a living selling it."

Thoughts of red magic made Dylan's stomach turn. The topic must have had the same affect on Lali, who looked distant and troubled.

"So you're an orange magician?" Kio asked, his tail curved thoughtfully. "You said something about being apprenticed to the Orange Oligarch."

"That's right." Lali came back from her distant thoughts and smiled. "I'll even be Oligarch someday, assuming we all don't get murdered before then."

Dylan was surprised to hear this. For an Oligarch to take on apprentices was not unusual, but normally an apprentice would achieve the rank of magician and move on. This meant less work for the Oligarch in the long run, but it was unheard of for a former apprentice to take over the position.

"He doesn't have any children," Lali clarified. "No family either, unless you count a handful of mistresses. I'm not the only apprentice, so it's not guaranteed, but I'd say I'm more likely than the other four."

"What exactly is orange magic all about?" Dylan asked. "I've never really understood it. Something about being egoistic?"

"Ego magic," Lali said and laughed. "Yes, some people call it that. It's about the personality and the mind, maybe even the soul. It centers on what makes us who we are."

"That's exactly the sort of thing I've been told before," Dylan said. "The thing is, the only time I've seen orange magicians, they've been acting as counselors. I don't see how that's magical."

"That is a very low-end version of it," Lali said with a frown, absentmindedly scratching the hand that had been wounded by the woodworm. "Real orange magic isn't so subtle."

"Well, you'll have to explain it to me later when my ass isn't throbbing with discomfort," Dylan complained. "I can't wait to get off this thing."

"I feel fine," Kio teased.

"Enjoy it while you can," Dylan said. "By lunch tomorrow we'll be on our own and you'll be draped over this mushushu like a hunting trophy until we get to the Cradle."

"Hey, speaking of which,"—Kio looked excited—"I told one of the wagon drivers about us heading there and—"

"YOU TOLD HIM?" Dylan and Lali shouted in unison.

"Yes, and you'll thank me for it if you'd shut up a moment. The guy just laughed about it and said there was no purpose in chasing legends. He's *heard* of it, you see."

"That is something," Lali admitted. "Did he know anything useful?"

"Not much. Said something about the gods. His wagon is stuffed full of books. He promised to dig one out about it for me tonight."

"That's a lucky break," Lali said. "We'll come along with you."

"Well, he invited me to dinner, but I'm sure he wouldn't mind you two looking through his books while he and I dine."

Lali laughed, but Dylan only rolled his eyes.

As it turned out, the big cat's story wasn't far from the truth. The man with the books didn't mask his displeasure at seeing Kio accompanied by two humans. He introduced himself first with the title of scholar, only adding his name as an afterthought. Considering his name was Rinkly, they could hardly blame him. He had prepared a sludge-like stew that smelled beefy, despite the unlikeliness of him having access to meat. Rinkly made it clear that he had prepared barely enough for two, much less four.

Dylan and Lali were both quick to lie that they had already eaten, neither of them too keen on the smell coming from the pot. Kio didn't share their reservations and kept his eyes locked on his dinner.

Rinkly didn't have much interest in discussing the Cradle, wanting instead to hear more of Kio's stories. After a few suspicious looks he agreed to allow Dylan and Lali to sort through his books alone. He said the book they were interested in was called "Origins" and had a red cover. This wasn't particularly useful advice since most of his books had red covers. In the end, the book in question turned out to have a blue cover. Luckily they found it before the last light left the day.

They carried their prize back to Rinkly's cooking fire. A bottle of wine had been opened, and neither was surprised when they weren't offered a glass. Dylan took some satisfaction in knowing that Kio couldn't drink wine, the taste being far too bitter for his palette. The cat was in high spirits anyway, thanks to his captive audience of one, leaving them free to examine the book undisturbed. It was in poor condition with many pages missing, including the index.

"It's all creation myths," Lali said as she browsed the pages. "Like the one about the world being a pearl in a clam."

"That's a popular one in the Lakelands," Dylan said. "That and the one where a giant salmon laid the sun and stars as its eggs."

"Where I come from, people can hardly imagine enough water for a normal fish, never mind a giant one."

Dylan laughed. "What do you believe then?"

"I don't know," Lali shrugged. "Maybe it's all just always been here. Maybe there's no real beginning or end to anything. Everything starts from somewhere, but it all has to come from somewhere else first."

"Like the whole chicken and the egg thing, except in a never-ending loop?"

"Something like that." Lali gasped and nearly dropped the book in her excitement. "Here it is!"

"Well, what's it say?" Dylan said impatiently as Lali read silently.

"You don't expect me to read it out loud, do you?" she asked.

"Yes!"

"All right, but it's your standard fare so far. You'll wish you asked me to summarize. It says: 'When the gods made the first land, they split chaos into light and dark. They were displeased with its simplicity, so they created another. When they created the second land, they made the sky from the light, the earth from the darkness, giving the world form, but they were displeased with its lack of motion. In the third land, the gods created the sea from a mixture of earth and sky, the waves making wind and setting the world in motion. They were displeased with its solitude. In the fourth land, the gods added fire, causing life to spring up from the other three elements. The gods were at first content with this land, but displeased with its lack of direction.'"

"Maybe you'd better summarize it," Dylan conceded.

"Told you," Lali said. She read ahead silently before speaking again. "Basically, for the fifth land, the gods created us and were finally happy. They did whatever gods do in their free time before changing their minds once again." Lali scanned ahead before continuing. "They decided that beauty shouldn't be restricted by physical form and made a sixth land, based on this concept, where they chose to live. They decided to erase all their earlier botched attempts, which would have meant no more us if it weren't for a handful of the gods who had grown sentimental toward humans. They rebelled against the wishes of the majority in order to save us. In the end, the sympathetic gods saved the Five Lands from being destroyed, but the price was that they were exiled from their own kind. A small piece of the divine world was broken off and attached to ours, so that the good gods could live there. They sleep away their days in this land, dreaming of us and our little lives. Thus the place where they sleep is called the Cradle."

"Which is where exactly?"

"I'm afraid it gets rather weird," Lali screwed up her face in confusion. "Apparently it's at the end of the road each man is destined to walk on."

"Right," Dylan said after a moment's thought. "So we just choose a road and walk to its end, and we magically get there?"

"Nobody can travel there, you idiot," Rinkly chimed in, causing Dylan to jump, unaware that the scholar had been listening. "It's allegorical. The only way anyone gets there is by dying. You return to the Cradle at the end of your life, which is where each person begins life as a baby. It's a circle of life and death."

"Well, I hadn't had time to reflect on any of it yet," Dylan said defensively.

"I told you to get the red book, stupid girl, not the blue one." Rinkly scowled. "That one doesn't even talk about the stones."

"Stones?" Dylan asked before Lali could react to Rinkly's rudeness. Realization crossed her features. She was thinking the same thing he was. Surely the stones referred to the lokas!

"Yes, used to open something or other. A door was it?" Rinkly waved an arm in an effort to help himself remember. *"Five stones to open the gate, five wills to alter our fate, five souls to make it hold true, five gods to…* erm, something that rhymes with true. It's all a load of nonsense."

"Then why was it written down?" Lali demanded. "If it doesn't mean anything, why would anyone remember it?"

"They don't," the scholar countered. "That's why you had to go digging through my books. It's no different than salmon eyes, kraken root, and lizard feet."

"What do you mean by that?" Kio said.

"That's another thing some fool wrote down in one of those books," Rinkly answered, his tone much more civil when addressing Kio. "You're supposed to grind all three together and burn them to talk directly to the salmon. You know, *The* Salmon. Just another load of superstition that is all but forgotten."

"But have you ever tried it?" the cat inquired.

"Of course!" Rinkly said matter-of-factly. "If those three spices worked, you and I would be talking to the Great Salmon right now." He nodded toward the pot of stew.

Suddenly, Dylan and Lali were very glad not to have been invited to dinner.

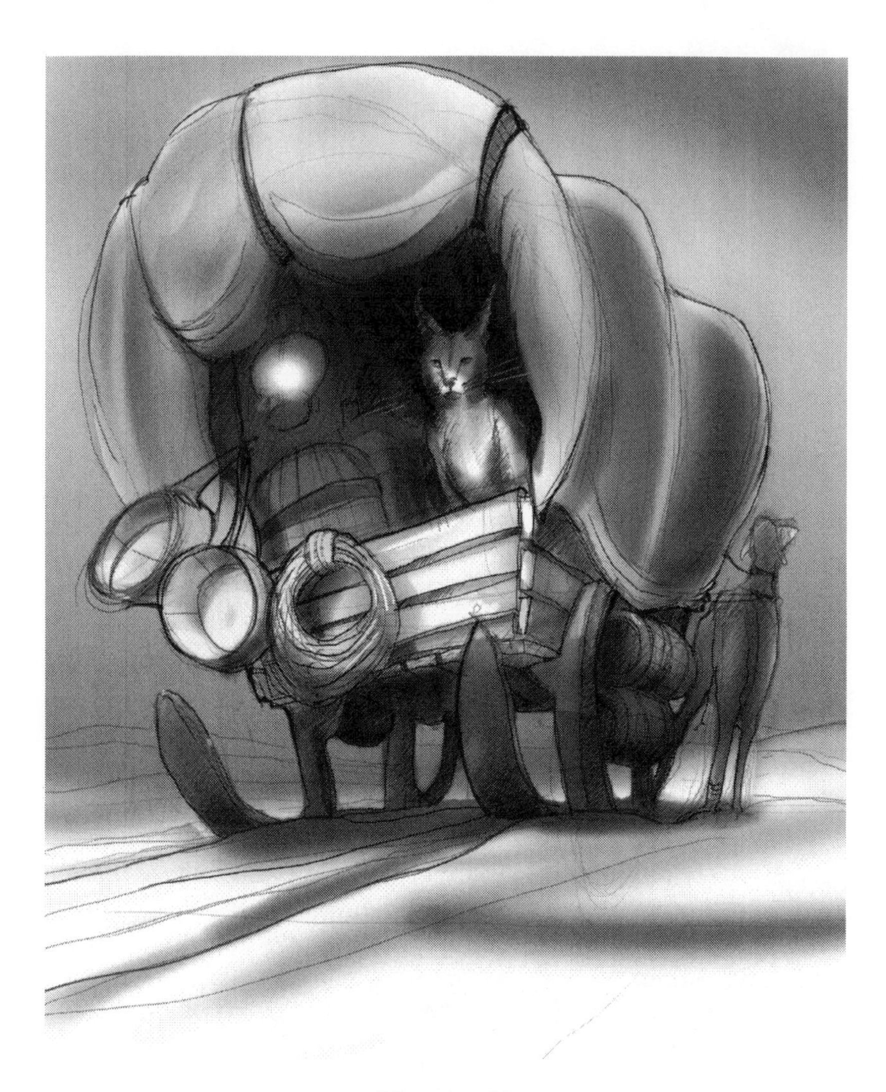

Chapter 12
Life's a Drag

Striking out on their own across the Drylands, with neither Tyjinn's magic nor the limited comforts of the caravan, was a miserable experience. Even though the mushushus did all the work, the riders sweat as though they were laboring to the fullest. Conversation was limited, and Dylan didn't try making any, choosing instead to drown his discomfort by losing himself in his thoughts. That alone was a testament to the unpleasantness of his surroundings, since his thoughts were as tormented as the desert was barren.

He tasked his mind to unravel what had happened in the Empress's garden. He couldn't imagine what had sparked the confrontation between Tyjinn and the Empress, but the gruesome details came all too easily. He envisioned Tyjinn engulfing her in a torrent of flames as she wrapped his neck in choking vines. Tyjinn then turned the earth into lava, unleashing a primal howl of victory as the Empress's body melted into the magma. The scene changed to an overhead perspective, the green oasis slowly fading to brown as the influence of the Green Oligarch's magic lost its hold.

He snapped out of his dramatic narrative. How was her garden still alive? In the days following her death, not even the slightest hint of wilt was visible there. When the Yellow Oligarch had been murdered, the effect was instant: The magic holding the windmill aloft had ceased, sending it hurtling toward the ground. Why had the gardens survived the Empress's death?

"She's still alive!"

"Who's that?" Kio grumbled from his draped position in front of Lali's saddle.

"The Empress! She can't be dead. If she were, the gardens would have died along with her!"

"How do you figure?" Lali asked.

He told her what had happened the night the Yellow Oligarch was murdered. Even Kio set aside his discontent to add details and a few exaggerations. Once they were done, Lali's eyes were wide with surprise.

"That's just… wow!" she said, still impressed a few moments later.

"Hard to believe it's true, huh?" Kio said proudly.

"A few of your parts weren't," Dylan pointed out. "The part about the magic giving out when Krale died is true though. Obviously the same thing would have happened in the oasis if the Empress were really dead."

Lali looked unconvinced. "That part of your story didn't make much sense," she said. "Surely the magic supporting the windmill was created with nodes. I find it hard to believe that any Yellow Oligarch would be able to maintain the concentration necessary to pull off such magic, while still being able to eat and sleep, or whatever."

"Nodes?" Dylan asked. "Like the ones that maintain the lakes in the oasis?"

Lali shrugged. "Probably. That's how all the top dogs do their big magic. I'm sure many nodes were used to create the oasis. That the gardens still live doesn't mean the Empress does too. Magic nodes continue working without their creator, until they lose their charge."

Dylan, unwilling to let his theory be proven false, tried one last time. "If that's true, why would the windmill lose power so soon?"

After a few seconds Lali came up with an answer. "It was deliberate. Whoever took the yellow loka used it to shut off all the magic. They wanted to destroy the windmill and all the evidence along with it."

"But that would mean the murderer was there with us!" Dylan remembered for the first time how the sound of arguing had woke him. Where had the murderer been? He mentally replayed their flight up the dark stairwell and the closed doors they had passed, each a potential hiding place for the Oligarch killer who may have lurked behind one of them, holding his breath as they passed. Or had he given chase, but fallen as the windmill shook? Dylan had barely survived the windmill's destruction, and he couldn't imagine what power the killer possessed to achieve the same. The thought sent chills down his spine.

The setting sun brought the cold of night, but that was soon dispelled by the red wood they were given when they left the caravan. The name could have been inspired by the style of magic needed to create it, but more likely it was because of the eerie red flames created when the wood burned. The magically enhanced timber lit easily and grew into a full blaze within seconds, accompanied by a circle of radiant heat extending almost twenty feet in diameter.

"They gave us the expensive kind," Lali said. "Must have been all that water you conjured up for them. The normal red wood barely creates enough heat to stretch out in."

"And this is really going to keep the boogie men away?" Kio asked.

"The draggers? Yeah."

"What if one of us has to use the litter box?"

Lali shrugged. "There's no such thing as modesty in the Drylands. All the shy people get eaten up."

"Is this how it is where you live?" Dylan asked. He couldn't imagine having to live with constant suffocating heat during the day and flesh-eating beetles during the night.

"Not at all. The western desert is all hard ground and rocky plateaus. The draggers can't dig through it. They only live out here, thank the gods." She paused, her eyes distant for a moment. "You would have liked Dringend, the city I'm from. I'm sure we would have traveled there next to warn the Orange Oligarch if everything wouldn't have gone all—" She waved her hands helplessly. "Well, you know."

"Sounds like Orange already has all the warning he needs, if he went into hiding," Kio said.

"Perhaps. Hasam is strange, but he's a good man. I hope he hid somewhere safe." Lali scowled. "All these gossipers call him a coward and assume he's run off, but what if something happened to him? What if he's already dead?"

"Do you think he is?" Dylan asked.

"Dead? Who can say?" She scratched unhappily at her hand as she considered the idea. Dylan noticed the wound was much larger than it had been. Although the strange firelight made sight tricky, he thought the scabbed skin was spreading outward.

"You'd better stop scratching at that. It looks worse," he said with concern.

"It's fine," she said, hiding the hand beneath one of her crossed legs. "So how long have you and Tyjinn been an item?"

The question hit him like a wall of cold water. He looked with panicked eyes back and forth between her and Kio. Their expressions remained neutral, but he still felt threatened.

"Very funny! I thought you two were together," he retorted.

"I wish," Lali responded unabashedly. "I've spent too many years getting to know the subtle pain of unrequited love."

Dylan was taken aback by her frankness. He had been put off by her initial flirtations with Tyjinn, but had since learned he had no reason to feel threatened.

"So how come you two never hooked up then?" Kio asked.

"Well, surely you know," Lali said, looking at Dylan. "Or not," she added hastily.

Dylan could barely bring himself to look at Kio, knowing the cat's reaction to this news would be a fraction of what it would be if Dylan were the subject of this conversation.

"You mean he's into guys?" the cat inquired.

"Exactly."

"Well, that explains why he's always making eyes at Dylan." Kio's tone was not sarcastic or amused. Dylan was uncertain how to interpret this. He made eye contact with Lali. She blushed, realizing that Tyjinn and he weren't together, or perhaps thinking that Dylan wasn't like Tyjinn after all.

The blue mushushu pawed the ground restlessly and called out in its strange honking voice.

"I guess they're hungry." Dylan jumped to his feet to retrieve their feeding bags, grateful for the distraction. His gut twisted uncomfortably as he mentally reviewed the conversation. Kio had been his best friend since as early as Dylan could remember. It felt wrong to keep the truth from him, but there was so much to lose. The love he felt for Kio urged him to confide, but that same love was at risk if Kio found the truth unacceptable.

He glanced at the fire and found the cat's eyes on him. They reflected disappointment, making Dylan's stomach sink even more. Kio must be considering what Lali had inadvertently revealed, but there was still room for doubt. As long as the subject didn't come up again, the idea would fade away. Dylan busied himself with mundane tasks as the night progressed, unable to bring himself to interact with the big cat. Already his feelings for Tyjinn had created a gulf between those he loved, and it made his heart ache—a sensation he was becoming quite used to.

Dylan tossed and turned in his sleep, tormented by images of Tyjinn as his enemy, of becoming the victim of his magic. He called out to Kio as white-hot flames threatened to consume him, but the feline merely turned his back and walked away.

He awoke with a jolt, his heart racing. The night was pitch black except for the red wood's eerie crimson light. He was lying on his stomach and tried to roll over, but found himself pinned down by Kio's warm bulk on his legs. The cat sleeping in his favorite sleeping place comforted Dylan, a reminder that his worst fears hadn't come to pass yet. He enjoyed the tranquility of the moment, until something rough and scaly nudged his forehead. He yelped loudly, causing Kio to spring into the air. Dylan rolled over, raising his arms defensively in front of his head. Above him a puzzled green mushushu face peered back.

He almost laughed before realizing that Mushi shouldn't be so near to him. The beast had been tied up on the other side of the fire, nearer to Lali. A rope dangled loosely from the animal's harness.

"Mushi?" came Lali's sleepy voice.

"Over here," Dylan replied. "He got untied somehow."

"Where's the other one?" she asked.

He scrambled to his feet and spun around, looking for Sapphire. She wasn't anywhere within the light of their campfire.

"She's over there," Kio said, peering into the darkness. Dylan needed a few more moments to spot her with his inferior night vision. She was thirty yards away, pawing at a small plant.

"Oh gods," Lali breathed. "We've got to get her back before—"

The sand around Sapphire erupted. Four large dark forms launched from the ground as if the desert had spat them out. Draggers! Dylan tried to rush forward to help the mushushu, but a strong hand on his shoulder held him back.

"Take fire with you," Lali said. She released him and turned toward the fire, reaching in with her bare hand and pulling it back in pain a second later. She kicked at it in frustration, trying to dislodge a thin log for him. Dylan looked over his shoulder to see Sapphire rearing up on her hind legs in shock as one of the giant dragger beetles snapped a pointed claw toward her abdomen. A flaming red stick was shoved into Dylan's field of vision. He took it from Lali and ran into the night.

Sapphire was further away than he realized. In his haste his feet slipped on the sand, causing him to fall to one knee, but he kept his eye on Sapphire. The mushushu struck at one of the beetles with her scorpion tail. The sound of a hard shell cracking ricocheted through the air, giving Dylan hope as he regained his feet. If she could fend them off until he reached her, the magical heat of the torch would drive the draggers away and he could lead her back to safety.

He swore as more of the draggers appeared, sand running off their backs like water. Sapphire spun in a circle, outnumbered and unsure where to turn. Dylan screamed as he ran, hoping to distract the beetles, but they paid him no heed. Two of the beetles grabbed the mushushu's hind legs with their massive claws. Seconds later, Sapphire was pulled beneath the sand, a shocked rusty honk ringing out before her head disappeared.

The beetles vanished one by one, all but the one that Sapphire had killed. Dylan reached her location a few seconds too late. Through angry tears, he struck repeatedly at the dead dragger, screaming his frustration. His torch sputtered, almost extinguishing before he came to his senses. Fanning the flame back into life, he began the slow walk back to the others, struggling with guilt over being the one who had tied the mushushus down that night.

He was halfway back to camp when the sand exploded in front of him, revealing two more draggers. He growled at them, happy to have his chance for revenge, thrusting the burning red wood forward like a sword. The beasts recoiled slightly but didn't flee like before. Instead they took two hesitant, almost reluctant steps toward him. He saw a glint of purple light in their eyes just before one launched at him. Dropping the torch in shock, Dylan stumbled back. One of the beast's pincers brushed across his leg and snapped closed a split second too late to catch him. He scurried to reach the torch with outstretched arms, grabbed it, and rolled over to find one of the draggers directly above him.

Dylan shoved the burning end of the stick into the dragger's maw. It squealed in pain and retreated backward but didn't leave. The purple magic driving it had overruled its natural instincts. The other dragger shuffled sideways to take the place of its wounded comrade.

Kio dashed to his side, hissing and spitting. This terrified Dylan more than it comforted him. The cat's claws would be useless against the beetles' hard exoskeletons. Now his dearest friend's life was at risk, as well as his own. The first dragger had recovered, and together the beetles lunged forward.

Dylan grabbed Kio, lifting him as he tried to run, the sound of skittering legs sending mad panic through his body. The draggers' legs were much more suited to this environment, and they soon overtook him. He was knocked forward, Kio flying away from him as he let go to avoid crushing the cat under his weight. A claw fastened around his ankle; Dylan cried out in pain as the beast sunk beneath the sand and began pulling him under.

A crack echoed across the dunes, the sound of a shell breaking. Lali, mounted on her mushushu, was successfully attacking one of the beetles. Unfortunately, it wasn't the one dragging him downward. Already his entire left leg was below the sand, but the other was still trapped above ground, likely to break before it could be pulled under as well. Sand scraped across his cheek as he tried to think of anything he could do to save himself, but his mind was a blank slate of fear.

Heat filled the area, so powerful that it forced Dylan to shut his eyes and threatened to burn his skin. The claw around his ankle trembled and then let go. The ungodly temperature smoldered a few seconds longer before ceasing as instantly as it had begun.

He opened his eyes to find that both draggers had gone, but he brushed the thought aside. That was Tyjinn's magic! Pulling himself from the sand, Dylan scanned the horizon. Was Tyjinn near enough to see? He had to be, but Dylan couldn't see him.

The little group ran back to the campsite, aware that draggers still lurked. Dylan cried Tyjinn's name, calling it over and over again, barely stopping to listen for a response. He wanted to run, feeling that Tyjinn could be just over the next sand dune, so very close to where they waited helplessly for daylight.

Lali was the first to notice that the ropes used to tether the animals had been chewed through. This wasn't normal behavior, and could only be the influence of purple magic. The mushushus had been the bait to lead them away from the fire where the draggers could finish the job. Luckily, Mushi had the sense to stay close to them, or Lali would have lost a friend as dear to her as Kio was to Dylan.

The sun rose less than an hour later, but it brought little comfort. The draggers had been unnaturally fearless toward fire last night, and he didn't see any reason it couldn't happen again during the day. The thought made him uneasy. Was traveling in the Drylands safe at all anymore?

Travel was tense until late afternoon when, from the crest of a dune, they were able to see the end of the desert in the distance. They reached the edge by sunset and pushed on until they found a plain covered with grass and trees, albeit sparsely. Here they made camp.

Kio managed to catch a slow rabbit, and although its death

grimly reminded them all of Sapphire, the nourishment it provided lifted their spirits. By the time they lay down to sleep, they were all feeling more like their old selves. All except Lali, who stared uneasily at the spreading wound on her hand before finally giving in to sleep.

Chapter 13
Mother

Travel the next day was an absolute pleasure for Dylan. Cool, refreshing wind blew over their skin, rather than the harsh, cutting wind of the desert. Trees increased in size and number as they made their way north, shiny green leaves waving away the memory of the barren landscape behind them. Kio was in high spirits, with the return of soft grass beneath his feet. Lali, on the other hand, was too preoccupied to enjoy the Longlands' improved surroundings.

Her aloofness increased until midday when they came to

the river. Kio and Mushi drank their fill, and the three-days' worth of grime that caked Dylan's skin made the allure of a bath irresistible.

"I don't care how urgent our journey is," he said, digging in his pack for his chunk of soap. "I refuse to take one step further before bathing."

"Mushi's been doing all the stepping," Lali chided him, "but I share your sentiment."

Unselfconscious as ever, Lali undressed and walked to the water's edge before jumping in. Not sharing her comfort with public nudity, Dylan waited until Lali dived beneath the surface for an opportunity to undress privately. He was halfway out of his shirt when her head emerged from the water and pivoted to face his direction with disturbing accuracy. He froze a moment before tiring of the game and stripping the rest of the way.

The water was bracingly cold when he jumped in, but his body soon adjusted to it. He imagined he could feel every grain of sand soaking loose from his skin and being swept down the river. Dylan swam contentedly before returning to shore to soap up. He was faced with being naked in front of Lali again, but at least now he could have his back to her.

"You have a nice body," she said as he was lathering himself.

He forced away a blush and laughed nervously. "Eyes to yourself," he said in mock sternness. "And thanks," he added a moment later.

"He always worries that he's too skinny," Kio said from on top of a rock where he was lazily grooming himself.

"Why don't you rattle off all my other insecurities while you're at it?" Dylan snapped.

"If only there was enough time in the day," Kio quipped.

"Not all girls like muscles," Lali replied.

Dylan dived underwater to escape the intensity of her gaze. When he re-emerged, Lali was on the shore helping herself to his soap. He took the chance to check her out as she had done him and found himself impressed again by her body. The tone of her skin in contrast with her platinum hair was striking. Dylan found her beautiful, but in a distant sort of way. Seeing her naked didn't make his whole body tingle with excitement like it would if Tyjinn had been there instead. He pushed the image from his mind. That train of thought would make leaving the water difficult without creating another sort of embarrassment.

As Lali leaned forward to set the soap down, he noticed the brown glove on her right hand. Dylan did a double take and realized it was some sort of rash or infection caused by the woodworm's wound. She must have been taking great pains to hide something so obvious from them. He knew he would have to confront her about it, but was unwilling to do so while they were both nude. Insisting on examining the wound now would lead to awkwardness, not to mention endless jokes from Kio.

Their stop at the river was almost too relaxing. When they continued traveling, they did so half-heartedly, barely riding another hour before stopping to make camp. They could have managed another couple hours before sunset, but their bodies and spirits were still weary from crossing the desert.

Kio napped as they set up the camp, sleeping until nightfall, then waking to hunt. Dylan was glad for it, too. They still had a fair amount of rations, but nothing he would willingly choose to eat. The game Kio hunted gave them at least one decent meal each day.

Lali watched Kio leave with transparent eagerness. Dylan thought at first that she was waiting until they were alone to tell him about her hand. He was partially right. She was waiting for privacy, but the topic she had in mind was completely different.

"So Tyjinn really isn't your boyfriend?" she asked.

"No!" Dylan stammered, his face flushing. "At least, I don't think so." He picked up a twig and drew with it in the dirt. "How would I know if he was?"

"Same way you would know with a girl," Lali laughed.

"Well, no one has said anything about being anything. It's a moot point now anyway, isn't it? He's not around to be anything to either of us." Dylan had more to say, but his emotions were rising dangerously and so he stopped himself.

"Fair enough," Lali said, "but do you want to be his boyfriend?"

"I don't know." Dylan sighed. "Yeah, I guess. I just—" He looked meaningfully toward the direction that Kio had gone.

"Worried about what he'll think, huh?"

"About what everyone will think."

"I wouldn't bother. People will judge you no matter what you are. Too fat, too thin, too nice, too independent; you'll never please everyone."

Dylan tossed the twig into the fire. "No, but I'd like the people closest to me to keep loving me."

Lali rolled her eyes. "Well, I think you're lucky. I'd love to be in your shoes. Hey, if I weren't so moral, I actually could be."

"How do you mean?"

"I mean that I could take over your body."

Dylan started to laugh, but Lali looked serious. His amusement quickly turned to unease. "You can't," he insisted.

"I can, but I won't. I am an orange magician after all."

Dylan thought of the counselors who occasionally strode through town looking for some easy money. They only practiced a low version of the magic, the way blue fortune tellers could scry up some scattered images and interpret them. He couldn't imagine how therapeutic magic could allow them to take over someone's body.

Lali sensed his confusion. "Orange magic is that of the ego," she said. "It's about manipulating the personality, changing who we are by reshaping, relocating, or even by altering the body itself."

"Relocating? Like teleportation?" Dylan asked.

"No. Relocating means swapping personalities with another person, or in the case of an unwilling participant, forcefully entering and engaging in a battle of wills with your opponent, until one of the parties is subdued to the point of—"

His attention faded as her words rattled on. "Not to be rude, but could you just lay out what you can do? You keep losing me."

Lali smirked. "All right. I can swap bodies with you. You'd be in mine and vice versa."

"Simple as that?" he asked surprised.

"No, but you wanted me to keep it that way."

"Right, sorry."

She gave a friendly smile. "Orange magic also can be used to change the body. To shapeshift."

Dylan's mouth fell open. "Seriously?"

"Yes, but I can't do it myself. It takes decades of study. If I had the orange loka already it might be a different story, but until then, I have to learn the hard way."

"But if you could do it, you could change into anything you wanted? Anything at all?"

"Within reason, yeah."

"That's amazing. I will totally trade lokas with you when you get the orange one."

Lali smiled. "Not a chance. If you don't lay claim to Tyjinn by then, I'll use it to become a man and seduce him."

Her tones were light, but he knew she wasn't joking. She obviously had considered this before. The level of emotion she felt for Tyjinn impressed him. He couldn't say he would become a girl for Tyjinn, if that's what his preference had been. "You'd really do that, huh?"

Lali nodded. "Boys lying down together. Could there be anything sexier?"

Dylan found himself daydreaming about that very subject. When his thoughts became too arousing, he began fantasizing about the different shapes he would assume if he were an orange magician. A big cat like Kio was at the top of his list. After that he would want to be a giant bird, if he could fly, of course. When he changed back to himself, he would definitely go for bigger muscles. That would certainly boost his self-confidence. Maybe that's why it was referred to as ego magic. He asked Lali if this was so.

"To an extent, yes," she answered. "Orange magic used to be called the magic of change. Ego magic is a more philosophical title. After all, do you really think you'd be the same person if you had the body of a two hundred-pound woman with one eye and four arms?"

"Probably not," Dylan laughed.

"Aside from that, being able to enter someone else's mind is useful for therapeutic reasons and can be instrumental in stabilizing or altering the personality."

"Roo rndn't wnttob my 'ed," came a voice from the darkness. Kio entered the circle of firelight, two dead pheasants dangling from his jaws.

"What?" Dylan asked.

Kio dropped his catch for the night on the ground. "I said, you wouldn't want to be in my head. Get plucking you two, I'm starving."

Lali reached forward to help but hesitated to reveal her hand.

"There's no sense in hiding it," Dylan said kindly. "It's hard to miss."

"You mean the hand?" Kio asked. "Smells wrong, too."

Lali sighed and held up the offending appendage so she could examine it herself. The wound looked even worse than it had a few hours ago, the patches of bare skin now reduced to tiny spots. Seeing it this close revealed it was much more than a rash. Her entire hand was scabbed over with what appeared to be tree bark. The areas where it peeled back looked like wood shavings.

"I keep hoping it'll go away on its own," Lali said, voice shaking. Her chin trembled before she pulled herself together. "Do you know what this is?"

"It's from when the woodworm stuck you," Kio said. "It smells like they do."

"Right, but do you understand what it really is?"

Kio and Dylan exchanged puzzled glances and shook their heads. "It's serious then?" asked Dylan.

"It could be," Lali said. "The woodworm have a notorious method of self-defense. If they choose, they can inject a splinter into an animal or person. This splinter is alive and looks like a small worm, thus the name. Once the worm is placed, it burrows beneath the skin and rests there, spreading its infection." She held up her hand. "This will continue spreading until—well, it's not pretty."

Dylan's jaw clenched. "There must be something we can do about it!" He hadn't known Lali very long, but he liked her. Not only did they both love Tyjinn, but she had received this injury while defending him. "Screw going to the Cradle. This is more important!"

"I agree," Kio said. "Do we need to find a healer?"

Lali struggled with herself before nodding. "I saw a sign earlier this afternoon."

Dylan had almost forgotten the faded green ribbon tied around a tree they had seen earlier in the day, the universal sign of the green mothers, the healers of the Five Lands. He realized with some irony that the most powerful of these healers was the Empress, who was now dead.

"The bow was facing us directly as we passed," Lali said, "so if we keep going in this direction, we should come to her sooner or later."

"Maybe we should pack up and go now. We could get there before dawn if we travel all night."

"One night won't make a difference," Lali said. "It's not

contagious at this stage, so don't be afraid."

"I wasn't worried about that." Dylan said.

Lali shook her head, dismissing the topic. "Let's get these birds plucked."

Dylan decided not to press the matter, but he swore to himself he would take care of her, feeling it was what Tyjinn would have wanted.

The home of the green mother was in the center of a small village of no more than two dozen houses—a village so unaccustomed to outsiders that when strangers arrived, every resident left their homes and work to stop and stare. And stare. When they tired of staring, they moved onto gawking, gaping, and ogling. When their eyes had their fill, they narrowed them and let their mouths take over, muttering uneasy suspicions to anyone who was near enough to listen.

Dylan felt certain these people's minds were as small as their town. He took some solace in Kio's uniqueness and Lali's beauty drawing all the attention, but not very much. Part of him was tempted to flash his loka so they would see that he too was worthy of their scrutiny. Even the mushushu was pulling a larger audience than he was.

Lali halted them in the midst of the villagers and offered a greeting that wasn't returned. Obviously they weren't going to receive much of a welcome, but one spry old woman saw opportunity and scampered up to the group, ignoring the disapproving expressions and tuts of her neighbors.

She smiled up at them. "Something I can be helping you with?"

"Yes, we'll need food and supplies," Lali said, unperturbed by their surroundings. "Oh, and a brief council with your green mother," she added as if it were an afterthought and not what had brought them here.

The old woman raised her eyebrows and increased her smile, but didn't yet move.

"We have money," Lali said.

That set the old woman in motion. She listened and patiently repeated the list of supplies that Lali dictated, before she gave them directions to the green mother's home. She then promised to meet them there with their items.

The thatched hut of the green mother was compact and squat, rather like the person dwelling there. The woman who opened the door was short and plump, possessing a proud chin and an expert scowl, which she turned on them. She continued staring, comfortable in her silence.

"Hello," Dylan tried. "Are you the green mother?"

Rather than respond, the woman brought out a smoking pipe, which she placed in her mouth. She pulled on it deeply and exhaled the pungent stink toward them, unmoved by their repulsed reaction.

"Sorry, I think we've made a mistake," Lali said.

"No wait!" Dylan pleaded, trying to prevent Lali from walking away.

"Woodworm's got ya," the green mother muttered. "Nasty stuff."

Lali stopped and turned. Her hand had been obscured underneath her crossed arms, a posture that she had adopted to hide it from view.

"Can you help her?" Dylan asked hopefully. "We have money," he added, remembering how effective that phrase had been with the old lady.

"Mm," the woman grunted. "But you don't pay mothers. Would you pay your own mother for helping you? No, you wouldn't. Not with money, anyway."

Of course. The green mothers were like Dylan's father in this regard, preferring favors over monetary rewards. A village always took care of its mother, providing her with food, clothing, and shelter. In return for such favors, the mothers never turned away the sick. Usually, travelers were expected to perform some labor or other deed once they were healed.

"How long is this going to take?" Kio said with a yawn. "I could use a nap if it's going to be more than an hour."

The green mother's eyes swiveled down to the speaker. When she saw that the voice came from a cat, she had a coughing fit and dropped her pipe. She continued coughing and retching for longer than any healthy person should have. Embarrassed, Dylan retrieved her pipe while she recovered. She pointed a stubby finger at Kio while looking wide-eyed at Dylan and Lali, expecting them to be equally surprised.

"He's cursed or something," Dylan lied.

"You expect me to cure him, too?" the woman demanded.

"No!" Dylan answered quickly. "No, just Lali. Do you think you can do it right away? We're sort of in a hurry."

"I can start today," the green mother said, forcing herself to look away from the cat, "but it will be weeks before she's better."

"I thought as much." Lali's face looked ashen, but not surprised. "I guess this is where we part ways," she said, turning to face Dylan. "Temporarily, I hope." She held up her infected hand to ward off his protests. "I have some business to take care of," she said to the green mother, "but I will return in the afternoon. Is that all right?"

The portly woman shrugged and retreated into her home just as the old lady with their supplies found them. She was hauling two canvas sacks, each almost as big as she was. They ran forward to relieve her of her burden and Dylan paid her generously. Then she disappeared down the road in great haste, as if afraid he might change his mind and ask for the extra money back.

"Well," Lali said, peering into one of the sacks, "we can at least have lunch together before you leave."

Traveling had given Dylan a new appreciation for fresh fruit and vegetables. Foods not dried or preserved had taken on an almost divine quality to his taste buds. Soft cheeses were also sorely missed, but he would have to keep on missing them since Lali had ordered a hard cheese that would last for weeks. All in all, it was a satisfying meal. The old woman had even included a bottle of milk for Kio, something they hadn't requested. Dylan was glad that he tipped her almost as much as the supplies had cost.

But now his mind was as troubled as his stomach was contented. The idea of leaving Lali behind seemed somehow irresponsible. He couldn't help feeling Tyjinn would be disappointed in him for abandoning his friend, but saw no other choice. He and Kio could split up, one of them staying with her and the other going ahead to whatever awaited them, but Dylan found the idea unbearable.

"We could travel to a different town together, further down the road," he said. "There's a green mother in almost every village."

Lali shook her head. "Don't tempt me. It was hard enough getting me to admit that I have a problem."

"I just don't like the idea of leaving you here with a bunch of strangers, and it's not like we're in any real hurry. We don't even know why we're going to the Cradle."

"We're going there because Tyjinn wants us to." Lali frowned and looked in the direction that Dylan and Kio would soon be heading. "We're doing it for him, but there are things that you need to know. Things I'm going to tell you now."

Dylan's stomach sank at the sudden seriousness of her tone. "All right. Tell me."

"It's possible that…" Lali hesitated and looked as if she were about to change her mind and not talk at all. She bit her lip before continuing. "It's possible that Tyjinn killed the Empress."

"Well, yeah," Kio said. "Anything's possible but there's no proof that—"

"He's killed before," Lali interrupted.

Dylan's entire body stiffened. He had searched so hard for an acceptable reason Tyjinn might have killed the Empress, and this revelation made that all the more impossible. Was now the time to tell the others what he knew? Did he really plan to keep it a secret, just to protect Tyjinn's reputation? He wasn't sure anymore.

"Who exactly did he kill?" Kio asked.

"Not a good person," Lali answered, "and he was just a boy at the time."

Dylan's mouth fell open. "Tyjinn or the victim?"

"Both. They were the same age, thirteen."

"Well, was it in self-defense or what?" Kio asked.

Lali shook her head before changing her mind and nodding. "Did Ty ever mention his dog, Fenric? No? Well, he was crazy about that dog. He'd had Fenric since he was little and would take him everywhere—even to school when the teacher would allow it. They were really close, just as you two are. Fenric sometimes roamed the nearby woods on his own, which was usually not a problem, since he always found his way back home. One day, Fenric had a run in with two boys, one of which Tyjinn—"

"Killed," Dylan filled in for her as she struggled with the word.

"Tyjinn was always something of a social outcast," Lali said, trying a different approach. "His talent and brains alienated him from most of the other boys, and his looks made enemies of the girls once they realized that he wasn't interested. Even being a son of the Red Oligarch didn't earn him any popularity, since his brothers and sisters could claim the same status and were much more accessible.

"So these two boys were out bow hunting, and they shot Fenric. They said it was a mistake, and that they thought he was a deer. Fenric was a big dog, but he wasn't *that* big." She shook her head. "Still, mistakes do happen, and they made two more that day. The first was leaving Fenric there to bleed to death."

"He was still alive?" asked Dylan.

Lali nodded. "Tyjinn followed Fenric's howls as best he could, but he didn't make it in time. I think if Tyjinn had been with his dog before he died, even if it had only been a minute, things might not have gone so wrong. Tyjinn became obsessed with the idea that Fenric died alone and afraid."

"I'd want to kill them, too," Dylan said quietly. "If someone did something like that to Kio." His jaw clenched, and he shook his head.

"You'd want to kill them, sure," Lali said, "but would you? Would Kio even want that?"

"What was their second mistake?" Kio asked, changing the topic.

"The second mistake was leaving the arrow in Fenric. The two boys had their arrows initialed so they could later prove who had made what kill. Tyjinn figured out pretty quick whose name went with the initials, since he had a troubled history with these two schoolmates. Of course they lied when confronted, until Tyjinn showed them the arrow. That only made them laugh. They didn't even apologize."

Kio leaned forward. "So he just toasted them right then and there?"

"No. In a way it would have been better if he had. Instead he waited almost half a year. He intended to avenge Fenric, but needed to wait until he wasn't an obvious suspect. Bottling up his anger for that long almost drove him mad, but the boys who killed Fenric often made enemies. Over the course of six months, they got in enough fights that Tyjinn finally felt free to act."

Lali stole a swig from Kio's milk bottle before continuing.

"When the parents of one of the boys went on holiday, Tyjinn saw his opportunity. Naturally the two boys were making the most of having an empty house to themselves, sleeping over and getting into more trouble than usual. Tyjinn approached the house in the dead of night, peering through the windows to find them sleeping in the same bed." Lali's eyes darted to Dylan and away again. "He was surprised, but such concepts were hardly alien to him. Besides, it made what he intended to do easier. He broke in and wasted no time in setting the bed on fire, feeling he was killing two birds with one stone, if you'll pardon the expression. That was when he heard the girl's screams."

Dylan swallowed. "It wasn't two boys in bed."

Lali nodded in grim confirmation. "The boy that lived there had his girlfriend over. Tyjinn didn't know about her and was sent into a panic. He tried to extinguish the flame, but he had underestimated his own magic, how strong six months of pent-up emotion would make it. Tyjinn never set out to kill them, you see, only to hurt them. In calm practice he could always extinguish the fire he created, but not then. By the time the screams stopped, half the room was on fire, and Tyjinn could do nothing but run."

"But she lived, right?" Dylan asked. "You didn't say he killed two people."

Lali's face was pallid. "He didn't mean to."

Dylan's stomach lurched. "And the other boy?"

"I wish he had been in that bed instead," Lali sighed. "He'd been lucky, exiled to his own home for the evening so that his friend could have privacy. Tyjinn never went after him, having lost his taste for revenge."

Dylan and Kio considered the tale, while Lali chewed her nails and watched them. Dylan felt disturbed by the tale, but also relieved. Tyjinn had a reason for what he did, and that it had gone so far was only an accident. Whether it was right or wrong was a different matter, but Tyjinn wasn't some mindless killer. He must have had a reason for killing the Empress, although it was still too hard to imagine what that reason could be.

"Did he ever get caught?" Kio asked.

"Obviously not," Lali said. "The townspeople thought it was an accident. A lantern left burning in the night or who knows what. He thinks his mother might have suspected and even helped cover it up, but she never said anything. The deaths left

Tyjinn shaken, and he retreated into himself for many years. He even moved outside of town once he was old enough and spent much of his time traveling. That's how we met. His mother made him Oligarch a year ago, probably hoping the responsibility would force him to rejoin society, but I don't think it did any good."

Lali regarded them with a guilty expression, obviously feeling that she had betrayed her friend by revealing so much. Dylan could understand those feelings. He felt as though he were betraying his friends by not telling them what he already knew, but still felt reluctant to do so without knowing Tyjinn's reasons. If Lali had simply told them Tyjinn had killed two people and not the story behind it, what would he and Kio have thought then? Without the full truth, others would judge Tyjinn harshly.

Unsure of what more to say, Lali began packing up their supplies. Dylan moved to help her as Kio began licking a paw thoughtfully.

"Thanks for telling us," he whispered to her as they worked.

"You can trust him, you know," she said, as if to dispel it all with one sentence.

Dylan shrugged. "I know," he said, even though he didn't really.

I won't hold back, Dylan. The next time you see me, I'll be your enemy.

Lali's tale had unsettled him. He loved Tyjinn, but now he feared he didn't truly know who he was. Was it possible to love someone without knowing them? He would have once argued that it wasn't, but now he was risking his life just to find Tyjinn again. In truth, he didn't care if Lali's tragic story was just one of many. All Dylan wanted was to hear them from Tyjinn's lips and not those of another.

He looked toward Lali, noticing how her brow was creased with worry and wondered if it mirrored his own. She too, had decided to love Tyjinn, despite his history. Suddenly he was glad that she wasn't coming with them. Facing Tyjinn as a possible enemy would be difficult enough without seeing Lali's heart broken in the process.

Chapter 14
Sacrifice

With a heavy heart, Lali watched Dylan and Kio leave, wishing she had found better words to tell the story. She had hoped to instill trust, but feared she had left suspicion instead. Tyjinn had always been a loyal friend—such as the two weeks he spent at her side, after she broke her leg. She should have told them how he had cooked for her, helped her hobble around, and even had cleaned her home. He had done it out of the kindness of his heart, never once complaining or acting as if she were in his debt. Lali wished he was here with her now. She wasn't looking forward to what she had to face.

She returned to the green mother's hut, considering it sullenly for a moment before letting herself in. She wasn't sure what inspired such informality. Perhaps the slipshod appearance of the woman suggested even a simple knock on the door would be too formal. Or maybe she was hoping to cause offense and be sent away; thus having an excuse to rejoin her friends. If her impromptu discourtesy had any effect on the green mother, she never found out, because she was so startled by the interior.

The hut was more spacious than it appeared from the outside and crammed full of furniture, books, and odds and ends. The books implied her would-be hostess was intelligent or had a curious mind. The worn furniture suggested a love for comfort. Along the left-hand wall was either a bed or a sofa, or possibly both, covered in thick blankets sprinkled randomly with pillows, books, and a dinner plate that might have slipped off an adjacent table. Directly ahead, a narrow pathway wove through the little home to a simple wooden ladder, leading up to a loft just big enough for a second bed. Despite the general clutter of the hut, it had a cozy feel and the allure of sleeping in a real bed was very appealing.

"I'd like a good look at your hand when you're ready." The green mother was standing in front of a massive set of shelves, each burdened with old jam jars filled with dried roots, a rainbow of powders, and thick, syrupy liquids. The woman shifted the jars around, shoving them wherever space was available and reaching for a beige powder. "Grumble tea," she said once she had it. "The good stuff," she added with a chuckle.

Lali stepped precariously over the knickknacks on the floor to reach her hostess, who still hadn't turned to face her. "I'm really glad we were able to find you," she said, deciding to make the best of her circumstances. "I'm Lali."

The green mother grunted as if the information was unimportant, but eventually offered her own name.

"Delia."

"Well met." Lali extended her hand in greeting, a habit that she had forgotten to override after her hand had become infected. Delia spun around and took hold of her wrist, tightening her grip when Lali tried to pull away.

"You've left it for too long," the green mother muttered. "But then I suppose you don't know what you're dealing with."

The sound of splintering wood and slime flashed in Lali's memory. She knew all too well what she was dealing with. "Is it bad?" she asked, knowing it was but still holding out for a miracle.

"Could be worse," Delia shrugged, letting the hand drop. "Could have got into your arm."

An unwelcome question arose in Lali's mind, and she let it linger there, unwilling to ask in case it somehow could manifest her fears. Instead she focused on Delia, who shuffled over to a tiny stove next to the door. She poured water from an old chipped vase into an equally battered pot and struggled to get the wood beneath lit.

"Don't suppose you know red magic?" the woman asked.

"No, sorry," Lali said, yearning even more for the comfort of Tyjinn's presence.

"Bound to get a red magician sooner or later," Delia said. "Then I'll have them magic this piece of junk into something serviceable."

Lali was unsure what to say and unwilling to reveal what magic she did have. She would negotiate whatever service she had to perform once she was on the other side of what was to follow.

Delia hummed tonelessly as she waited for the water to boil. She obviously was used to being alone. Lali could appreciate that. She was a loner at heart, but had learned to be outgoing and social in her apprenticeship to Hasam. Since she began her studies, almost six years ago, she had lived in the same quarters as his four other pupils. Much of her training, in particular the aspects involving counseling, required her to interact with the citizens of Dringend.

"Had a brush with a woodworm?" Delia asked as she poured a generous portion of the beige powder into the now-boiling water.

"Yeah, I guess I got a little closer than I should have."

"Nasty creatures." Delia shook her head. "You see, what you've got in you is a worm, and it squiggled down into you and—"

"I know," Lali snapped, clenching her jaw. "Someone on the road noticed my hand and told me," she lied, trying to make her tones more pleasant.

"Well, don't worry yourself about it now," Delia said, unabashed by her behavior. "Just get some of this tea in you first. It makes even the worst news sound a treat."

Grumble tea, as the woman had called it, looked more like mud as it was shaken and dumped into a mug. "Normally I have honey." She shrugged in what might have been an apology.

"I'm sure it can't be that bad," Lali said as she accepted it.

The concoction was, in fact, worse. The brew sludged into her mouth and coated her tongue with a taste both sour and rotten. She gagged involuntarily as the first drops reached the back of her throat. Steeling her resolve, she chugged down the rest of the drink. It slid down her throat much slower than she would have liked, and as it proceeded further into her system, nausea slowly took hold of her stomach.

"It'll be much worse for you if you don't keep it down," Delia advised.

The solemn look on her face was enough to make Lali heed her advice, not that she had much choice. She grasped desperately for happy thoughts, hoping that her mind would be so distracted that her stomach would forget to throw up. She thought first of Tyjinn, but forced him away. She was tired of being obsessed with him.

Next, her mushushu came to mind. She had insisted Dylan and Kio take Mushi with them, and now her heart ached for the familiar. They needed him if they were going to reach Tyjinn in time, but this wasn't the only reason for her to send her pet away. She knew she wouldn't be able to properly care for Mushi with what she was about to go through. Still, it could be worse. It could have been like Eddin's family.

She shuddered at the memory. Eddin's disappearance was one of the first assignments Hasam had given to her. Eddin was a strange man, but also one of the few hunters in Dringend who was able to lure and kill draggers. The meat from their claws was a valuable delicacy, but nowhere near as precious as the medicine that could be extracted from their brains. Despite Eddin's success, he remained aloof, keeping his wife and three children away from the city. He entered Dringend only to trade and collect his profit, always immediately returning to his home outside of town.

When Eddin hadn't been seen in town for over a month, Lali was sent to visit him. The dragger brain he regularly provided was crucial in treating three of the most common desert ailments, so his continued efforts were crucial. Her mission was more suited to an ambassador, but Lali was sent in the hopes that her orange magic might give her an advantage in dealing with the unpredictable man.

Upon her arrival at the family's home, she was immediately aware that something was wrong. The family lived in a self-built shelter, a series of huts connected to form one building. Eddin referred to this as his ranch. The ramshackle estate was curious, considering how much money Eddin earned from his trade. Were he not antisocial, he could have hired artisans to construct something nicer, but he trusted no one outside of his family.

The absence of Eddin's usual paranoia was her first clue that something was amiss. She had been warned he would have vicious dogs tied up outside. Not only were there no dogs, but the front door was wide open. A dusty silence in the air made her feel the home had been abandoned. All she could imagine was that Eddin had decided to leave Dringend with his family and not return.

Lali called out as she entered but didn't receive a response. Enough sand filled the entryway for her to calculate that the door had been open for about a week. She explored the main room and the kitchen area, but found no signs of life among the squalor. A glance in another room revealed nothing but hunting equipment and the dried husks of giant beetle-crabs. As she investigated, she felt more uneasy. Nothing was missing from any of the rooms. If Eddin and his family had left town, they had done so without their possessions.

She approached the only bedroom. What she found there confused her. Gathered around the bed were rough-hewn wooden sculptures obviously intended to represent people. The nearest sculpture looked like a child on its knees, arms outstretched pleadingly. Another small figure lay curled up on the floor. The largest sculpture portrayed a woman cradling a child. The sculptures all had a desperate quality to them, especially the child with its arms extended. Lali's skin crawled as she examined each one in turn. The material was unusual and bark-like, flaking at her touch. She struggled to understand how wood could be sculpted like this without first removing the bark.

Her attention was drawn to the unusually wide bed where

even more wood was on the pillows and underneath the sheets. Pulling back the blankets she saw a mess of scraps and shavings. In the center of the bed was a trunk-like piece of wood, hollowed out and caved in.

A mix of terror and agony tickled her mind, but it wasn't her own. Her orange magic was picking up on someone else's emotions. She immediately focused on it, willing a connection between her center and the other's. She spun around once she realized how close the other person was. In a moment of dizzying confusion, she approached the sculpture of the mother and child. The life signs were coming from the mother.

She reached out disbelievingly just as the life signs faded, followed by a noise like an egg cracking open. The head of the mother sculpture caved slightly and broke open as brown maggot-like worms spilled out of the hole. The pieces came together in her mind then, stories she had heard when she was a child, but later dismissed as too outlandish and terrible to be true. Lali pulled her hand away before any of the slimy worms could touch her and ran from the room. She escaped through the back door and was brought to an immediate halt. Standing in front of her was a woodworm, just like she imagined them when she was young. It stood impassively, its beady sap eyes focused on her.

The makeshift cage imprisoning it did little to avail her fears. Its prison was a combination of wood and twisted wire. The creature inside was too weak to escape. One of its arms had been broken off. Lali felt a strange mixture of sympathy and revulsion. She backed away, her eyes on the woodworm until she reached the corner of the house. Once she was around it, she turned and dashed to Mushi so she could ride to safety. The memory of that day had haunted her dreams ever since.

A squadron of Hasam's crimson knights were sent to the ranch to burn it to the ground, along with everything in and around it. But first an investigator sent with them had examined the grounds. He concluded that Eddin had captured the woodworm while hunting and come into contact with it. The infection had spread throughout his body until he died in his bed. His over-sheltered and naïve family left him there, unsure what to do until his body spawned the creatures that would infect them.

"That's how they reproduce, you know." Delia's voice

sounded muffled as if she were speaking from beneath a pile of blankets. Lali's head swam as she turned to face her. The green mother was pointing at her hand. "The little splinter worm in you will produce others, a few of which will live long enough to grow into full-sized woodworms. If they get enough of ya to eat, that is."

Lali found she didn't really care either way. She had to stifle a laugh as Delia brought her chubby face close to her own and nodded with satisfaction. "Looks like my tea has kicked in." She struggled to help Lali to her feet, but Lali couldn't feel any of her limbs.

"C'mon outside with me now," Delia said as she half-helped, half-dragged her to the door. "We'll see to your hand then before it spreads even further."

Even through the haze of drugs in her mind, Lali felt momentarily sobered by her worst fears. She panicked and struggled against Delia's grip, but the woman easily overpowered her. The drugs seemed to rise in response to her exertion, pulling her back down into an ocean of numbness. She was vaguely aware of the bright daylight stinging her eyes and the distorted faces of the curious townsfolk. She was grateful when she was allowed to sit down in front of a tree stump and relax, her infected hand placed thoughtfully on its flat surface and held secure by the green mother's strong hand. A glint of metal caused her to look skyward, but it was already gone. The curious sound of meat splitting caused Lali some puzzlement; then she began screaming.

Tyjinn never would have guessed that this was the Cradle's location. He and the man who had taken him hostage—or perhaps accomplice was a fairer description now—were standing in a grassy field indistinguishable from any of the adjacent fields. No special landmark marked the spot, no white-barked tree or rock formation that looked like something else when viewed from the right angle. Nothing but coarse green grass and dirt.

And yet something was there, something woven into the fabric of reality; a subtle difference in the way the light cast shadows and a barely perceptible change in the way the air tasted. Tyjinn reached down and put his hand on the ground, expecting to feel power thrumming beneath it. He felt nothing, aside from a slightly cooler temperature than he expected.

"Rather disappointing, isn't it?" his companion said. "For such an important place, that is."

Tyjinn shrugged. "You certainly took your time bringing us here. It can't be all that important."

"Don't play dumb, my friend. You know as well as I the significance of this place, although I doubt you understand how to utilize it."

That was true enough. Tyjinn had a vague recollection of the Cradle's legends, but couldn't understand what purpose coming here would serve. Considering how much power his "friend" had already secured by obtaining three lokas, chasing old legends seemed like an amusingly trivial pit stop. Perhaps not though, considering the way the tips of his fingers were beginning to tingle.

"You know, I think I'd rather like to give your loka a try," the man said in idle tones.

"Sorry?"

"No need to be. Just hand it over, please."

Tyjinn stared at the palm extended toward him, his heart thudding. Until now he believed he had been kept alive as a mercenary, to be used in future battles with other Oligarchs, but now his captor had changed his mind. "You brought me out here to kill me."

"This is where I am supposed to laugh maniacally and confirm your worst fears, is it?" The man sighed, and let his hand drop. "I assure you, I am much too pragmatic to go about things in such a way. Had I intended to kill you, I would have done so as you slept."

Tyjinn stared at him.

"I haven't given the signal to those holding Mama that she should be fed today. It was terribly forgetful of me." The man raised an eyebrow, his mouth set in a cold, flat line. "Good enough for you?"

Anger boiled within Tyjinn. For a moment he considered killing the bastard, consequences be damned, but knew he couldn't. He had already killed to protect his mother, and giving into temptation would mean that the Empress had died in vain. Tyjinn removed his necklace and gave his loka one final glance before handing it over.

"Thank you for cooperating," his captor said as he considered the gleaming red jewel. "We don't want another incident like what happened in the desert with the draggers, do we?"

Tyjinn didn't respond. The night in question, the Oligarch killer had insisted they begin backtracking, offering no explanation as to why. Eventually they crested a dune to find a campsite below them. Tyjinn's stomach had sunk when he recognized Dylan's form by the fire. How had the killer known they would be in pursuit? Even worse, why were they alone? He had expected them to rally help, not come chasing alone.

His captor had wasted no time in attacking. Watching the scene play out below had been excruciating. Tyjinn had held the red loka in one hand, Mama's necklace in the other, grasping them both so tightly that they cut into his skin. When one of the draggers began pulling Dylan beneath the sand, Tyjinn acted on instinct, sending a heat wave so powerful that it overrode even the purple loka's magic.

His companion had been furious. The only way to pacify him was to explain that Dylan had the blue loka, and that if he was dragged beneath the sand, his loka would be lost too. The man considered this for a moment before laughing and motioning for them to retreat. It had unnerved Tyjinn that he had found it amusing.

"I'm afraid we have some leisure time before our guests arrive, but we can while away the hours by you teaching me your wonderful style of magic. Red loka, awaken for me."

Tyjinn barely felt the power leave him. "Guests?" he asked.

"Your friends, of course. You instructed them to come to this very spot."

Tyjinn's blood ran cold.

"Did you really think that I of all people wouldn't detect such magic? That the message you sent their way would go unnoticed?" The man regarded his new loka with satisfaction. "Don't worry. I couldn't be more pleased. You've saved us an extra trip. Dylan will deliver the fifth loka directly to me."

Tyjinn couldn't speak. His mind raced with the implications of this revelation while he tried to ignore the guilt crawling up from his stomach. He had summoned his friends to their doom.

Chapter 15
Of Gods and Men

"We should have just stayed with her," Dylan said. The sun had set, and Mushi's pace had slowed to an amble. "We made it, what? Three whole hours away?"

"I don't think I could have slept in that town," Kio said from below. He had dismounted from the mushushu half an hour earlier, when it had slowed enough for him to keep pace. "Not with all those creepy people. I bet at night they gather around in a circle and stare at each other until they collapse from exhaustion."

"Probably."

The woods around them were dense, the shadows thick as tar. They had abandoned the road when it veered off in the wrong direction. They hoped to find a clearing where they could set up camp, but they weren't having any luck. By the time they stopped, the woods were so dark that they could barely see their surroundings, until they had a fire kindled.

"You want me to hunt tonight to save our food?" Kio asked once they were settled.

"No," Dylan said quickly. He didn't want to be left alone, even though he would have Mushi to keep him company.

The evening was chilly, and they crowded close to the fire for warmth as they ate. The meal passed in almost total silence. Dylan was increasingly uncomfortable with this and grasped for something to speak about, but every topic that came to mind was one he didn't want to discuss. How could he talk about his fears and hopes when they all revolved around Tyjinn? The meal finished without a word exchanged.

"This is going to be a boring trip," Kio said as he licked his mouth clean. "Is the secrecy really worth it?"

Dylan was so taken aback that he didn't know how to respond.

Kio ceased grooming and stared at him. "I'm your best friend! Why are you hiding yourself from me?"

Dylan tried to laugh carelessly as if he had nothing to hide, but the laugh caught in his throat. "You overheard me talking to Lali."

"I didn't overhear anything," Kio growled, "but now you've just confessed that you confided in Lali instead of me and that infuriates me twice as much!" The cat's tail lashed furiously. "Do you really think I don't know you well enough to tell when you've fallen in love? It couldn't be more obvious, but I thought it best to let you tell me in your own time. Well, I'm fed up with waiting!"

"I knew you'd be mad." Dylan's voice cracked. "I don't want to lose you, Kio."

"Then stop acting like a jackass." The cat's voice softened, even though his tail still flicked back and forth. "I don't care if you fall in love with a rock as long as you tell me about it."

"You don't care that I love Tyjinn?"

Kio's tail stopped moving. "Wait a minute," he said carefully. "I thought you were in love with Lali."

Dylan's heart almost stopped. He opened his mouth to explain, but nothing came out.

Kio howled with laughter. "Gods, you are such a sucker! I totally had you."

Once Dylan found his voice again, he called Kio a number of names.

"I think Tyjinn is great," Kio said once he had finished laughing. "He slings some mighty impressive magic, and for a human, he isn't so ugly. The whole suspected murderer thing isn't exactly ideal, but I'm sure it's not true."

Dylan's relief at Kio's acceptance quickly faded as he realized that he had kept more than just his sexuality hidden from his friend. He was about to confide in Kio when something in the distance caught his eye. A glow was moving through the woods, an orange light growing in size as it neared. He pointed wordlessly toward it.

"The fire," Kio hissed.

Dylan extinguished the flames with handfuls of soil. By the time the fire had gone out, they could see the spectral light was not only closer, but was one of several. The lights were moving steadily nearer, traveling single file like a parade of ghosts.

Somewhat guiltily, Dylan and Kio crawled over to Mushi to hide behind his bulk. By the time they looked over his shoulder, the glowing lights were no more than six yards away. They were huge four-legged animals, their burly bodies packed tight with muscle. The bright light radiating from their fur made looking directly at them difficult, but they could make out features similar to bears.

"Solar bears," Dylan breathed in wonder. His father had once told them of seeing solar bears when he was a small child. Jack had been so awed that he never forgot the details, which was apparent when he recounted his description. As accurate as his story had been, it failed to fully capture the ethereal wonder of the beasts.

The procession of bears halted, lifting their noses and sniffing. Dylan wasn't sure what a solar bear's diet included, but he couldn't rule out mushushu steaks, cat tartare, or human kebabs. Maybe the dissipating smoke from the fire covered their scent, or maybe they simply weren't on the menu. Either way, the solar bears resumed their plodding march.

"Must be heading back north," Kio whispered.

That made sense. The bears left the frigid climate of the icy northern mountains in the summer, migrating to the southern deserts where they spent months soaking up and storing sunlight within their unique fur. Once they collected enough heat, they returned to their natural environment where they would be kept warm throughout the winter.

Dylan and Kio silently watched the bears as they passed, enraptured by their beauty. The wisps of warm light they radiated were reminiscent of Lumin, the fifth season between winter and spring when all magic was visible to the naked eye. Even after the light from the bears had retreated into the distance, their spirits felt buoyed by the experience.

Part of Dylan was tempted not to tell Kio the rest of what he had been hiding about Tyjinn, but he felt determined to make amends for not confiding in him. Steeling his willpower, he set about restoring the campfire. Once he was done, he told his best friend everything he knew.

"The mushushu ran away," Kio reported.

Dylan looked up from the map to assess his friend's level of seriousness. "I tied him up!" Dylan exclaimed. "Really well, too. After Sapphire, I've been obsessively careful with that."

Kio thumped his tail in a way that Dylan had learned to interpret as a shrug. "The ropes are gone, too."

Dylan swore. "I guess we should try finding him."

"I wouldn't bother," Kio said. "He's faster than either of us. Besides, his smell was headed back the way we came. Probably trying to get back to Lali."

"I hope so."

"Can't really blame him for wanting to leave."

Dylan nodded in agreement. Things were starting to feel weird. The air was becoming thick and heavy, like the promise of a thunderstorm. Their skin was prickling, and every hair was standing on end—which in Kio's case was overwhelming. Even their voices sounded a few octaves too deep.

"How much longer?" Kio asked.

Dylan consulted the map again. "An hour maybe. Or we could already be there. I don't know. We're too close to say." Looking around he only saw an unending field of grass dotted with the occasional scrawny tree. Was this the Cradle?

"So where do we go from here?"

"Good question." Dylan squinted while turning in a circle, searching for anything significant on the horizon. As he was turning, he felt the strange buzzing in the air intensify momentarily on his face. He stopped and slowly turned to face that direction again and took a few steps forward. The tingling sensation increased slightly.

"This way," he said, rubbing his nose to stop the tickling.

"Dylan, wait," Kio said pleadingly. "Are you sure you want to go through with this, knowing everything we do?"

Kio too felt that Tyjinn wouldn't expect them to chase after the killer alone. Instead, they were meant to rally reinforcements, Tyjinn's threat designed to keep Dylan from joining said party. Unlike Dylan, Kio wasn't head-over-heels in love with Tyjinn, and lacked the blind determination to reunite with him. All Kio saw ahead of them was danger, and he had tried his best to make Dylan recognize it.

Kio wasn't completely critical. He too sought rationale for Tyjinn's murder of the Empress. He wove a tale in which the Empress was the mastermind behind the Oligarch murders. In a brave confrontation, Tyjinn had battled her in the gardens, only losing through some foul play on her part before becoming her unwilling hostage.

The story was pure escapism, and despite their greatest wishes, they knew it wasn't true. If only Tyjinn had used his message to explain his reasons, or at least given clear instructions on what they were to do. Instead it had been an apology, an emotional goodbye—and ultimately a threat, one Dylan felt certain was empty.

"We've got to go on," Dylan said, answering his friend's question at last. "There's probably nobody there, anyway. It's not like they've been sitting around waiting for us to show up."

The cat didn't reply, but did follow when Dylan started walking again. Another half hour and they were considering turning back for a different reason. The strange environmental effects were now uncomfortable. There was a delay of a few seconds between speaking and hearing the words. Distances were also askew. At times they seemed to be moving forward at a snail's pace before suddenly snapping forward and ending up much farther along than they should have been. Perhaps that was why they were suddenly standing near Tyjinn and his companion before they had any warning.

Dylan recognized them both immediately and was so

confused by what he saw that he stood dumbfounded for what felt like an eternity. His vision blurred momentarily, either from the shock or because of the strange effect of the Cradle.

"Welcome, my friends," Krale said cordially. His mouth moved out of synch from the words, his voice so deep it sounded like a croak.

"You're—" Dylan stopped, the equally distorted sound of his own voice surprising him into silence. He didn't understand what was happening. He felt as if he had been drugged. He looked down at Kio, who also appeared disoriented.

Krale took a step toward him, his face serene. "I know you must be rather surprised to see me, but I assure you, I mean no harm."

"You're dead," Dylan answered. For one insane moment, he wondered if they all were.

"Hardly. What you saw was merely an illusion."

The image of a stone beak crushing a skull like a grape replayed in his mind. Dylan knew it had been no illusion. The wind picked up, bristling Kio's fur and making Krale clutch his robes. All four present stumbled in the gale, nearly losing their footing.

An almost-comical look of realization spread across Tyjinn's features. His mouth opened, shaping words that didn't reach their ears until he had finished speaking. "There are too many lokas here," he warned. "You have to get out of here, Dylan. Run! Both of you, run!"

A chill ran up Dylan's spine. He turned to run, his head swooning with the effort.

"Purple loka, awaken for me," Krale's voice rumbled from behind him.

Dylan kept running, wondering what the madman was planning to do with his magic. Purple magic was only good for controlling and communicating with animals, which couldn't do him any harm. His mouth went dry, a purple light flashing as he turned to check on Kio. The cat was facing him, his body in a running position, but he was no longer moving.

"The only way you are leaving here is without your cat."

"Let him go!" Dylan shouted. Anger flooded his mind. He stormed back toward the former Yellow Oligarch, breaking into a charge as he neared, his fists balled in fury. He was knocked down from behind before he could reach Krale. At first he thought it must have been Tyjinn, but then he felt the familiar prickling of Kio's claws on his back.

"This is turning ugly so quickly," Krale tutted. "You are among friends here, son of the Blue Oligarch, but I can easily make those friends into enemies."

Kio's claws dug further into his back, drawing blood.

"You've made your point," Tyjinn snarled.

"That I have," Krale conceded.

The weight on Dylan's back disappeared as Kio stepped off.

"No more outbursts, young man. I can stop the beating of his heart if need be."

Dylan fixed Krale with a hate-filled gaze as he stood up, but the monster was completely unaffected. Dylan looked instead to Tyjinn. His anger melted away, replaced by desperation. "Please," he whispered, begging for his help. Tyjinn lowered his eyes but didn't look away, not completely.

Maybe there was still hope. The techniques they had practiced together! His mind raced to remember the code words. "Cloud bomb!" he shouted, indicating they should work together to create the steam that would obscure everything from view.

Tyjinn didn't grab his loka like Dylan did. He just shook his head sadly. "I don't have it anymore."

"Aren't you a curious pair?" Krale said with amusement.

Dylan turned on him, holding the blue loka threateningly but unsure what he should do with it.

"Oh dear. I was looking forward to the part where I rant about all my plans," Krale sighed, "but all this drama is making me weary. Simply give me the blue loka, and all of you can go free." He turned to Tyjinn. "*Even* your mother."

Dylan's head spun. What did Mama have to do with any of this? "I don't trust you."

Krale wearily pinched the bridge of his nose. "You don't have a choice." His hand glowed purple before Kio leapt on Tyjinn, knocking him down and clawing his face. Crimson beads of blood showered into the air. To Tyjinn's credit, he lifted his arms only to shield his face. He didn't strike back.

In his panic, Dylan practically threw the blue loka at Krale. As soon as he did so, Kio ceased his attack. Tyjinn rolled onto his side, his now-bloodied arms still protecting his head. Dylan ran to him, tears threatening to blind him. He wanted to comfort Tyjinn, but didn't want to hurt him further by touching him. He reached out to Kio instead, who was completely unresponsive.

"The gods must love the number five," Krale said, although reality was now so distorted his words were nearly impossible to understand. Dylan turned to look at him and saw four lokas in one hand, his blue loka in the other. "Five seasons, five planets, five wells, and to unlock the door to their domain, five lokas."

He added the blue loka to the others and suddenly the world went still. The distortion ceased completely, leaving them momentarily in a boring, empty field. Then the sky above them spun, the ground below them disappeared, and they all spiraled into eternity.

Wind buffeted Dylan as he fell, the extreme air pressure causing him to draw his arms near and curl his legs. He couldn't open his eyes long enough to see clearly. His fall lasted long enough that he had time to call out more than once, but the roaring wind in his ears whipped away any response. He plunged into shockingly cold waters, glad his fall had finally ended somewhere survivable. This feeling was soon replaced by memories of falling from the Yellow Oligarch's windmill and almost drowning.

Holding his breath, Dylan waited for his lungs to start aching as he began kicking in a direction he hoped was upward, but the burning sensation in his lungs never came. More than a minute had passed, but Dylan felt fine. Acting recklessly, he opened his mouth. Water rushed inside and down his throat, but to his amazement, the sensation felt as natural as inhaling air. He exhaled the water just as easily and laughed. He was breathing water!

The surface continued to elude him. With breathing no longer an issue, Dylan decided to stop moving and let his body's natural buoyancy take over. He began to rise, butt first, revealing that he had actually been swimming horizontally instead of vertically, but he hadn't been far from the surface. He broke through a handful of seconds later, righted himself, and wiped the water from his eyes. The water in his lungs poured out with a sensation that was uncomfortably similar to throwing up. Dylan paddled in place and took in his surroundings.

He was back home. He didn't understand how that could be possible, but he was back at his and Kio's favorite lagoon. Dylan looked to the shore, expecting to find Kio sitting there with a bemused expression on his face.

"Kio!" he shouted and stilled himself as much as possible in order to better hear any response. Possibly the cat was still underwater, as Dylan had been. He wondered if the cat could breathe water, too. The absurd thought normally would have made him laugh if he hadn't been so concerned.

"Don't worry, Kio is safe," a voice said from behind.

Dylan spun around and saw an old man looking down at him. A simple gray robe hung off his thin frame. His long beard was gray too, but a mixture of so many shades that it resembled storm clouds. Two perfectly green eyes twinkled at him, but behind their friendliness was an intensity that made clear that this man was not to be taken lightly.

"My toes are getting wet," the man said.

The toes in question were bare and almost at eye level with Dylan. They waggled in greeting.

"You're walking on water," Dylan said.

"Easier than treading it," the man replied, bending over and offering a hand.

Dylan took it without hesitation. With a strength belying his appearance, the stranger hauled him completely out of the water until his feet were dangling above it. Then Dylan was gently lowered, and this time his feet landed on the water as if it were solid.

"This is amazing!"

"Sort of ruins the fun of having a boat though," the man mused as he strolled toward the shore. "What would the world be without them gliding gracefully across the water's surface? I'd miss that. Then again, it might be charming to see deer, squirrels, and all manner of wild animals scurrying over the ocean."

"Yes?" Dylan offered.

"Yes. I imagine the bears would look especially amusing."

Dylan stopped in his tracks. Sensing this, the man halted and looked over his shoulder with a smile.

"You're him, aren't you?" Dylan asked in reverent tones.

"Refresh my memory," the stranger said.

"You're Orbsen. Orbsen, son of the wave!"

The god simply nodded and gestured for Dylan to continue following him. Dylan did so, but with difficulty. His mind was so full of thoughts and questions that he wanted to sit down for a few moments to sort everything out. He did the best he could while continuing to walk.

Orbsen was the god of his people. That is, the people of the Lakelands. He was the god of rivers, oceans, lakes—anything watery. Even rain. He was an easy god to follow since no religion surrounded him. No rules or commandments, no hymns or dusty old books, just a god. There were only myths, most humorous if not lewd. These stories told and retold—usually by people in a drunken state—had kept the name of Orbsen alive.

And here he was in the flesh, walking on water just a few feet ahead and gesturing for Dylan to do the same. This meant an end to his every problem. A god, *his* god, had stepped in and rescued him from the disaster that Krale had conjured. And now he was home.

"You aren't home," Orbsen said. Having reached the shore, he turned and waited for Dylan. "Forgive the intrusion, but your thoughts are quite loud. This isn't really your lagoon, but I thought this environment would be most comfortable for you."

Dylan nodded. So much for blissful self-denial. He forced himself to face the truth. "So we're in your world then?"

"Yes. Krale was successful in opening the gateway, the first to do so in almost three hundred years."

"But where is he? For that matter, where are Kio and Tyjinn?"

"I can show you." The old god turned and walked into the surrounding trees with Dylan rushing to keep up. They stepped over fern-covered ground and reached a large willow tree that Dylan recognized from the real lagoon. He and Kio liked to walk beneath its thick canopy of drooping branches that curtained off the rest of the world. Beyond was farmland that they would cut across to quickly reach their home. Orbsen held a handful of branches aside, creating an opening to fit through.

On the other side was not the drab field of beans that Dylan expected. Instead, a vast ocean stretched to the horizon. Its azure waters rocked gently, building into waves that pounded the little beach.

"You can see Kio if you look that way," Orbsen said, pointing across the water.

Dylan looked, at first seeing only the endless ocean. His vision was pulled forward, away from his physical body, and then he saw Kio. The cat looked no worse for wear and was staring upward with rapt attention.

"Is he all right? What's he looking at?"

"He's fine," Orbsen answered, "and he's looking at his god."

"But—" Dylan turned to face Orbsen and stopped. The old man had been replaced with a man in his prime. He wore a blue tunic and dark pants, light chain mail resting against his well-muscled chest. A simple cap of chainmail hid part of his short-cropped black hair. His handsome, tanned face was clean-shaven, and his eyes were now blue. "Orbsen?"

"A different guise for a different aspect of water," the god explained, nodding toward the ocean. "You were saying?"

Orbsen was so distractingly attractive that Dylan needed a moment to remember his question. "Kio. He doesn't have a religion. How can he have a god?"

"There's not much room in a feline's philosophy for religion. It must be a thankless job, being the god of cats."

"Can we go to him? Or bring him here?" Dylan begged, desperate to be reunited.

Orbsen shook his head. "You're stuck with me, son. Sorry."

"What about Tyjinn?"

The god pointed again, and this time Dylan saw a much different scene. Tyjinn was on his knees, facing a goddess. Her skin was as pale as milk, her hair made of slowly waving flames. She too was kneeling and smiling at Tyjinn as if he were an old friend. The goddess noticed Dylan and nodded in his direction, causing Tyjinn to look over his shoulder and catch Dylan's eye.

Then Tyjinn was at his side, intimately close, but before he could speak the scene changed around them both. They were dressed in formal clothing and preparing for an important moment, Tyjinn grinning proudly. Again the world shifted. Now they were lying nude together, caressing, exploring each other's bodies. Sitting in a grove together, reading silently. They were old, they were young, they were happy, crying, arguing, laughing and playing like children. They were together. A hundred possibilities continued to express themselves, each of them a situation that Dylan yearned to experience.

Then Tyjinn looked away, and it was over. Dylan was

standing next to Orbsen again, the horizon revealing only an empty blue sky.

"What was that?" he gasped.

"Hope." Orbsen put his arm around Dylan's shoulders and began leading him down the beach.

Dylan sighed. "Are we dead?"

"No!" Orbsen laughed. "The afterlife is much more interesting than this stale old world that we gods built for ourselves. Let me explain. Krale's crackpot scheme to open the Cradle worked, but it's not just a simple door that opens up for one or two people to step through. Every living thing from half a mile around was brought here. Somewhere here a grasshopper is meeting its maker. Gods only know what sort of questions it will have."

"You mean we get to ask questions?"

"Haven't you been already?" Orbsen replied, but he seemed distracted. He shaded his eyes with one hand, watching the horizon where a storm was brewing. The coming storm looked particularly nasty, the clouds so pregnant with rain that they were black. "Now that takes some gall," the god muttered. "In my own element, even. And look there, in the water."

Below the storm, the waters were darker than the sun-drenched areas but something else appeared beneath the surface. Something so large that its silhouette darkened the water completely.

Dylan's skin crawled despite the distance. "What's down there?"

"Shadow," the god said. "The same as what lurks in the clouds. Pure shadow. I believe the dark god Krale prays to is hoping to cut our visit short. Onto the boat."

Where nothing had been before a long, narrow pontoon boat rested half in the water, half on the shore. Leaving the safety of the beach and entering the darkening waters seemed like a bad idea, but second-guessing his own god had to be a worse one. Dylan clambered onto the boat. Orbsen leapt onto it gracefully, and immediately it launched itself into the ocean.

Except they were no longer in a boat or on the ocean. Dylan found himself sprawled on a humble raft made of weathered logs bound together by frayed rope. He looked up at Orbsen to find a figure completely covered in rags. Each long rag was a variety of faded colors, the long strips wrapped loosely around him but somehow staying together as one piece of clothing. The only break in the garb was at the eyes, one brown, and the other hazel. Orbsen's strange new guise held a long wooden reed that he used to pole them along in the water.

The river they traveled was surrounded by forests, the water clear enough to see fish swimming through the lazy current. Dylan was relieved to see no sign of the approaching storm or shadows beneath the water.

"Where were we?" Orbsen said. "Oh, yes, questions, that was it. The point of coming here is to ask questions. We gods can't interfere in your physical world. Universal laws and all that. We can't grant wishes or perform great feats of magic for you, not without first utilizing a number of loopholes that greatly limit the result. I'm afraid the only thing we are good for is information."

Dylan was disappointed. He felt safe in Orbsen's presence, despite the chasing darkness, and had assumed the god would set everything right by ending Krale's plans. This thought gave him an idea. Perhaps information could be useful after all.

"So you could tell me how to defeat Krale?"

"Exactly." Orbsen removed the pole from the water and set it on the deck, allowing the current to take over. "But I won't."

Dylan was incredulous. "Why not?"

"Because it wouldn't work. A series of events could happen that would stop Krale, but if I explained them to you and you intentionally tried to reenact them, it wouldn't be the same and thus wouldn't work. Understand?"

"No."

"Well, say for example I tell you that there's a magical sword that you could use kill Krale. You then go directly there to retrieve it and end up dying fighting him anyway. But if I hadn't told you about it, you would have bumbled along before finding it, meeting a friendly giant who is crucial in helping you succeed against Krale."

Dylan looked skeptical. "But couldn't you just tell me to be sure to meet this giant first?"

"That was a very simplified example," Orbsen said with a sigh. "I don't suppose you could just take my word for it?"

Dylan shrugged. He didn't have a choice.

"Ask me about another one of your problems instead."

Dylan let his mind wander. There must be some helpful questions he was allowed to ask.

"We saw Krale die," he said. "Kio and I both witnessed it. Was that just an illusion?"

"No, I'm afraid not." Orbsen shook his head. "But it wasn't Krale you saw die. It was his son."

The blood drained from Dylan's face. "Rano?" He realized that he had never actually seen the dead man from the front, not clearly. The head had been blood-soaked, but the owner had worn ceremonial robes and wielded the yellow loka.

"You saw what Krale wanted you to see," Orbsen continued. "Rano had come home that night while you were sleeping. Krale had already planned to fake his own death at the cost of his son's life, and rather than delay that plan because of your presence, he saw it as an opportunity. He presented Rano with the robe and loka. The poor boy thought he was inheriting his father's legacy. Krale already had the purple loka by then and used it to control the wyvern he had waiting."

Dylan took a while to digest the news. Rano had been his friend and now he was gone. Even though they had fallen out in recent years, it still hurt terribly. "Why?" Dylan whispered. "Why do that to his own son?"

"To have the freedom of movement that anonymity provides, perhaps. He also needed an excuse for the telepathic communication between Oligarchs to cease. Otherwise word of their systematic deaths would have spread immediately. Some still have no idea that so many of their colleagues have fallen. He also had a personal grudge against the boy. He never believed that Rano was really his child. His wife had been indiscriminate during their marriage, so he assumed the boy was a bastard. The sad truth is that he killed his own flesh and blood."

They floated down the river in silence, Dylan lost in his thoughts. Blood or no blood, killing another person to gain more power was unthinkable to him. He never would have thought the Yellow Oligarch capable when he first met him. Krale had appeared to be so sound of mind. He recalled Krale's explanation of how both he and Dylan's father had two equally valid views on how the world should be run, and how it was sometimes frustrating to compromise. Apparently Krale had decided to compromise no longer.

Poor Rano. He had never done anything to warrant such a violent ending. No one deserved to be murdered. Dylan thought of Tyjinn. Had he been wrong to kill in retaliation for his dog's death? It didn't seem like a fair solution, but every time he replaced Tyjinn's dog in the story with Kio, his own anger rose dangerously. Wouldn't he have done the same? But the Empress, what had she done to deserve death? He realized that he was in a rare position to find out.

"Why did Tyjinn kill the Empress?" Dylan asked.

"Now *that* is a good question, with an answer that is the solution to more than one of your problems." Orbsen explained to him how Tyjinn was acting under Krale's orders to prevent his mother from being killed. What relief Dylan would have normally felt was buried by the concern he felt for Mama.

"Where is she being held?" he asked. "How can we save her?"

"Mama isn't being held anywhere," Orbsen said. "It was another of Krale's deceptions. The necklace belonging to Mama was stolen by a magpie under his control. Tyjinn was falsely manipulated into doing what he did."

Dylan was beginning to despair. So far, the only thing he had learned was that too many unjustified murders had been committed. That, and the one person who probably deserved to be dead was, in fact, alive. "How is any of this a solution to my problems?"

"Krale wasn't the only one to fake their own death. Oh, for crying out loud!" This last comment was directed at the shore where Orbsen threw the raft's pole.

A sinister darkness was in the trees, creeping within their shadows, stalking the little raft as it made its way down shore. It left the shelter of the trees, slinking out to the river's edge and allowing them to see it clearly for the first time.

More than just darkness or shadow, it was the total absence of light—opaque blackness, solid but without any true form. Stopping once it reached the water's edge, two tendrils of darkness began extending towards them.

"You know as well as I do that you can't best me in my own realm, Thaedon." Orbsen put two fingers in his mouth and whistled sharply.

Two enormous forms burst from the river and landed on the shore on either side of their aggressor. Wild pigs, but not just any ordinary wild pigs. They were each the size of a small house. Dylan remembered that the pig was sacred to Orbsen. Boar was always served on the first day of summer when the Lakelands held a feast in the water god's honor. Dylan had always thought it odd that a water god would have pigs as his sacred animal, instead of some form of marine life. And it was equally odd that they paid tribute to the god by eating the very animal he held dear. Dylan certainly hoped there were no hard feelings, because the two tusked beasts before him bristled with hairy muscle.

Each of the boars tore into the shadow, ripping away great chunks as if it were made of cloth. The darkness appeared helpless against the attack, lifting its tendrils in defense only to have them torn off. The pigs continued their relentless attack until the shadow was reduced to a pile of dark strips, in the middle of which sat a pudgy man with messy black hair. His face was indignant as he stood up and moodily shoved one of the pigs away. To Dylan's surprise, the pig actually stumbled backwards.

"Well?" he demanded. "Aren't you going to introduce me?"

"Dylan," Orbsen sighed, "meet the patron god of the competition, Thaedon."

"God of the underworld," the strange man added when he realized Orbsen wasn't planning on doing so himself.

So this was Krale's god? He didn't look like much now that his shadows had been ripped away. Still, Dylan felt some apprehension about the god's intentions. Could Orbsen protect him from another deity?

"Oh, ho! Your loud thinker is having a crisis of faith!" Thaedon laughed.

Dylan blushed, embarrassed that his thoughts had been exposed. He desperately tried not to think of anything else embarrassing.

"Now he's thinking of what he wants to do with his boyfriend!" Thaedon announced gleefully.

"You have about thirty more seconds before I set the pigs on you again," Orbsen warned.

The other god wasn't intimidated. "I just came to speak some sense into this young man here."

Orbsen looked to Dylan, his gaze asking if this was all right with him. Dylan had to admit he was curious, so he nodded.

"Excellent," Thaedon clapped his hands excitedly. "I just thought it in your best interest to know that Krale means you and your friends no harm."

Dylan snorted in disbelief.

"I mean it!" the dark god protested. "You're no longer of any use to him. He has the red loka now, as well as yours. Thanks for giving it to him, by the way."

Dylan's stomach sank. So much had happened so quickly that he had completely forgotten about surrendering his loka to save Tyjinn.

"Anyway, Krale's got no quarrel with you as long as you stay out of his way. Otherwise—" Thaedon glanced nervously at Orbsen and let the threat remain unspoken.

"What's he planning to do?" Dylan asked "I can hardly stay out of his way if I don't know what he's going to do next."

"He's going to raise an army, of course," Thaedon answered. "An army of goblins that shall march out from the east and conquer every town until the Five Lands are his. Starting with the Lakelands."

Dylan's increasing sense of dread was interrupted by the dark god's sarcastic laughter. "You actually believe all that?" Thaedon snorted and turned to Orbsen. "Where did you find this guy? You really want this chump to go head-to-head with my man Krale? An army from the east... please!"

"Charming," Orbsen said. "Now if you'll excuse us, we have more pressing matters to attend to in realms where you can not follow."

"I've already sent Krale back! He's long since on his way. By the time you two stop chattering—" Whatever else the dark god had to say was interrupted by one of the pigs turning and sitting on him, although a muffled voice could still be heard from somewhere beneath the beast's butt.

Orbsen snapped his fingers, and the ropes of the raft frayed further and broke. The logs spread beneath Dylan's feet until he had nothing left to stand on, plunging him into the water. He reached instinctively for one of the logs to keep from going under, but the logs were gone. As his head submerged, he felt something grab his ankle and drag him down. He panicked for a moment before remembering he could breathe underwater.

Dylan was pulled downward at an alarming speed until whatever was dragging him hit bottom. The grip around his ankle let go and took hold of his thigh and then wrist, pulling him down until they were on the same level.

He faced a boy not many years older than he was, his hair blond and his body lean, tan, and naked except for a necklace of shells. Golden eyes regarded him with amusement.

Dylan looked around at the underwater realm, partly in an effort not to stare at the other's nudity. They seemed to be at the bottom of the ocean, judging from the large amounts of seaweed, coral, and schools of fish surrounding them.

"There's isn't much time left now, so just listen," Orbsen said, gently grasping Dylan's chin and turning his head until their eyes were locked. "The Empress isn't dead. She's a talented magician, even without the green loka, and not entirely human. She buried herself beneath the earth to save herself from the fire, but she is wounded and will soon die without the magic of the green loka. If you want to save her and redeem Tyjinn in the process, you must take it back from Krale and return it to her in no more than five days."

Dylan opened his mouth to speak, but the hand on his chin moved to cover his mouth.

"There's one more thing I can do for you. The entrance to the Cradle is never the exit. It's up to me to decide where in your world you are returned to. I'm going to send you where you most need to be, even if it's not where your friends are." The hand on his arm and the hand on his mouth both withdrew, and Dylan found himself floating upward.

"I don't want to be alone," he said as rose through the water.

"You won't be, not for long." Orbsen smiled up at him. "I'll be watching over you. Don't forget, I am also the god of storms."

Dylan opened his mouth, a million questions all clamoring to be spoken, but the water god was no more than a tiny speck far below him, the ocean full of much more light than it had been a moment ago. He looked up to see the reflection of the sun dancing above him. Reaching his arms up, he kicked and broke through the water's surface.

Chapter 16
The Cat in the Cradle

Kio found himself falling, but like all cats, he handled it well and landed safely on all four feet. The grass where he landed was lush green and longer than the struggling dry grass he had seen just moments before. His ears had already picked up the rustling of mice from more than four of these tufts of grass. As he instinctively turned to hone in on the nearest, a family of pheasants rose from their hiding place and took flight. Kio's mouth salivated, his tail whipping back and forth at the prospect of so much prey. He hunched down into a stalking pose, his body as close to the ground as possible, before his higher functions took over.

Where was he exactly, he wondered as he sat upright again, and more importantly, where was Dylan? He struggled to remember what had happened. The world had gone crazy, his senses betraying him the further they had progressed toward the Cradle. Then Krale was there, and so was Tyjinn, telling them to run. After that, nothing. He strained to remember and had a vague impression of purple light and Tyjinn's face bleeding.

Trying to remember wasn't doing him much good. He needed to find out where Dylan was and make sure his friend was safe. Testing the air with his nose, he was surprised to smell salt water and followed the scent to the low grassy knoll ahead of him. Mice, birds, and large insects scuttled and flew tantalizingly out of his path with every step. As soon as he found Dylan, he was going to return here and hunt until he was exhausted! He never had seen such grounds before. Surely this territory already belonged to a cat. Or did it have so much prey that even a greedy feline couldn't deplete the stocks? Maybe the previous owner had eaten himself to death.

Once he crested the knoll, he saw the source of the salt water smell. A calm, gray sea was directly ahead of him. A small port town sat to the right. There was something odd about the scene, although he couldn't decide what. Regardless, it was the most likely place Dylan would have headed, so Kio veered toward it, batting aside a couple of the slower mice as he walked.

Halfway to town, the scent of fresh fish tantalized Kio. He increased his pace, noticing a fish market by the waterside. Even though he didn't see any people, the booths were fully stocked. Then he realized what was wrong with the harbor—no ships could be seen, neither out at sea nor docked in port. His keen eyes couldn't spot even a single rowboat or dinghy.

As he entered the town, he noticed a number of other elements crucial to a fishing village also were missing—no rope on the docks or wagons to load and unload goods from the ships, not a single scrap of litter from bags, paper, or gutted fish. Even the air was clear of the typical city noises. No humans were here, only stall after stall of irresistible, juicy fish for the taking.

Kio was no fool. Fields full of mice and rabbits and now the harbor without humans to stop a cat from stealing lunch. This was a cat's paradise, which meant he had left his world behind and entered the world of the gods. Or was it the afterlife? Was there a difference? If this was where cats went when they died, surely more cats than just him would be around. Then again, he didn't see any gods here either.

Kio strolled up to the nearest stall and snatched a live sardine swimming in a bucket of water. He chewed it thoughtfully as he considered his options. He wasn't sure if Dylan would have arrived at such a place. Did humans have a paradise, too? If so, Dylan was probably surrounded by pastries and naked women. Or men, in his case. But how could they find each other again? If he kept walking in one direction, would the paradise of cats eventually meet up with the paradise of humans? He wasn't sure, but he was determined to do something besides eat.

He decided to walk through the center of town, which was as deserted as the harbor had been. Every door and window was cracked open enough for a normal-sized cat to gain entry. The area had more ledges than usual too, including ones that led from window to rooftop. A suspicious amount of milk bottles sat on doorsteps waiting to be spilled. Rats ran rampant through the town, all just careless enough to attract his attention. Kio was becoming frustrated by all the distractions when he entered the center square.

Unlike the rest of the town, the courtyard maintained the illusion of normal life. A wheelbarrow was placed to one side and a few crates and barrels had been scattered about. These props couldn't lie to Kio's nose, though. He immediately smelled that they had never been used. However, they were good for giving rodents places to hide, making hunting more exciting. As if to prove the point, a cat shot from behind a barrel, streaked across the courtyard, and pounced on a small rat. It grabbed the rat gleefully in its mouth, tossed it into the air, and batted at it repeatedly until it hit the ground. About to have another go at the trembling rodent, the other cat noticed Kio.

The cat was male; Kio could smell that much even from this distance. Like him, the cat was white, but his fur was broken by a black spot or two. His tail was a swirl of both colors, and the fur on his head was black as well, reminding Kio of a little toupee. The cat widened his golden-green eyes in surprise and kept them locked on Kio as he approached. When the cat was near enough, it yowled a long warning cry that was surprisingly high-pitched.

Kio laughed. This was a normal house cat challenging him.

Kio was easily three times his size. He could probably knock the cat out cold with a single swipe of his paw, but instead he yowled his own warning and finished with a definitive hiss that showed he meant business.

The other cat didn't back down. Instead, his slightly angled ears and aggravated tail showed he was seriously considering pouncing. Kio was bracing himself defensively when the other cat stood and walked in three wide circles. The first loop already showed a massive change occurring. Its black spots began to spread like paint, turning more of the white fur black—but the cat's physical increase in size was more impressive. By the second round, the cat's fur was more black than white, and the cat was now Kio's equal in size. By the time the cat walked its third circle, it was not only completely black and three times larger than Kio, but significantly more muscled as well. It sat, scowled with emerald green eyes down at his challenger, and hissed.

The wind power from that hiss flattened Kio's whiskers against his face. He immediately rolled onto the ground and exposed his belly. This situation required the ultimate show of prostration. He wasn't facing just another cat. He was facing the god of cats and had been stupid enough to challenge him in his own territory!

Kio needed a long time to work up the courage to look directly at the other cat, and when he did, he made sure to only do so briefly. To his relief, the massive cat had relaxed his display of dominance and had his ears forward in an inquisitive expression. He wanted to know what Kio wanted.

Kio rolled back onto his belly but remained as flat as possible. Craning his neck, he tried to look around the other cat to communicate that he wanted to pass through his territory.

The god of cats thumped his tail in irritation, knocking a considerable amount of dirt and stones into the air. He obviously didn't like the idea, but was generous enough to curl his tail in just the right way to ask why.

Kio sat up cautiously and tried to figure out how to explain his desires using only body language. He repeated his craning movement and followed it up by kneading the earth with his paws, a gesture of affection. He then rolled over on his back again and pawed at the air, as if he were playing with a friend, feeling like a royal idiot during the entire process. To his surprise, the god of cats began laughing in a voice as human as his own.

"Wait, you can talk?" Kio asked dubiously.

"Yes," the cat god answered in a rumbling voice, "although I don't enjoy it like your kind does."

"My kind?" Kio asked. "I thought I was the only one."

The giant cat huffed his impatience, his mood of amusement having passed already. "There's never one kind of anything in your world."

Kio had considered the idea only in his most secret fantasies. Of course the topic of his origin had come up many times, occasionally between Dylan and himself and more often from strangers, but Kio always played it off as unimportant. "Do I have parents? Where are they?"

The cat god was already longingly eyeing a far-away rat. An age seemed to pass before he answered the question. "I can take you to them."

"Yes!"

"Or I can take you to your friend."

"Oh." Kio slouched despondently. "You can't do both? There's not an option 'C' where we pick up Dylan first and then go meet the rest of my kind?"

The god of cats looked at him as if he hadn't understood a word.

"Ah, well. Take me to Dylan. He needs me to protect him, especially now. That's the most important thing."

The cat god blinked thoughtfully. "Then I will take you somewhere else. Somewhere to help your friend."

"What do you mean?" Kio asked, but the big cat stood and turned to leave. He shrank as he walked across the courtyard. By the time he reached the nearest street, he had returned to the size and color he had been when Kio first saw him. The cat god stopped and looked back at Kio before continuing on his way, cat language for "follow me."

Kio followed the cat god down more streets than he thought the town could possess, considering how small it looked from the knoll. They walked for so long that the sun set and a thick fog began to fill the streets, making the cat ahead of him difficult to follow. Eventually he couldn't see the god of cats at all. Kio called out, asking for the other to wait, but heard no response.

Time lost all meaning in a gray world without sky. Kio

continued walking in what he hoped was one direction. He didn't tire in the slightest, not physically, but he quickly became sick of the fog, which was too opaque to be natural. Even the ground beneath his feet was lost to sight. Disoriented but determined, he pressed on, not knowing if he was making any progress. Relief came when he began ascending a steep hill. At least it was something different from the monotonous, flat terrain. His legs tired as he made his way uphill, a sure sign he had left the world of the gods and had returned to his own.

The fog ended at the hill's summit, an invisible barrier separating it from the area beyond. On the other side was a stretch of manicured lawn leading to a stone, two-story house. The open windows of the well-maintained home combined with the scent of freshly baked goods suggested it was occupied. The sun twinkled, still chasing the morning dew away. Had he truly walked all night, or did time function differently in the Cradle?

Enjoying the feeling of the short grass beneath his paws, Kio trotted happily toward the house. Normally he would have felt more apprehensive about approaching a strange home, but he was convinced he was here for a reason. To help Dylan, the cat god had said. Obviously someone was inside who could do just that. When he was about halfway across the yard, he looked back and saw the fog was a swirling wall of clouds that circled the yard. Powerful magic was at work here. Quite possibly the work of an Oligarch.

The door to the house was divided in two halves that could swing separately from one another. Currently, the top half was open, but the bottom was closed. He couldn't imagine what use such a design could have, besides being great for people who couldn't make up their minds whether or not to shut the door. Kio called out a greeting as he stood before the door, and although he could hear movement from within the house, he received no reply. He called out again with the same result, beginning to feel less confident.

Still, the god of cats had led him here. Maybe whoever was inside was bound and gagged and needed help. Considering what had happened to other members of the Oligarchy, the idea wasn't all that far-fetched. Deciding to take action, Kio hopped onto the closed portion of the door, balancing precariously for a moment as he took a cursory glance inside. He had the vague impression of a lavishly furnished room but saw no sign of life. There wasn't an immediate threat, so Kio sprang into the room.

"I'm in the house," he called cautiously. "I know someone's in here, and I'm worried you need help."

Still no response, and yet he could smell someone had very recently been in this room. Two different people, in fact. They obviously weren't restrained, so what sort of game were they playing? He looked around for a clue. The room was nicely decorated but didn't seem to serve any purpose. Kio saw three options. The kitchen was obviously to the right, since alluring smells were drifting from it. Straight ahead was a living room and a stairwell, leaving only the room on the left, which was hard to see into.

Kio was considering leaving when a zapping noise from behind startled him. He jumped and twisted, landing in the direction of the noise, fur bristling. A miniature black cloud rumbling with thunder was floating toward him. It looked so ridiculous that he couldn't help but laugh—until it shot another bolt of lightning that came dangerously close to striking him.

Slinking backward and no longer amused, Kio turned and scurried toward the living room to avoid the little storm. An identical cloud emerged from that room as well, soon joined by another from the kitchen. All three zapped menacingly as they closed in on him, lightning bolts striking the wooden floor and causing tiny wisps of smoke to rise. Kio's only hope was the room to the left. Nothing appeared to stop him as he passed over its threshold. He realized, even as the door slammed shut behind him, that he had been corralled here on purpose. The sound of metal bolts sliding closed confirmed it.

"I got you!" a male voice shouted triumphantly from the other side of the door. "Ohoho! I got you all right!"

Kio glanced around the room. He was, for the time being, safe and alone. This was an artist's studio, fully equipped with all the tools necessary to paint, sketch, sculpt, and even weave. Painting was the dominant art form, a style Kio wasn't familiar with. The artist appeared to have loaded half a dozen brushes with paint before entering a self-induced seizure. The results weren't recognizable, but the eclectic mix of colors was appealing.

"I said I've got you," the voice repeated, sounding disappointed by the lack of response.

Kio maintained his silence. Maybe his captor would become curious enough to open the door, giving him a chance to escape. A second door led out of the room, but it too was closed and probably locked. That didn't really make a difference since he couldn't turn a doorknob—paws be damned—but there was one other alternative. Behind a vaguely sinister sculpture was an open window. He would be out of here in no time! Stepping over a wooden carving of a dog wearing a turtle shell and leaping over a stack of charcoal sketches, he reached the window, cautiously poked his head out, and was greeted by a rumble of thunder. The once spotless sky had turned to a swarm of dark, angry clouds. His fur stood on end, and his skin prickled. He ducked back in a few seconds before lightning hit the ground, passing through the air where his head had been.

"Aha!" the voice shouted victoriously. Footsteps clattered through the house, followed by a door slamming shut before a tall, potbellied man appeared at the window. He was balding, but what little brown hair he had left was sticking out in all directions. His beard matched this hairstyle, framing his grin full of crooked teeth and threatening to swallow his nose and ears completely. The man regarded Kio with wild, round eyes. "I've got you!" he shouted again.

Kio stared. Surely this man would see that he was just an animal who had accidentally strayed into his home and would shoo him out accordingly.

"Well? What do you have to say for yourself?" the man demanded. "I know you can talk!"

"How the hell do you know that?" Kio asked in surprise.

"Aha! Aha!" he screamed. "I knew it!" The strange man hopped in a circle, pulling at his hair in an expression of vindicated celebration. "In my own home! You tried to assassinate me in my own home!"

"What? No! That's not what I was doing at all!" Kio was becoming more distressed by the second. Obviously this person was both delusional and dangerously powerful. "Look, I don't mean you any harm."

The strange man stopped his dance. "Then why did you sneak into my home? In disguise, no less!"

"I didn't sneak in, I called—Wait, what do you mean disguise? I'm not in disguise."

"Nice try, Orange," the man snorted. "A giant talking cat is hardly subtle, you know. Next time why don't you try shape-shifting into an opera-singing gazelle?"

"It's a cat?" a female muffled voice asked from behind the door.

Kio sighed as the pieces fell into place. "You might be an Oligarch, but I am not."

"If you're not Orange, who are you?"

"A giant talking cat." Kio left it at that, refusing to give the man any more fuel to feed his mad furnace.

The man mulled this over, as if it was a sensible argument. Just when Kio thought he was off the hook, a malicious look of determination came over the man's face.

"You're forcing me to be drastic," he said, holding out his left hand. A sinister gray mist formed there and slowly floated toward Kio.

Kio thought it was another lightning cloud, but one much too thin to have any real electrical potential. He eyed it warily as it neared, a sense of fear welling up inside him. The feeling intensified into such terror that he raced across the room, sending art supplies flying in all directions. By the time Kio reached the farthest corner of the studio, he felt comparatively calm.

What had he been so scared of? He turned to see the mist making its way around a sculpture that lay between them. The cloud didn't look very threatening, but once again as it neared he became overwhelmed with fear. The mist was directly in front of him now. Kio pressed himself into a corner, too panicked to do anything else.

The tiny shred of logic left to him realized that the fear originated from the mist and was not his own. This was magic, not his true emotion, but this realization did nothing to comfort him. He was too terrified to even move.

"Who are you?" asked the Oligarch as he climbed through the window.

"Kio! That's all! I'm just a cat!"

"Very well. If you won't be truthful…"

The mist crept forward slightly, brushing against a whisker. Kio yowled.

"Stop it, Diggory!" a woman shouted as the door was thrown open. "Leave the poor thing alone!"

"He's an assassin," Diggory insisted.

"Oh, you are such an idiot!" She stomped over to Kio, walking through the gray mist without consequence, and attempted to pick him up. She had to heave a couple times before he completely left the ground. She turned angrily on the Oligarch, cradling Kio to her chest. "Stop this at once or there won't be any supper for you."

"Oh, fine!" Diggory clenched his fist, and the mist dissipated.

The newcomer gently set Kio down and tenderly stroked his head. "You'll have to forgive him," she cooed. "He's as mad as they come."

"That's no way to speak to an Oligarch!" Diggory boomed, but the woman continued to ignore him.

"My name is Yasmine," she said. "I'm the caretaker of this house and of the Gray Oligarch."

Kio didn't normally find humans attractive, and this homely woman was no exception. Her hair was a dull brown without any sheen, her body bony, and her features too masculine. Her humble clothing attested to her status as a servant, but her expressive brown eyes overcame it all. They shone with the light of kindness, lending her a much more authentic kind of beauty.

"He must be a magician," the Gray Oligarch said, peering over Yasmine's shoulder to get a better look at Kio. "How else could he have reached the island?"

"It's a long story," Kio muttered, "but I guess it's easiest just to say that a magician brought me here."

"Aha, but for what purpose?" Diggory asked, working himself into another paranoid fit.

"To seek your help!" Kio shouted, not sure if this was true, but it sounded logical. The cat god had brought him here to help Dylan. Surely he was here to enlist the magic of another Oligarch. Diggory might not be completely sane, but he had already shown that he was a force to be reckoned with.

"Help you with what?" Gray asked suspiciously.

"There's someone going around killing Oligarchs one by one—"

"You see, Yasmine?" Diggory said. "I'm not crazy!"

Kio wasn't sure about that, but was eager to get on his good side. "You aren't crazy at all. Three Oligarchs have already died. Well, one of them just faked his death and is actually the killer."

Diggory nodded, no stranger to convoluted plots. Perhaps he was the right man for the job, considering how unstable the situation had become.

"Which one is the killer? Orange? Black? It's Black, isn't it?"

"Nope, Yellow."

"Yellow." The Gray Oligarch whispered the name slowly, drawing it out. He clenched his fists and narrowed his eyes. "Yellow," he repeated. "I hate that bastard. He's nothing but a cheap imitation of me."

"My friends and I hate him, too," Kio said with an air of conspiracy.

"So much that you want him dead?" Diggory said.

Kio swallowed. "I guess so, yeah."

"Yasmine! Please get dinner ready for my new friend and me," the Gray Oligarch grinned. "We'll be in my study until then."

The Gray Oligarch led him upstairs to a room that looked nothing like a study. The room did at least contain a desk, although it was crammed full of cogs, weights, and a heavy-looking mallet. If the Gray Oligarch was a clockmaker, he wasn't a competent one, since not one complete clock could be seen. Drawers lined the walls, many of them hanging open, exposing a variety of glass vials and bottles. A storm churned outside the small glass window set in the ceiling.

"So you do weather magic?" Kio asked.

"I *am* the weather," Diggory said. "Look here." He pointed at a device hanging on the wall too high for Kio to see clearly. "This barometer says it's going to rain."

"Seems reasonable," Kio conceded, realizing now that the clock parts were actually pieces of different weather machines.

"No, it's not reasonable at all!" the Gray Oligarch disagreed. He dug in his pockets, his tongue sticking out with effort. Kio expected him to reveal an old piece of candy, but instead Diggory held up a loka. Even though it was surely the gray loka, its light was silvery. The clouds above dissipated almost immediately. Then Diggory went to his desk, retrieved the mallet, and began bashing the barometer until it fell to the floor in pieces.

"Damn gadgets are never accurate," he complained.

Kio looked anew at the pile of broken devices, deciding it was time for another change of topic. There had to be at least one that was safe. "What was that fear mist thing?" he asked, hoping the question wouldn't prompt a demonstration.

"Emotion," Diggory answered. "It's my secondary power. Do you want to see my collection?"

"Sure," Kio said, even though he wanted quite the opposite.

The Gray Oligarch turned to the drawers and pulled one open, sending debris sliding across the floor. He chose a jar that looked as though it had once stored preserves. A hastily scribbled label identified the contents as 'Agitation.' The mist that swirled inside was yellow and pulsed impatiently.

"This is my secret armory," Diggory said in a stage whisper. He dug some more and held up another jar labeled 'Despair,' its mist black and still.

Kio had to admit that the fear cloud had been an effective weapon. Bottling up these emotions was not only a terrible pun but brilliant as well, since the jars could be lobbed at enemies while leaving the gray loka free for other purposes.

"Which one do you want to try?" Diggory asked him.

"Are you kidding me?" Kio winced at the idea.

"They're not all bad," the Gray Oligarch said, digging through his collection. "There's love, that's always nice. I give those as gifts to Yasmine, but she never opens them. Then there's elation, or let's see, contentment, or hysteria. I rather like that last one."

"You like being hysterical?"

"It's of the laughing variety, not the panicked sort. Here, try it."

Before Kio could protest, the Gray Oligarch opened the jar and shook it, freeing a sparkling lavender cloud that tickled Kio's nose as it spread wide and dissipated into the air. The effect wasn't immediate. Not until one final piece of the barometer fell to the floor were they both overcome with uncontrollable laughter. Then Diggory started putting as many broken pieces of weather gauges into his nose as he could fit.

"Your ears! Do your ears next!" Kio howled as he rolled on the floor.

Soon enough, the Gray Oligarch's nose, ears, and mouth were stuffed full of bric-a-brac. Kio was wearing the man's socks on his front paws and his shoes on his hind paws, and they had torn down a light blue curtain and fashioned a toga for Kio to wear. They were conspiring to raid Yasmine's room for more clothing when the effects of the magic wore off.

"Potent stuff," Diggory said after spitting everything onto the floor. "I do that one about a dozen times a day."

No wonder you're off your rocker, Kio thought. His lungs and a number of muscles ached from the exertion of laughing. He watched as the Oligarch used his magic to refill the jar. Rather than use fear against their opponents; hysteria would render them equally ineffective and would be much kinder.

"We could really nail Krale with some of those," Kio said.

"We'll do more than that to Yellow." Diggory wiped the sweat from his forehead. "If he's running around killing other Oligarchs, we have all the excuse we need to finish him off."

"Yeah," Kio agreed half-heartedly. He didn't really like the idea of setting out to kill Krale, but this was a 'do or die' situation. The idea of capturing him and taking his lokas sounded better, but not very realistic.

"After dinner then," the Gray Oligarch said enthusiastically. "We'll track that huckster down and give him a taste of his own medicine. He thinks he knows air magic? Just wait until he gets a taste of my winds!"

"He won't be easy to find," Kio said. "He's been on a roving rampage for a while now."

"Oh, we'll find him," Diggory said, holding up a jar labeled 'Introspective.' "After some serious thinking, one of us will figure out where the rat is hiding."

Chapter 17
Transformation

The round stones of the church walls had been softened by time. The great arches overhead disappeared into darkness, revealing no hint of a ceiling. Candlelight filled the room, hundreds of dancing flames chasing away the cold and transforming it into a warm place of comfort.

Tyjinn knelt in front of his goddess, the Bride of Fire. She matched his position and regarded him with amused eyes. The fire that was her hair waved gently around her head, separate locks that curled into question marks. He resisted laughing, which would be inappropriate considering recent circumstances. Here he was, facing his goddess's judgment after committing murder and betraying his friends. This was no time for amusement.

"Lighten up, little dragonfly," the Bride chided. "She's not actually dead."

"The Empress?" Tyjinn asked, not daring to hope.

The goddess nodded. "She's not exactly in the best condition, but she might pull through. Did you know she's half-elemental? Earth, obviously."

"That's impossible!"

"Not as impossible as you might think," the Bride said and laughed. "So you see, there's no reason to be upset. Even your mother is fine."

She explained how Krale had tricked him, the flames of her hair sputtering in agitation, her anger mirrored in Tyjinn. He had nearly killed one of the finest magicians of their time, helped Krale to reach the Cradle, and left his friends alone and defenseless. So much treachery, all because he foolishly believed a lie.

"This is the part where you are supposed to feel happy and relieved that everything is all right," the Bride said, leaning forward and placing a warm hand on his cheek. "Don't torment yourself over the past."

How could he not feel disappointed in himself? He had betrayed Jack's trust and failed to protect Dylan. His heart ached, both with the pain of his mistakes and his love for Dylan. If only he could go back and choose a different path so they could still be together, even if his feelings never were reciprocated.

"He's handsome," the goddess murmured, looking over his shoulder. Tyjinn turned. Where there had been only shadows before was the object of his heart's desire. Dylan looked just as surprised to see him, his trusting gray eyes full of emotion.

Desire became manifest, bringing Tyjinn close enough to Dylan to hear the sound of his breath. Tyjinn wanted to grab him, embrace him and never let go, but it was Dylan who reached out first to take his hand. Reality began to shift around them, different scenes playing out, each experienced as if real. They lay sleeping together, a tangle of arms and legs. As old men they walked together, laughing about how difficult the simplest of tasks had become. Middle-aged, they argued with each other, but passion remained behind the words. Next they were being married, their friends and families surrounding them, lending their support. In a fraction of a second, countless situations played out, all of them aspects of love.

He turned back to his goddess, the vision fading. "Was that real?"

She nodded. "Given the chance, it could be."

Tyjinn looked back over his shoulder, but the shadows had returned. "Take me to him," he said. "I need to be with him, to protect him."

"Dylan must walk his own path," the goddess said, "at least for the time being. He can't always look to you or others for protection. He'll only overcome Krale if he finds his inner strength. It's not my plan, but then he's not one of mine."

Tyjinn tried to hide the anger in his voice but failed. "Whose plan is it then?"

"Someone I respect very much."

"And if Dylan doesn't find his inner strength?"

"Then he faces death."

"No!" Tyjinn was on his feet. "I won't allow it! There has to be something I can do!" He couldn't stand the thought of Dylan coming to harm. All of this was his fault! Nothing should have made him leave Dylan's side, certainly not trickery. "Please," he fell back to his knees, his voice hoarse. "I'm begging you."

The Bride frowned, reached for one of her flaming locks and twirled it around a finger. "When I return you to your world, it can be to any place of your choosing," she said.

"Could you send me to Krale so I may kill him?"

The goddess nodded.

"No," Tyjinn said. "Not like that." Recent events had threatened his sanity, and he had only just been granted redemption in regard to the Empress. To kill Krale in direct defense of Dylan was one thing, but to assassinate him would bring back that poisonous taste of murder. There had to be another way. "I would give my life to save Dylan, if given the chance."

The goddess sighed. "The future remains uncertain, but should a time come when Dylan faces no option but death, I can send you to him."

Tyjinn assented immediately.

"By doing so," Bride cautioned, "you will be placing yourself within death's reach."

"If Dylan were to die, then my own life would mean nothing. Please. Let me do this."

"Then until that time, you must sleep in a place between both worlds."

The Bride's warmth enveloped Tyjinn as he sank into a deep and quiet place. As his last vestiges of consciousness gave way to dream, he wondered how long he would sleep before Dylan needed him. Days, weeks, maybe even years for all he cared. He was tired and was finally being given a chance to rest. Contentedly, he sighed and let himself worry no more.

Sunlight poured through the open window, warming Lali's resting face and illuminating the green mother's otherwise dingy hut. She lay in bed, enjoying the sun's warmth, the scent of fresh air, and most of all, the silence. Delia had left hours ago to help deliver a baby and had yet to return. Hopefully the labor would be long and difficult. This was an unsympathetic wish toward the woman giving birth, but Lali was desperate for some time alone.

The green mother had warmed up to her during the last few days and decided to make up for years of solitary living by embarking on conversation marathons that lasted for hours. These mostly one-sided discussions were occasionally about Delia's life, but more often featured gossip. The green mother reveled in spinning tales about her fellow townsfolk.

For instance, she claimed the young man who delivered her groceries increased the prices when delivering to less savvy elderly customers. Delia said the money he skimmed was being saved so he could run away with his cousin with whom he was in love. Lali didn't put too much stock in these tales. After all, when Delia had stepped outside to collect her food, she whispered that Lali was a princess from the south who had run away to escape an arranged marriage. Lali found this behavior more amusing than not and had pretended to still be asleep when her hostess reentered the hut.

Despite her personality flaws, the green mother knew her craft well. The amputation of her hand had been quick, if not painless, and Lali had mercifully passed out within moments. Since then she had been well cared for. She had been well fed, and most important, continually supplied with the grumble tea that kept her pleasantly apathetic about her situation. It helped with the pain too, reducing it to a dull throb, but mostly it was the blissful hum in her mind that provided relief. In fact, she was about due for another drink. Maybe the laboring woman shouldn't have such a difficult delivery after all.

The sun was suddenly replaced by shadow, causing Lali to open her eyes. A large head loomed in the window. Instinctively, she pushed herself up to a sitting position and winced in pain, having forgotten one hand was missing. She could already feel the stump beginning to bleed. Ignoring her pain as best she could, she focused dizzily on the visitor in the window.

"Mushi!" she exclaimed. She reached up with her good hand to stroke her dearest companion's face. "What are you doing here? Are the others with you?"

"No, I came alone."

Lali froze. Her mushushu had just spoken, his lips moving with a flexibility she had never seen before. Grumble tea was potent, but so far it hadn't caused her to hallucinate.

"I was worried about you," Mushi continued, looking as guilty as his reptilian face could manage. His voice was oddly familiar.

"You aren't Mushi," she sputtered. "A talking cat is weird enough, but I know my mushushu can't talk."

"I know. I have a lot of explaining to do. Look, can you open the door? A small crowd of peasants are eyeing me like I'm their next meal."

She recognized the voice and knew exactly with whom she was dealing. "You son of a bitch," she snarled. Her anger gave her enough of an adrenaline boost to reach the door and open it. The mushushu squeezed into the room, knocking over a number of things in the process.

"You'd better change before you do any more damage," she said, slumping down in the nearest chair.

The mushushu became infused with an orange glow as its shape began to change. Lali watched unimpressed as the neck shortened and the front legs reshaped into arms. In less than a minute, the mushushu was replaced by a fat man with dark skin and darker hair. He shrugged apologetically, unperturbed by his own nakedness.

"Damn you, Hasam! Where the hell is the real Mushi?" Lali hissed.

"Safe! He's safe, trust me. He's still in the palace stables and being treated like he's… well, me!" The Orange Oligarch kneeled down and opened the saddlebag that hadn't transformed along with him. He turned it inside out, contents spilling everywhere. He felt the leather carefully until he found a lump. Tearing it open revealed the orange loka, which he examined happily. "Think I can fit into some of Dylan's shorts?" he asked.

"I hope for both our sakes that you can," Lali sighed. She was too tired to maintain her anger. Wearily she crawled back into bed. "Are they okay?"

"A little tight," Hasam answered. After a tearing noise, the shorts managed to cover the essential parts.

"Not the shorts, Dylan and Kio."

"Oh, yes, I think so. I took them almost as far as the Cradle. Any further and it would have defeated the purpose of doing all this."

"So the rumors of you being in hiding are true." Lali shook her head. "You should have appeared once you were in the presence of the Empress."

"Fat lot of good that would have done. If I had, I'd be as dead as she is." Hasam joined her, sitting on the edge of the bed and causing it to tilt dangerously. "It was hard leaving you here," he said gently, taking her arm and examining where her hand had been.

"I would have been glad for your company," she said. Hasam might be a coward, but he was also a kind and intelligent man who had become a sort of foster father to her.

"I could have done nothing against the woodworm's infection, but now I can help you." Hasam stood so suddenly that the bed bounced and caused Lali's body to hop a little.

"Help how?"

"With orange magic, of course." Hasam examined one of Delia's bookshelves. "You haven't forgotten what I've taught you about shape-shifting and mass displacement, have you?"

Lali forced herself to think, which was becoming easier as the tea wore off. The Orange Oligarch was referring to the impossibility of shape-shifting into something of significantly more or less mass than the shifter. Human beings didn't have enough bulk to turn into something as large as a mammoth. Likewise, becoming a fly was impossible because all the excess body mass would have to go somewhere. However, turning into a 150-pound fly was completely possible. Of course this wouldn't function well as a disguise, but would certainly terrify the enemy. All this was interesting, but she didn't see its relevance in her present situation.

"What are you getting at?"

"Your hand," Hasam said. "You transform into another form, and when you transform back, you make sure to change into a Lali with two hands instead of one."

Her mind raced as she considered the idea. "Will that work? I thought you said that changing back to a human was just letting go of the animal form and automatically reverting back to what's natural."

"Yes," Hasam said, "but you can guide it with a little bit of willpower. You should have seen my nose before I became Oligarch. It was huge!"

Lali laughed, buoyed by this good news, but the feeling left her as she realized one problem. She had never successfully shape-shifted before.

"Don't look so down," Hasam said, picking up on her thoughts. "You can use the orange loka to help you. We'll have you back to your old self in no time. Well, after we change you completely of course."

Hasam smiled, and Lali couldn't help but smile back, feeling for the first time in weeks that things were going to be all right.

Chapter 18
Brown

Dylan clambered out of the water, stones pressing painfully into his hands. The discomfort was even more intense on his bony knees, so he stood and coughed a few times to clear his lungs. Turned to examine the water he had been swimming in, he found little more than a murky puddle. He stepped back into it experimentally. At its deepest point, the water barely reached his ankles. He shrugged, unimpressed. After everything he had lived through today, this hardly seemed strange at all.

Wiping the water from his eyes, he surveyed his surroundings and gasped, the air notably thinner. Mountains surrounded him in every direction, majestic, timeless, and elegant. The top of each mountain thinned as it rose, finally spiraling as it reached for the sky. That was the entirety of this world, countless graceful spires and an open blue sky. From his current position—twisting stones at his back and a sheer drop ahead of him—the horizon was limitless, the mountains becoming gray silhouettes before fading away into infinity.

Dylan was content to lose himself in the silence. He felt tiny, insignificant in comparison to his surroundings. This was a welcome contrast to how he had felt recently. No decision he made here could change the permanent surroundings or put his friends at risk. He was a solitary ant lost in a giant world, no longer able to make a difference.

But that wasn't true. He had to stop Krale, reclaim the lokas, save the Empress, and redeem Tyjinn. All this alone, without even the blue loka's power. Without it, he could barely conjure up a handful of drinking water. He sighed, wishing for Kio's company. The cat would listen to his problems patiently before making light of them, diminishing how daunting they seemed.

"Enough self pity," he imagined Kio telling him. *"Time to get on with it so we can be home in time for dinner."*

The wind blew, carrying the gentle sound of a piano. This was his sign, what he was sent here for. The song was coming from directly ahead of him. Dylan approached the cliff, his head swimming with vertigo from the idea alone. He crawled on his hands and knees, and when he was close, looked over the edge.

Below, hewn out of the mountain, was a balcony made of stone. A petite wooden chair and planting boxes full of herbs completed this unlikely scene. He couldn't see a doorway, but the increased volume of the music confirmed its existence.

He estimated a twelve-foot drop would get him to the balcony. Normally a jump of that distance wouldn't terrify him, but if he missed his target, he would be falling much farther than that. Didn't this place have a front door? Couldn't Orbsen have started him out on the balcony? This was probably his god's idea of a character-building exercise. Dylan decided to lower himself over the edge. The only risk was slipping and falling on his ass, assuming he didn't break his back on the balcony's edge. He mulled over this idea long enough that a third song began, this one loud and powerful. Now was the ideal time to make his attempt, because the song would help camouflage any noise he made.

He brushed all the loose soil off the rock to reduce his chance of slipping. Heart thudding in his ears, he got down on his stomach and lowered his legs over the edge, worming backward until only his arms and shoulders kept him in place. He could no longer hesitate, because the piano-playing occupant might see his legs dangling in the doorway at any minute. He increased his grip on the rock, raised his elbows, and let gravity do the rest. His head knocked painfully on the rock wall as his whole body swung over. The pain in his head was nothing compared to the aching in his fingers. He had little choice but to let go.

By some miracle he landed on his feet, but not before pinwheeling his arms ridiculously to regain his balance. He had done it, but he didn't have time to celebrate. Behind him, a great opening in the rock functioned as a doorway, one as wide as the balcony itself that left no room to hide. Realizing he was in plain sight, Dylan hurried into the interior in the hopes of finding cover and almost ran headlong into a bookshelf.

He was in a library. Row upon row of bookshelves extended before him, forming an aisle that led to the source of the music. He could see the edge of the piano beyond the dozen or so rows of bookshelves ahead. He cautiously made his way down the aisle, pondering where he was.

Was this some sort of scholarly institution? In the middle of nowhere? More likely it was a secret society. That would explain its remoteness and difficult entrance. Perhaps he had stumbled upon a magical cult. He glanced at some of the book titles as he walked. One dealt with knitting, another was titled "Royal Romances, Bloody Betrayals." Not exactly the sort of books he would expect mages to hoard away in a mountain hideaway.

He cast these thoughts aside as he ducked into the last row of bookshelves. The music stopped—causing his heart to leap in the certainty that he was caught—but soon another song started, this one fast and complex. He could barely imagine how someone could move their fingers so swiftly. Pressing himself against the corner bookshelf, Dylan peeked around the corner.

The woman playing the piano was ancient. Her skin was as dark as Tyjinn's, but wrinkled and stretched over her boney arms. Over her slender frame she wore a simple white robe that appeared ivory next to her short, stark white hair. Her face was both proud and thoughtful, head tilted slightly upward. For a moment, Dylan thought she might be blind and stupidly waved a hand back and forth to find out.

The woman's eyes locked onto him, the music halting with a resounding thud. She didn't move to attack him, or cry out for help. She was too dignified for either action. Having already been spotted, Dylan decided to fully reveal himself. He stepped into the aisle and stood exposed.

The woman played the same discordant note that had ended her song, as if it were an intentional part of the composition before resuming the piece, her eyes locked onto his. She played the entire song in this manner. Dylan didn't know how to react. The music was loud enough that he couldn't speak over it. He tried smiling sheepishly, but his smile wasn't returned. By the time she finished playing, he was squirming.

The woman stood and walked to the front of the piano, regarding him coolly.

"I couldn't find the front door," he said.

"That's because there isn't one."

"Oh."

"I've narrowed it down," she said. "You are either the son of the Blue Oligarch, a new representative of the lizard clan, or a rather silly air elemental. I rather think it's safe to eliminate those last two, don't you?"

Dylan was dumbfounded. What sort of magician was he facing? He hadn't seen her work any magic. Perhaps the music had disguised her spell. Or maybe he was facing another Oligarch. But which one? He didn't know much about the others he hadn't met. Still, the white robe with the white hair implied who she might be.

"Are you White?" he asked.

"Are you blind, or haven't you ever seen a black woman before?"

Dylan's mouth fell open. How could he have phrased his question so stupidly? Now he'd surely insulted and alienated her, with one simple sentence.

"No, I'm sorry. I meant—"

A smile seeped across the woman's stoic face. "I am, in fact, the Brown Oligarch. I'm sure there are a few good jokes we could make about that too, if we wanted. It's probably best if you call me Lucile."

He grinned and exhaled in relief. "I'm Dylan. Uh, how did you know who I was?"

"Familial resemblance combined with your father being one of the few people with the capability to locate where I live. You're very far from home, you know."

"I don't, actually," Dylan admitted.

Lucile looked puzzled. "How did you get here? There aren't too many possibilities. One of the lizard men? A pegasus is possible, but unlikely. Surely you didn't travel here by land and sea. If you had—"

"Wait," Dylan interrupted her. "What's a lizard man?"

"The natives of this continent and the only people, aside from myself, with the power of teleportation."

"Continent?" Dylan repeated "I'm on a different continent?"

"One far south of your home. How could you not realize that?"

Dylan opened his mouth to speak but only shook his head. "It's a long story, and one that you aren't likely to believe." He felt completely flabbergasted. "I honestly don't know where to begin."

"Do you know the nature of my magic?"

"Teleportation, you said."

"Yes, but also thought." Lucile leaned against the piano as she spoke. "I was able to discern who you are because of my magic. My loka represents speed. Not only the speed of physical movements, but the infinitely greater speed of thought. Ideas and concepts come to me much faster than they do for other people. Not only faster but simultaneously. What would take an hour for another person to think takes me minutes, if not less."

"So you're saying you could handle hearing the gist of my story without me explaining it?"

Lucile nodded. "There's a more interesting option, if you are willing. With my magic, all you have to do is think it, and I will see it as if it were happening. We both would."

The idea sounded brilliant. If what she was describing was

true, he would be seeing something like a play of his own life. Dylan agreed, and she led him down a cold, stony hallway to another room. Doors, windows, and walls were all carved from stone, and yet he saw no sign of chiseling on the walls. They appeared impossibly natural, as if wind and water had conspired to wear a mountain down into an apartment. Lucile closed the door, shrouding them in darkness.

"It's easier this way," she explained as she guided him to a chair he couldn't see. Dylan sat and waited, the sound of another wooden chair scraping the floor to his right, before brown light infused the room, revealing Lucile sitting beside him with her loka glowing in her hands. Dylan had never seen brown light before. It was, he decided, like holding a glass of maple syrup up to the sunlight and looking through it. The thought made him hungry for one of Ada's lavish breakfasts.

"The magic is attuned to you, as you can see," the Brown Oligarch said.

Dylan snapped out of his daydream and had a fleeting glance of a table laden with food. It faded out of existence, leaving only the blank cave wall. "That's amazing!" he exclaimed.

"It can be entertaining, especially if I ask people to imagine something embarrassing."

Dylan reacted by trying not to think of anything, but his mind betrayed him and conjured up an embarrassing thought.

"That's funny," the Brown Oligarch said, nodding at the image that had appeared. "Most people think of themselves naked instead."

"Really?" he gritted between his teeth, willing the image of himself using the outhouse to fade as quickly as it had appeared.

"Down to business," Lucile chuckled. "Why don't you start from the beginning?"

Glad to change topics, Dylan wondered where to begin.

"I suppose it all began when we were staying with the Yellow Oligarch," he said. Images filled the space before them. He and Kio were running down the spiral staircase to discover the source of the disturbance. His heart ached momentarily at the sight of the cat. He wished they were still together. Kio would love this.

The wyvern crushed what was supposed to be Krale's head. Lucile didn't seem perturbed by the gore. Instead she stood and walked to the image to get a better look. "Too young to be

Yellow," she said as she pointed at the corpse's exposed arms. "Unless his son has recently taken over."

Dylan was shocked that she so quickly saw what he had missed, but focused on continuing his tale. He watched with fascination as he plummeted from the windmill and sped toward the waters. The images then faded to black.

"How am I able to see all this from outside my perspective?"

The Brown Oligarch shrugged. "It's how you choose to remember it. What we are seeing isn't a perfect recollection. Hindsight, contrary to popular opinion, is never perfect."

The next memory was of Dylan accepting the blue loka and then traveling to meet Tyjinn. Lucile observed their journey to the Purple Oligarch without comment, expressing neither surprise nor disdain at his death.

Dylan's mind leapt to the campfire where Tyjinn had first confessed his feelings. He wished he could step inside the image, take over from his past self, leap over that fire and kiss Tyjinn. They would then be together during the desert trip and perhaps everything in the garden would have played out differently.

"Which of those scenarios were true?" Lucile asked.

Dylan realized that both reality and his desire had taken visual form. "I never got a chance to tell him," he answered. "You aren't surprised about us?"

Lucile's tone was compassionate. "You aren't the only two to discover such a love."

The desert journey passed in a blur, as did the time spent with the Empress, since Dylan rushed to the part where Tyjinn first kissed him. His heart beat twice as hard now, both with passion and his fear of revealing what had come next. The images froze in place. Did he want another person, especially another Oligarch, to know that Tyjinn had attempted to kill the Empress?

In the end, he decided to divulge the full truth. Orbsen had sent him here for a reason. The Brown Oligarch might know how to stop Krale or what Dylan should do next. She was silent through the rest of the retelling, impassive except when he entered the land of the gods through the Cradle. This part of the story enraptured her, her face exposing surprise and wonder.

"And then I ended up here," he finished as the image of him on the mountain range faded into neutral brown light. "So what do you think?"

"About what?" Lucile asked as if she were surprised she should have an opinion.

"Well, about all of it," he said. "What do you think I should do?"

"I suppose you mean in reference to putting an end to Krale and his plans." She leaned back in her chair and considered him. "To be quite honest, I don't have anything to worry about."

"Nothing to worry about? Krale is picking us off one by one!"

Lucile shrugged. "He'll never be able to reach me here."

"What about—what was it you said? Lizard men and elementals or something?"

"Fair enough," Lucile nodded. "But even if he did find me, I could teleport away the second I saw him. I could teleport so far away that it would take months, if not years, for him to locate me again."

"Even in your sleep?" Dylan said.

"My, my, don't you have a morbid imagination?" Lucile regarded the image that accompanied his thoughts. It was of an old lady sleeping peacefully while a multitude of monsters crawled through the window. "I don't actually have a window by my bed, but it would be nice."

"Look, maybe you are safe, but what about the others?" Dylan pleaded. "Aren't you at all concerned about them?"

"You'll probably think me cruel for saying this, but I'm really not." The Brown Oligarch put her hand companionably over his in a gesture completely opposite from her words. "Have you asked yourself why I live so far away from the rest of the world?"

He hadn't had much time to wonder, so he shook his head.

"I'm not much of a people-person on the best of days. I prefer to be alone with my thoughts, but considering how many I have, I'm in good company. As for the Oligarchs, I've never been able to stand the lot of them. Half are mad with power, the other half would do anything to gain more."

"Present company excluded, I'm sure," Dylan muttered.

Lucile narrowed her eyes but shrugged a moment later. "Perhaps I have become just as crazy as the rest of them. That doesn't mean that I'm willing to get involved. Nor should you. Do you really care that Purple had his power taken from him, no matter how harsh the methods?"

Dylan had to admit he didn't. From what he saw of

Purple's treatment of the animals, the man had gotten what he deserved. But it would have been better if someone had taken away his power by other means and begun helping the animals immediately. Instead their suffering had grown worse without the meager care he had provided them.

"You may think my neutrality self-serving," Lucile continued, "but aren't your own desires just as selfish? You want to save the Empress, but ask yourself, are you more concerned with saving her life or absolving Tyjinn of his guilt?"

She had him there. His excitement at hearing that the Empress was alive *had* been because Tyjinn could go back to being his old self. But it wasn't as simple as that. He found much to like in the Empress. Sure she basked in the glory of her own status, but she also played hostess to countless people and asked nothing in return. Without her, the wonderful desert garden would return to sand.

"The blue loka," the Brown Oligarch said. "Krale has promised to leave you alone, and yet you mean to risk your life to take it back from him. Like all Oligarchs, you have become addicted to your own power."

True, Dylan felt obligated to take the loka back, but he didn't want to keep it. His father was the real Blue Oligarch. He just wanted this whole affair to end so he could go back to being Dylan and not a mostly incompetent Oligarch. If Brown wasn't willing to help him, he wasn't going to beg or force her to see things his way.

"Look, I don't have to explain myself to you," he said angrily. "Just tell me how to get home, and I'll leave you alone."

Lucile didn't respond. She was staring straight ahead at a wavering image. Dylan looked and saw himself handing the blue loka back to his father. He had forgotten that his thoughts were still being broadcast by the brown loka. He blushed with the revelation.

"You don't have to explain yourself," she said. "You genuinely care about others. To be honest, I wish you felt otherwise. It would have made my decision much easier."

"Will you help me?" he asked. "Please?"

Lucile thought for some time, probably longer than someone with her power needed to, but in the end she nodded. "I think I can assist you without becoming directly involved, if only to satisfy my own curiosity."

Dylan smiled. He had a feeling the Brown Oligarch wasn't quite as cold-hearted as she liked to portray herself.

"Let's run through it once more, slower this time."

Dylan groaned. Twice now, the Brown Oligarch had made him remember his desert scrying attempt. She pored over it obsessively, trying to discern the meaning in the images as Dylan automatically reviewed it in his mind, causing the images to play out again in front of him.

He felt oddly proud of the vision. He hadn't realized before, but he had accurately predicted the future. The Yellow Oligarch had first taken purple, the yellow clouds and purple birds merging symbolically before they moved to green. The jungle was taken next, partially due to the red flames. All four colors were then mixed into one as Krale claimed the lokas for himself. Next blue was taken, rather effortlessly, he had to admit. What followed was just as unclear as the first time he experienced it. A variety of colors paraded onto the battlefield, but before he could focus on them, gray bled through the images like ink soaking through white cloth.

"Sorry," Dylan said as the gray faded into the strange brown light of Lucile's magic.

"No matter. I feel we still have learned something important." The Brown Oligarch pursed her lips. "Power, when assigned to one individual, can change hands very quickly. Whoever is able to wrest it from the current holder inherits it in addition to what they already possess. We know there will be a war of magics, one that ends with a single color."

"You mean Gray, as in the Oligarch?"

Lucile nodded, causing Dylan's stomach to churn nervously. What sort of Oligarch could stand against Krale's amassed powers so effortlessly?

"Of course my interpretation may be incorrect. The best course of action would be to prevent the war from coming to pass."

"Which brings us back to stopping Krale," Dylan sighed. "Any ideas?"

"Yes. Arrange a meeting with him."

Dylan laughed before he could stop himself. Arrange a

meeting with Krale? Ridiculous! Maybe they could share a polite drink at a tavern before brawling with chairs and mugs.

"What's your plan then?" Lucile challenged him. "Do you know where to find him?"

Dylan had to admit that he didn't. With the strange exit policy of the Cradle, Krale's god could have put him down anywhere beneficial to him. He was probably sent to kill another Oligarch and steal their loka, but which one? They could travel to the remaining Oligarchs immediately, staying only momentarily to search for any sign of Krale. He suggested as much to his hostess.

She shook her head. "It won't be as easy to visit them as you might imagine. We could try, if you insist, but I don't recommend it."

"How does your plan work, then?" he asked.

"We name a time and a place for him to meet us and confront him there with as much support as you can muster in the meantime."

He nodded. They couldn't take action against Krale if they couldn't find him. The Brown Oligarch had surely thought this out thoroughly using her magic. Dylan only saw one flaw with the plan.

"How can we contact him if we don't know where he is?"

"Easily enough, I imagine. Krale used to be the telepathic link for the entire Oligarchy. When he 'died' he made sure to sever that link to further his illusion, but I suspect the old methods still function. Whether he responds is another matter. Just a moment."

The Brown Oligarch left him alone. With nothing to do, he conjured up more memories, starting with Kio and then his father and Ada. Dylan felt homesick. He had spent so long wanting to get away from the world he knew, but now he would give almost anything to be back there again.

When Lucile returned, she was holding a slim yellow wand. Dylan's father owned one as well. They were used to contact the Yellow Oligarch telepathically when he was still the hub of communication.

"I'll use my magic so you can hear what he and I are conversing about." Without further explanation, Lucile closed her eyes in concentration.

"Krale," she said, her mouth not moving. Dylan realized he was hearing her voice from the brown light that had previously played back his memories. "Krale, it's Lucile," she continued. "Jack's son is here and has explained everything to me, so there's no sense in pretending."

"I wouldn't dare," Krale's voice replied, sounding so near that Dylan cast a nervous look around the room. "What can I do for you?"

"The boy wants a meeting."

"I have no doubt that he does." Krale chuckled. "Unfortunately I'm quite done with him and his friends. You know, why don't we talk about this in person?"

"A rather dubious request," Lucile replied.

"You can bring the boy along if you like."

"He'd rather meet you in three days."

"Now *that's* dubious," Krale said with good humor. "You have the power to bring him to me now, but he wants three days to—oh, I don't know—rally some reinforcements? The remainder of the Oligarchy perhaps?"

Dylan began to sweat. Krale was no fool.

"You can hardly expect him to meet you defenseless," Lucile said reproachfully.

This remark was met with silence, enough that it appeared Krale had finished with them. Eventually, a response did come. "Very well. Three days time. Where?"

"My home," Dylan said impulsively.

"His home, the tower of the Blue Oligarch." Lucile opened an eye and looked at him inquisitively. He nodded to let her know that she was correct.

"The *former* Blue Oligarch, but very well. Three days from now at noon."

Lucile set the yellow wand on her lap. They sat in silence for a moment, considering what had transpired. "We teleport first to Black," she said. "With his power we could end this whole mess in an instant."

As good as that sounded, only one thing sounded more appealing to Dylan. "I'm starving," he said apologetically.

"Very well, then," the Brown Oligarch sighed. "First you eat, then you save the world."

Chapter 19
Black

Two moons glared through an overcast sky, dark clouds occasionally obscuring them in their sluggish journey across the heavens. Dylan shivered and regarded the clouds warily. Were they heavy with rain or snow? Even during the summer, icy weather was possible in the northern Steeplands.

Behind them lay a deep valley, ringed on all sides by mountains. Unlike the southern continent they had teleported from, the mountains here were hulking giants; clung to by stubborn trees. Steep gray stone rose triumphantly above these forests, blocky and serrated. The great bowl they circled was filled with forests, farmland, and two villages.

Ahead of them was the castle of the Black Oligarch, pressed between two forbidding mountains, as if the castle had shoved the twin peaks aside before settling down for all eternity. Every wall was topped with spikes, every window protected by bars. Alert soldiers manned each tower and walkway. Dylan felt a dozen or more pairs of eyes on him and shivered from more than just the cold. He remembered the Brown Oligarch and turned to find her standing behind him, suddenly thankful he wasn't alone.

"It doesn't look like the friendliest of places," he said, failing to conjure some humor into his voice.

Lucile shrugged. "These are dangerous times. At least I'm sure that's what the mind behind this place will claim. There's nothing that invites war more than preparing to defend against one."

"Let's get to it then," Dylan said, stepping toward the portcullis and its dual guardhouses.

"Best of luck," Lucile said, not following him. "You'll find me here shortly after sunrise, should you need me."

He whirled around to face her. "You're leaving me?"

She nodded. "You may have convinced me to help you, but I still have no desire to become more involved than I already am."

Brown light swept her away before he could argue. Dylan sighed and looked back toward his goal. If the fortress appeared intimidating before, it was positively daunting now. He decided to approach the gates before his loitering attracted suspicion. As he walked, he tried thinking of a plan, but none came. He was going to have to wing it.

Two guards awaited him. The first looked brutal. He was squat, sported an uneven mustache, a prodigious beer belly, and managed to swagger while standing in place. This man was clearly eager for distraction and a chance to flaunt his authority. The other guard was his opposite. His thin frame and hunched posture showed he was interested only in doing as little work as possible.

Dylan instinctively wanted to head toward the lanky guard, but knew this tactic would fail. Instead he headed directly to the aggressive guard, putting on a haughty air.

"Inform the Black Oligarch that I am here to see him," he said, adding extra emphasis on the "I" in the hopes of trumpeting his self-importance.

"And who are you?" the guard sneered, his beady eyes twinkling with amusement.

Dylan recoiled dramatically from this question before replying, "I'm the Blue Oligarch, you impudent slob!"

The grin slid off the guard's face and was replaced by a grimace. "You don't look like an Oligarch," he growled, putting a hand on his sword. "You look more like a runt with barely enough meat on his bones to be called a man."

"Don't provide me with the motive to prove my power to you," Dylan said with a tone that belied the fear in his belly.

The guard was unimpressed. "Show me your loka," he demanded.

"I won't take orders from the likes of you!"

The guard gave a bark of laughter. "I have full authority from the Blacksmith himself to deal with intruders in any way I see fit. Oligarchs included."

Dylan obviously wasn't going to get anywhere with him. He wished he still had the blue loka so he could make this obnoxious guard eat his words. He did have some blue magic at his disposal, but not enough to protect him against a sword. Still, it might be useful. Channeling his anger, he sent a small ball of water splashing into the other guard's face, shocking him into alertness.

"Inform your master that I am here," Dylan commanded. "I want him to know how I've been treated by your colleague."

The thin man started toward the gates, but stopped for confirmation from the other guard.

"Bring the overseer here," the big man snarled. "He'll sort this idiot out soon enough."

The thin guard scurried away, leaving Dylan alone with the brute. The next ten minutes passed awkwardly for him. Annoyingly, the guard didn't take any discomfort from the situation and spent his time staring directly at Dylan, occasionally spitting close to his feet. Dylan felt he should act offended, but was too preoccupied with trying not to shiver. He still wore shorts and a thin shirt, when he should have been in trousers and a jacket.

After an excruciatingly long wait, a small door in the gates opened and a lean man in military uniform stepped out. He looked tired. His dark hair was heavily speckled with gray, his face lined. He took one look at Dylan, and his weary features became more so.

"Rufus," the man said, extending a calloused and scarred hand.

Dylan shook it while wondering how to proceed. He wasn't about to try the same haughty act that he had with the guard, knowing this man would respond poorly to such treatment. "Dylan, acting Blue Oligarch," he said evenly.

"Acting, eh? Well that explains the age. You'd better come in." Rufus extended an arm toward the door. Dylan shot the guard a satisfied look as he walked by.

Just beyond the gates was a large, open courtyard devoid of frivolous decoration. The only items visible were of a practical nature. Wagons, tools, firewood… and roughly one hundred soldiers, all armored and bristling with weapons. The troops paid no attention to Rufus and Dylan as they passed. The soldiers were listening to a speech given by an officer of some sort. From the sound of his oration, they were on the verge of heading out on a campaign.

Dylan was led to a small building that had probably once been a stable, but was now an office and living quarters. The interior was charming, in a rustic sort of way, with oil lamps casting a cozy glow. Without this warm light, the room would have appeared as bare and practical as the courtyard outside.

Rufus motioned him toward a large oak desk, cluttered with scrolls and maps, and took a seat. Dylan sat across from him and waited. The man's questions never came, meaning that he was expected to begin.

"I apologize for the suddenness of my appearance," Dylan said, trying to sound diplomatic, "but I'm afraid I have some bad news." Rufus gestured for him to continue, but looked impatient, so he decided to be as direct as possible. "There's a renegade member of the Oligarchy who is killing the others in a bid for power. The Black Oligarch's life is in danger."

"Where are you from?" the officer asked.

"The Lakelands," Dylan answered after a surprised pause. Had the man not heard him?

"How did you get here? My scouts should have picked you up before you reached the pass."

"Teleportation," he answered.

Rufus wrote something down and sighed. "Well, I thank you for your concern. Will you be teleporting back to your home? If not, you will need a pass."

"But the Black Oligarch—"

"I'll deliver your message to him."

"You don't seem very concerned," Dylan said, his frustration growing.

"About the Black Oligarch's life?" The shadow of a smile crossed the officer's face. "I'm not concerned in the slightest."

"I'd like to speak to him myself," Dylan said firmly.

"That's not possible," Rufus said. "Not just anyone can barge in here and meet the Blacksmith. If that were possible, I'd be a lot more concerned about him. Not for his safety, but for his state of mind."

"I see," Dylan said in a strained voice. Obviously he wasn't going to be granted permission to see the Oligarch. He would have to find a way to see Black on his own. "Well, I still need a place to stay. I can't teleport myself, you see, and the person who brought me here won't return until morning."

Rufus regarded him steadily. "Right, well, I'll just set you up in an unguarded room for the night and answer a few casually placed questions as to the Blacksmith's whereabouts. Then I'll leave you to it, shall I?" The sarcasm left his voice. "That army outside is about to embark on a campaign so important and confidential that I should kill you just for seeing them. I have a battalion returning in the morning that is going to need medical care, food, and rest, in that order. I know you mean well, but we're aware of what's happening in the south. The Yellow Oligarch has picked off a few easy targets, sending people like your father into hiding, and the rest of the Oligarchy into fits over someone having more power than they do. Should Yellow show up here, we'll kill him and send his lokas back so you can all squabble over who gets what. Until then, we have more pressing matters to attend to. Understood?"

Dylan nodded, defeated. He didn't know what to say. He was surprised that they were equally well informed and apathetic about the situation. Maybe he should leave after all.

"I can set a tent and some warm bedding for you outside the fortress. You'll be safe there, and if you should need—"

A roar interrupted Rufus. At first Dylan thought it was from another of Krale's possessed beasts, but he soon realized the sound was cheering from the soldiers outside. He couldn't imagine what they were so happy about, unless their leader had decided to pay them a visit before they marched to battle. Dylan stood so suddenly he knocked his chair over and reached the door before Rufus started shouting.

Bursting into the courtyard, he saw that the soldiers were all facing away from him and toward the center of the fortress. Dylan darted to the right, hoping to circle around the soldiers to see where the Black Oligarch was. He reached the end of their formation and turned the corner they formed, aware they would see him. The soldiers let out another cheer, startling him.

Far ahead and in front of the battalions, he saw a brawny man dressed in a heavy black apron turning to walk away. Dylan increased his speed and shouted for his attention.

"Stop him!" Rufus shouted from behind.

Every soldier turned to look at him, but so did the Black Oligarch.

"I need to talk to you," Dylan shouted before a foot shot out and tripped him, sending him face first onto the ground. He lifted his head just as the hilt of a sword came down. He barely had time to register the pain before losing consciousness.

A hammer was pounding, both inside and outside his head. Dylan winced as he opened his eyes and discovered a blacksmith's workshop. He was feverishly hot, but this was because of the huge furnace across the room. A large burly man with his back to him was hammering a piece of metal on his anvil.

Dylan sat up as silently as possible. He wasn't tied up and didn't see anyone guarding him. He glanced down at the furs and pillows arranged around him. Obviously some attempt had been made to keep him comfortable. This was a good sign. Now if only the loud hammering would stop echoing the throbbing in his skull.

He waited for a brief pause between hammer swings to speak. "I'm awake," he said in a croaking voice.

The Blacksmith turned to face him with a hammer and soon-to-be sword still in his hands. He had a wide expressive face and a completely bald head. His massive square jaw was heavily fortified with black stubble that matched his thick eyebrows.

"All right then?" he asked gruffly.

"Yeah, just no more hammering. Please."

The Blacksmith held up the unfinished sword. A shadow

exploded into existence, enveloping the hot metal and bathing it in darkness. When the black light disappeared, it revealed a perfectly formed, sharp, shining blade. The Blacksmith regarded it critically.

"So that's your magic?" Dylan asked as he pulled himself gingerly to his feet. "Manipulating metal?"

"Metal, stone, any of the lifeless elements. You're Jack's boy?"

Dylan nodded, sending a wave of dizziness through his body.

"He's a good man, Jack is. Met him once, many years ago." The Black Oligarch scratched his chin thoughtfully. "Can't say that he and I have the same philosophy, but I found him respectable."

Previously Dylan would have found this comment encouraging, but it was too similar to what Krale had said. Apparently respecting someone else's philosophy didn't rule out waging war against them.

"We searched you while you were out," the Blacksmith added. "Didn't find the blue loka."

"Yes, well, someone is going around helping himself to everyone's lokas, as you apparently already know."

The Black Oligarch shrugged. "It's not the first time, and it won't be the last. Mighty kind of you to come all this way just to warn me. It wasn't necessary with all my informants, but without your father around, I suppose you couldn't have known that."

For someone who knew so much about what was happening in other lands, the Blacksmith seemed oblivious to his people's apathy for his well-being.

"Your life is in danger; not that Rufus seems to care," Dylan said, hoping for a reaction of surprise but not getting one.

"Rufus is a practical man." The Blacksmith began rubbing oil onto the blade he had just completed. "He knows I have more important things to worry about."

"Like what?" Dylan asked.

"Like seven infestations of corpse sludge, all within riding distance," was the angry response. "The Steeplands are being taken over by the stuff, with me and my men the only resistance. Not to mention another village full of bandits who have taken advantage of the chaos."

Dylan had no idea what corpse sludge was, but obviously it was some sort of combatant or soldiers and swords wouldn't be needed. "You won't be much use to anyone dead," he pointed out.

The Black Oligarch stopped his work and regarded him before shaking his head. "I can't be killed."

"That's a little optimistic."

"It's the truth. Death is my magic. I won't be dying unless it's on my own terms. The Yellow Oligarch can come here and do his worst, and it won't make a difference. I'm as impervious to magic and weapons as any stone is."

Dylan didn't find this analogy effective since he had witnessed Tyjinn reduce a stone floor to molten lava, but the point was made—and complicated things. The Black Oligarch had much less to lose if his life wasn't at stake. An army was even there to defend his people, should Black's magic fail. That raised another question.

"If death is your domain, why the ongoing battle with corpse sludge? Why not just use your magic to kill them and be done with it?"

"I know what you're getting at." The Blacksmith strode closer to Dylan and crossed his arms over his considerable chest. "You're wondering why I can't just use my magic to kill Yellow and solve all your problems."

"Well, yeah."

"I'm going for a ride," the Blacksmith said. "This is all starting to remind me of one of those intolerable meetings the Oligarchy is so fond of. Instead of taking action, they just want to talk about it the whole damned day. You can join me if you like."

Dylan didn't see that he had much choice.

The two horses were just as brawny as the blacksmith himself. Dylan's steed had a torso so wide that he felt as if he were doing the splits while seated in the saddle. He became more uncomfortable as they rode, but at least he was no longer freezing, thanks to the loaned cloak and trousers he was wearing. The thick forest they galloped through obscured the moonlight, shrouding them in darkness, but the horse seemed to know its way along the road.

The woods eventually gave way to open land, a farmhouse appearing on the horizon. The Blacksmith slowed as they approached, stopping his horse before they reached the house.

He dismounted and helped Dylan do the same after realizing the younger man didn't know how. The people of the Lakelands relied solely on boats for transportation, using horses only for pulling carts and doing farm work.

The Blacksmith hooked his thumbs in his apron and surveyed their surroundings. "This valley and the two neighboring it used to belong to the Buggane. You know of them?"

Dylan nodded. He had only heard of Buggane in legend. He knew they were humanoid, had sickly transparent skin, and a vicious appetite for human flesh. Especially babies. Buggane were intelligent enough to be effective thieves, sometimes even magicians. They used any skill at their disposal to mercilessly plunder and kill.

"My ancestors came here and fought for this land, more of them dying than living."

"Why didn't they just go somewhere else?" Dylan grumbled.

"Because they saw the same potential here that the Buggane did. They took this valley first and blocked off the pass, building a small fortress where the current castle now stands. Over generations they continued to fight—in addition to life's daily struggles—until the last Buggane was purged from the Steeplands."

The Blacksmith was clearly inspired by his history, and as much as Dylan could appreciate that, he didn't see what it had to do with him. His skepticism must have been obvious because the Black Oligarch explained further.

"In truth, this land belongs to no creature; not man, or Buggane. We fought for possession of it, and should a more powerful race come and do the same, then the land will pass to them."

Dylan finally saw where this was leading. Krale fought for the lokas and won, and in the Blacksmith's philosophy, this made him the rightful owner. "I'm asking you to join such a fight," Dylan pleaded. "Krale is just as ruthless and conniving as any Buggane. All we want is to return the lokas to kinder hands."

The Blacksmith shook his head. "You misunderstand me. I haven't yet made my point. Come."

They stopped to tie the horses to a scrawny tree before proceeding. Instead of approaching the house directly, the Blacksmith led them toward a barn on the left. He held a finger to his lips as they neared. At the side of the building the Blacksmith pointed out a small hole in the wood, just large enough to look through, which he did. Then he stood aside and motioned for Dylan to do the same.

Dylan felt like he was about to see a peep show as he bent down to peer inside the barn. At first the darkness made seeing difficult, but he could smell something foul, like rotting meat. The interior of the barn was cloaked in shadows. He realized with a start that the shadows on the ground were shifting and moving. He could hear a wet, squishing noise, and see faint light reflecting off the surface of the black things.

The Blacksmith placed his hand on Dylan's shoulder and led him a short distance away. "If you could see the cow in there, you'd be sick."

"I didn't see anything except, I don't know, it was like black slime I think."

"That's close enough," the Black Oligarch said. "We call it corpse sludge. Ever heard of it?"

Dylan shook his head.

"Nasty stuff. It gets inside of you. One touch on your skin paralyzes you. Once you are helpless, it seeps into your body through your nose, ears, even straight through your skin. After that, you don't live much longer. We hope."

"What do you mean?"

"You sure you didn't see that cow?" the Blacksmith pressed.

"I didn't."

"Well, come on, I have to do this anyway." The Black Oligarch crept back toward the main house with Dylan in tow. To see such a large and capable man act as cautious as a rabbit surrounded by wolves was disconcerting.

When they reached the front door of the house, the Blacksmith took an old iron key out of his pocket and placed it in the lock. "I should have done this weeks ago," he whispered. "I just didn't have the heart."

Dylan nodded, even though he didn't understand. The Black Oligarch struggled with a lamp. Once the light flared, a large room was revealed, one with the sole purpose of receiving guests and providing access to the wooden stairway and long balustrade above. Up these stairs they went, the Blacksmith once again placing a finger to his lips. He led the way to a door at the end of the hallway where he used his tinderbox to light another lamp.

"Stay and watch from here," he whispered so quietly that Dylan could barely hear him. "Don't come in."

He used a smaller key to unlock this door and drew his sword before flinging the door wide open. "Stay back!" he shouted as he charged into the room.

Dylan's first impression was a floor covered in black goo. The Black Oligarch stormed through it, sending great puddles flying wherever he trod. The slime reacted instantly, rising up and wrapping around his legs, but had no paralyzing effect on the Blacksmith. The big man continued his exploration of the room, running back and forth in search of something.

Abruptly a different shape filled the doorway—a man of similar size to the Black Oligarch, but quite clearly dead. Large clumps of his flesh were missing, as was most of his hair and an eye. Black sludge dripped from the empty socket.

Dylan stumbled backward, terrified of the apparition and wishing that he had been given a sword. Then he did the only thing he could think of—he screamed.

"Richard!" the Black Oligarch bellowed. The walking corpse turned away from Dylan. A moment later a gleaming blade erupted from the back of the zombie's head. The sword withdrew but soon returned, striking a blow from the side, severing the neck from the head. Dylan leapt back just in time, the head narrowly missing him before it landed with a wet smack. The remaining body swayed before falling forward, revealing the Black Oligarch with his teeth bared like a rabid animal.

"Be free, my cousin," he growled, his eyes wild and distant. Slowly they regained focus and he glanced around, as if surprised by the strange surroundings. "Are you all right? None of it got on you?" he asked Dylan, who checked himself and shook his head. "Good, get out of here. Wait out front; I'll join you."

The Black Oligarch lifted the lamp from the wall and threw it into the room, sending flaming oil spilling across the floor. Then he stepped directly into the fire, turned, and glared angrily at Dylan for not yet retreating. That was all it took. Dylan spun around and raced from the house.

Dylan collapsed on the front lawn, sucking in the cool night air in great gulps. He looked back at the house and saw flames flickering in the upper windows, but no sign of the Black

Oligarch. He was beginning to wonder if the man was really as unkillable as he claimed, when the Blacksmith came striding out of the house. His clothes had been almost completely burned off his body, leaving only the collar of his shirt and enough trousers to remain dignified. The pants were charred and smoking, but the man's skin was unblemished and unharmed.

"It's the only way to get the stuff off," he said as he neared. Dylan offered his cloak but the big man shook his head. "Sweet gods, he responded to his name!"

The Black Oligarch was clearly shaken, but Dylan didn't know what to say. "At least he's free now," he attempted.

"Yes. Come, let's deal with the barn." The Blacksmith returned to the porch where he had placed another of the oil lamps.

Dylan kept his distance as the Blacksmith opened the barn door and threw the lamp inside. Silhouetted by the fire, his brawny shoulders shook. From a distance it could have been mistaken for manic laughter, but Dylan knew he was sobbing. He wondered why the Oligarch had waited until this night to finally dispatch his cousin. He didn't know the effects of corpse sludge, but as far gone as his cousin was, Dylan guessed he had been infected for quite some time. The Blacksmith could have sent his soldiers to burn the buildings down, but had probably wanted to do it himself. Perhaps he didn't want to do it alone, but also didn't want to appear weak in front of his men.

The Black Oligarch turned, all signs of vulnerability gone from his face as he strode toward Dylan. "This is why!" He gestured to the devastation behind him. "This is the reason I won't join your fight."

"I know you have your hands full—" Dylan began, but the Oligarch interrupted him.

"When I first told you how my ancestors fought for this land, you said they should have gone elsewhere. I agree with you! They secured the first valley and spilled ten times as much blood trying to take the other two, but they never could. Not until the Black Oligarch came to them."

The Blacksmith winced as if in pain before continuing. "He used the magic of the black loka to slaughter the remaining Buggane and was revered as a god for his genocide. Do you know where they say corpse sludge comes from?"

Dylan shook his head, feeling intimidated by the intensity of the other man's speech.

"From the bodies of Buggane, the marrow from their rotten bones seeping into the earth. The greatest concentration of corpse sludge pools at their mass graves. If that's not evidence enough for you, my magic is ineffective against them. The black loka helped create them! Do you see? Corpse sludge was created through our madness!"

"I'm not asking you to wipe out an entire race," Dylan said carefully. "All I'm asking you is to stand against one man, to help me find a way to stop him. We don't even have to kill him, but if we don't do something, he will kill again."

"And who will fill his shoes?" the Blacksmith demanded. "Who will be the next Yellow Oligarch? Who will replace Purple or Green for that matter? How do you know that they won't be twice as bad as Krale? Like the Buggane, we thought we had seen the worst, but no! You cannot know a man completely, and the next Oligarch to come along may want more than just power."

Dylan gritted his teeth. "What good are you then?" he shouted. "Give me the damn loka if you don't have the guts to use it."

For one crazy moment it looked as though the Blacksmith was going to do just that. His eyes were wide, almost hopeful before returning to their previous determination.

"Look," Dylan said, "I'm sorry your ancestors messed things up, but I'm sure your predecessor was only trying to help. At least he was man enough to take action instead of sniveling over the mistakes of the past."

The Black Oligarch backhanded him, spinning him around and knocking him to the ground. "I was that man!" the Blacksmith shouted. "Five hundred years ago I was the one to slaughter the Buggane! I've lived long enough to see the result of my actions! You are nothing more than a child in my eyes, playing at games beyond your comprehension. If what you saw tonight won't convince you, then I pray you live long enough to be haunted by the very ghosts you create."

The Black Oligarch strode to the horses. Dylan called after him, apologizing and begging him to stay, but the man wouldn't listen. He mounted his horse, took the reigns of the other, and disappeared into the night.

Chapter 20
White

Dylan took nearly two hours to walk back to the Black Oligarch's castle. For most of this time, he was occupied with quelling his own imagination, images of corpse sludge spurring him on. Passing through the pitch-black woods near the farmhouse was the worst. Normally innocuous noises, such as the foraging of woodland animals, became stalking monsters in his mind.

Dylan forced his thoughts to another subject: the Black Oligarch, an immortal man hounded by his own history. How long had he lived, and how much longer would he continue trying to set things right? Did Tyjinn feel equally tortured by his actions? If there was anything Dylan could do to make either man forgive himself, he would do it, but try as he might the solution evaded him. Weary, both physically and mentally, all Dylan wanted was to meet with Lucile and teleport somewhere more familiar.

The sun was beginning to rise when he reached the fortress. To his relief, the Brown Oligarch was waiting for him. He didn't bother with any formal greeting. Instead he asked her to bring him somewhere he could sleep, which she did. He didn't know where they went, only that it was dark and had a bed.

When he awoke, the room was as dark as it had been when he arrived. He lay in bed until the Brown Oligarch reappeared, asking her then to take him somewhere to bathe. She teleported them to a landscape of massive rocks that held pools of steaming, bubbling water and left him there to soak in comfort. Dylan thanked her profusely for her kindness and patience when she returned. She didn't believe in his cause, and yet she continued to support him.

Their next goal was the home of the White Oligarch. Lucile took him by the arm, and after a syrupy swirl of brown light and the lurching of his stomach, their surroundings changed.

Lush green grass blanketed gently rolling hills. Friendly puffs of white cloud sailed idly through a cerulean sky, as trees sighed and waved in the light summer breeze. Dylan breathed in happily. They were still in the Steeplands, but much further south and closer to home.

A large village was within walking distance, but the old rickety house in front of them was much more interesting. Its dull white paint was beginning to peel. The wooden poles supporting the large wrap-around porch were painted with festive stripes that had faded into a dreary reminder of happier times.

The first floor was fairly conventional, no more than a large rectangle supporting the upper floor. The second story went wild with rounded towers, bulging windows, narrow balconies, and arched gables. The roof was just traditional enough to make the mess below look somewhat respectable.

"I will meet you here in two days time," Lucile said.

"Two days?"

"You'll need time to convince the White Oligarch, and frankly, I don't know where to find any of the other Oligarchs. This is your last chance to recruit an ally."

Before Dylan even had a chance to reply, she was gone.

Glancing at the porch, he steeled himself, taking solace in having no guards to contend with this time. He crossed the lawn and climbed the worn, wooden stairs. A rope was hanging next to the door, so he pulled it a few times, causing a bell to sound in the distance.

The door opened almost instantly, revealing one of the most aloof-looking men Dylan had ever seen. His face was long and pinched, the nostrils of his hawk-like nose flaring in distaste as he looked upon his visitor. The powdered wig on his head was just as pale as his skin. He wore a starchy red coat with a high collar and two long coattails that almost reached the floor. The man's black pants poofed out bizarrely at the waist, but were otherwise tight on his skinny legs. His dusty clothing, like the wig, had been out of style for several centuries.

Dylan was about to introduce himself when the man's frown deepened. "Well?" he demanded. "I suppose you feel guilty and have brought it back? Well, have you? Let's see it, you filthy urchin!"

"Sorry," Dylan stammered. "I'm just—"

"A thief! I know what you are!" The man stomped once for emphasis. "The bag is no good to the likes of you. Is it money you want? You won't have it! Now give it back to me!" A hand was thrust out expectantly.

"Look, could you just summon your master?"

"My *what?*" The expression on his scandalized face turned to pure surprise as he noticed something over Dylan's shoulder. "Oh, dear heavens!"

Dylan turned and saw a cloud in the sky, a rather large one that hung much too low. The cloud continued descending as it blew toward them at a startling rate.

"Inside, inside!" the pale man hissed.

Dylan didn't need to be told twice. Fearing that Krale's magic had found him, he darted into the house. He had the briefest impression of walls lined with red fabric, vases on pedestals, and large paintings of stuffy gentlemen or buxom women, before the agitated man ushered him into an adjoining room. He was led to a window where they both squatted on the floor and peered out the window, like children waiting for their father to come home.

The cloud, much closer now, hovered mere feet above the ground. Dwarfing the house they were in, it halted before lowering the rest of the way to the ground. As it made contact, a thud shook the house to the very foundations.

"What is it?" Dylan whispered.

"I haven't the slightest," the man answered. "Maybe the thieves who stole my bag?"

"I sure didn't," Dylan said.

"No, perhaps you didn't." The man tore his eyes away from the window to look at him. "I'm Crimson Barry," he said, extending a hand. "The White Oligarch."

"Oh!" Dylan exclaimed, embarrassed about his earlier comment. He hastily took Barry's hand and introduced himself.

"The son of Blue, eh?" Barry nodded appreciatively. "How is old Zane?"

"He was my grandfather. He died some time ago." Nearly twenty-five years now! Dylan tried to return his attention to the window, but another voice sounded from behind.

"Are you playing hide and seek?" This was said by a little boy, no more than five years old.

"Your grandson?" Dylan asked Barry.

"Gods no! Just another ghost. Scram, you little brat!"

"I don't wanna!" the child cried.

"What's going on in here?" This time a rather rotund lady spoke. Dylan swore she hadn't been there a second ago. "Have you looked out the window, Barry? Something strange is happening."

"Who's the new boy?" croaked an old man who somehow had managed to creep up on Dylan.

"He's not one of us," the White Oligarch said testily.

"Look at the cloud!" the child shouted in awe, pointing out the window.

A dark-haired boy of Dylan's age floated into the room and began speaking in a language he couldn't understand.

"He looks like he could be dead," the old man said skeptically, prodding Dylan experimentally.

"I wanna ride it!" the child demanded.

"I don't like the look of it," the fat woman said worriedly.

"Probably will be dead sooner than later," the old man insisted.

"Quiet!" Barry shouted. "Zandy, go get Natasha. We may be needing her. The rest of you, *out!*"

The last word carried weight, causing all but the fat woman to instantly disappear. Zandy hovered off the floor and rose directly up, passing through the ceiling and disappearing.

"Welcome to the ghost house," Barry muttered.

Crimson Barry spent a few minutes explaining his home to Dylan. The ghost house was a space in neither the physical world, nor in the spiritual. He claimed it was the only place in the entire world where ghosts once again became solid, if they wished, and where the living could become insubstantial if their minds were open enough. Both space and time functioned differently in the house. The number of rooms was at times uncountable and at others severely limited. Likewise, it was possible to stay in the house for an hour and leave to find that only a minute—or an entire day—had gone by in the real world.

His narration was interrupted several times by various spirits popping into the room and disappearing. News of the mysterious cloud outside had spread, and the ghosts all had the same question as he did: What was it?

Eventually they were joined by a young woman who was clearly still alive, though Dylan wasn't sure how he knew. Something was simply more vital about her than the others. She was in her teens, probably a few years younger than he was, and attractive in a witchy sort of way. Her shoulder-length hair was black and her bangs almost hid her eyes. The girl was thin and carried herself as if she didn't wish to be seen. With her arms crossed over her chest, she slipped into the room and sighed.

"Hey," she said.

"Hi," he answered. "I'm Dylan."

"Natasha."

"It's about time," Barry sniffed. "There's a situation brewing outside, and we may have need of the loka."

The girl scrounged in a tiny black purse around her waist and pulled out a milky white loka. She closed it in a fist and returned her arms to their self-hugging position.

"Your apprentice?" Dylan asked, wondering why she had

the loka and not Barry.

"Not really," Barry said dismissively.

Dylan risked making a puzzled face at Natasha, who rolled her eyes and shrugged.

"Something's coming!" declared the ghost of an old lady as she shot into the room.

"Kitty!" the little boy ghost cried in delight.

Dylan returned his attention to the window and saw a familiar white form squatting outside the cloud and urinating. "Kio!" he cried, jumping to his feet and running to the door. He ran straight through three ghosts in the process, but scarcely noticed.

"Kio!" he shouted again once he was outside.

The big cat was covering his mess by kicking dirt over the spot, but looked up when he heard his name. He growled in glee when he saw Dylan and raced across the yard, leaping into Dylan's arms and rubbing his face against that of his friend. Dylan laughed with joy, tears streaming down his face.

"I missed you so much," he said when he could speak again.

"I missed you twice as much!" Kio said with a grin, hopping to the ground.

"How did you get here?"

"I'm with the Gray Oligarch," Kio explained. "That cloud ball hides his entire house and island. It's like Yellow's windmill but twice as cool!"

Dylan stared at it in awe. The flying windmill was amazing enough, but a floating island was unbelievable. The Gray Oligarch must be powerful indeed.

"How did you find me?" Dylan asked as he scratched behind Kio's ears.

"Mostly luck. I figured that you'd keep visiting and warning the Oligarchs. White was nearest, so here we are!"

"Is everything all right here?"

Dylan turned to see Barry standing on the balcony with Natasha behind him. He was about to assure Barry that everything was fine, when another voice boomed across the yard.

"Watch your back, cat! They're sneaking up on you!" The speaker was a tall man with electrified hair. He was nervously popping in and out of the cloud, as if he were trying to dodge an attack.

"It's fine, this is my friend," Kio called back, then whispered to Dylan, "That's Diggory. He's a little nutty."

"Not him!" the Gray Oligarch shouted. "The creepy man on the porch and his girlfriend. They have the look of Oligarchs about them. Watch yourself!"

"How dare you, sir!!" Barry retorted. "I don't care for your tone! You're on my territory, and if you continue in this manner, I shall have to ask you to leave!"

"I'm on *my* territory!" the Gray Oligarch declared, stepping back into his cloud and sticking his head out to speak. "I should ask you to move that junky old house off my front lawn."

"I'll teach you some manners!" Crimson Barry stormed angrily off the porch and disappeared. He reappeared a moment later, walking back up the steps. "If I weren't already dead!" he shook his fist angrily. "I'm not helpless though." He rolled up his sleeves and turned to Natasha. "Are you ready?" he asked her.

"I was born ready," the Gray Oligarch screamed.

"Wait!" Dylan yelled. "No fighting. Just, uh—" His mind raced, trying to find a way to defuse the situation.

"Keep them apart," Kio advised in hushed tones. "There's no reasoning with Diggory."

Dylan took on what he hoped were commanding tones. "Barry, Natasha, back inside! I'll have a word with Gray and rejoin you later." Barry scowled at this command but complied. Diggory made a rude gesture as White reentered the ghost house, but thankfully Barry didn't notice. Natasha did, but found it humorous and grinned.

Once the others were safely inside, Dylan and Kio exchanged bemused glances and walked across the lawn to meet the Gray Oligarch.

Diggory was, without the slightest doubt, completely insane. He greeted Dylan with enthusiasm that turned quickly to suspicion, followed by confusion. He ushered them both into his house, taking them to a room filled with a model village. The quality of the models was quite impressive but each was missing its roof. This was in order to keep an eye on what the little wooden occupants were up to, they were told.

Standing over the village like giants, Diggory's mood became somber. For once, Dylan had no trouble persuading an Oligarch to join them. The only problem was convincing Diggory to wait until the prearranged meeting time.

"I say we strike now!" Diggory said, slamming his fist on the table and causing little wooden men to topple over.

"I agree," Dylan said carefully, "but we don't know where he is. We have to wait for Krale to show himself before we can do anything."

Diggory appeared on the verge of throwing a tantrum.

"We'll travel separately," Kio said, "each taking a secret route so that Krale won't see us coming."

"A secret route?" Diggory pondered this for a moment. "Oh, I like that! I can be quite stealthy, you know."

The cat had obviously learned to manage the Oligarch, since this diffused his anger and had him excited about the plan. Kio kept Diggory on track as they went over further details and discussed strategy. As their business drew to a close, Dylan found himself glad to be leaving. Talking to Diggory was like running through a forest blindfolded—at any moment, you just knew were going to smack into a tree.

"Where are you going?" Diggory asked as they were stepping out the front door.

Dylan was about to patiently explain that they were leaving when he realized that Diggory was speaking to Kio.

"I'm going with Dylan of course," the cat replied.

"But I thought you were *my* friend." Diggory's offense was apparent. "Why would you travel with him instead of me?"

Kio hesitated, trying to find the right answer. "Just for the night," he said. "I want to sleep in that house just once, so I can keep tabs on the White Oligarch. Tomorrow morning, I'll come back with a full report. Then we'll head out. Deal?"

Diggory grinned like a happy child, but Dylan only felt afraid. He didn't want to leave his friend in the hands of this madman. He barely wanted Diggory's support, but without him, Dylan would be on his own. When they were finally allowed to leave, Dylan couldn't shake the feeling that he had gained an ally more dangerous than his enemy.

Kio and Dylan entered the ghost house to find Crimson Barry still flustered over his encounter with the Gray Oligarch. Around him was a small army of ghosts, listening to his angry rants with transparent amusement. Barry distractedly directed Dylan to the kitchen when they expressed hunger. There they found Natasha cooking, a large man with an ample stomach directing all of her actions.

"He used to be a cook," she said with a lopsided shrug. "He could do all this himself, but he insists it's unsanitary for the dead to cook for the living."

Dylan pitched in to help. He didn't know much about cooking, but felt it was the right thing to do. The chef eagerly instructed him, which helped greatly. The simple vegetarian meal didn't involve much more than a little pan frying, but Dylan felt he was getting in the way more than he was being useful. He took an eternity to dice an onion, and he peeled a carrot with so much enthusiasm that hardly anything was left.

They ate their meal in a formal dining room, sitting in uncomfortable wooden chairs with long straight backs and narrow hard seats. A number of ghosts floated in to join them, including Crimson Barry, but none of them ate. Obviously they didn't need to, but Dylan wondered if they were even capable. He couldn't imagine not eating again, even if he were dead. He enjoyed it too much.

"I'd kill for a steak." Natasha sighed as she prodded the vegetables on her plate. "Too often, though, the ghost of the animal shows up halfway through cooking it, or even worse, during dinner. I can't tell you what an appetite killer that is."

"Wouldn't bug me," Kio said. Aside from milk and toasted bread crusts, he wasn't too pleased with his meal.

"How long have you been—" Dylan hesitated, "Oligarch?"

"Trying to figure out the whole loka thing?" Natasha took a final jab at her food, then pushed her plate away. "I *am* the White Oligarch, since you're wondering."

"Technically maybe," Crimson Barry said, "but it's my expertise and ability that allows you to step into the role."

"Well, you couldn't do it without me either," Natasha said, shooting him a glare. "Anyway," she continued, turning back to Dylan, "I've been here since I was twelve, so three years now."

"Orphan?" Kio inquired.

"No, just couldn't stand my parents. *And* I'm highly psychic," she said, pushing the issue with Barry once more. "That's important."

"Indeed it is," Barry said, sounding proud of her. "She's

exceptionally gifted, even without the loka boosting her powers."

"So that's the white loka?" Dylan asked, not sure what the first was.

"Sort of." Natasha placed the loka on the table and flicked it carelessly, spinning it like a top. "It's all about the soul, obviously." She gestured to Zandy who gave a little wave. "Even before I became Oligarch I could see the dead, but now I can talk to them, hear their responses—even smell them."

"Outside this house, too?" Kio asked.

"Anywhere and everywhere." Natasha sounded bored with her power.

"Great, once again I'm feeling loka-envy," Dylan muttered.

"She can see and hear much more than that," Barry added excitedly. "She's quite the little prophet."

Dylan shook his head. "Seeing the future is blue territory."

"Scrying," the old ghost nodded, "but Natasha's gift allows her to speak with the spirits. I know, we're all ghosts here, but these spirits exist outside of time, and have knowledge forbidden to those trapped in the mortal realm. What about it, Natasha? Feel like giving them a demonstration?"

"It could be useful," Kio mused. "If we can still change what's going to happen without paradoxes and that sort of thing."

"Who knows?" Natasha shrugged. "Usually you can't tell what the prophecies mean until they've already happened, so I wouldn't worry about it."

"Very well then. Lights first." Crimson Barry gestured with his hands, and all the candles in the room extinguished at once. They were left in darkness, except for the glow from the loka. Barry floated over the table, stopping behind Natasha's chair as she took hold of her loka and closed her eyes.

Crimson Barry leaned forward, his arms and head passing through the high-backed chair. He placed his hands on her shoulders and gave his audience a moment's attention. "Don't be alarmed by this next part; we're both quite accustomed to it," he said before falling forward. Barry didn't appear on the other side of Natasha's body. Instead he disappeared into her.

The moment he did so, the loka blazed to life. Natasha opened her eyes. They were glowing just as brightly as the loka. "All settled then?" she asked.

"Indeed," she answered in Barry's voice. "So tell the boy what you see in his future."

Her head whipped up, those eerily glowing eyes locking onto Dylan's. The hair on his arms began to tingle as energy built up in the room. The sensation intensified until his skin was crawling. He wanted to look away from the girl—whose hair was floating as if she were in water—but couldn't.

"The cat," she croaked in a disturbing conglomeration of Barry's voice and her own. *"The cat shall continue betraying you until the wolf takes control."* She moaned suddenly, as if this revelation caused her pain. *"The one you love will lose himself when he takes the life of another, never to be found again."* This time she wailed. She raised a hand and pointed directly at Dylan. *"You! You will let one of your own kind die and let one against you live. The end of the Oligarchy shall be on your head."* Instead of moaning, this time she laughed, slowly and deliberately. *"That is all."*

"No, it isn't," Barry's voice spoke again, but sounded strained as if it were fighting to be heard. "Find out if he has the bag."

Natasha's eyes blazed even more fiercely, and Dylan suddenly felt his mind invaded. The sensation was unbearable, like someone had removed his eyes to allow rushing water to fill his head. Thankfully it didn't last long. The force left his mind, leaving his eyes burning with the afterimage of light. When they cleared, he found the room returned to its previous state. Crimson Barry was separate from Natasha, and the candles had been relit.

"What the hell was that?" Dylan demanded.

"I'm sorry, but I had to be sure you didn't have it," Barry apologized.

Dylan shook his head and rubbed his eyes. "What is it with you and this stupid bag?"

"It's not just any bag, it's—" Barry stopped suddenly, remembering the other occupants of the room. "Well, perhaps later," he finished. The other ghosts babbled their disappointment, but Barry's expression showed he had no intention of revealing his secret to any of them.

"Sorry the prophesies are always so weird," Natasha said. "Don't worry about them too much. Even the most mundane thing comes out sounding dramatic. I once told my father he would lose what held him together. All he ended up losing was his belt."

Dylan wished he could laugh, but what she had said hardly

sounded promising. Kio was to betray him, Tyjinn was to be lost, and he was going to make a mess of everything else. He mentally repeated the prophesies a few times to memorize them, each time hoping to see a double meaning that was more optimistic.

"Do you mind if Kio and I explore the house a little bit?" he asked their hosts. He wanted to get away from them so he and Kio could talk openly about what they had just heard.

"Not at all," Barry said amiably. "Just don't wander more than fifteen doors in any direction."

"Right," Dylan said, barely hearing him. His head burdened with thought, he and his cat left the room.

Chapter 21
The Ghost House

"I'm not going to betray you," Kio said again.

Dylan reached down to stroke his head. "I'm more worried about you going back to Diggory. Are you sure it's the only option?"

"I wish it wasn't," Kio admitted, "but he's powerful and might be the only friend we've got. Of course, we could forget about meeting up with Krale and hightail it for the hills."

"And live in a cave the rest of our lives?" Dylan shook his head and sighed. "I miss Dad."

"Yeah. So do I."

They walked through the hallways of the ghost house while they talked, and even after half an hour had not exhausted their options. So far they had discovered a massive ball room, two libraries, and an indoor archery range. The house had four different courtyards, each with a sky that indicated a different time. They wanted to explore further, but were continually having to backtrack because of Barry's "no more than fifteen doors" rule. His reasons for this rule were becoming clear: They could disappear for days if they lost their way. One hallway they found stretched farther than the eye could see. Dylan counted fifteen doors before they stopped. The hall still showed no sign of ending.

"We could go a little further," Dylan said.

"It's not like we'll have any trouble finding our way back," Kio agreed. "You can't get lost on a straight path."

"Exactly. As soon as we reach the end we'll come right back."

Neither was a stranger to the thrill that came with breaking rules. Suddenly it was like they were back in the Lakelands, getting into trouble once more, stealing one of Ada's pies from the oven, or sneaking out in the middle of the night to sleep under the stars.

"Barry probably keeps his moonshine down here," Kio joked as they increased their pace.

"Or a harem."

"A harem? Doesn't seem the type to me."

"A collection of powdered wigs then," Dylan laughed as they broke into a run.

The hallway remained endless, but changes were gradually occurring. The lights that lined the hallway were losing their color, fading from orange to icy blue. This matched the temperature well. The ghost house had been chilly before, but now it was freezing.

"I can't see my breath," Dylan realized. It was so cold that his fingers were beginning to cramp. He should have been able to see his breath.

"Look at the walls," Kio said warily. "They've gone all ghosty!"

Not just the walls, the floor, doors, everything had become transparent. All that could be seen beyond was a gray haze. The world around them had become a phantom, and Dylan feared they had too. Wordlessly they turned back. Dylan walked two steps before something cold and hard wrapped around his neck and yanked him backward.

"Ki-" is all he managed before he fell onto his back. The sound of chains rattled in his ears as he began sliding down the hall. Kio turned, his eyes terrified as he gave chase. It was futile. Whatever had Dylan was too fast. Kio couldn't keep pace. The cat skidded to a halt and began running in the other direction, no doubt in search of help.

Dylan's hands went to his throat, his fingers touching metal. Chains wrapped around his neck like a collar. He twisted painfully in an attempt to break free and ended up flopping onto his stomach. This allowed him to see what was dragging him away, but Dylan instantly wished he couldn't.

The chains around his neck connected to a suit of armor bristling with spikes and ornate curves, forged from dark metal eaten through with rust. Through the holes Dylan could see the skin of the demon dragging him; for he was convinced it was no man. The visible skin was pink and raised with scars and blisters. Eyes like hot coals burned through the horned helmet covering its face.

Dylan's mind reeled. The creature was facing him but flying backward, its arms and legs spread in the air as if it were free-falling. Dylan's body slid off the floor and into the air, his stomach lurching as together they plummeted through a void. The halls had disappeared, the ghost house no longer there. Instead there was darkness, broken only by two swirling vortices of light. One was white and pure, causing Dylan to think fondly of home, but the abomination dragging him howled with mad glee as they changed direction and headed toward another sort of light. This one was dim, like a grim ember on the verge of extinguishing, but Dylan knew its light would still burn him once he was there. The white light of hope was but a pinprick now as they continued to fall. Dylan knew he would never know its comfort, not when anchored to a hellbound demon.

Then Barry was there, barely recognizable, dusted off, young, and blazing with a light of his own. He flew over him to tackle the demon, the ensuing fight mostly lost to Dylan as he was jerked back and forth like a leaf in the wind. The screams were terrifying but ignited hope within him once more.

Another figure came now, a large woman whose friendly face was transformed by determination. It was Zandy, Barry's trusted friend, and like him, she was now younger, radiating with a power that hadn't been apparent before. She reached Dylan, placing warm hands on his shoulders to steady him as Barry and the demon continued to wage their war.

"You are a ghost now," she said, her hands moving to his neck and jerking on the chains. "These bonds can no longer hold you."

But they could! He could feel the metal biting into his skin, burning as if on fire and itching with infection.

"It's only an illusion," Zandy said, reading the wild panic in his eyes. Her voice was commanding, her eyes every bit as fiery as Tyjinn's. "Nothing can hold you now. You have the ultimate freedom. The freedom that comes with death."

The truth made his heart ache, but Dylan had no choice but to accept it. He was flapping in the wind between two eternities. Of course he was dead, which meant he wasn't any more substantial than Zandy or Barry. Nothing could hold a ghost. His confinement was only in his mind. Dylan sighed with resignation and the chain passed through his neck. He was free.

Zandy nodded in approval before her eyes moved back to the battle. Dylan followed her gaze and witnessed Barry wielding a rapier of golden light, his youthful form twisting to avoid more chains snaking from the armor. One nearly wrapped around his head before he ducked, his strawberry blond hair barely escaping before the chain loop closed. Barry jabbed with the rapier, striking the demon in the stomach and causing it to howl, but the foul apparition recovered quickly, dark magic building around its form.

Dylan flinched as Zandy swore and grabbed the chain that had once been around his neck, wrapping it around her wrist. She tore her eyes away from the battle to speak to Dylan.

"Tell Barry— No, never mind. He already knows."

Zandy stole one longing glance in Barry's direction before taking off, zooming toward the pinprick of light above with such speed that Dylan could barely follow her progress. The demon was yanked after her, towed against its will. Barry was left behind, shock registering on his face as he cried out Zandy's name. If she heard, she didn't respond as her journey toward the white light continued. The demon howled and struggled, ripping pieces of the armor off, but before it could jettison it completely, the two figures disappeared into the light's center—and were gone.

Dylan turned to Crimson Barry, and for a moment he thought he saw tears in his eyes before the noble figure snapped his fingers.

Gravity returned with a vengeance and Dylan hit the floor. Around him the halls of the ghost house had returned, although they were still transparent. When he looked up, Barry's hand was extended toward him, his appearance old and dusty once more.

Dylan took his hand, surprised to find it solid before he realized what this must mean.

"I'm dead," he moaned.

"You aren't dead." Barry pulled him to his feet with an indignant expression. "I told you, ghosts can become solid here, although it's a habit I'd rather not return to."

Barry began moving down the hall, leaving Dylan to stumble after him. They were walking along the endless hallway, the walls slowly regaining their solidity again.

"What happened?" Dylan asked. "Was that normal?"

"Normal?" Barry snorted. "No. But then again, he and I have done battle countless times before. That was the Drake you ran into. At least that's what he calls himself. It's not the name his mother gave him, I promise you that. Gods only know what the Drake wanted with you. Some foul magic, no doubt. I told you two not to wander so far. Imagine a mortal being dragged to the afterlife instead of dying properly!"

"Sorry." Dylan withered under the lecture before remembering who had released him from his chains. "Zandy! Is she—"

"Gone to her final reward, I imagine." Barry turned his face away. "She was a true friend. I shall miss her terribly."

"She wanted to tell you something, but then said that you already knew."

Barry's only response was silence.

"I'm sorry," Dylan mumbled again. "It's all my fault."

"Nonsense, nonsense," Barry tutted softly. "The Drake has been crawling out of the inferno decade after decade, ever since I killed him. Another conflict was inevitable. Perhaps Zandy's sacrifice finally put an end to our vicious cycle. I can only pray that it has."

Dylan glanced sidelong at Barry. Despite being back to his aged appearance, he still had a remnant of light surrounding him. Who had he been in life, and what sort of man was he still?

These thoughts were interrupted by Kio's arrival. The cat had run to seek Barry's help when he couldn't catch up with Dylan, and he was desperate to know what had happened. Kio made Dylan tell his story twice on the way back, but Dylan did so with some reverence. He had barely known Zandy, but felt that she had given up much to help save him. Barry maintained his silence throughout this, escorting them to a bedroom in the main part of the house before quietly taking his leave.

Once awake, Dylan and Kio were puzzled to discover that it was still night, even though they had both slept long and deep. Knowing that time flowed differently in the ghost house, Dylan was concerned that they had somehow slept through the day, but Crimson Barry confirmed that sunrise was still many hours away. Dylan and Kio celebrated this extra time by raiding the kitchen, helping themselves to the pancakes and honey left over from Natasha's breakfast.

After eating they continued exploring, making sure to be careful this time. The most interesting thing they found was a room full of portraits of previous Oligarchs. Quite a few looked like Barry, with the same powdery wigs and pinched expressions. Dylan searched for a portrait of his grandfather but wasn't able to find one. The paintings were probably too old to include anyone he would recognize from his family.

By the time they returned to the front room, the sun had risen and the pink of early morning was beginning to leave the sky. Dylan's heart filled with dread at the prospect of saying goodbye to Kio again. That wasn't all that hung over his head, since he knew he must ask Kio to do something difficult.

"I don't want you there," Dylan blurted out.

"When you confront Krale?" the cat asked, picking up on his thoughts. "Forget it. I'll be there."

"Think about what Natasha said."

"Cheap fortune telling," Kio said dismissively. "When have I ever turned against you?"

"You don't remember, do you? At the Cradle. I thought you hadn't mentioned it because you felt bad but..."

Kio looked lost, so Dylan explained what had happened, how Kio had lost his will to the purple loka and attacked Tyjinn. The cat's ears flopped guiltily as he listened.

"Tyjinn's face was bleeding, wasn't it?" Kio said. "I can just barely recall."

Dylan nodded, a lump in his throat. "Krale will have the purple loka when we meet. Nothing can stop him from turning you against me again." He swallowed. "Please stay away. For both our sakes. Just until the battle is over. You make sure Diggory gets there. That's already enough."

The cat agreed reluctantly just before they began their emotional goodbye. The fur around Kio's neck was soaked from Dylan's tears by the time he walked across the lawn and vanished into the cloud. Dylan waited, watching until it rose into the sky and disappeared.

There was time to spare before his rendezvous with Krale, but Dylan didn't know how much. If time kept running slowly, it could even be a week before he had to go. According to Barry, time could shift at any moment, running normally again or even so fast that he would have to leave instantly. The constant uncertainty caused Dylan's stomach to bubble with nervousness.

The extra time had its uses. Between Kio's return and their run-in with the Drake, he had nearly forgotten about Krale and the need for White's support. Having Gray as an ally eased the pressure, but Dylan still needed all the help he could get, even if Barry wasn't likely to get along with Diggory. Odd how Barry had never asked him the meaning of Diggory's visit. Or Dylan's for that matter. He sought the old ghost out, finding him relaxing in the front room.

"Barry?"

"Hm?" Barry pulled his considerable nose away from the book he was reading.

"Aren't you curious as to why I'm here? Since I arrived, besides wondering if I stole your bag, you haven't asked why I came."

"I could ask why you hadn't told me already," Barry countered with a yawn.

Fair enough.

"The ghost house is quite used to visitors," Barry continued, turning back to his book. "You may leave whenever you please."

"But—"

"I assure you," the ghost interrupted stiffly, "that if I have any questions, I will ask."

Dylan considered this behavior. He had only known the Oligarch for a short time, but already knew that this was uncharacteristic. Crimson Barry reigned over the house with the nerve-wracking attention of a bored monarch. He directed the activities of the other ghosts as if they were his helpless and rather stupid subjects, leaving nothing to chance. Yet here was a guest in his home whom he chose to ignore. Why?

"You already know, don't you?" Dylan said.

"Know what?" came the innocent reply.

"Oh, come on!"

Barry carefully marked his page, closed the book, and tossed it onto the nearby table, sending a cloud of dust flying. "Fine. If you are determined to make this an issue, yes, I know all about the little civil war you are brewing up."

"So you know about Krale's plan to become a one-man Oligarchy?"

"Yes, yes," the old ghost droned. "That idiot Purple showed up here not long after his murder and raised a fuss about it. He was seething that his would-be partner turned on him so early in the game. He wanted me to help him get revenge by blowing the whistle on Yellow's plans."

"Why didn't you? You could have saved a lot of lives."

"Has anyone else died?" Barry asked, his tones implying he already knew the answer. "I haven't seen any dead Oligarchs here except him. They're such an arrogant lot. I think they'd all prefer the purgatory in this house to moving on. I practically had to shove Purple into the light."

Dylan was reminded of both Black's and Brown's attitudes. No one in the Oligarchy wanted anything to do with each other, feeling superior while dismissing their colleagues as reprehensible.

"Before you continue being judgmental," Barry said, "I'm not much good outside the confines of this house, as you've seen. I couldn't have warned anyone."

"You could have sent Natasha."

"Oh yes, excellent. Send a fifteen-year-old girl to locations where a murderer is likely to be. That would have been brilliant."

Dylan wanted to argue that he was barely older than Natasha and had put himself at risk to warn others, but he knew it would be fruitless. "Isn't Natasha in danger if Krale shows up here?"

Barry paused for a moment. "No. Did you notice the transparency of the house when you first arrived? The way you could see through it, I mean."

Dylan admitted he hadn't. There was so much to take in when arriving via teleport. By the time he had noticed the house, it had looked as solid as any other.

"It wasn't," the ghost assured him. "I can phase the ghost house out of the physical world if need be. Although you can't tell from the inside, no one could possibly enter right now unless I allow them."

"Then why did you let me in?"

"Because I thought you had my crane bag!" Barry said impatiently.

Dylan thought for a moment before replying. "Could someone leave the house while it's phased out?"

"Well, yes. They would be dumped into the physical world and unable to return, but yes."

"Then I think you'd better tell me why your crane bag is so important."

"Why ever should I do that?" the ghost demanded.

"Because not only do I know another way into your house, even with your security measures, but I have a pretty good idea who robbed you."

Even for a ghost, Crimson Barry looked quite pale and shaken. They were sitting in an office not unlike that of Dylan's father. This was the only place in the house where Barry had complete privacy. Dylan told Barry of his experiences in the Cradle, believing his story would be met with a healthy dose of skepticism, but the old Oligarch took it in stride.

"I figure that the world of the gods probably connects with the afterlife," Dylan said. "I mean, it's all the same place, right?"

"I've never seen any gods here." All hint of arrogance had disappeared from Barry's voice. "It doesn't matter. If the gods can set you back down anywhere they want, they could have put him down here. Oh, I've been such a fool!"

"Why would Krale want the crane bag?" Dylan asked.

"Because it gives him the needed advantage to go from powerful to invincible. He's formidable enough with five lokas, but can only use them singularly. Time and space, much like in this house, aren't the same in the crane bag. With it, he'll be able to invoke all of his lokas at once."

Krale had invoked the purple loka shortly before taking control of Kio at the Cradle. Dylan hadn't considered the implications then, but if Krale could only utilize one loka at a time, it might have been possible to trick the renegade Oligarch into using one type of magic that they could readily overcome with another. This small weakness was now gone, and Krale would only get stronger with each loka he acquired.

"Wait! Why didn't he try to take your loka while he was here?"

A bit of arrogance returned to the old ghost's face. "With the exception of the Black Oligarch, there is no more formidable Oligarch than White. Soul magic is quite powerful. I could have separated his soul from his body, had he confronted me."

"But what if he caught Natasha alone? Would she still be able to defend herself?"

Barry's face became gaunt. "I know I appear to bully her and dispute that she is, in fact, the White Oligarch. The truth is, I feel as protective toward her as I would my own child. I have always downplayed her role in order to keep her safe. I've gone to great lengths to maintain this illusion. I dare say that Yellow believes I am the White Oligarch and didn't fancy going up against a ghost."

Dylan was startled by his frankness, but also relieved to find that Barry had a more sensitive side. "You're sure he couldn't have known? You didn't keep it very well hidden from me."

"I was shaken up when you arrived because of the theft. I was against the magical demonstration at dinner, but Natasha insisted. I rather think she likes you."

That would be an awkward conversation for another day, not that there was much he had to explain. Natasha had told his future and seen that he loved someone else. He hoped the revelation hadn't hurt her, but he didn't have time for such complexities now.

"You have no way of telling who has left the house recently?"

"Not at all," Barry answered. "For all I know Krale could still be here."

Although the comment was idle, once they both considered the implications they shot into action. Barry called his most loyal ghosts together and organized a search of the house—a substantial effort, considering its dimensions. Dylan was charged with finding Natasha and ensuring her protection.

He found her reading in her room. She was glad for his company and didn't seem upset with him at all. They played cards while they waited. Dylan noticed her eyes lingering on him longer than was normal and grasped how obvious his affection for Tyjinn must have been to others. He tried to steer their conversations away from any potentially romantic topics, but she was too determined to talk about boys.

"Does he know how you feel about him?" she asked.

"No," Dylan answered, trying to ignore the pain in his chest. "At least I don't think he does. I chased after him, hoping to tell him, but now he's gone."

"Sleeping," Natasha nodded.

Dylan leaned forward. "What do you mean? Do you know where he is?"

She shook her head. "When the spirits were speaking through me and they mentioned him, I saw him sleeping. There was light, like from a candle or a distant fire, but nothing else. Not even a bed below him."

Dylan swallowed. "You make him sound dead."

Natasha shook her head. "Believe me, I know what dead looks like and he's not. Besides, if he were, you two would probably be together right now."

In the ghost house. For one morbid moment, Dylan wished it were true, if only to have the comfort of his presence again.

"Will I see him again?" he asked.

Natasha returned her eyes to her cards. "I don't know. I only see the future in bits and pieces and it's always changing."

Sleeping. Dylan tried to imagine what this could mean. There had to be some way to find him again. Maybe when Dylan met with Krale, he would discover Tyjinn still travelling with him. If so, he knew they could win. Together, he was convinced that they could do anything. His optimism didn't bear scrutiny, but it went a long way toward keeping him sane.

When Barry finally arrived to report that the entire house had been searched with no sign of Krale, Dylan found he didn't want to leave Natasha's company. They spent the rest of the evening together, whiling away the time.

As pleasant as this was, all of Dylan's problems came rushing back as he lay sleepless in bed that night. The news that Krale was now more powerful than ever sat like a stone in his stomach. He didn't know what he was going to do, and had little time left to think of something.

Chapter 22
Orange

Lali's reptilian body slowed to a brisk trot and then to walking speed. She exhaled in great coughing bursts through her long, fang-filled mouth, her body dispelling the accumulated heat quickly and efficiently. Then she strolled for ten minutes to allow her muscles to slowly relax. This was the way she always rode Mushi. Years of taking care of her beloved mushushu had made being one much easier, because she knew how to maintain and care for the animal.

In fact, she hadn't taken long at all to get used to the form. Who would have thought that having two pairs of mismatched legs and a stinger for a tail could feel so natural? Becoming a different creature was exhilarating. Having now experienced it, she was surprised that Hasam didn't spend more of his time as an animal.

The human form did have its advantages. The height that came from standing on two legs was one, not to mention how useful hands were. She slowed to a stop and began to focus, calling on the power of the orange loka that was, for the time being, hers.

The process was slow. This was only the fourth time she had shape-shifted. The procedure wasn't at all painful like she imagined it would be. The body went numb and tingly as it changed, so any discomfort from bones growing or muscles twisting and reforming wasn't felt. After a quarter of an hour, she had completed the transformation back to her human self.

Left panting and covered in sweat, she lay naked in the grass beside the saddle she had been wearing. She decided to rest before trying to move, idly fingering the ribs that protruded much too far now. Under Hasam's guidance she had regrown her lost hand, but the price had been taking material from other body parts to reform the limb. She had to use up quite a bit of her own fat and muscle to replace the much denser bone material.

Now she looked like she was starving. In the last village she had visited, people had certainly stared. Lali had stopped by the local tavern and eaten enough for three men. She needed to put weight back on as quickly as possible, but she was also burning much of what she ate as she traveled.

Lali had been running almost three days now. First she traveled to the Cradle. Hasam had grudgingly reverted to his role as Mushi and allowed her to ride him again. The big coward had been shaking as they approached where the Cradle was supposed to be, but they found nothing there, no sign of a struggle or anything else strange. Nothing to see except a nondescript field.

Lali was at a loss as to where to search next and decided to head across the Longlands to Tyjinn's home, with one detour along the way. The home of the Blue Oligarch was on the same route if she veered north. She might find Dylan there, or maybe find out if he and Kio had passed through. She could then charter a boat to take her down to Brandwald, which would give her time to recover. If she didn't have any luck there, she could head south to the oasis to see how things were faring before heading west to her home.

Sitting up, she opened the saddlebag to retrieve her clothes. The orange loka rested on top of them. She hesitated before picking it up, still not believing that she had been given this responsibility. The honor that Hasam had bestowed upon her was slightly tarnished by his reason: He wanted nothing to do with Krale and feared for his own life. He preferred to go back into hiding, but Lali wouldn't join him without first learning the fate of her friends. Hasam had given her the loka for protection. She suspected he was also relieved to no longer be a target.

Either way, the loka was now hers. She didn't dare call herself the Orange Oligarch, but she secretly enjoyed the idea. In truth, she would have to hand it back to Hasam some day and resume her apprenticeship, but she didn't mind. This experience would put her leagues ahead of the competition, almost ensuring her the position.

Lali dressed and opened the other saddlebag to find food to snack on while she set up camp. Once that was done she sat down to a proper meal. She ended up eating all her rations, leaving her with nothing for breakfast. That didn't worry her, though. She couldn't have slept on an empty stomach, and the next village wasn't too far away. Her belly full and her body exhausted, she decided to turn in early, even though the sun wasn't yet down.

Lali slept as a human but dreamt the dreams of animals. She explored the world in many guises. Sometimes she was a mouse nestled warmly in its desert burrow. She was a stray dog, wandering the streets of Dringend, the city of the Orange Oligarch. Great square buildings rose up chaotically around her, leaning out over the endless cobbled streets. She sought food from the garbage and companionship from the pack following her.

Then she was a cougar, stepping carefully across the stone plateaus looming behind the city. She crept along silently, inching toward a rabbit when the rocks gave way and sent her sliding over the edge. She hit bottom, landing on her back despite her feline equilibrium. Rocks avalanched onto her, pinning her four legs. She struggled and yowled as shadowy forms crept into her field of vision.

Lali awoke with a start, trying to sit up but was instantly forced back to the ground. Her arms *were* pinned down, just like in her dream. Her legs, too.

"She's awake now anyway," a man's voice growled.

Foul breath hit her face. Lali squinted at her oppressor through the darkness. The face in front of her was covered in a grisly beard and surrounded by unkempt greasy hair, the skin ravaged with pock marks.

"Hello, my pretty," the man rasped. "We're going to have some fun with you tonight."

"You aren't going first again, Amos," a stupid-sounding man said from near her legs. "You did both times before. It ain't fair!"

"Shut your trap, Jacob!" the man on top of her snapped. "Luke, get over here and hold her arms."

Lali lay dumbfounded for a moment, thinking she had escaped from one dream into another, but the details were too grimy and ugly to be anything but real. Her heart began to thud, sending adrenaline into her bloodstream. She heaved upward with all her strength. The man barely even budged. She cursed her recent loss of muscle mass.

"Don't struggle or we'll get ugly," Amos rasped while staring lustfully at her.

She spit in his face, and he responded by grabbing her chin and slamming her head against the ground. The back of her head connected painfully, causing her to see lights. Orange lights.

The loka was still in her saddlebag, her only hope. She didn't have to be physically touching it, but things would be much easier if she were. Lali tried to calm herself and make a mental connection. Not an easy task in her present situation. The other man, Luke she thought he was called, had taken control of her arms, freeing Amos to begin rubbing his hands over her body. She allowed herself to feel revolted for a moment before mentally reaching for the loka again.

She felt it, only faintly, but she had contact. Now what to do? She couldn't change forms quickly enough to be of any use. They would probably kill her as soon as they saw her changing. She squirmed as her legs were slowly pulled apart, almost losing her connection with the loka. A face loomed in front of hers—the man with the idiot's voice. He looked even dumber than he sounded.

He was trying to kiss her. She looked directly into his eyes. Then she moved, but not physically.

Drawing power from the loka, she sent her mind into his body. His own feeble mind had no choice but to trade places. The change of perspective was so sudden that she almost fell forward. In that instant, she looked down at her own body. To her delight, she saw that she didn't look like a terrorized victim. She looked as vicious as a cougar.

This changed when the idiot took over her body. Then she looked confused and frightened. Lali didn't have time to enjoy the expression. Amos was tearing at her shorts, all resistance gone with her body vacated, and she didn't intend to let him get any further. She released her own arms and stood up.

"Me first," she shouted as she kicked Amos in the gut.

The man fell and rolled over onto his side in pain, but recovered surprisingly fast. He was on his feet in seconds and attacked her, punching her in the face repeatedly and once in the chest. The pain was phenomenal, but she just kept reminding herself that it wasn't her body. She put up enough of a fight to encourage the man to keep attacking her. Her nose crunched, sending blood flying, and one of her eyes was swelling shut. She threw herself at the larger man, knocking them both to the ground. He rolled over and took control of the fight, choking her and slamming her head against the ground.

During this, her real body was on the ground, arms flailing as the third man tried to subdue her, and she yelled in a voice both familiar and strange. "Stop! What's going on? Hey! Stop!"

Lali was on the verge of passing out. Doing so would leave her vulnerable and in the wrong body, so she reached out to the loka again. A second later, her mind and her assailant's switched. She was now in Amos's body, looking down at a thoroughly beaten man. She knew that Amos wouldn't be much use inside Luke's body, so she stood and turned on the third man.

"You want some, too?" she screamed as she laid into him. She was surprised by how powerful this new body was. Adrenaline and blind fury coursed through its veins, and she found it easy to run with its impulses. The part of her that was slightly detached noted that Amos's penis was still hard, even though he had spent the last few minutes fighting. The man clearly had a few issues to work out.

She pulled back on her anger to let the other man get the best of Amos. As the most dangerous of the three, she wanted Amos to receive the most damage. Control of a situation like this was difficult. Once anger was triggered, a chemical response took over. Even though the body wasn't hers, self-preservation was ingrained into it. Ignoring the body's natural instincts wasn't easy.

The third man knocked her to the ground, but must have feared Amos's retaliation because he fled into the night. Meanwhile, her natural body had stood and looked to be on the verge of fleeing as well. Worried that she would quite literally lose herself, she reached out to the loka and set everything right again.

Her body was shaking with panic when she returned to it, but her training allowed her to recover quickly. Amos, now back in his own body, seemed to be thinking about getting to his feet. She went over to him and stomped on his face a couple of times, making sure to hit both eyes. She was fighting dirty, but nowhere near as dirty as what they had planned.

Keeping her eyes on both groaning forms, she slipped on her boots and picked up the saddlebag. She slipped into the night, making certain they didn't see which direction. Not that they were likely to give chase in their condition, but she couldn't be sure. Changing back into a mushushu was the safest course of action.

She stopped a couple of times, thinking that she would attempt shape-shifting, before a twig snapping would send her running again. The situation was frustrating; she wished she had killed the bastards, but it wasn't in her nature. Eventually she found a secluded glade. After standing still five minutes and hearing nothing out of the ordinary, she shape-shifted without interruption. Feeling tired but proud of the way she had defended herself, she broke into a leisurely trot, heading toward the Lakelands.

Tyjinn slept within the heart of a flame. Inside its secure warmth he felt no discomfort, had no disturbing thoughts. There was nothing but blissful heat, the same warmth that melted the winter's ice and gave plants life in spring. This was the warmth a baby felt when cradled in its mother's arms. Here he slept, unaware of his past or his future.

Eternities passed before coolness seeped into his harmonious state. At first it was welcome, like a thirst-quenching drink on a hot summer day, but soon the cold became uncomfortable. Tyjinn stirred in his sleep, skin prickling as he reached out for a blanket that wasn't there. He shivered as the white cold overwhelmed the orange heat, fading its color into apricot, beige, then eggshell before disappearing. His teeth began to chatter, and his body started to shake.

No longer able to sleep, he opened his eyes. Tyjinn was surrounded by darkness. Though there was no light, he could see a man who wore the shadows like a cloak.

"Thaedon," Tyjinn whispered.

"Ah, you remember me," the dark god replied. His eyes glowing scarlet, he squatted down to get a better look at Tyjinn.

"How is it that I know you?" Tyjinn felt confused.

"It's easier to remember dreams here," Thaedon replied. "All those worlds that exist just outside human perception, but run parallel to normal life regardless. I almost had you, you know. You were almost one of mine. You spent your childhood alone, an outcast just like me. I was with you during all those lonely hours. Do you remember?"

He did. The memories came like a flicker just outside his vision, disappearing whenever he tried to look directly at them, only to return when he looked away. The dark god had been there with him when he skipped school to sit by the river. Those solitary times were like a salve on his soul, his invisible friend whispering comforting words—telling him not to rejoin the others, not to try, not to care. Tyjinn was meant to be alone, he would never fit in, and he preferred it that way. That's what he had chosen to believe during that miserable time in his life, until Fenric came along.

"Ah, your dog," the dark god said nostalgically. "I was glad when he came, glad you didn't need me as much. I stepped away, happy to allow you the comfort your dog provided you. But then what happened, hm? They took him away from you. And who stepped in? Who did you turn to in your time of need?"

The flame. Tyjinn had turned to fire and used it to take revenge. He had always worshipped it in a way. For him, fire was the most alluring and yet untouchable of all elements. The other three elements nurtured life. The world depended on them to survive. What water, earth, and air created, fire destroyed.

"You turned to her, the Bride of Flame," Thaedon said. "Look what it did to your life! Look what it did to others!"

He didn't need to be reminded. Tyjinn lived with the memory every day. He had taken two lives, including one who was innocent, but he hadn't meant to. He truly hadn't. When he set the bed on fire, he meant only to burn them, scar them; make their outsides match the ugliness inside their souls, but he hadn't properly understood his magic back then. In practice, creating and extinguishing fire had been easy, but rage and the panic that followed had made control impossible. An accident, like Fenric's death was purported to be, and maybe it had been. Tyjinn couldn't be sure. All he knew was that in his attempt to punish them that night, he had become one of them.

He had contemplated suicide countless times after that, feeling that he should punish himself by sharing their fate, to pay for two lives with his own. Eventually he did try. Overcome with guilt and self-hatred, he turned his magic on himself. Instead of burning him to death, the flames wrapped around him, refusing to touch him but causing him to lose consciousness from their intense heat. That was when he first saw her.

"The Bride saved me from the fire," Tyjinn said. "She found me and showed me the other side of the flame. The sun that lights the darkness, the fire that cooks our food, the—"

"Love that burns inside?" Thaedon mimicked. "Let me tell you something, son. The brighter a flame burns, the darker the shadows it casts."

"Not if there is more than one fire."

The dark god frowned. "You're going to die. Has she told you that? The fire is going to turn on you like it does everyone. You are going to die and for nothing."

"It's going to be for him," Tyjinn said. "For him and to take down Krale. It won't atone for what I've done, but—"

"But nothing!" Thaedon stood again, his anger manifesting as black wings that unfurled from his back. "This scheme will damn you forever and for what? He doesn't even love you!"

That didn't matter. Tyjinn loved Dylan and would give anything to protect him. The mistakes of his past had tarnished Tyjinn's soul, but Dylan was innocent. He deserved a chance to live his life, and Tyjinn intended to give it to him, even if that meant sacrificing himself.

Thaedon paced away and then back again, silent and thinking. The only sound was from his footsteps, echoing into oblivion. "There are of course, other alternatives," he continued. "Your power, your special gift that allows you to be both a mage and an Oligarch, you have only begun to explore that potential. Just think what you could do with the other lokas. You could reshape the world in your image, punishing the Fenric-killers while rewarding those who please you. I could give you that power!"

A chance to change the world. Tyjinn had thought on that often. He had done everything in his power to serve his community and atone. Doing so had exposed him to the less fortunate in life. Many times their misfortune was of their own making through drink or poor decisions. More often it was simply fate. They were born into a life of poverty that they couldn't find a way out of. What he soon realized was how owning the loka could instantly change any of their lives. Success bred power as much as power led to success.

What could be done? As Krale had so recently told him, someone had to have power and someone didn't. That's just how it was. The renegade Oligarch believed if he had all the power, he could set the world right for everyone else. Tyjinn had once entertained the same idea, until he accepted that there was no one paradise to suit the needs of every man. Not in this world.

He was disturbed by how much of himself he had seen in Krale. They were both loners. Tyjinn, despite his charitable deeds, had kept himself distant from everyone. Lali was the one exception. She was so head-over-heels in love with him that she had broken down his barriers and ignored all his defense mechanisms. She had struggled for years to do what Dylan had done so easily. Tyjinn didn't feel as alone anymore, but he could still remember how it felt. Being around Krale had been a constant reminder of the monster he could become.

Tyjinn forced himself to stop shivering and looked the dark god squarely in the eye. "So Krale is one of yours? And you would toss him aside so easily so that I could take his place?"

Thaedon licked his lips "Krale is ambitious, but he lacks your talent. Surrender your will to me, and you will have your every desire. Even the boy. He was impressed by your little yellow magic trick. Just think how he would worship you when you become the most powerful mage in the Five Lands."

Tyjinn's grin was wicked. "I could use the power for anything, couldn't I?"

"Oh, yes!"

"I could kill Krale?"

"Most certainly!"

"And then you?"

Thaedon was on top of him faster than a shadow fleeing from the sun. His icy hands were around Tyjinn's neck, lifting him into the air, the burning scarlet eyes threatening to devour him.

A wave of summer warmth burst through the darkness, filling it with a golden light and softly spoken words. "That is enough."

The dark god hissed, releasing Tyjinn. "You'll come to my realm when you die," he snarled. "I promise you that!" In the light he didn't look so intimidating. He was little more than a potbellied man with a piggish face and bad hair. "I hate you, Bride!" Thaedon screamed before disappearing.

Tyjinn turned to see his goddess. She placed one pale hand on his throat, washing away the cold and pain.

"Why did you let him in?" Tyjinn asked, for he knew her power was great enough to protect him even from other gods. The only way Thaedon could have reached him was with her blessing.

"I wanted to give you one more chance," she answered. "To show you that there are other paths available to you. The fate you have chosen for yourself worries me."

"Am I really going to die?"

"Some things are worse than death. One is losing yourself to the darkness. Another is going so far you can never find your way back." She brushed a hand across his cheek. "You must learn to control yourself while restraint is still an option."

"I don't see any options," Tyjinn said, lying back down. He may have killed accidentally, but Krale had done so intentionally. It took a murderer to kill a murderer. If he didn't do it, no one else could. "There's only one path ahead of me." His voice was weary, his eyelids heavy. The warm embrace of the goddess led him back toward a tranquil slumber.

"Sleep my friend," came the Bride's voice, distant and fading. "Sleep and dream of other roads."

*****

"The little maid in the little house knew someone was lurking behind the curtain, but didn't want to let on that she did, so she started baking instead. She decided to bake a cake in the shape of a shield to defend herself and cookies in the shapes of daggers in case she needed to fight back. Once the goodies were complete, the thief behind the curtain couldn't resist coming out for a taste. What he didn't count on was how pretty the maid was. He'd only seen her from behind, you see."

Kio grimaced inwardly. The Gray Oligarch had kept him and Yasmine hostage at the dinner table until well past midnight, forcing them to listen to fairy tale after fairy tale. First the idea was charming, but after a while, the predictable nature of the stories began to annoy.

"Wait," Kio interrupted. "By chance does the maid turn out to be a long-lost princess and the thief some sort of prince who just happens to be single? One or both of them enchanted?"

Diggory scowled at him over the book before disappearing behind it again. He silently turned the next few pages. When his face reappeared over the top of the book, he looked very surprised. "How did you know?" he asked. "Have you already heard this one?"

Kio rolled his eyes. "That must be it."

"There's another one here," Diggory said.

"About a contest with half the kingdom for a prize? One that is won by a prince under an enchantment?"

"No need to ruin it for us," the Gray Oligarch scolded. He became introspective for a moment, then announced, "I have to pee."

Diggory rose and stumbled out of the room. The second he left, Yasmine underwent a transformation. She had been distant and detached the entire evening, responding to her employer's insanities as if they were no more than polite trivialities. Now that he was out of sight, she was more awake, sensing her chance to have one sane conversation.

"One more glass of wine should put him to sleep," she said. "The fourth usually does it."

"Thank the gods," Kio muttered. "If only he drank faster."

"Sometimes I over-salt his food so he does." Yasmine giggled.

"Should he really be drinking? I mean, we're in a flying house. That can't be safe."

"Oh, it's not flying because of him," Yasmine said dismissively. "He likes people to think that it's his magic, but it's not."

"Really?"

Yasmine nodded. "He told me once. He was a little drunk at the time. I don't think he would have admitted it if he hadn't been."

"How does it work, then? What kind of magic keeps it flying?"

A slightly embarrassed look crossed her face as she smiled. "Sometimes I think it used to belong to the sky people. I know it's just an old legend, but I think it's romantic."

Kio vaguely recalled hearing that legend. An entire kingdom was said to be in the clouds, full of beautiful and kind people who never aged. It sounded ridiculous, but being on a flying island disguised as a cloud did wonders for changing one's perspective.

The Gray Oligarch returned in a foul temper. For some reason he was no longer in a sociable mood and suggested they all retire. Kio was shown to a room on the second floor. As soon as he entered, the door was shut and locked behind him.

Kio sighed and decided to go to sleep without worrying about it. He was certain that he would be let out in the morning to play whatever games Diggory had lined up before the big meeting. He hopped onto the bed and groomed himself, enjoying the silence before drifting off to sleep.

In the morning, he barely had time for a satisfying yawn before there was a polite knock on the door.

"It's me," Yasmine said. "I need you to stay away from the door. Don't try to escape or anything."

Kio wasn't planning on it, but now knew that he should have been.

"Just trust me, okay?" she added.

"All right," he said. "Come on in."

Yasmine entered with a food tray. He could smell bacon and sausage, which greatly improved his mood.

"So now we're playing prisoner?" he asked conversationally as she set his breakfast on the floor.

"Yes," she answered. "He wants to keep you here, just in case your friend turns on him."

"Nice," Kio said easily, but inside he was beginning to panic.

If he was trapped here all day, he wouldn't be able to back Dylan during his confrontation with Krale. Of course he had promised to stay away, but he never really intended to do so. He *had* to be there. He knew Diggory wouldn't listen to reason, but maybe he could convince Yasmine to help him. "I need you to let me go," he whispered, putting on his best sad kitten face.

"You will stay here in this room until Diggory returns," she said in a voice so angry and loud that he flinched. Her face didn't match the emotion though. In fact, she looked as though she were about to laugh.

She walked over to the one window in the room and carefully opened it. Tiptoeing to a chair, she carried it over to the window. Appearing satisfied with her work, she returned to the bed and brought her head close to Kio's. "There's a huge tree outside," she whispered. A puzzled look crossed her face. "Cats can climb down trees, can't they?"

"I'll manage something," he whispered back.

"Good. Don't leave until he's already gone. I'll knock on your door. I would just let you out, but I don't want it to look like I helped."

Kio felt it would still be obvious that she had helped, but hoped she wouldn't come to any harm from it. "Thank you," he said.

She got up to leave, but then hesitated. "Can I… can I pet you?"

"You may," he said with a grin.

He was then treated to one of the best behind-the-ear scratchings he'd ever had. After she left the room, he hopped down to enjoy his breakfast, which had cooled nicely. All in all, it was a very good start to a very dangerous day.

Roughly an hour later he felt the island touch down, the entire house shaking. When Yasmine's signal finally came, he said a hasty goodbye and jumped out the window. The tree was easy to scale, and in less than a minute he was down, across the lawn, and through the wall of clouds.

Freshly harvested fields surrounded the cloud island. To the south an old dirt road ambled toward town, and to the west was a wall of thick trees. All Kio had to do was travel through those woods to reach home. *Home!* How inviting the word sounded! He only wished he were returning with Dylan at his side.

He bounded across the field without bothering to be cautious, certain that the Gray Oligarch had headed into town first. Kio's way was shorter, an advantage of being on home turf. Ideally, he would arrive at the tower before Diggory did.

Despite his confidence, it was a relief to reach the safety of the trees, but the feeling didn't last. Something was amiss. The birds were silent, and the smell was all wrong. Something was here, something that didn't belong. His nose was having trouble identifying what it was. It was alive, an animal of some sort, but with too many mixed signals. Scales, fur, feathers, dung, fire, fear, sweat, and more—all mixed together and squeezed into too tight a space.

Kio slowed his pace as the smell intensified. He began to hear noises. The exhalation of breath. Shuffling in the leaves. A hiss. Kio crouched low, cautiously crawling forward. His muscles froze when he saw the glint of sunlight on red scales. The beast was barely larger than himself, small, as all red dragons were, but he knew they could be the most deadly. Near it was a lion and a vicious-looking ape, neither taking any interest in the other. Shouldn't there be some territory disputes here? They should at least be preying on the horse or avoiding the dangerous chimera. Kio's keen eyes spotted two enormous falcons in the tree, so large even he wouldn't dare hunt them. They waited patiently, just as the other animals did. Something was very wrong here.

Kio stared long and hard at the chimera. The last time he had seen one was at the nightmarish home of the Purple Oligarch. Krale must have returned there to gather reinforcements. Without the blue loka to protect him, Dylan would be in a world of trouble. He had to warn him. To tell him not to—

"I was hoping you would join us," Krale said from behind.

There was a flash of purple light, and Kio found his body was no longer his to control.

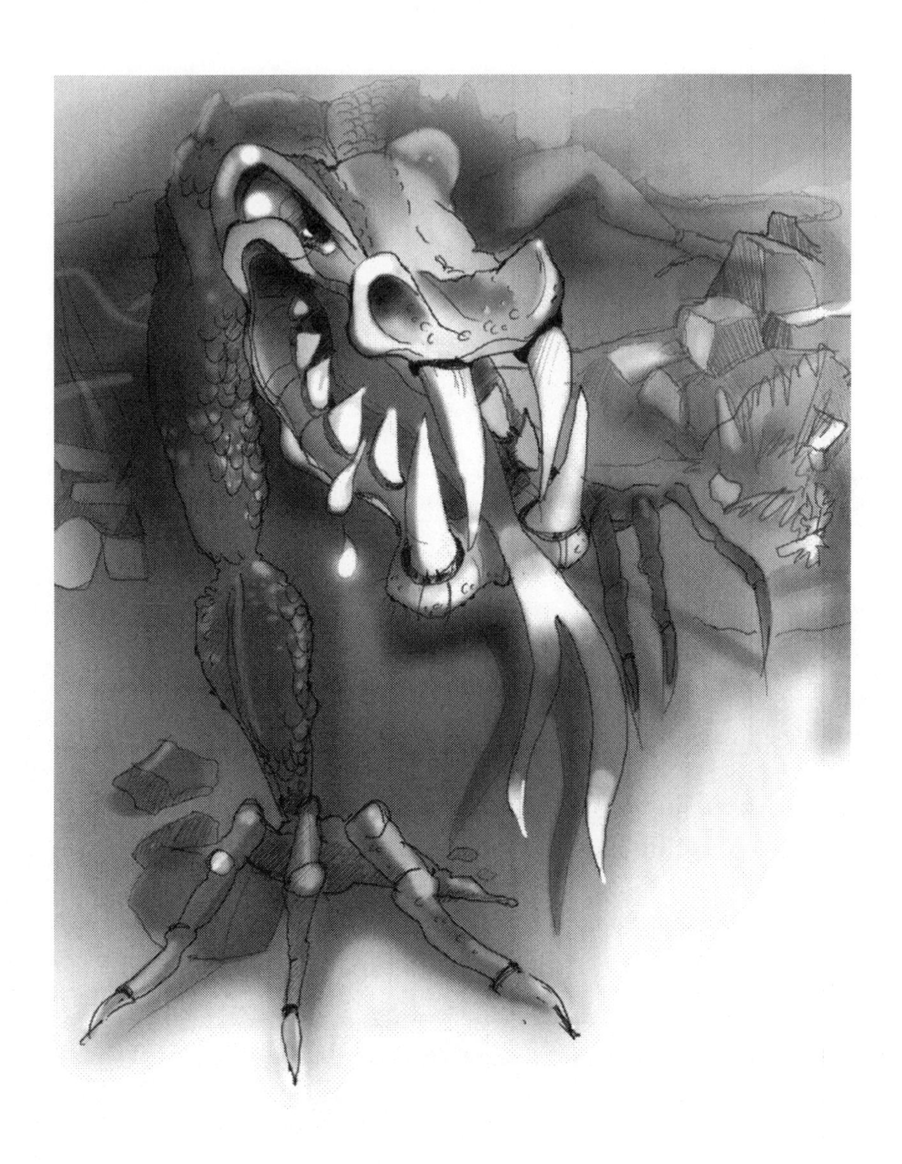

Chapter 23
Confrontation

Transparent and wavering, the ghost house now lived up to its name. Outside of its sanctuary, Dylan regarded it as he awaited Lucile. Odd how he could see through it to the soft blue of the morning sky and the hillocks beyond, while the interior remained invisible. Should he fail in his quest, would his soul pass through its endless halls on the way to eternity? That would provide a strange feeling of satisfaction. Crimson Barry's concern for himself and Natasha didn't extend to the rest of the world, but he would have something to fear when he learned that Dylan and his allies had fallen. That would mean Krale had gained even more power.

Dylan sighed, his anger toward the old ghost evaporating. White joining as an ally would mean inviting a fifteen-year-old girl onto the field of battle. Barry was useless outside the confines of his home unless he possessed her, and the idea of putting such a young girl in danger was wrong. Except that Dylan wasn't much older. He wished that someone more capable would tell him that he couldn't go, that he was just a boy, and that they would take care of everything.

"Are you ready?"

After nearly jumping out of his skin, Dylan turned to find the Brown Oligarch a few steps behind him.

"You should wear bells or something," he complained.

There was a hint of a smile. "Anyone joining us?"

"No. I didn't have any luck here either."

"I'm not surprised. To the Lakelands then. I need you to choose an exact location. Thinking about it very hard should be enough for me to pick up on it."

It didn't take Dylan long to choose. Closing his eyes, he imagined a tall stone tower, its every detail familiar to him. He visualized the long green lawn stretching out to the surrounding lake, the blue water lapping against the docks, his father's ships, and the long wooden bridge that stretched to a distant shore. Yes, his home would be a fine place to arrive.

He opened his eyes to discover they were there, the massive stone tower in front of him looking as majestic and welcoming as always. The decorative flags still hung from it, the plant boxes in the windows were still thriving with colorful blooming flowers, and the grass of the lawn was still short and well maintained. For some reason, he had imagined the tower instantly deteriorating into a cobweb-covered mess after he and his family had abandoned it.

What would have been an emotional homecoming was ruined when Dylan turned around. On the other side of the bridge was the unmistakable figure of Krale on horseback. This wasn't as upsetting as the menagerie of animals that flanked him. At the fore was the considerable bulk of a chimera, joined by a red dragon whose long, low body spoke of vicious and deadly speed.

"You can teleport us out of here before he sets those animals on us, right?"

The Brown Oligarch was about to say that she had no intention of staying, but one look in Dylan's pleading eyes softened her stony demeanor. "If you stay close to me," she answered. "You'll want to meet him in the middle of the bridge. That way he can't surround you with beasts. We can't do anything about the falcons, but I'll try to keep an eye on them while you speak."

Dylan looked up and saw two huge birds circling in the sky. Krale certainly was well prepared. He hoped no nasty surprises waited for them in the water as well.

Lucile placed a bony hand around his arm. "Are you ready?"

He wasn't. Dylan had no idea what he was going to do. He wasn't armed, he saw no sign of the Gray Oligarch, and he had no plan. What was he doing here? He was just a boy, and he was about to face the most powerful man in the Five Lands. What could he try besides politely asking Krale to stop doing what he wanted to do?

"I'm ready," he lied.

The world shifted, and they were on the bridge, close enough to clearly see Krale's face. The man looked momentarily taken aback before smiling greedily. He kicked his horse, prompting it forward, his ragtag group of animals following. Their movements were sluggish and unnatural. Dylan took careful note of this, hoping that being under the purple loka's spell inhibited their natural prowess, a potential advantage in a greatly skewed situation. The dragon didn't seem to be suffering as badly as the others, making Dylan wonder how fast the creature was normally.

The narrowness of the bridge forced the chimera to fall in line behind Krale and the dragon, eliminating one immediate threat. The Brown Oligarch's advice had already proven useful. He wished she had been more forthcoming about what was supposed to transpire here.

The renegade Oligarch rode slowly toward them, his eyes

examining them with cautious interest before scanning the terrain behind them for any sign of a threat. Dylan used this time to size up his opponent as well. He was surprised by the normality of Krale's appearance. This was still the same thin, old man he had dined with all those weeks ago. In his mind, Dylan had built him up as being larger-than-life, but he looked no more threatening or evil than he had before.

Krale's robes were still ceremonial, but now they were of white silk. In his hand he carried the crane bag, which actually looked to be made from the pelt of a bird. Krale clutched the bag so tightly his knuckles were white. As a further precaution, the silver chain that tied the bag shut was wrapped around his wrist. Dylan could never take it from him, not that he had expected as much. The lokas, according to Crimson Barry, would be inside, the power of all of them at Krale's disposal.

Krale stopped his horse close enough to see and hear them but far enough away that he couldn't be reached. His face was impassive and calculating. This wasn't a lunatic mad with power; it was an intelligent and experienced politician. He was in full control of himself and aware that he had the upper hand, while remaining cautious to avoid the mistakes made by the overconfident. He was, in his way, more frightening than any monster Dylan had faced.

"It's a pleasure to finally meet you." Krale's eyes were on Lucile, who didn't dignify his greeting with a response.

"You *are* aware that I am in possession of five lokas?" Krale continued.

"I am," the old woman answered.

"Then you understand you cannot best me magically."

"I understand that, despite my age, I'm notoriously hard to catch."

"Yes, yes indeed." Krale nodded. "I've given some amount of thought to that. I don't believe I could take your loka from you by force." Purple light played about the bag and the beasts stirred restlessly.

"There's no need for the animals," Dylan said, deciding to interject himself into the conversation. He was beginning to feel invisible.

"That's just the point I was coming to." The renegade Oligarch considered Dylan with little interest. "If I want to, I can set these animals on the Lakelands and have them ravage the people living here. I can call on many more than these if need be."

"There's no need for that!" Dylan said angrily.

"It would teach you to stay out of my affairs, which is reason enough." Krale's attention returned to Lucile, a smirk playing about his lips. "However, should I set the animals upon the people of Woodruff, I think the effect might be more dramatic. You were born there, weren't you, my dear? I believe your extensive family still resides there?"

Dylan risked a brief glance at the Brown Oligarch, who was beginning to show signs of anger. In a blur of brown light she disappeared. He heard Krale's gasp of surprise as she reappeared between him and the dragon. She placed her hand on the dragon, and they were both gone. A large splash came from the water next to the bridge. Something under the water's surface increased in size as it moved toward the bank. The red dragon's head broke the surface, coughing up water.

"Next time that will be you, except you'll be in the middle of the ocean." The Brown Oligarch was once again standing at Dylan's side. She was completely relaxed, as if what she had done hadn't taken any effort. "Give the boy his loka," she said. "You'll give the others to me, and I'll return them where they belong."

Krale's face twisted with rage as he held the crane bag aloft. Its iridescent surface reflected yellow light. The Brown Oligarch's mouth opened with a choking noise and yellow light poured out, taking the air from her lungs. In the same instant, her robes burst into flame. Dylan jumped away from her, unsure of what to do. Then, fire and all, she was gone.

A look of concentration remained on Krale's face for a moment before faltering. "Damn it! She's too far away. I should have used the lizard." He scowled down at Dylan, anger creasing his face. "Well? Is that all you managed to bring? Just one Oligarch?"

"Just one," Dylan lied, wondering again where Diggory was.

"I should have known you'd be useless to me. I thought you might manage to draw more of them out, but you've wasted my time." Krale sighed irritably. "Very well. You won't interfere with my plans again." He snapped his fingers, and the animals rearranged themselves. A white cat stepped forward. "Kill him," Krale ordered impassively as he turned his horse to leave.

A terrible mixture of fear and love filled Dylan. His cat, his best friend, was stalking toward him, eyes blinded by purple light. "Kio, please," he whispered as he backed away.

The cat replied with a low, guttural growl.

"Kill him!" Krale shouted impatiently.

Kio leapt into the air. Dylan fell backward, his hands raised in defense. Water dripped onto his arms as something large and red flew over him. The red dragon, with uncanny speed, had launched itself at the cat. It snapped Kio out of the air with its jaws and turned, skidding through the grass as it landed. Hissing, the cat fought back, but his claws were useless against the dragon's scales. The dragon ran toward the tower, Kio still in its mouth.

Not understanding what had happened but terrified for his cat's welfare, Dylan scrabbled to his feet and sprinted to catch up. He was halfway across the lawn when the door to the tower opened, revealing Jack and the Gray Oligarch.

Fire exploded behind Dylan, singeing his hair as it launched him forward through the air. He landed on one knee, jumped up, and kept moving. The dragon had already plowed through the two men in the doorway, knocking them backward. By instinct, Dylan swerved to the right, another explosion of fire appearing where he would have been, but still close enough to leave a painful burn on his left arm. With a final burst of speed he raced into the tower, falling over the Gray Oligarch as he did so.

Dylan stayed on the floor, panting heavily. Familiar arms wrapped around him and hauled him up. He turned and looked into the blue, spectacled eyes of his father before he was pulled into one of the best hugs of his life.

"The dragon, the dragon!" shouted the familiar voice of the Gray Oligarch.

Dylan pulled away from his father to see Kio and the dragon tangled together in the corner. Kio fought fiercely to escape the dragon's mouth, his white fur wet with saliva and blood. The cat's purple eyes were still locked onto Dylan. He was struggling to escape the dragon, but only so he could kill Dylan. The dragon, in an impressive move, released the cat from its jaws and moved fast enough to trap the feline under its heavy bulk. Once this was accomplished, the dragon turned its head to them and growled in a disturbingly human way.

"No, don't!" Jack yelled as the Gray Oligarch wielded his loka.

"I won't kill Kio," Diggory assured him. "Just the dragon."

"It's not a dragon." Jack grabbed Diggory's wrist and forced his hand down. "It's an Oligarch."

Diggory understood immediately. "I should have known. They run around in disguises all the time; believe you me! Anyone could tell that's not a dragon! Couldn't they?" He rubbed his nose thoughtfully. "How did you know?"

Jack's eyes looked much bluer than usual before fading to their normal color. "I just can," he said as he moved forward and crouched before the dragon. "You aren't Hasam though, are you? If you were, you'd be able to talk."

The dragon shook its head, causing Diggory to gasp in amazement. The dragon looked next at Dylan and held his gaze.

"Lali?" he asked.

The door to the tower exploded inward in a mess of flaming shards. Krale was still on the bridge, the crane bag held high, but his beasts were just outside. Then the strangest thing happened. Where the door had been, a thick wall of ice grew, sealing it. The two windows in the entryway also shattered and were instantly replaced by icy equivalents.

"You have the blue loka?" Dylan asked his father.

"You don't?" Jack responded incredulously. Then the entire tower began to shake, accompanied by a number of loud, cracking noises that sounded like trees being felled. His father didn't appear perturbed by any of this. "Do you have it?" he repeated.

"No, I lost it!"

"Damn!" He shoved his slipping glasses back in place. "We'll never get the tower back up without it."

"What's going on?" Dylan and Diggory asked at the same time.

"Security protocols," Jack answered. "Magic nodes I set up long ago. In an emergency, the entire island will sink into the lake, taking the tower with it."

"Is it deep enough?" Diggory asked.

"I made it deep enough. Not many enemies can follow us down there. We'll be safe for the time being, but I'm afraid that the spell is going to backfire. We need the blue loka to maintain the magic and to get the tower back up." He looked at his son, the frustration disappearing from his face. "I'm glad you're okay."

"I'm glad you are too. What are you doing here?"

"I never left," Jack admitted. "I only said I was leaving so you wouldn't return."

Dylan found that hard to believe. His father had always been completely honest with him. That he had lied about going into hiding stunned him. Krale could have come here at any time, and his father would have been defenseless without the loka.

"You could have been killed!"

Jack's response was calm. "I couldn't abandon my people."

"Touching, touching," Diggory snapped, "but how much time do we have before the spell backfires?"

"A couple of hours at best."

"And then?" The Gray Oligarch's eyes darted wildly around the room as his panic intensified. He was already constantly on edge, and the stressful situation only made him worse. Dylan tried to signal to his father not to answer, but Jack did anyway.

"In a few hours the ice will have melted, and the entire tower will flood."

Kio yowled angrily from underneath the dragon, providing a welcome distraction.

"Is there something we can do for him, Dad?" Dylan asked.

"Not without the purple loka. Unless you think you can calm him, Diggory?"

"Not if he's under another loka's spell." The distracted Gray Oligarch stared in wonder through the ice of the door. The water had already risen higher than the first floor. The growing darkness showed that they were falling fast.

Jack lit lamps while Dylan checked on Kio. He couldn't see much of him under the dragon's bulk. The cat's head was sticking out, ears flattened and eyes an unnatural violet color. He was incapacitated enough that Dylan could pet his head without being bitten or clawed, but this made Kio growl with an unholy fierceness.

Dylan worried about Kio's injuries. Lali had surely done her best when subduing him, but the struggle against her sharp teeth had wounded him. He attempted to check the extent of his friend's injuries, but it was difficult with him being pinned under a dragon. While bending over, Dylan noticed a pouch tied around the dragon's back leg. He squeezed it and felt the familiar shape of a loka inside. Lali had taken a huge risk being so near to Krale.

"We're going upstairs," Jack announced.

"We are? What about Kio? We can't move him."

"That's why we are going there." Jack turned to address Lali. "Once upstairs we'll shut ourselves in a room. When you hear the door, I want you to release Kio. He'll probably follow but won't be able to reach us. This will give you the time you need to transform. Agreed?"

The red dragon nodded.

"Good. Once you are yourself again, try to join us. If you can get around Kio, that is."

"Check him!" Dylan pleaded. "I think he might be hurt."

"He's not the only one," Jack said, examining Dylan's burnt arm. "Come upstairs. Ada can tend to this."

Dylan didn't like leaving Kio behind, but his father's idea was the best so far. He left with a longing glance over his shoulder. He hoped Kio would be all right, but the truth was they were all in danger. Even if they escaped from the tower, Krale and his monsters had to be to dealt with. They were now two Oligarchs strong, but that didn't seem enough to overcome what they were facing.

Ada was crying, overjoyed that Dylan was home. She immediately set to work on his arm, applying ointment and bandages. Dylan winced as she worked, begging her to tend to Kio instead. Jack argued it was too dangerous, but when finished, Ada brushed by him and out the door.

When Ada returned her hand was bandaged. She reported that Kio was stable but would need to see a doctor as soon as possible, causing a pit to open up in Dylan's stomach. Lali returned with her, looking thinner and paler than before, but Dylan was happy to see her hand no longer infected. Ada had loaned her clothing that wasn't complimentary to anyone under sixty, but it was better than nothing.

He and Lali managed to catch up while waiting for the others to find a solution to their predicament. The first question out of their mouths was about Tyjinn; both disappointed with the other's lack of information. Dylan told her a truncated version of his adventures before asking about her own.

He laughed with amazement when learning that Mushi was really Hasam in disguise and grimaced when hearing about her would-be rapists. Two nights after her successful escape, Lali had lodged with an old woman who rented a room to travelers. The old woman told her of the previous tenant, a strange man and his motley collection of docile beasts. Acting on instinct, Lali had run all night to overtake him. Bravely using herself as bait, she transformed into a red dragon and allowed herself to be captured. Krale's magic had some effect on her, but not enough to steal her free will.

"I couldn't believe who it was!" Lali said. "Krale had visited Hasam on more than one occasion. I've even dined with him before, the bastard. While chasing him down, I had more than one fantasy of how I would kill him and put an end to all of this... but knowing him somehow made it harder. I just couldn't bring myself to do it." She hesitated. "I don't know if I could kill anyone."

The tower trembled, bringing their reunion to an end.

"It took us that long to hit bottom?" Dylan asked disbelievingly.

"We touched down before we came to this room," Jack said, his face lined with concern. Together he and Diggory went to one of the icy windows, which were becoming alarmingly clear as the ice melted away.

The tower shook again, a loud bang coming from above them.

"There's something out there!" Diggory exclaimed. "Did you see that?"

"Yes, I'm afraid I did," Jack said after watching a moment longer.

The previously dark window was now aglow. Dylan rushed to the window to get a closer look, seeing a strange spotted texture sliding by before it narrowed and disappeared. He realized with a start that he had seen a massive beast swim by. Eventually the creature came back, swimming lower, which allowed them to view it from above. It looked like a giant eel except its body was covered in fine scales, its head decorated with fleshy tendrils, horns, and six pearl-white eyes. The monster glowed with a ghostly luminescence.

"A leviathan," Jack breathed. "Krale must have called it here."

"From the ocean?" Dylan remembered reading about these

creatures, and they didn't live in fresh water.

"His telepathy combined with purple magic. Maybe even blue magic to map out the underwater cave between here and there." Jack shook his head. "He has to be stopped."

"I'll fry it!" Diggory exclaimed, his loka already in hand. "I'll call my storms and hit this water with so much lightning that we'll be eating leviathan steaks for weeks."

"Will that work?" Ada asked.

Jack shrugged as the Gray Oligarch set to work. They didn't see much aside from the eerie silver light emanating from the loka. Meanwhile, the tower continued to be pummeled by the underwater behemoth. After it struck for the fourth time, they could hear water pouring in from below.

"Kio's down there!" Dylan shouted, running for the door.

Jack caught him before he could reach it. "He won't drown yet," he said, struggling to hold his son. "Diggory?"

"It's not working," the Oligarch spat. "Something is holding my storms back."

Dylan continued to struggle with his father, the image of Kio drowning on the first floor driving him to despair. He couldn't break free from his father completely, so in desperation Dylan punched him square in the face, sending his glasses flying. The blow was enough to make Jack release his grip.

Running to the door, Dylan threw it open and ran headlong into the Brown Oligarch. He managed to catch himself, and her, before they both fell. She looked terrible. She was soaking wet; her clothes and patches of her skin burned, her face ashen and exhausted.

She opened her mouth to say something when a feral Kio came snarling down the hallway. She reached out her hand as he leapt and a pleasantly syrupy light took all three of them away. Dylan had a brief impression of a forest, then they were moving again. When they stopped, he was in a familiar room made of stone.

The Brown Oligarch sat wearily on her piano stool and caught her breath. "So much for not getting involved," she rasped.

"Where's my cat?" Dylan demanded. "He's my friend! Don't drown him!"

"I remembered Kio from your memories," Lucile assured him. "He's somewhere safe."

"He was under—"

"I know," she said, waving a hand tiredly. "Is anyone else hurt?"

"Not seriously, but we have to go back for them. The whole tower is flooding."

"Very well."

"Wait! Listen, I want you to take my father and Ada away first. Take them somewhere safe. The other two there are Oligarchs. I want you to teleport them and me to face Krale." He hesitated, thinking about Lali, tempted to send her away with the others, but they needed all the help they could get. He started to see a way her magic could be useful to them. More useful than he was at the moment. He needed to arm himself. "Do you have a sword?"

"No weapons. Just the poker there," she said, nodding toward the fireplace.

Dylan took it. It would be enough to get Krale's attention, and he didn't know how to use a sword anyway.

"Anything else?" she asked.

"Yeah," he said after a moment. "Can you teleport the other animals away?"

"I can try, but I can't promise I have enough strength to succeed."

"Just do your best. Don't kill them though," he added. "It's not their fault."

The Brown Oligarch's smile was brief. "Care to tell me your plan?"

"I wish I had one." He hesitated. "Maybe you could drop Krale into the ocean like you threatened," he suggested with guilt. Asking someone to commit murder felt unsavory, but it had been her idea originally.

"The lokas would be lost, including the green one," she said. "It would cost the Empress her life."

Dylan swore, loudly. "All right, but there must be somewhere we can take him, somewhere we would have the upper hand or where we could trap him until he agrees to surrender."

The Brown Oligarch sighed heavily. "It was an empty threat, although I didn't know it at the time. I can't teleport him anywhere, and he knows that."

"Why not?"

Lucile pointed to an open book resting on the top of her piano. Dylan walked over and examined it. It showed a sketch of the crane bag with three paragraphs of text underneath it.

"I came back here after I recovered from his attack. I knew I'd seen that bag somewhere. Read the second paragraph."

He did and experienced an all too familiar sinking sensation. The paragraph said the crane bag absorbed all magical attacks. Not only had Krale acquired the ultimate weapon, but he had the ultimate defense as well.

"It doesn't specify that it can defend against the attack of another loka," Lucile said, "but I wouldn't bet that it couldn't. Especially with five lokas inside it."

"At least it doesn't protect him against pokers," Dylan said, trying to sound brave, but it was hard to keep his spirits high. This revelation meant that Lali's ego magic wouldn't work on Krale. Otherwise she could have switched to his body, tossed Dylan the crane bag, and returned to herself. He supposed she could shape-shift into some sort of animal to attack Krale, but he would only use his purple magic on her. It hadn't been entirely effective before, but now Krale would be suspicious and redouble his efforts. That could turn her into as much of a liability as Kio had been. Better Lali join Jack and Ada somewhere away from the action. He asked the Brown Oligarch to also take her away

So this was it. No Oligarch could stand against Krale. Even Crimson Barry's idea to separate his soul from his body would fail, the magic deflected by the crane bag. With the white loka, Krale could then use that very trick on the Blacksmith. Brown, like Orange, would fall when caught.

The Gray Oligarch wasn't likely to be of any use either. Then again, his vision had shown Gray triumphing over all. Maybe there was a chance yet. He gripped the poker tightly. "I'm ready when you are."

When they returned to the tower, they found Jack nursing a bloody nose and trying to coax his broken glasses onto his face. The ice barrier over the window in this room had shattered as well, and water was pouring in.

"I was worried about you!" Jack said. "The leviathan broke through upstairs and we have to—" He disappeared with the Brown Oligarch, who returned quickly to take Ada.

Dylan exhaled loudly, trying to calm himself while willing

his shaking hands to be steady. "Are you ready to face Krale with me?" he asked Diggory.

The man responded with frightening enthusiasm. Dylan explained how they would teleport to where they could confront him. Lali overheard and immediately offered to go with them. He agreed rather than argue the point until Lucile returned. All it took was a single gesture from him, and the Brown Oligarch wordlessly took her away.

"Well, it's just you and me now," Dylan said to Diggory. "You have your loka, and I have a poker."

"Then there's no way we can lose!" the delirious Oligarch responded.

Chapter 24
Gray

Dylan wanted to escape, to hide behind his father's legs like a frightened child. He wanted to feel safe as he had with Tyjinn, to run away from it all like he and Kio had once planned, but there was no turning back now. Krale had taken everything from him. His father was no longer Oligarch, Tyjinn was lost to the world, and Kio had been turned against him. There was nowhere safe for him to run, nobody to protect him anymore.

His home had been taken from him as well. The island had sunk completely, swallowing the tower and destroying the bridge in the process. The surface of the lake was cluttered with scraps of wood, shingles, and plants from the garden; the last remnants of the home he grew up in.

Unfortunately, Krale had not gone down with the bridge. He was near its ruins on the opposite side of the lake, still surveying the surroundings from atop his steed. With foresight, the Brown Oligarch had wisely brought them to the opposite shore. Her opponent had also planned ahead, commanding his animals to disperse further along the lake's bank in case anyone surfaced. The lion was nearest, already leaping through the air with a vicious roar. It disappeared in brown light along with Lucile. She returned shortly after, moving to take the next beast away.

"What's wrong with my clouds?" the Gray Oligarch complained.

Dylan looked up and saw a circle of clear weather directly above them. Thick black storm clouds surrounded the blue sky, an invisible force preventing them from entering. Occasional wisps of storm were carried up into the sky as they hit the unseen barrier.

"Air pressure," Dylan realized. "Krale is using yellow magic to push it so high your clouds can't get near."

"Then I'll just have to create them from the ground up," Diggory growled. "Take us closer!" he shouted to the Brown Oligarch.

They were behind the renegade Oligarch before Dylan could prepare himself. By the time Krale reoriented, the Gray Oligarch had already whipped up a wicked black cloud the size of a large room. It hovered no more than a foot off the ground and was beginning to rise. Lightning arced from it, hitting the ground around Krale's horse, which started to buck and whinny in fear.

This was the weakness Dylan had been searching for. He now knew how this battle was going to be fought. Magic might not be effective directly against the Oligarch, but it could be used to affect his surroundings.

Krale calmed his horse and counterattacked with yellow magic, sending biting winds that dissipated the small storm almost immediately. Dylan and Diggory stumbled backward, the maelstrom threatening to knock them over.

"Spook the horse!" Dylan shouted, remembering Gray's power over emotion. It would only work if Krale wasn't using purple magic on his steed, but horses were already tame. Why expend the extra concentration to control it?

Diggory screamed, an angry whip of gray mist lashing

out from his loka and striking the horse in the face. The horse reacted instantly, launching into a panic and bucking and kicking, throwing Krale off in the process. The winds stopped as the old man hit the ground with a dry snap that could only be a broken bone.

Dylan's heart rose with elation. They had managed to defeat Krale already! Now all they needed was to take the crane bag from him. Dylan and Diggory rushed him at the same time. Ahead of them the Brown Oligarch appeared, exerting considerable effort to grab onto the still bucking horse and teleport it to some unknown destination. She returned without it just as they reached Krale's fallen body.

The old man's face contorted in pain as he clutched at his neck. His collarbone, white and glistening with blood, had broken through the skin. Dylan didn't hesitate; he reached down for the crane bag. Green light exploded from it, and the soil around Krale. Fat, vicious vines unraveled from the earth and sprouted thorns oozing with poison. The first of these whipped sideways, striking the Brown Oligarch across the face and sending blood flying. She swayed from the impact but managed to stay on her feet, teleporting them all a safe distance away before a far away look came into her eyes. Then she fell to the ground with the controlled grace of a ballerina.

Diggory was summoning another cloud when the same harsh winds blew in to destroy it. Krale was now standing, the unsightly injury near his neck already healed by green magic. The Gray Oligarch, in his frustration, began to approach their enemy. His loka was cradled in his palm, producing a miniature storm that he shielded with his other hand. Powerful lightning that belied the storm's size tore into the waving tendrils, reducing them to shreds.

Dylan, in the meantime, edged around to the right, hoping to sneak up on Krale while he was distracted. He wished he could get behind the man completely, but Krale's back was against the water's edge. The best he could do was to come at him from the side. Dylan had moved significantly closer to his target when something in the air changed. The winds had halted. Looking up, he saw the storm clouds beginning to move forward again, free from the pressure that had kept them at bay.

Dylan stopped in his tracks, uncertain what this meant.

Krale's free hand delved into his robes as he searched for something. He pulled out his hand to reveal a small wooden box.

"I was saving this for the Black Oligarch, but I'll try it on you first," Krale announced, as if he were discussing an experiment with a colleague.

The box had a hinge on its lower back that took all but the base with it when it opened. Tied to this bottom plate was a tiny serpentine form with two leathery wings that flapped in agitation as it tried to free itself. Its strange birdlike head was tied down, forcing it to look forward.

Dylan realized with a cold jolt of fear that it was the legendary cockatrice, whose gaze could turn any living creature to stone. He turned to shout a warning to Diggory, but hesitated. Krale's attention was momentarily distracted, and warning the Gray Oligarch would give away Dylan's position. With still so much ground to cover, now was his only chance.

Diggory sensed his magic was no longer inhibited and ran toward Krale, eyes locked onto the lizard. The small storm around his loka was gone, replaced by great swatches of silvery light. Electricity was growing in the air as Diggory used his magic to gather his forces. Lightning blitzed forth from the loka in his open palm, setting the box and cockatrice on fire and temporarily blinding Krale in the process. But it was too late. The animal had worked its magic.

The Gray Oligarch, with one foot still in the air, went completely stiff, his skin turning the color he represented. His rigid body fell forward and hit the ground, his limbs not bending as they struck the earth.

Krale, who had dropped the box before it could burn his hand, rubbed desperately at his eyes. Not wanting Diggory's sacrifice to be in vain, Dylan charged forward, poker raised above his head and screaming in the heat of battle. If only he had been silent! His shout warned Krale, who sent great plumes of scarlet fire twisting toward him. Dylan continued running forward, his momentum too great to stop in time. The fire seemed to lick the air in slow motion, as it sped toward him—and he toward it.

Then Tyjinn was there, so close that Dylan could smell his skin, see the fine hairs on his neck. Out of nowhere he had come, placing a hand on Dylan's chest to stop him and push him away. Tyjinn's other hand beckoned to the flames. They crashed into him, and he grunted in pain, but then the fire changed color, becoming lighter, more natural in appearance. The flames spun around him, forming a cylindrical barrier.

Tyjinn spared a second to look at Dylan. His face still bled where Kio had attacked him, as if no time has passed. He grinned wildly and turned his attention to his opponent, sending the flames hurtling back where they came from.

The flames collided with Krale, and for a moment the old man appeared to be finished, but the fire collapsed into the crane bag like air sucked through a reed. The fire must have caused him some discomfort, because a green light poured over his body, healing the burns and providing proof that the crane bag wasn't an invincible defense after all.

Tyjinn, a competent red magician even without his loka, sent two more spiraling streams of fire toward the old man—one toward his head, another at his feet. Krale hastily whipped the crane bag around. The fire was absorbed as it had been before, but now he was on the defensive.

Krale's air-stealing trick came next, but Tyjinn reacted calmly. His hands glowed yellow with light which he then placed over his mouth to keep from suffocating. This counter-magic saved his life, but also rendered him harmless. Tyjinn was an unusually gifted mage, but even he couldn't perform two types of magic simultaneously.

Dylan ran forward, only feet away from Krale when he swung the poker down, but the old man was too quick. Wind, condensed and forceful, struck Dylan's chest and tossed him to the ground. The air was knocked out of him, unable to return, as Krale's magic slowly suffocated him.

Dylan forced himself to sit up, his eyes watering as he desperately tried to inhale. Then Tyjinn was leaping over him, flinging flames from his hands as he launched a new assault on Krale. It was enough of a distraction that the spell on Dylan ended, allowing him to breathe again.

Tyjinn had the upper hand for a moment, but vines snaked out of the earth and entangled around his feet. Thorns as thick as nails grew out of the vines and skewered his flesh, trapping him where he stood as blood gushed over his feet. Invisible forces knocked him around, sending his body lurching back and forth, the concentrated air as effective as fists. Tyjinn was still trying to send fire at his enemy, but the wind around him caused most of it to burn him instead.

Dylan panicked, scrambling on the ground for the poker when something else caught his eye. Lying in the grass less than an arm's length away was the gray loka, having spilled from Diggory's hand when he fell.

Tyjinn's scream stole Dylan's attention. Still being brutalized by blasts of air, the wound on Tyjinn's face ripped open wider as one of his arms caught fire.

Dylan leapt forward and scooped the gray loka up. "Gray loka awaken for me," he intoned. The energy exploded inside him. The experience was totally different than what he had known with the blue loka. Instead of being a tool he had to reach out to, the gray loka was already a part of him. His energy and that of the stone were one. The gray loka's magic drew from an emotional well, manifesting his every feeling, and right now Dylan was very, very angry.

The storms above churned in response. Fifteen bolts of lightning ripped through the sky and into the earth directly in front of Krale's feet. The resulting explosion threw the old man into the lake with a splash. Dylan waited until Krale stood before he sent three more bolts of lightning into the lake behind him. The dispersed electricity wasn't enough to kill Krale, but did send his body into painful spasms.

Dylan called on hail next, summoning monstrous chunks of ice the size of his fist that pelted into the lake's surface. Krale sent yellow magic into the air, trying desperately to blow the storms away, but he was too late. One of the ice balls collided with his right shoulder; the arm holding the crane bag went limp. Immediately afterwards, another ice stone ricocheted off his head. Krale swooned and fell face-first into the water.

Dylan commanded his storms to cease, and they obeyed immediately. He spared one glance to make sure Tyjinn was okay. He wasn't, but Dylan knew he had to disarm Krale while he had the chance. He ran and pulled the old man from the lake. Krale began retching up water. Dylan dropped him as soon as they were on the shore and wrested the crane bag from his wrist.

"Lokas, awaken for me," Dylan said in order to render them useless to anyone but him. His body was filled with so much power that he dropped to his knees, overwhelmed. The sensation almost made him throw up, but he forced himself to breathe deeply. Tyjinn stumbled to his aid, lifting him from the sandy shore and walking him further inland.

"I'm fine," Dylan gasped, fighting back another wave of nausea. "Make sure Krale doesn't get away."

"I'll do better than that," Tyjinn said. He limped to the shore and dragged Krale up by his wispy gray hair. Tyjinn sneered, his eyes full of hate as he forced Krale to look at him before he threw the old man forcefully to the ground. He stooped to pick something up. A feeling of panic washed through Dylan as he realized it was the poker.

"The one you love will lose himself when he takes the life of another, never to be found again."

Dylan heard the words of the White Oligarch as if they were being shouted in his ear. The prophecy Natasha had made would be fulfilled.

"Ty, stop!" he cried. "Don't hurt him!"

Tyjinn turned to him, one hand on Krale's neck, holding his head to the ground. In the other was the poker, still wavering in the air and ready to strike, but he lowered it as he regarded Dylan. Tyjinn's face was ravaged, bruised, and bloodied by what he had been through. "If we don't kill him, he's going to kill us," he said, as if explaining something to a child. "Don't look, okay?" He turned away again, raising the poker high.

The instrument that would cost Tyjinn his soul was already swinging downward when Dylan said the only thing that came to mind. "I love you!" he screamed.

The poker stopped an inch away from Krale's skull. Tyjinn turned toward Dylan with an incredulous look. "You what?"

"I love you," Dylan repeated between sobs, "so please let him go. For me."

Tyjinn stared at him a moment longer before he released Krale, dropped the poker to the ground, and hobbled forward. He wrapped his arms around Dylan, bear-hugging him and laughing as he lifted him into the air. When he set Dylan back down, Tyjinn kissed him on the forehead. "I hope you weren't just saying that to get my attention," he said.

Dylan shook his head and started laughing himself. "I mean it!" He would have kissed Tyjinn if his poor face weren't such a mess. Doing so would only injure him further. Instead, Dylan pushed him gently away. "We have to help the others," he said "The Brown Oligarch is hurt and—"

"Even without my loka," a voice from behind Tyjinn croaked.

Together they turned to see a broken and beaten Krale on his knees, his head a bloody mess where the hail had struck him, his robes wet and muddied. One pupil was heavily dilated and his lips were pulled back, revealing a broken tooth. "Even without my loka," he snarled. Yellow light surrounded the poker and lifted it into the air. Before either of them could react, it shot forward and buried itself in Tyjinn's stomach with a sickening squelch.

Tyjinn turned and looked at Dylan, his eyes and mouth wide open with shock. He tried to say something, but his voice came out as an airy squeak before his legs buckled, and he started to fall. Dylan caught him but struggled under his weight. Unable to support him, the only thing he could do was to make sure Tyjinn fell on his side instead of onto the poker.

Krale laughed maniacally behind them, but Dylan ignored him. "No, no, no," he whispered. "Not Tyjinn, please no!"

With shaking hands, he brought the crane bag as close to the gaping wound as he dared. "I'm going to fix you," he whispered.

He needed the healing power of the green loka, but finding it was difficult with so many types of power coursing inside him. He hoped focusing on what he needed would be enough to activate the right loka. Dylan didn't have to dig deep to find the power he needed. Inside him was a raging storm of conflicting emotions. He tapped into these and began his magic.

Green light slowly trickled forth, the flow of blood around the poker slowing. He realized that he was being stupid. He couldn't heal the wound while the poker was still there. A flicker of fire lashed out from his hand, and the storms above grumbled ominously. He pulled away from Tyjinn with a gasp, realizing that his emotions had almost triggered other kinds of magic.

Krale's laughter doubled in volume. "Not easy, is it?" he cackled. "As if someone like you could handle such power. Not even the Empress could heal such a wound! But I could. Give the lokas back to me and I will save him for you."

Dylan turned to Krale, rage building inside. He could still control one loka, the one he was destined to wield. The clouds opened and rain hammered down as Dylan poured his emotions into the loka. All the fear, all the anger, all the desperation, uncertainty, sadness, loneliness, and hopelessness he felt, he gave it all to the loka where it combined and festered, waiting to be released.

"Better to let him die," Krale snarled, "and rid the world of your disgusting love."

Dylan's emotions exploded from the gray loka, manifesting as thick silver cords that wrapped around Krale like a spider capturing its prey. Krale's back arched as he began wailing. His eyes bulged in panic, and he screamed before collapsing into a sobbing heap. Krale rolled on the ground clutching his head as the emotions fought for dominance over him. He begged for forgiveness and help one moment, before screaming in terror for Dylan to stay away the next. The old man got to his feet and ran, falling several times, clawing and beating himself as he stumbled in an effort to sever the silver cords. It made no difference. The emotions Dylan had expelled stuck to him, all competing at once for his attention and driving him insane.

Purged of all of his emotions except one, Dylan turned back to Tyjinn. He braced himself for what he had to do next. Rolling Tyjinn onto his back as gently as possible and bracing one foot on Tyjinn's hip, he grasped the poker and pulled. Tyjinn screamed and lost consciousness. The blood flow increased, but Dylan didn't panic.

He reached into the crane bag and, without looking, pulled out the green loka and reinvoked it. He tossed the bag aside and knelt before Tyjinn. Placing the loka just above the wound, Dylan called upon the only emotion he had left. Love. Sparkling emerald light bathed Tyjinn's entire body. The raggedness left his breathing. The blood stopped flowing, and the swollen bruises on his face disappeared. The claw marks that Kio had left were erased as if time had turned backward. The gaping wound where the poker had been was replaced by flesh, new skin darkening until it matched the rest. Even when every wound had disappeared, Dylan allowed the light to linger, letting it search Tyjinn inside and out for any other injuries. When he was finally satisfied, the light faded.

Tyjinn's eyes flickered open. "What happened?" he mumbled.

"I did," Dylan said. Then he leaned over and did something he had been wanting to do for weeks. He kissed him.

Chapter 25
The Empress and the Wolf

The gardens of the Empress had changed. Silence dominated its pathways, the people who had once come to celebrate having abandoned it. The delicate flowers and fruits had wilted or spoiled in the desert sun. The forest trees, while faring better than more delicate forms of flora, were beginning to show signs of brown on their leaves. A handful of brave people had stayed and tried to do what they could, mostly bringing water from the lakes to the inner gardens, but their efforts weren't enough to hold back the desert's claim on this land.

When they arrived, the woodworm were still standing vigil over the nest where the Empress had once reigned, not having moved since the day of the fire.

"I suggest we hurry," the Brown Oligarch said. "She can't be in good health—or very comfortable for that matter."

Dylan looked at Lucile with concern. He had managed a little more green magic to get her back on her feet, but it hadn't been nearly as effective as what he had done for Tyjinn. Poison was still coursing through her system. Something would need to be done about it soon.

"Do you think fire would scare the woodworm off?" Tyjinn asked.

"Maybe." Dylan didn't want to provoke them, especially after what happened to Lali. "Let me try talking to them first."

He opened the crane bag and fished out the green loka, the purple and yellow stones catching his eye. One was good for telepathy, the other for communicating with all creatures. He hoped that one or both would help him get his message across. He held up the green loka, and the reaction was instantaneous. Every woodworm's attention was focused on him. "We've come to bring this back to its rightful owner," Dylan said.

The wall of woodworm opened without hesitation, allowing them inside. They walked through, the chain of creatures closing behind them once they passed. Little was left of the nest. Most of it had burned completely, leaving only the occasional black skeleton of a tree and heaps of ashy earth. Because they didn't have to navigate a maze this time, they reached the center in minutes.

The massive seed had fallen over and was half buried under ash, its once-pearly hue darkened by the flames. They saw no sign of the Empress. As a group, they turned defensively when a sound came from behind them. One of the woodworm had followed and was staring at them with its sad, sap-colored eyes.

"I don't know what to do," Dylan explained to it.

The woodworm tottered forward on its stiff wooden legs until it reached a spot where it stopped and bent over with a creak. It rubbed away the burnt leaves and twigs until bare earth was exposed. Then it righted itself and backed away. It looked at Dylan again and shifted its body with another creaking sound.

Dylan's ears tingled at the noise, giving him an idea. Had he just understood the language of the woodworm? The only way to find out was by trying what he thought he was supposed to do. He walked over to the marked spot and placed the green loka there. Nothing happened.

"Relinquish your power over it," Lucile suggested.

"Right. Uh, green loka, I give you back to the Empress." Still nothing. "Awaken for her." A hand burst free from the earth below the loka, capturing it. Green light built in intensity as a figure began to rise from the earth. The arm came first, like a serpent responding to a snake charmer. Next came the head. Like the arm, it was so caked in dirt that the features were hidden. Regardless, it was feminine and familiar.

Tyjinn's guilty expression deepened as he watched. Dylan reached over and took his hand before turning his attention back to the Empress. She was visible to her waist now. Both arms were free, although she wasn't pushing herself out of the ground. She was rising as if being elevated from a platform below. Her legs came next, but she stopped with her feet still buried. At this stage she looked like a human tree, until her features took on more detail and softened.

"An earth elemental," Lucile said appreciatively. "I should have guessed."

"Half-elemental, actually," Tyjinn said.

The Empress now looked as she had before, but was entirely the rich brown color of soil. Her skin was slowly changing, the browns fading into different shades depending on the area of the body.

"That was very, very close," she said, her voice not yet human. She turned, her now-green eyes focusing on Dylan. "Thank you for returning my loka to me, Dylan, and for bringing with you my aggressor."

She raised a hand as if to begin magic, but Dylan was ten steps ahead of her and had positioned himself in front of Tyjinn, reaching his arms behind to hug him protectively. "You can repay the favor by forgiving him," he said. "He was acting under duress."

"I don't know if that is a favor I can grant," the Empress said.

Lucile moaned, her legs collapsing beneath her. Dylan could have sworn that she winked at him as she fell.

The Empress was distracted for the next couple of minutes, healing the Brown Oligarch while gradually becoming more human in appearance. As she worked, Dylan explained how Krale had tricked Tyjinn and how he had later almost died trying to defeat the renegade Oligarch. He nudged Tyjinn after this speech, prompting him to apologize, which he did numerous times.

By the time her attention was free from Lucile, the Empress looked as she had when they had first met. Perhaps her human side had reasserted itself, making her much more gracious and forgiving, because her anger toward Tyjinn had diminished. Dylan had a feeling that Tyjinn would never be welcome in her gardens again, but it was a small price to pay in the name of peace.

Even as they spoke with her, little green sprouts speckled the ground around them. Dylan had no doubt the entire oasis would soon return to the way it had been before. He would have liked to watch it happen, but more pressing issues were at hand.

"Take me to Kio, please," he said to the Brown Oligarch.

They bade farewell to the Empress, and as a group, teleported to a much different environment. Bird song filled the once silent air, the dry desert heat replaced with the rich humidity of the Wildlands. They arrived before a ring of cages. A chimera stood in one, a lion in another.

"You brought them here?" Dylan asked, feeling momentarily upset. The home of the former Purple Oligarch was one of the least happy places he knew of. While he understood bringing some of the more dangerous animals back here, he didn't like the idea of Kio being in one of these cages.

After a moment, he realized how much the place had changed. Gone was the scent of filth and death, replaced by the comforting, musky smell of animals. Many of the cages were empty and large enclosures were in various stages of construction. Someone had been hard at work improving life for the animals.

"Hello, Dylan," said a sullen voice from behind him. "You should probably keep your distance, just in case."

Dylan turned to find the most downtrodden expression on Kio's face he had ever seen. His ears were so low that they flopped over each side of his head, and his eyes were focused on the grass, too ashamed to look up.

Dylan laughed so hard he almost wet himself. Kio quickly moved from humble to angry before laughing himself. Dylan ran to him and hugged him as tightly as he could without hurting him. Then he backed up a little to examine the cat. There were a few bandages on his stomach, but other than that, he looked as healthy as always.

"Krale is finished, so there's nothing more to worry about," Dylan assured him. "Look, even Tyjinn's face is fixed."

The cat perked up and noticed the others for the first time. "It's really over?" he asked.

"Yeah. Everyone is all right, too, aside from a few scratches." His stomach sank as he realized that wasn't completely true. "Diggory is dead, I'm afraid," he added solemnly. He hadn't really cared for the strange man, but felt a sense of sadness and personal responsibility for his death. If he had called out a warning, Dylan would have given himself away, but Diggory might still be alive.

"You will let one of your own kind die and let one against you live."

And he had. His judgment had caused an ally to die, and he had spared Krale's life. These were decisions that Dylan would have to live with. He struggled silently with mixed emotions before Kio spoke again.

"The others are inside. I'm sure Jack would want to see you right away."

They entered the squat little house together, even Lucile deciding to come along. Jack was on his feet and hugging Dylan as soon as he heard the door open, tearfully kissing him on the cheeks and forehead. Ada was next, and as soon as she was done, Jack was hugging him again. Over his father's shoulder, Dylan noticed that Lali had risen to hug Tyjinn as well, but quickly returned to a couch where she sat with an unfamiliar man.

He was tall and wore a tight gray shirt that strained against his well-defined muscles. The shirt complemented his oddly tinted, charcoal-gray hair, even though the man appeared to be no older than thirty. His ruggedly handsome face wasn't familiar to Dylan, but the silver eyes that peered up at him were. That, and the two wolf pups dozing happily on his lap.

"Nikolai?" Dylan asked. "Wow, you look... Wow!" Tyjinn cleared his throat noisily, causing Dylan to grin sheepishly. "You look different," he finished lamely.

"I had to change back to human form," the werewolf explained. "The murderer you were looking for came back for more of the animals. He had the magic of the Purple Oligarch this time. The only way I could resist him was as a man. I tried to stop him—"

Dylan noticed the broken arm. "You're lucky that's all that happened."

"Lucky, too, that werewolves heal quickly," Lali said, patting Nikolai's good arm affectionately. She let her hand linger a moment longer than necessary. Dylan suspected that she would have gladly traded places with one of the wolf pups.

Nikolai, on the other hand, looked rather uncomfortable in his current form. "I will change back soon," he said, reaching up to ruffle his own hair as if to reassure himself that he was still hairy somewhere.

"Tell us what happened," Jack said, dragging in a few extra chairs from the kitchen so they could all sit.

Dylan told them everything. When he reached the part of the story where he confessed his feelings for Tyjinn, he decided not to censor himself. By the time he reached the end, Ada had her hands over her mouth, and tears were running down her face. Dylan thought his worst fear was realized, until she ran over and embraced Tyjinn.

"Oh, I'm so happy!" she said giddily. "He finally has someone!" Her face and tone suddenly became stern. "You *do* love him back, don't you?"

Tyjinn laughed and caught Dylan's eye. "Yeah, but don't let on just yet. It's best to keep them guessing."

Dylan looked at his father, who appeared taken aback but not upset by this revelation. Then Ada bustled into the kitchen, and before long the smell of a home-cooked meal was making their stomachs rumble. It was only after they ate that Dylan remembered something important.

"Krale is still out there," he said. "He got away in the chaos."

"He is powerless without the lokas, but still dangerous," Jack said. "If he ever recovers mentally, that is. Regardless, we'll find him and see that he stands trial."

"You're going to need this then," he said, handing his father the blue loka.

Jack invoked it in his name, and Dylan felt some of the power leave as it had when he had given back the green loka. Restoring his father's title was a great relief and made him eager to be rid of the other lokas. He dumped them onto the dinner table, wondering how to go about it. Removing them from the crane bag made them feel more distant. He hoped if he didn't return the lokas to the bag, the power would leave him altogether.

He handed the red loka to Tyjinn, who hesitated before taking it. "I'm giving this back to Mama," he said. "I have enough power without it, and I'm tired of the responsibility."

Dylan understood why Tyjinn refused to resume his position. He still felt guilty about having been tricked by Krale, attacking the Empress, and putting his friends in danger. Dylan wanted to relieve his conscience on all accounts, but there would be time for that later. He regarded the remaining lokas: gray, purple, and yellow. There wasn't any debate in his mind about gray. It suited him so well that he wanted to keep it.

"He didn't have any children to pass it on to anyway," Kio said once Dylan had expressed his desire. "There's Yasmine, but she wasn't related to him. I have a feeling she'll be happy he's gone, even though she's out of a job."

"She can keep the flying island and the house," Dylan said. "If she wants to, that is."

"I wanted it!" Kio complained, but no one paid him any attention.

"The purple loka is the one for the animals, right?" Lali asked rather pointedly.

After a moment Dylan understood and had to admit her idea had merit. He slid the purple loka across the table to Nikolai, who stared at it.

"This should make your work here easier," Dylan said. "If that's what you want. There's no pressure, but you're obviously determined to stay and help the animals. With this you can communicate with them and help them to get along with each other."

Nikolai hesitated but took it. "I'm honored," he said. "Although I don't know the first thing about magic."

"You'll pick it up as you go along," Jack said. "Necessity breeds invention, as they say." He thoughtfully pushed up his poorly repaired glasses on his still-swollen nose. Dylan wished he had brought the Empress along with them, but he supposed his father's nose would heal on its own. "I have to caution both of you boys," Jack continued. "While I think you are both ideal candidates, officially the Oligarchy has to vote on who receives displaced lokas."

"Oh, to hell with the Oligarchy," Lucile said. "It's all but finished anyway."

Dylan realized it was true. By tradition the lokas were passed on to blood relatives, but if it were up to Dylan, that was never going to happen again. He wouldn't be inheriting the blue loka from his father and didn't have any siblings, so it would have to go to someone else. If the previous Purple Oligarch had relatives, Dylan refused to see the loka go to any of them. What sort of people would allow his cruelty to go on? Natasha's final prophecy was coming true.

"It's time for the Oligarchy to end," he said to his father. "You always let your people vote if you are allowed to stay in power, now everyone else can do that as well. We'll take the yellow loka to the region Krale used to serve and let the people elect someone to have it."

"I'm sure Mama will agree to that as well," Tyjinn said. "One of my siblings is bound to win anyway. As for the purple one—"

"I officially elect Nikolai on behalf of the animals," Kio said.

"I'm sure he'll get the vote of the other animals here as well," Jack said and smiled. "That just leaves you, my son. Who gets to vote you into power?"

"Well," Dylan stammered, panicked at the idea of having to give up the gray loka, "I got my loka before all these new rules, so I'm the last of the old regime."

The others laughed, and he was glad. He didn't know where he was going to live in the future, but supposed when he did choose somewhere, he would have to allow the people there to decide if he was worthy or not. He hoped he would be, but keeping the gray loka wasn't as important to him as his family and friends. As long as he had them, nothing else mattered.

Tyjinn stood back and beamed proudly at his achievement. *The Unsalvageable* now had a mast and a sail... of sorts. The mast was constructed from two branches scavenged from the jungle floor, green leaves still sprouting here and there. It was charming in a rustic sort of way, which is more than could be said for the sail. Formerly one of Ada's blankets, it was pink with white ruffled lace running along its edge. There were much more suitable blankets to choose from in the cabin, but Kio had insisted.

"Well?" Tyjinn said loudly over the cat's laughter. "What do you think?"

What Dylan thought was that he had finally discovered a limit to Tyjinn's talents. He struggled to find a response that was complimentary without being a lie.

"I doubt I could do too much better," he said. When Tyjinn didn't look pleased, Dylan hastily added, "*and* it's going to be extremely helpful!"

That much was true. What meager blue magic Dylan once possessed was now lost, replaced by the power of the gray loka. It was definitely a trade up. Conjuring wind to fill their sail wouldn't take any effort at all, although creating one tame enough not to destroy Tyjinn's shoddy workmanship might prove difficult.

"Let me take a quick dip, and then we can try it out." Tyjinn stripped off his shirt, thoroughly soaked in sweat from his labor, and dived into the lake.

Dylan watched the ripple of Tyjinn's muscles as he swam until his gaze was felt. He had no need to look away or to feel ashamed. As they grinned goofily at each other, all Dylan felt was pride, both in who he was and in the amazing person he had fallen in love with.

Kio nudged against Dylan's legs for attention. "I still don't see why we couldn't get a ride back with Lucile like everyone else did," he said.

"Because this is more romantic."

"More adventurous, too," Tyjinn added as he returned to the boat, dripping water all over the deck.

Dylan raised a suspicious brow. "There's nothing adventurous about going home."

"True, but we *are* in the Wildlands, and there are some amazing sights if we head east instead. There's that tribe of animal-headed people, or the temple of the swamp witch."

"Or there's home," Kio said. "You know, the place that isn't swarming with monsters?"

"Home is good," Dylan agreed. "No monsters is better."

"No need to worry about monsters," Tyjinn said, pulling Dylan close. "Not with a big bad Oligarch like you to protect us."

Dylan's protests were silenced with a kiss. Thunder rumbled in the distance.

"Let's give it a go," Tyjinn said. "The sail," he added when Dylan blushed.

"Better go inside first," Dylan said. "Just in case I mess things up."

Or in case the mast falls on top of us, he added silently.

They took shelter in the boat's cabin, sitting comfortably on the pillows and blankets. Dylan grasped the gray loka, hanging now on the same chain Tyjinn had once used for his own. It wasn't hard for Dylan to call on his emotions. Feelings of love, friendship, and contentment magically translated into a steady wind. The sail filled, white lace fluttering as the boat gently glided forward.

"I knew you could do it!" Tyjinn said, rewarding him with another kiss.

More grumbling thunder, closer this time.

"Do that again," Kio said.

Tyjinn grinned. "You mean this?"

The kiss lasted twice as long and so did the thunder. They pulled away from each other, surprise mirrored in their eyes.

"I noticed that before," Kio said. "The timing was too perfect to be coincidence."

"Must be a side effect of my emotionally powered magic," Dylan said sheepishly. "I'm sure I'll get it under control."

"I hope so," Kio said. "Until then, I'll be a strict chaperone. The last thing we need is a hurricane just because you two can't keep your hands off each other."

Kio pounced, shoving himself between them. The two boys laughed as they wrestled with the big white cat, the wind carrying them to adventures unknown.

Dylan and company return in:

From Darkness to Darkness

From the cradle to the grave...

The Black Oligarch is dead. Some call his successor a boy. Others see him as a threat. Cole lost everything the night he became Oligarch: his family, his home—even Jonah. Now he's all alone, left only with painful memories and the power to destroy the Five Lands.

When Dylan is sent to the Steeplands to help Cole, he finds in him a kindred spirit. Together they return home, intent on building a new life for Cole, but dark forces have other plans for them. The dead are rising, old enemies returning, and secrets from the past unraveling that threaten to change their lives forever. Can Dylan bring a young man out of the darkness and keep those he loves safe, all without making the ultimate sacrifice?

From Darkness to Darkness, the second novel in the Loka Legends series, continues the adventures of Dylan, his boyfriend Tyjinn, and their talking cat Kio. The book features original art by Andreas Bell and is gearing up for release in 2012.

Also by Jay Bell:

Hell's Pawn

John Grey is dead… and that's just the beginning.

Purgatory should have been a safe haven for souls that belong neither in Heaven nor Hell, but instead John finds himself in a corrupt prison, one bereft of freedom or pleasure. Along with his decedent friend Dante, John makes a brave escape, only to fall straight down to Hell and into the arms of Rimmon, a handsome incubus. John is soon recruited as Hell's ambassador, visiting the afterlife realms of other cultures to enlist an army strong enough to stand against Heaven. As interesting as his new job is, John's mind keeps returning to Purgatory and the souls still trapped there. Somehow John must stop a war he doesn't believe in and liberate Purgatory, all while desperately trying to attract the attention of an incubus whose heart belongs to another.

For more information, please see:
www.jaybellbooks.com

Also by Jay Bell:

Something Like Summer

Love, like everything in the universe, cannot be destroyed. But over time it can change.

The hot Texas nights were lonely for Ben before his heart began beating to the rhythm of two words; Tim Wyman. By all appearances, Tim had the perfect body and ideal life, but when a not-so-accidental collision brings them together, Ben discovers that the truth is rarely so simple. If winning Tim's heart was an impossible quest, keeping it would prove even harder as family, society, and emotion threaten to tear them apart.

Something Like Summer is a love story spanning a decade and beyond as two boys discover what it means to be friends, lovers, and sometimes even enemies. This full-length, gay romance novel is available in paperback, Kindle, Nook, and other eBook formats.

For more information, please see:
www.jaybellbooks.com